Prophecy's
Pawn

Richard R Draude

NewLink Publishing

Henderson, NV 89002
info@newlinkpublishing.com

Prophecy's Pawn

Richard R Draude

Line/Content Editor: Janelle Evans
Interior Design: NewLink Publishing
Cover: NewLink Publishing
p. cm. — Richard Draude (Science Fiction / Fantasy)
Copyright © 2019 / Richard R Draude
All Rights Reserved

ISBN: 987-1-948266-70-3/Paperback
ISBN: 987-1-948266-06-2/E-Pub

1.   Fiction/ Science Fiction/ Adventure
2.   Fiction/ Science Fiction/ General
3.   Fiction/ Science Fiction/ Space Opera

NewLink Publishing

Henderson, NV 89002
info@newlinkpublishing.com
Printed in the United States of America
1 2 3 4 5 6 7 8 9 10

ACKNOWLEDGMENT

I would like to thank all those who encouraged me and have been patient with me while creating this, the third book in the MacKenna Saga. To Janelle, my editor, who is constantly reminding me about expressing the characters' emotions. To Marty, who has truly helped me appreciate her patience. To my beta readers, many thanks for slogging through the rough manuscript. To all those in our writers' group, your comments, critiques and criticism are wanted and welcomed. And finally, to Kalen, Mayla, Dani, Connor, Russell and the others, without whose meticulous journals this story could never be told.

Books by Author

The MacKenna Saga
Dreams and Deceptions
Plots and Prophecies
Prophecy's Pawn
(Watch for)
Prophecy's Knight
Prophecy's Queen

Almost A Whisper

The Tyranny Series
RR Draude and JA Wilkins

Tyranny's Outpost
(Watch For)
Tyranny's Prisoner
Tyranny's Alliance

Prophecy's Pawn

Chapter 1
I Can't Fight This Feeling Anymore

Amid the scents of baking bread, roasting meat, the boisterous conversation of her friends, and warm night air, a chill crept up Dani Santiago's neck. This new sensation reminded her of her aunt's and parents' warnings to remain alert for danger. Her eyes darted from doorway to street as she scanned her surroundings.

Tucked into the shadows of a shop doorway, two figures watched her companions. Dani stepped away from her friends and moved toward them. The moment she did, the two faded into the shadows and hurried up the walkway.

The inviting aromas carried by the warm post-sunset breeze twisting its way along the semi-dark city street reminded Dani of their reason for being here. Her stomach rumbled. Shrugging off the feelings of dread, she pulled her long raven black hair over her shoulder and examined the tips. *Ugh, these split ends need to go.*

Asilyn, the oldest member of their clique, stepped away from their knot of schoolmates and spoke into her comm unit, "I'll be home in three hours." She rolled her blue eyes and huffed in disgust. "Mother, Dani, Carmen, and Carolina are havin' last meal with our friends. I'll be catchin' a transport when we're through." Asilyn rolled her eyes heavenward and shook her head. "Yes, Mother, Jimmy's here." The tall, slender redhead winced. "Mother, whatever 'tis you're doin', stop, it's right in me ear." The grimace in her blue eyes faded while she listened. "No, Mother, I won't mute me comm. You can get hold of me if you're needin' to. Yes, I've heard the rumors about the missing women, and they're just

1

rumors, but I'll be careful." Asilyn tapped the device behind her ear, and rejoined Dani, Carmen and the rest of their friends.

Out of the shadows two women appeared, hurried down the street, and pushed their way through the middle of the group. Dani squinted at the two. *Are they the two women I just saw?*

'Tis rude ya are." Jimmy O'Hanlin took hold of Asilyn and pulled her away. "How 'bout an apology?"

The women ignored him. One of them stared over her shoulder at Asilyn and the other at Dani for a moment, then they continued heading toward Auiray Street without so much as an expression of regret. Jimmy slid his arm around Asilyn's waist.

"You all right, Luv?"

"Yes." She smiled up at the tall lanky redhead. "Let's eat."

Their clique entered the Double Moon Café. A twinge of jealousy hit Dani. *Why hasn't Connor called?*

The ten friends took their places in their usual booths at the back of the eatery and punched in their food orders. Completing their requests, they fell into more boisterous conversation.

Asilyn glanced at the chronometer over the front door. "Oh gimmish, Jimmy, I've got ta be goin'."

"Stay." Dani touched Asilyn's arm. "My mother will be here in a few minutes. We can take you home after we drop off Carmen."'

"I can't, Dani. It's an hour past the time I told me Ma I'd e home." She inserted her iden-disk into the booth receptor and paid her portion of the tab. Amidst complaints about her departure and her friends' goodbyes, she stood to leave the café. Jimmy put his arm around her waist, pulled her close, and kissed her.

The group made their usual oohs and aahs. "Good one, Jimmy," said Marco.

Carmen elbowed him.

The young man flinched, but kept grinning.

Asilyn paid no attention. When their lips parted, she made her usual, weak protest, "Jimmy, I've got ta be gettin' home."

"Then I'll be walkin' with ya ta the transport stop."

Asilyn shook her head. "You do and I'll not be gettin' home anytime soon."

More laughter and teases erupted from the group.

2

"It's just down the street." She gave him a quick peck on his cheek. "I'll be fine. Now let me out. I'll be seein' you tomorrow anyway."

She put her hand up and fended off his next attempt, laughed, hurried out of the eatery and ran down the walkway heading toward the business district. Asilyn rounded the corner of Auiray Street in time to see the public transport glide away from the stop. "Wait! Wait!" The big gray vehicle never slowed.

"Oh gimmish! Mother will 'ave me head." Asilyn activated her comm. "Link. Home. Mother." She tapped her foot while waiting for the call to connect.

"Asilyn, where are ya?"

"I'm sorry, Ma, I lost track o' time. I just missed the transport."

"I expected you home an hour ago, girl."

"Mother, 'twas our last time together as schoolmates, we were talkin'."

"Of course, ya were, and how's Jimmy?"

"Mother!" Asilyn clenched her teeth. She let her have her loudest, most exasperated sigh. "He's fine. He's comin' over tomorrow to work on our cruiser."

"I know." Her mother laughed. "I've a lovely midday meal planned."

Asilyn bit her tongue to hold her retort. "Be careful and I'll see you in a bit."

"I will, Mother. The next transport will be along in two shakes."

"Hurry home."

Asilyn terminated the link. I don't know why I fight it, everyone knows. I wish he'd ask and get it over with. She scanned the empty street and spotted two women down the block. They remained in the shadows between the light cast by the hololamps.The units, floating on both sides of the street, kept the area well lit, at least that is what she used to believe.

Asilyn stared into the shadows. I think those two are the ones who bumped into us. Something about the women's presence made her back away from the transport stand. One of the women pointed in her direction. A chill crawled up Asilyn's back. In her head she heard Jimmy shout. *Run!*

Keeping to the shadows, the women moved toward her. Another

moment of indecision passed before Asilyn's legs got the message. She bolted, tore around the corner, and ran toward the café. The echoes of hurried footfalls, reverberated off the buildings. Her heart raced. Asilyn broke into a sweat and a full run in the same instant. Taking a quick glance over her shoulder, she spotted the two women half a block behind, and pumped her legs harder.

The echoes of the women's footfalls accelerated.

She raced along the empty walkway toward the eatery. At the far end of the street, the café door opened and she called out, "Jimmy, Dani, help!"

She heard a soft hiss, then felt a sting in her back. Her legs grew wobbly and her vision blurred. She forced herself to stay in motion until she could no longer move her legs. Asilyn tried to cry out again, but her voice would not work either. She tumbled forward and rolled over several times.

The two women caught up to her, grabbed her arms and lifted her off the walkway. "We've got her, go ahead and grab your girl," Asilyn heard one of the women say to no one in particular. Through the fog, Asilyn heard Dani say, "Jimmy, it's Asilyn, she's hurt!"

"'Ey, leave 'er be!" Jimmy's shouts and the sound of hurried footsteps grew closer.

The women released Asilyn.

She slumped to the ground, unable to stop herself.

The women raised their pistols. The air filled with the sharp crack of pulsar fire, confused shouts and running. The outcry faded and someone lifted and cradled her head. Through the fog she saw Dani's and Carmen's worried expressions before the lights went out.

Dani stood alongside her mother, staring into a hallway through a window in the far wall. They turned in unison when they heard Asilyn stir and try to sit up. Dani came to the bedside, and took her hand.

"You stay put until the med-tech checks you out," Lily said.

Asilyn settled her head onto the pillow and looked into her friend's concerned eyes.

"Dani, what happened?"

"We're not sure, but you're safe now." Dani brushed the hair from Asilyn's face.

"Where are we? How long have I been out?"

"We're at the Northern Escarza Med Center." Lily paced alongside the bed. "You've been out for two hours."

"Two hours!" Asilyn stiffened and tried to sit up. "Me Ma!"

With a gentle push Lily settled Asilyn into a lying position.

"My husband went to get your mother. They should be here shortly."

"Thanks, Missus Santiago." Asilyn settled back.

"You should have waited," Dani said. "We could've avoided this."

"Those women, what did they do ta me?"

"We don't know." Lily turned and peered out the window.

"Dani and your friends saw you fall, and the two women trying to carry you off. Jimmy and the other boys gave chase.

They shot Jimmy with the same drug they used on you.

When he fell, the other boys stopped chasing them."

Before Asilyn could make sense of the incident or ask about Jimmy, the room door slid open. A tall, slender man dressed in a Roving Patrol officer's uniform entered. The dark circles under his brown eyes and the stoop of his shoulders told Dani he suffered from the same ailment that killed Asilyn's father, too much work and too little sleep.

The officer ran his hand through unruly dark brown hair. "Excuse me, Missus Ryan? I'm Lieutenant Castellano of the Central Valley RP Command. With your permission, I'd like to have a word with your daughter."

Lily turned and put herself between the officer and the girls.

"Officer Castellano, I'm Lily Santiago. Asilyn is not my daughter, but Dani is."

Officer Castellano glanced in the girls' direction and Dani smiled and raised her hand.

The officer extended his hand. "It's a pleasure to meet you, Mrs. Santiago."

"The Ryans are close friends." Lily shook the officer's hand.

"We're waiting for Asilyn's mother to arrive. Her friends already told the local RPs everything they know. Those women drugged Asilyn. When my daughter Dani and her friend Carmen reached Asilyn, she had already passed out. I don't believe she can be of any further help."

"I think she can, Mrs. Santiago. She may know more than she thinks she does."

"I know Asilyn's old enough to question alone, but I would prefer if you waited until her mother arrives."

The officer pointed to the door. "May I speak to you?"

Lily turned to the girls. "I'll be right back." "We're not going anywhere," Dani said.

Asilyn forced a smile, and the adults stepped into the hallway. While they watched Lily speak to the officer, the door on the other side of the room opened. Jimmy's crop of red hair poked through, followed by his green eyes and brilliant smile. Asilyn waved him in.

"I'll go see if I can find out what that officer wants." Dani stood and crossed the room.

Thanks, Dani." Asilyn sat up and tried to straighten her hair. Jimmy came to her side and took hold of her hand. "Are you okay, Luv?"

"I am now." She smiled up at him.

Dani reached for the door.

"You gave me a scare. You should have let me walk ya to the trans-stop," Jimmy said. "I could 'ave looked out for ya, besides I...I had something I...I wanted ta talk to you about."

The sudden tremor in Jimmy's voice made Dani alert. She shot Asilyn an amused look, stepped into the corridor, paused for a moment, then hurried to the waiting room.

Carmen Arriere called out, "Dani, is Asilyn all right?"

"She's fine." Waving her arms, she beckoned her friends to her side. "Quick, follow me. I think Jimmy's finally got his nerve up! He's going to ask her!"

Over the protests of the admitting nurse, the entire group rushed through the door, up the corridor, and approached the window.

Lily turned away from the RP officer. "Dani, what's going on?"

Pointing toward Asilyn's room, Dani grinned as Jimmy wiped his hands on his pant leg.

"Go on, Jimmy, ask," Marco, Carmen's present interest, said. "She's not goin' ta say no."

"Shush!" Carmen elbowed the curly-haired young man in the ribs.

"If me Ma asks," said the young man, "I'm gonna tell her why me ribs are bruised."

"Shush." She cocked her arm.

Marco grinned and backed away.

Jimmy opened his left fist and Asilyn's eyes lit up. The lanky lad dropped onto one knee next to the bed.

"It's 'bout time," said Ed Delahan. "He's been carrying that blasted ring about for over a cycle."

A noise down the hallway distracted Dani. She saw her father and Della Ryan hurrying toward the group.

Lily stepped toward them and stopped Asilyn's mother.

Della, Asilyn's fine, she just needs a moment."

"Why, Lily? What's goin' on?"

Lily drew Della closer so she could see into her daughter's room.

Asilyn's eyes glistened. Her hand went to her mouth and she started to cry.

A pang of envy hit Dani when Jimmy slipped the ring on Asilyn's finger. The collective sniffles of the other girls brought a smile to Dani's face. She heard Della Ryan whisper, "He's a good lad. Her father would've approved."

The girls giggled when Asilyn pulled Jimmy close for a long kiss, stopping him from looking around. Over his shoulder she waved her friends off.

"All right, Carmen, Marco, all of you get out of here." While her friends headed down the hall, Dani stole a sideways glance at her father. *I wonder if he'd approve of–*

Her mother's voice interrupted her thought, "No, mi amor, she's not too young."

She's three years older than me. Dani swallowed hard and returned to watching Asilyn. *This could be a problem.*

7

Selwyn Colony
Atwood Estate

Chapter 2
All I'm Seeing Now is Red

Out of the corner of her eye, Jenna watched Maria Atwood's hand hover over her desk, while the comm chirped its annoying beeps. Maria's mood, like Selwyn's weather, had turned stormy and unpredictable. Jenna knew her boss dreaded the call from her father. She had no progress to report and word of recent failures had already reached him. She also knew the brunt of Maria's anger would fall on her for not cracking MacKenna's encryption.

Jenna snapped her gaze to her lap when Maria ignored the beeps and turned toward her.

"Have you come up with a way of Breaking the encryption on MacKenna's data modules?"

"No." Jenna didn't dare look up from her computer. "He lied!" The comm panel chirped again. Maria continued ignoring it. "MacKenna lied to me!"

Let the blame fall on MacKenna. It's because of him and his father, my father plays lackey to this woman.

"Answer me, Jenna! Why not?"

Jenna held her tongue for a moment longer, but she knew better than to withhold the truth, it only made the abuse worse. "I'm not defending him, but he didn't lie. I don't think he told you everything. The module order he gave us is correct, but no matter what system I use, I keep getting this message."

Despite the comm's incessant chirps, Maria left her desk. In half a dozen heavy steps she crossed the office and stared over Jenna's shoulder. On the screen the message flashed in time to the water dripping outside the window. *Computer Configuration Mismatch.*

"What's that mean?"

Jenna dropped her hands into her lap, stared at the floor, and did not answer.

"Well, Jenna, what does it mean?"

The comm's irritating chirps stopped.

"I think it...means we need a specific computer system in order to access these modules."

"Specific system? What specific system?"

Rubbing her sweaty palms on her pant legs, Jenna remained silent.

"Spit it out, Jenna. What system do we need?"

With her gaze riveted on the floor, Jenna whispered, "When we searched MacKenna's flyer, there was this very old computer system in it."

"What? That was probably his father's system!" Maria stepped back and struck Jenna open-handed across the back of her head.

The tall blonde's head snapped sideways and she tumbled off her chair.

"You knew his father's system disappeared from his lab. You had it in your hands and you left it behind. I told you to take everything!"

"You told us you wanted all traces of MacKenna to vanish." Softening her hate-filled stare, Jenna stood, straightened her chair, glanced at Maria, and sat down. "Teresa and I figured we'd take his flyer with us. She wanted it, so we eft everything in it, except the modules."

"How could you be so stupid?"

"You know what happened. While Teresa waited around to make sure MacKenna and the Santiago woman died, his friends caught up with her."

Maria's hand stopped in mid-swing, and she flinched when the comm's chirp restarted. From behind clinched teeth she said, "I suppose you think it's my fault they still have the computer!"

It is. Jenna didn't meet Maria's gaze. *You should have killed him when you had the chance.* She shrank away, continued to stare at the floor, and remained mute. She knew better than to try and avoid Maria's beatings. When she drew closer, Jenna blurted out, "At least Teresa didn't betray us. She took her own life like she was supposed to!"

Maria's arm wavered in the air. "I told your father you're as worthless as your mother." She scowled, lowered her arm, glared at Jenna, then turned away from her and huffed in disgust.

Clenching her fists until her knuckles turned white, Jenna bit her tongue to keep from giving her usual flippant response. Maria paced around the room's perimeter. Jenna could hear her mood worsening as her ranting grew louder. "I won't let the MacKennas or the Santiagos interfere with my family's plans again! We've expended too much time, credits, and energy, and we're too close to remaking the colonies. Now get back there and find out where MacKenna has that damn computer hidden! We need to know what else his father figured out about my grandparents. Find out if they know about the blood hunters."

When the comm stopped its incessant beeping, Maria slipped into her padded seat, turned and stared out the window. After a minute she said, in a soft voice just above a whisper. "Jenna, I'm positive Russell MacKenna left more than one copy of this data around."

An icy chill ran up Jenna's back at Maria's sudden, soft-spoken tone. "Where could he have hidden it?"

Like a child playing, Maria spun her chair around to face her. "What about checking the Arrisian networks?"

Are you out of your mind? Jenna stared at her employer. "The Arrisians have at least ten xonabytes of data storage planet wide."

"I'm well aware of their online storage capacity. Get back there and set up six teams to drill into the Arrisian networks. Find out if and where MacKenna archived other copies."

"Send Lucinda or Kilina." A sour expression crept across Jenna's face. She waited for the comm to cycle through its beeps, then looked up from the floor. "I hate the Arrisians and their colony."

The comm ceased its annoying bleating. Maria narrowed her eyes. "I don't care what you like or dislike. You try pulling another stunt like you pulled on me at the Crystal Lake camp, and you and your father will find yourselves residents of Avalon with the rest of the peasants. You'll do what I tell you, Jenna." Maria's smile turned wicked. "Or should I start planning your wedding to Aedon Fuqua?"

At the mention of the fat old man's name, Jenna shuddered. "That's right, Jenna, he still wants you."

"Oh." Jenna hung her head, her stomach knotted. "All right, I'll go."

"That's better. Now, I want you back on Arriesgado in a fortnight! I want MacKenna dead. Find out why Skylar failed to take the Ryan girl. I want the Santiago woman taken, see to that one yourself. Feed her my father's beguilement drug, then see to it you teach her our truth about her family and her world. Once we have her, she'll bring the other women around to our way of thinking. With all the women on our side we'll control enough land shares to change their laws by legal vote."

The comm chirped again. Maria ground her teeth, scowled at her desk, and stepped toward it. "Take additional people, and have them place new pumps in the northern and southern mountains. I can't wipe those males off that stinking planet, but I can keep them busy and prevent anyone from finding out what we're really doing. My family's waited long enough. My great-great-great-grandfather started this over two millennia ago. I *will* finish it finally and put an end to the MacKennas and Santiagos."

"Why not just send the ships to finish them?"

"It's not the right time! I have to know what the MacKennas and Santiagos know. We cannot afford to have even one of them alive when we change the colonies, otherwise they will claim the crown." Maria stomped over to her desk and stared at the chirping comm. "The ships will fly when I say it's time. Once the Arrisians are gone, we'll prove how necessary it is to settle worlds under the guidance of the Theory of Ordered Colonization. Only then can we Now get back there and make sure Skylar's not taking a holiday. I want all our targets taken in the next two cycles."

"Who should I take with me?" Jenna shifted in her chair, kept her voice neutral and didn't look at Maria. "The only one I trusted was Teresa, and because of MacKenna she's dead."

"Take whoever you want, just get me results! I won't settle for any more failures. Search the networks, find Russell MacKenna's other copies. And get the encryption key MacKenna told us about or I'll start arranging your wedding. I'll join you in two—"

A knock at the door interrupted Maria. It slid open and two

blond-haired girls rushed in. "Mother, Mother, Daddy sent us to get you."

Maria turned away from Jenna and smiled at her girls, mirror images of one another. The girls stopped in front of her. She bent down and hugged each one. When she spoke, all signs of her waspish nature had vanished. "Now dear ones, what is so important? Your father knows I'm very busy right now."

"He said to tell you that–" the first twin started to answer, but her sister finished her sentence. "–that the Selwynian Minister is here."

"Sabrina, what did I tell you about interrupting?"

"Sorry, Mother."

"Now, Ariel, what–" The comm's continual chirping made Maria flinch. She refocused on the two girls. The smile and warmth she bestowed upon her daughters sent another icy chill up Jenna's spine.

"What else did your father say?"

Ariel brushed her white-blond curly hair away from her eyes. "He wants you to hurry downstairs. He said Minister Alwyn has something important to tell you."

Maria bent down and touched the girls' cheeks. "Please, tell your father I will be down momentarily."

The girls kissed her on her cheeks. "Yes, Mother." As they turned, their gaze fell upon Jenna. Both girls gave her a sour look, then ran from the room.

Jenna braced herself for Maria's change.

"Get back to Arriesgado now!" All gentleness in her voice gone, Maria stormed back to her desk. "Find out where MacKenna has his father's computer hidden, and then kill him!" She tapped the control on her desk. "Sorry, Mother, I was busy. How are you and Daddy?"

Jenna shut the computer down, collected the modules, stood, and slipped out of the room while Maria's mother distracted her. Once in the back hallway of the immense mansion, a wicked sneer spread across her face. *This time, MacKenna, you will die!*

13

Outlands
Half Moon Canyon

Chapter 3
I Feel My Nightmares Watching Me

Like a rag doll tossed aside by a careless child, he lay in the street where the explosion's concussion had thrown him. People gathered around and spoke, but their voices made no sound. When he tried to rise, someone's hand stayed his movement and kept him on the ground. He stared into the flames, the images of his father's burning home searing into his mind.

Movement in his peripheral vision caught his attention. He tore his gaze from the carnage and peered into the yards across the street. Like partners in some berserk dance, shadows and light cavorted on the walls of nearby houses. In the flickering madness he saw a pair of eyes, someone lurking in the shadows. The eyes stared at the devastation, a look of insane delight in the upturned lines around them.

Disembodied eyes, familiar, yet unidentifiable. They moved from shadow toward the light and then melted into the darkness, disappearing before he could place them.

The world around him shimmered and changed. He found himself in the barren Wastelands. A sense of being watched made him look up.

The same insane eyes floated above him.

The ground beneath him rumbled and an abyss opened before him. From the pit great flames leapt skyward, licking the dry air. Above him the fire's reddish glow reflected in the eyes, giving them an evil glint. He could feel the malice in their stare stab at his heart.

The land tilted up and he slid toward the pit. The eyes watched him slip toward oblivion. Like a drowning man, he clawed at the insubstantial air, but all attempts to halt his slide failed. He plunged toward the boiling chasm

15

and a fiery death.

The heat grew intense. He clawed at the ground to no avail. The searing heat withered his flesh. He cried out in pain.

He felt the flames lick his skin. Unseen hands grabbed him. "Kalen, wake up!"

When the familiar voice beckoned him, the sinister eyes retreated.

"Kalen! Kalen! Wake up!"

The voice wrapped around him like a lifeline, dragging him away from the flaming abyss.

"Kalen, wake up, mi amor!"

Kalen MacKenna forced himself awake, shattering his nightmare into a thousand burning fragments. He stared up into Mayla's lavender eyes and a calm washed over him. Shifting his gaze, Kalen stared through the door of his domed tent. The sun peeked over the rim of Half Moon Canyon, welcoming him back into the living world. The eyes from his nightmare, however, remained a haunting memory he could not place.

The sky morphed from slate-gray to silver-blue. Kalen and Mayla sat huddled together, outside their tents, watching in the pre-dawn light as nature again put herself on display.

"Kalen, are you sure you don't want to try to get some rest?"

"No, absolutely not." The memory of the last three nights sent shudders through his body. "I slept last night. That was more than enough for me."

"You can't call that sleep. You had that dream again, and more than once, I'll bet?"

"No, it only happened once, but it managed to entertain me all night." He wrapped his arm around her. "Forget it. I'm all right now."

"I'm not going to let this go. You need to sleep." Mayla curled her legs up under herself. "Tell me about your dream."

"Nightmare is more accurate. I really don't want to relive it in the daytime."

"How long have you been having these. . .nightmares?"

"You're not going to let this go, are you?"

"No. As your doctor, I want to help you. As your fiancée, I don't

16

want you flying around brain-dead from lack of sleep. Now, tell me what you see in your dream."

The sun's flaming brow peeked over the lip of the crescent-shaped canyon. The return of sunlight ignited the terra-cotta colored walls behind them. As if on schedule, a small blighted lizard scurried out from a bush and alighted on its rock to warm itself in the returning heat of day. The warm, dry morning air stirred, carrying with it the unending sounds of the three-tiered falls spilling into the north end of the canyon. The water's subdued roar called to him amidst the gentle breezes sweeping down the canyon. Nature began its daily housecleaning duties, and would, by week's end, erase any trace of their five-day stay.

"Would be nice to remain hidden here for another month." Kalen glanced around.

"It would, but you know we have to leave." Mayla laid her head on his shoulder. "Ignoring me this time isn't going to work. Start talking."

The sun moved along its arc, spilling more light into the canyon. Kalen took a deep breath. He let it out with a tentative sigh, then gave her the details of his nightmares, relating all he could remember. When he finished, he said, "So, does that give a hint of why I'm having these dreams?"

"It might." Mayla lifted her head. "I believe you saw more the night of the explosion than you realize. Your conscious mind may have blocked the memory, but your subconscious is trying to make you remember. That's about all I can tell you without some research. If we're going to get back before dark, we'll have to get started."

Kalen kept his eyes closed and pretended not to hear, until she pulled his blanket off him. "If we must." He grinned, stood, extended his hand, and helped her to her feet. Stepping over to the tents he gave their main struts a quick twist and collapsed the domed enclosures. He lifted the compact poly-fabric discs and headed to the flyer. When he reached the Lexicon, he circled to the pilot's door. "Vehicle access."

The flyer's wing doors rose. Reaching in, Kalen tapped a key on the center console control pad. The rear cargo bay cover popped open. He stowed the tents in the pods along with the other gear. Mayla laid their folded blankets and their bedrolls alongside the tents. Moving behind Mayla, he enfolded her in his arms. "Maybe we could stay just one more day?"

"You know we have to leave." She turned within his loose grasp and kissed him. "My parents have our engagement celebration planned for this evening."

"All the more reason to stay." When she pulled loose, he dodged her playful shove.

She slid into the passenger seat and secured her harness.

Kalen rounded the flyer, took a long look around the secluded canyon and sighed. Dropping into the pilot's seat he buckled his harness. His hand danced across the console. The Lexicon's engine started. After the power rose to a safe level, he pulled the yoke back, until the flyer hovered above the ledge the ship perched on. Tapping another key on the console, the landing struts retracted. With a slight pull on the yoke, the Lexicon lifted out of Half Moon Canyon.

"I'm worried about you." Mayla reached over and rubbed his neck. "That nightmare of yours hasn't let you get a full night's rest in the past three days. That's not healthy."

"If I can't sleep tonight, we'll try your remedy tomorrow, I promise."

"No, I want to give you the Nyrasal tonight."

"Let me try on my own. I don't want to become dependent."
"Kalen, for the tenth time, it's not a drug. You won't become dependent."

"All right, all right." He let out an exasperated sigh. "We'll do it your way." He checked the time. "We'd better hurry. We still have to stop in Solana and pick up our clothes for your parents' shindig." Kalen pushed the power up and the Lexicon rocketed eastward.

Chapter 4
Feels Like Coming Home

The town of Solana, nestled at the southern tip of Lake Solana, loomed in the distance. It spread east following the shoreline with grand homes on large lots dotting the lakeshore. To the south, more modest homes and shops spread out along the myriad of roads.

"Okay, where's this tailor shop?" Kalen slowed when the Lexicon approached the city's western boundary.

"Somewhere near the center of town on Cloven Street." Mayla leaned forward and punched the shop's address into the planetary positioning system. "That will take us right to the landing area across from the shop."

Kalen merged with the crosstown traffic. Off the ship's starboard side, he spotted another flyer paralleling their course. "Does your uncle have someone shadowing us?"

"No. If he did, I would've told you. Why?"

"You're going to think I'm paranoid, but I believe someone is following us."

"Where?" Twisting in her seat, Mayla scanned the sky.

"That dark blue flyer on our starboard side, aft. It's been running parallel to us since we came out of the wilds."

"Are you sure?"

"Let's find out." He moved to a higher attitude. Banking right, he merged with the southbound traffic, moving away from their

19

destination.

The other flyer followed.

"Readjusting for new course to reach destination," the planetary positioning system computer announced. *"Make legal U-turn in two kilometers."*

Kalen made the U-turn to port, melding into the northbound traffic.

"Make a right in half a kilometer," the computer's voice instructed.

After a minute he banked to starboard, and slipped into east-bound traffic. The other flyer fell behind, made the identical turns, and followed. "I'm sure."

"What do you want to do?"

"I'm not about to start a mid-air chase in all this traffic. Let's pick up our clothes. Maybe the pilot will get careless and we can get a look at him or her."

"You are approaching your destination on the right."

Mayla scanned the buildings and pointed. "That cluster of shops straight ahead. There's the landing area across the street." Kalen followed Mayla's directions while tracking the flyer tailing them. He settled into the flyer lot and shut the Lexicon's systems down. When the blue flyer disappeared behind the shops across from the landing area, Mayla slapped her door release. "That's too close for me. Let's find out who that is and what he or she wants."

Kalen slipped out of the Lexicon and caught up with Mayla running across the street. She avoided a collision with half a dozen small children and other adults on the walkway. Dashing down an alley between two shops, she reached the far end a few seconds ahead of Kalen, skidded to a halt, and searched for the flyer.

"Over there." Mayla pointed to movement in the woods bordering the town.

A man came out from between the trees.

Mayla and Kalen stepped away from the shadows of the alley into the daylight.

The man spotted them and froze in place.

When Mayla started after him, the man ducked into the woods. The sound of his running footsteps faded away.

"Kalen, what's wrong?" She stopped in mid-step when Kalen didn't follow, turned, and stared. "What's the matter? You look like you've seen a ghost."

He shook himself out of his daze. "Did you see his face?" They heard a flyer engine whine to life.

"I did. Why did that shake you up?"

The dark blue flyer appeared, hovered above the trees for a moment, the whine of its engine rough and uneven. It turned and disappeared into the southern sky.

"Mayla, he looked...ike my father. A younger version for sure, but he looked just like Dad."

Mayla turned and stared at the empty sky. "I guess I didn't get as close a look as I thought. Are you sure?" She turned, walked over to him, took his hand, and looked into his eyes. "Of course you are. Nothing we can do now. Let's go pick up our clothes and change."

Mayla and Kalen headed to the tailor's shop. Kalen glanced behind. *Who the hell was that?*

The Lexicon's 'End of Trip' alarm sounded. Kalen disengaged the navigator and slowed.

"That's our family's estate." A broad smile filled Mayla's face.

"Los Huertos de Cielos."

The sight of the immense mansion, appearing to float amidst a sea of lush green turf, left Kalen speechless. To the east, the deep, liquid-blue waters of Lake Solana rolled, reflecting hints of polished silver from the post-midday sun. To the south, west and north, orchards grew. The trees, like leaf-cowled monks with their arms lifted heavenwards, surrounded the estate.

"Los Huertos de Cielos." Kalen let out a low whistle. "The Orchards of Heaven, how very appropriate." He circled one more time. "Just how many people did your parents invite?"

"Just a few friends."

"More than a few!" He pointed to four dozen flyers parked along the northern border of the south grove. Kalen considered a hasty retreat until he spotted Mayla's parents approaching the landing area. Tightening his grip on the ship's yoke, he prepared to land. The Lexicon settled in among the other flyers. He tapped the controls and the wing doors rose. A warm breeze flooded the cabin with the rich scent of ripened citrus.

The couple stepped out of the flyer. Liana, Mayla's mother, came to them and hugged her daughter. Her lavender eyes flooded with tears and her voice tight, she whispered, "I thought I would never see you again."

"Nor I you." Mayla returned her mother's embrace. "Thanks for being so patient, we needed some time alone."

"Of course. It's been trying for all of us." Liana reached over and hugged Kalen. "Thank you for protecting her."

Quintin grasped Kalen's hand. "Russell and Alannah, were they alive, would take great joy in the son they raised and the man you've become. You're a welcome addition to our family."

Kalen swallowed the sudden lump in his throat. "Thank... thank you, sir."

"Come, everyone is waiting to celebrate your safe return and engagement."

In spite of his own misgivings about large gatherings, Kalen put on his best smile and tightened his arm around Mayla's waist. "Let's go. You heard your father. They're *all* waiting." He took a deep breath and looked around again, a warm feeling of familiarity helping him relax. *Feels like coming home.*

Through the library window in the east wing, Kalen watched while Caesar and Laney, the large Tyrian Setter he'd saved in the Barrera Mountains, played among the shade trees in the estate's courtyard. Caesar's mother came and stood beside him. "Good evening, Lily."

"Good evening." She gazed out the window at her youngest child. "I'm afraid my son has stolen your dog."

"No, Lily, he hasn't." He laughed, watching Laney trying to knock Caesar off his feet. The boy dodged her and pushed back. "Laney never was *my* dog. For a brief time, while I was alone in the mountains, I believed Michael Sandino had murdered Mayla. Then I found Laney, or maybe she found me. Anyway, she provided companionship, helped me to keep my sanity, and distracted me when I felt my thoughts slipping into a dark place. On top of that, she saved my life a number of times. Laney decides who she belongs to and I believe she's made her decision."

The large red dog managed to knock Caesar over, then licked

his face.

The boy's infectious laugher and giggles rippled through the courtyard, penetrating the dual-glazed window.

"Then you don't mind?"

"Look at them, Lily. Do you think I could, or would, break up that duo?"

"Caesar keeps asking when you're going to want her back."

"So that's why he's avoided me for the last two days." He gave her a gentle nudge. "Why don't we go ease his mind right now?"

They exited the library through the door in the outer wall and crossed the courtyard. Kalen drew Laney away from Caesar. Lily took her son's hand and helped him to his feet. In an instant the boy's face clouded up and he was on the verge of tears. "Are you going to take Laney away now?"

Kalen released his hold on the dog. "Well, Caesar, that depends." He reached for the boy and Lily let go of Caesar's hand.

"Depends on what, Kalen?" Caesar came to his side.

"I'm going to be busy from now on. I won't always have the time to look after her and give her the attention and love she needs. I'm looking for someone who will love her and take good care of her. Do you know someone who would do that for me?" With all the enthusiasm and self-confidence of a boy just turned seven, Caesar said, "I can, Kalen! I can do it! I love her! I can take care of her!"

Kalen scrunched up his face and rubbed his chin. "Hmmm, I don't know, Caesar. A dog like Laney's a big responsibility."

"I'd take good care of her, Kalen. I would. I can do it! I can!"

"Have you asked your parents?"

Caesar twisted around and looked at his mother. "Please, Mother, can I keep her?"

Caesar's blue eyes opened wide when Lily didn't answer right away. After a long pause, she gave her son a serious look.

"Kalen's right, Caesar. You'll have to care for her, clean her, and clean up after her. You cannot expect your brother or sisters to do any of that for you."

"I will, Mother, I will. I promise."

"All right, Caesar, but your father and I will hold you to that promise. If you don't take care of her, you won't be able to keep her. Do you understand?"

23

"Yes, Mother."

She pushed the mop of Caesar's blond hair out of his eyes. "Your father and I are serious, Caesar. You must care for her yourself, otherwise she'll go back to Kalen."

"Yes, Mother. I want to keep her! I'll take good care of her!"

Caesar turned to Kalen. "I'll take good care of her, Kalen. I will! I promise."

Kalen gazed upwards, pursed his lips and tapped them with his left index finger as if considering Caesar's fitness for the job. He could feel the boy holding his breath. Kalen relented and squatted down. He stroked Laney's red coat with his free hand. The dog panted, and moved closer to the boy's side. She stared at Kalen as if she understood the decision being made, and was making her own desires known.

"You know, Caesar, I believe you'll do a good job. All right, Laney is your dog now."

Caesar's breath exploded from his cheeks, and a broad smile split his round face. He jumped at Kalen, wrapping his arms around his neck. "Oh, thank you, Kalen! Thank you, Mother!"

Caesar let go of Kalen and took off across the courtyard. "Come on, Laney."

Laney looked up at Kalen.

He patted her, then with a slight tilt of his head, he said, "It's all right, girl. Go on. You belong with him."

She barked once, then chased after Caesar.

When the two disappeared into the house, Lily looked at Kalen. "You handled that nicely."

He stood and looked into her brown eyes. This tall, graceful woman possessed an elegance of spirit and an inner peace he'd seen in few women besides his mother. "I want him to take the responsibility seriously."

"He will. He was the only one she responded to when Zavier brought her here. He's already bathed her twice. He needs a playmate. Dani is too old for him. Sonia and Dulciana have each other and Lucas wants less and less to do with his little brother. Thank you, Kalen. She'll make a great companion for him." She kissed him on the cheek and whispered, "Mayla's right, you are a very special man."

Outlands
Santiago Estate

Chapter 5
You're the One

Kalen sat on a bench in the center of the courtyard, watching Caesar wrestle with Laney. Since he had given her to Caesar three days ago, the boy had stopped avoiding him. At the sound of approaching footsteps, Kalen looked up and spotted Mayla and Cal coming toward him, confusion clouding his fiancée's face. Cal, on the other hand, carried a mini-comp in his right hand and beamed with his usual self-satisfied smirk. When they reached Kalen's side, Mayla sat down next to him.

"What are you two up to now?"

"I have no idea." Mayla scooted closer to Kalen and took hold of his hand. "Cal just told me he needed to speak to us together. Something about securing our future."

"All right, Cal, we've been back for five days. Since our engagement celebration you've been avoiding us. I know that look, brother. What do you mean securing our future?"

"I have a little something to share with you. For the past seventeen years, all the mining operations I've run in the Verdes are due to surveys I found in Dad's lab after his death." Cal's grin spread across his face. "He did a lot of research around Armagh, but never turned his work into the Central Council."

"I didn't know that."

"Neither did I. After I spoke with Mayla's grandfather, he told me to use them to my advantage, and to make sure I took are of you."

Cal settled on the soft turf, opposite Kalen and Mayla.

"Over the past seventeen years we've removed enough gold,

platinum, and other rare minerals out of those five mines that we can all live more than comfortably. Shannan and I have placed twenty percent of each year's profits away for you. With the principal untouched since I started the business, and the interest adding up," Cal tapped the mini-comp's screen, "that's your account's balance."

Kalen took the comp and studied the screen, did a double take, reread it, then stared at his friend.

After a moment, Mayla placed her hand under Kalen's chin, pushed upwards, and then looked at the screen. "You've been holding out on me, my love."

"This is a little something, Cal? What would I do with all this wealth?"

"Anything you want. Call it compensation for your false conviction and imprisonment. You've a right to your happiness. I think together you and Mayla can figure it out."

Kalen's thoughts swam. When he left prison, he wondered what kind of future he had. Now he marveled at the kind of future he could make for himself and his future family, and he knew right where he'd start.

The estate quieted. After a week Cal found Kalen helping with repairs to the second-story porch. "Quintin, can I borrow Kalen for a few minutes?"

"No problem." Mayla's father smiled. "He's been working hard. He deserves a break."

"What's up?" Kalen handed the power nailer to Quintin. "Walk with me."

Kalen followed Cal down the access ladder and through the mansion. Cal headed toward the flyer's landing area. He looked over his shoulder. "I've been lazing about for three weeks. That's long enough."

"You've been conducting business every day." Kalen patted his friend's shoulder. "Take a break. It's been an intense couple of cycles."

"Conducting business by vid is not the same as being with me men. We'll be opening a new shaft in two weeks. I have to make sure the mines are running and our home is secure. Jenna knows where we're living. I'll not be risking her sneaking up on us. I'll be gone for a couple of cycles. Can you be staying out of trouble for that long?"

Kalen gave Cal a playful shove and smiled. "Where did Carla, Shannan, and Neela go?"

"Mom wanted time alone to be spoiling them proper like. It's been a while since she had the chance."

"I could tell how much she missed them the day I visited her. I didn't get the chance to ask about all the trouble when I escaped from the trap Jenna set."

"Don't worry. You can be asking her all those questions when we return. We'll have to take care moving forward, but there's no hiding now that Jenna knows I'm not dead."

"What's Paddy up to?"

"I've sent him and Connor to Erías. They're going to keep an eye on things. I want to know what our brother Sean is doing."

"What do you think he's up to?"

Cal's brow furrowed. "Nothing in particular." He stopped walking and leaned on his flyer. "Like I said, it's just a precaution."

"You've upset Dani, you know."

"I know. She's pretending she doesn't care, but she's pouting and wandering about like a moon-eyed calf. As soon as I can spare someone, I'll send Connor back here."

The two friends embraced, then Cal dropped into the pilot's seat, sealed his flyer and lifted off.

Over a cycle passed before Cal returned with his family. He greeted Kalen, spoke with Quintin and Liana, and then secluded himself with Shannan, Carla, and Neela in the west wing for the rest of the day.

Late on his second day back, he asked Kalen and Mayla to join them. Carla greeted Kalen with hugs, then filled him in on the events after he had escaped from her house. "You caused quite a stir. My heart stopped when that harpy's shot hit your Lexicon and you almost smashed into that tree by Connie's house. After you disappeared, those women cleared out fast. By the time the RPs arrived to ask questions, all we could do was give them a description of the utility van, but neither the women nor the utility were ever found. I turned over their spy gear. The RP later told me it was of no help tracking down the people we saw. Why the info feeds never picked up on the story is a mystery to me."

Carla put her arm around Mayla. She lifted Mayla's left hand and smiled, touching Alannah's ring on Mayla's finger. "Are you sure you know what you're getting yourself into?"

"Yes, I do."

"Has Kalen told you the MacKenna legend?" "What legend?"

"The one behind the ring the MacKenna men give their intended brides?"

"There's a history that comes with this ring?" Mayla looked at Kalen. "When were you going to tell me?"

"I hadn't really thought about it." Kalen scratched his head. "I'm a bit vague on the details. I'll tell you what I do know later." After some small talk, Carla called Neela into the room. "You four need some privacy. I'll take my granddaughter for a walk. We have a lot more to catch up on." She gave Kalen an impish smile and said to Mayla, "You and I need to have a long talk in private about these two."

"I'll look forward to that." Mayla grinned and laughed. "Maybe I can avoid some of his pitfalls with our children."

"She'll give you the real story on these two rogues," Shannan said, laughing when Kalen and Cal cringed.

Carla hugged Kalen. "I love you both." She took Neela's hand and they left the room.

The mood grew serious.

Shannan said to Kalen, "Cal told me the people who kidnapped ya played a copy of me Ma's meetin' with your mother."

"She did more than play it." Kalen rubbed his neck and sighed, "Jenna put the vid in a loop and let it run for hours. I think I have the whole thing memorized."

"I wonder how she got hold of it?" Shannan's face clouded over. "Me Ma swears she never showed it to anyone 'til she discovered Cal's connection to you."

"Shannan and I wanted to talk to you before you saw it." Cal fidgeted with his hands. "I wanted to ease you into this by viewing it together."

"It wouldn't have made any difference." Kalen shifted in his chair, uneasy with the subject. "I'd still think it's pretty far out there."

"Hmmm." Cal pursed his lips and tapped them with the forefinger of his left hand. After a moment he said, "Kalen, do you remember what Dad told us about the universe and the balance between good and evil?"

"I think I do." Kalen paused for a moment to gather his thoughts. "Dad said Shawn always believed the universe strives to maintain a balance between the two. Whenever evil upsets that balance, the universe tries to restore order. I know from Dad's journals that Shawn felt the fortuitous timing of his and Arturo's arrival at Kaladon Crossing and the plague's outbreak were no mere coincidence."

"Maybe Evelyn's experience," Cal said, grinning, "is the universe's way of reaching out to restore order through you?"

"Me!" He gaped at his friend. "Why me?"

For a moment Cal looked at Kalen, and then he burst out laughing.

"What's so funny?"

Cal continued to laugh, then tried to explain between gasps for air. "You. You sound like–like characters out of one of your father's–old stories. The hero is always asking 'Why, me?'" Cal held up his hand and cut off Kalen's protest. He caught his breath. "Think about it, Kalen. You've seen the vid. Can you explain how an eighteen-year-old girl could sit with a woman she'd never met before and accurately predict events taking place in your life now, more than forty years after that meeting?"

Kalen shook his head

"I know you're skeptical, Mayla, but can you?"

"No, I can't." Mayla shrugged and gave Cal a dubious look. "Me Ma would like ta meet ya, Kalen," Shannan said, "and tell you what she can recall about her meetin' with your mother." "Kalen, I can tell you this." Cal leaned forward and stared at him. "Some of what is in the prophecy has already come to pass."

"Like what?"

"Start with your birth. Your Ma always said you came early. You weren't due for two weeks. Yet the voice said, 'Behold, the Child of the Promise. This day shall he be born.' You were born that very evening. Makes me wonder how soon after Russell stopped the vid your mother went into labor."

29

Kalen shrugged it off, but Cal continued. "How about the preservation of your life? The failed attempts to kill you. And what about you finding Mayla after the storm?"

"Those could all be coincidences."

"No way. Like Shawn and Russell, I don't believe in coincidences, especially not in this situation."

"Come on, Cal, it's me, Kalen MacKenna." Kalen tried to laugh, but couldn't. "Do I look like the focal point of some great cosmic mystery?"

"I think what Cal is trying to point out is what Maria already knew." Mayla wrapped her arm around his shoulder. "It doesn't matter whether we believe it or not. The truth is, a lot of people are convinced you and I are at the center of something important. That's why she wanted to discredit you. Like it or not, we are going to have to live with it."

"My, my," Kalen said, leaning away from her. "Haven't we waxed philosophical?"

"No, sweetheart, not philosophical, just practical. I've seen how these people feel about you. All your protests aren't going to change their minds."

Just what I need. Something else making me the center of attention. Kalen shrugged and sighed.

Outlands
Town of Cooperton

Chapter 6
Working on Mysteries Without any Clues

"This looks like a good place," Kalen said, after a quick glance around. He and Mayla stopped in front of an ornate furniture store display. "Is he still there?"

"Yes, but he's keeping his distance." Mayla pretended to admire the arrangement behind a large plexi-panel window in the Cooperton store. "He's too far away to take him."

"I'm getting tired of being tailed and watched by strangers." Kalen tilted his head to avoid the sun's glare. "This is the fourth time we've left the estate and someone's followed us. It appears it's a different person again."

"Do you have any ideas? I'd love to put a stop to this."

"I think I do." He leaned in close and whispered in her ear.

Mayla stepped back, gave him a playful slap on the arm and giggled. In a loud voice she said, "You're so bad. Let's go in and find out if that's possible."

Entering the store, Mayla found a saleswoman. She introduced herself and Kalen. "Alicia, I want to ask you about that bedroom set on display."

"It would be my pleasure." While she headed toward the furniture in question, Kalen held back. "Sweetheart, go ahead. I need to use the bathroom."

"All right." Mayla pulled the saleswoman into a conversation, as they stepped around the display. Kalen darted to the rear of the store and exited onto the street behind the shop. He raced up the block, until he had moved well north of their tail's location. He turned right and ran toward the street the shop faced. Reaching the corner, he skidded to a stop, peered around the side of the building, and spotted the man tailing them. *This should be easy.*

While the man's attention remained riveted on the store, Kalen stepped out and moved into the pedestrian traffic on the walkway. When he had moved close enough, he lowered his head, waited for a clearing between vehicles, crossed the street, and moved into the parking lot. Ducking behind a parked cruiser, he made his way among the flyers and came up behind his target. "Looking for someone?"

The dark-haired man spun around. His brown eyes popped open and his lips moved, but no sound came out of his mouth.

"Who are you, and why are you and the others following us?" Kalen moved closer and grabbed the man by his coat.

The stranger yanked himself free, stumbled backwards, and turned to run.

Kalen tried to catch him again, but someone grabbed him from behind. This new assailant lifted him off the ground as if he were a child. Kalen flailed, but the second man tossed him over a flyer. He flew through the air, bounced off of the next vehicle, hit the ground, and rolled onto his stomach. Grunting, he pulled his legs under himself and sprang to his feet, looked for the two men and spotted them more than a dozen rows away, with Mayla in pursuit. He ran after his assailants. They dove into the same dark blue flyer he had seen before. Kalen continued running, skidding to a halt next to Mayla. The flyer lifted off and rose above their reach.

"Are you all right?" Mayla said between breaths. "Did you get a good look at them?"

"One of them." Kalen clutched his left shoulder and massaged it. "I didn't see the other guy's face. I was too busy trying to get my feet on the ground."

"These were different people like the last three times?" "Yeah, at this rate we'll never find out who's chasing us."

Kalen stood, his fists clenched, watching the flyer disappear in the eastern sky. "I didn't see a registration number, so we can't track it."

"Let it go." Mayla took a deep breath, let it out, and then hooked her arm in Kalen's. "One good thing came out of this."

Kalen tore his eyes away from the empty sky. "Oh, what might that be?"

"I found a lot of great furniture for our new house."

"Really? Imagine that."

Their arms still linked, Kalen made a playful attempt to steer her away from the store, but failed.

While Kalen and Mayla stood in the mansion's courtyard talking, a faint sound drew his attention to the gate. Over Mayla's shoulder, Kalen spotted Neil entering the courtyard. He gave Mayla a nod and pointed. "Your Uncle Neil's back."

Neil smiled when he saw them. As he crossed the courtyard, in his dress uniform, he walked with the stride of a trained and confident officer. A twinge of guilt bit Kalen, and he regretted ever having spoken down to him when they first met. *After all he's done, I need to apologize.*

Neil stopped in front of the couple. "You two look rested. Kalen, how are you feeling?"

"Better, sir. Still a little stiff, but we've gotten back into our sparring routine. The soreness will go away."

"You've been gone a long time, Uncle Neil." Mayla gave him a hug. "What have you found out about Maria and her operation?"

"Not enough. I am still waiting on a couple of reports. After I receive those, I will talk to the entire family. Right now I have something for the two of you." He reached inside his uniform coat and withdrew four data cubes, handing one to Mayla. "Your grandfather recorded this for you three months before he died. He left instructions to give it to you if and when this time came."

"What time are you talking about?" Mayla took the cube, turning it over in her hand.

"Later, when you two are alone, listen to it together."

Mayla looked at the module and then at Neil. "Uncle Neil...what's on it?"

"You will have to listen to find out, that is all I will say." He handed Kalen the three other data cubes. "I am sorry Maria got away with the original modules. My superiors feel you are right about keeping your partial backup copy off-world. These modules contain duplicates of your father's journals and other writings we have cleared. I apologize for prying, but our people have to go through every file to check it for relevant information. You should share these with Cal. Much of the time your father is speaking of you and him. He felt he had two sons, and he was proud of both of them. I know I would be. Also, your father left a vid that will be of special interest to you and Quintin."

"Neil, I've been wondering," Kalen said as he took the modules. "How did you track me in the Lexicon? You showed up just in time to save me when that ship attacked me after I escaped from Mesa Tyree. When Mayla and I were headed north from Escarza, again you appeared just in time." He hooked Mayla's arm with his. "Cal told me you led them straight to the camp in time to see Teresa leaving in the Lexicon."

Neil looked up into the night sky. "While you remained close to the Lexicon, I could always find you."

Walking to the center of the courtyard, Kalen and Mayla settled on the bench near a large Cereza tree. "How? I checked the flyer out after we got to the cavern home Cal built. I never found anything. Zavier had it rebuilt, and the bug still wasn't found."

"I would be disappointed if you had found it." The commander smiled and his blue eyes lit up. "It is a good thing my techs are not as clumsy as Jenna's people, or I might have been the one searching the east coast for you. As for Zavier's friend, I made sure Marcus replaced the CCMF tracker once he finished rebuilding the Lexicon."

"Why didn't you tell me who you were when I came out of stasis?" Kalen scratched his cheek. "I was feeling pretty desperate and lonely."

A pained expression crossed Neil's face. He settled on the bench across from them. "I regret that, Kalen. At the time I did not know whom I could trust. Later we were busy searching for the person who set the bomb in your room."

"Did you ever find the person or persons responsible?"

"We discovered some explosives in the possession of two rehab techs during a surprise security sweep. We arrested and questioned them, but so far they have said nothing that could help us."

Kalen thought back to his first days awake from stasis. He remembered the earliest attempt on his life and wondered if they were the same two women who tried to kill him. "Still," he said, "it would have helped to know someone was close by."

"I almost did tell you the day you came out of the coma and we spoke for the first time. However, I still did not know Doctor Stiller well enough. The only people in the prison I could trust were the ones I had placed there myself when I took over. It was all I could do to keep from telling you, when you asked me about my father on your release day. I wanted you away as soon as possible, and that is another mistake I made. I should have listened to Mayla and let her extract you at Edgeville."

"You had other people watching me?"

"Lieutenants Hidalgo and St. James were never very far from you."

"Lydia and Sandra are your people?"

"Both very fine officers. They send their regards and their congratulations. Kalen, I am sorry I did not tell you."

"Well, that clears up a lot of my questions." He rolled the modules in his hand. "As much as I want to know what Dad stored on the modules, I hope Maria and Jenna stay far away. If I never see either of them again, it'll be too soon."

Lake Solana
Santiago Estate

Chapter 7
Revelation

Mayla stared at the vid-projector, unwilling to view the data module vid she clutched in her right hand.

"Mayla, it's been three days since Neil gave you your grandfather's message," Kalen said. "Are we going to sit here again and stare at that viewer, or play it and find out what he had to say?"

Mayla bit her lower lip, reached for the viewer, then pulled her hand back. "I don't know if I dare. You heard what he said. My grandfather recorded it if this time came, but I'm not sure what 'this time' means. We didn't capture the people responsible for killing him."

"We're closer to getting the answers he sought." "But what could he have to tell me?"

"Maybe just how much he loves you."

Mayla reached for the viewer, but pulled her hand away, opened her fist palm up and said, "You do it."

"Are you sure?"

Mayla nodded, her lower lip pinched between her teeth.

After inserting the module in the viewer, Arturo Elano's image coalesced in the air above the device. Kalen adjusted it so Mayla's grandfather faced her. His image floated there without moving for a moment, giving Kalen time to study the man who saved his life. The ensuing years had not changed the judge much. He still looked as Kalen remembered him. Though his hair appeared a bit thinner, his eyes remained clear and penetrating.

The image broke the silence. *"Mayla, since you are listening to this message, it is obvious our enemies have managed to eliminate me. I'm sorry I cannot tell you this in person."*

Mayla put her hands to her mouth. A soft moan escaped her lips. Kalen wrapped his arm around her.

She laid her head on his shoulder.

Her grandfather continued.

"No matter, I've lived a full life. Mayla, as you're aware, I've made these recordings for you throughout your life. Some have guided you, and others, when Neil needed me to speak to you if I were unavailable. I had one prepared in case you resisted going home to help Mister MacKenna."

The old man shifted his stance before he continued.

"First, I want you to know how proud I am of you. I know you have not had a normal life or an easy one, quite to the contrary. I had Neil keep you busy so you wouldn't have time to form attachments on Wyndimere. I wasn't trying to be cruel, Mayla. I wanted your mind focused on your own world. The people who framed Mister MacKenna are dangerous. I feared if you were thinking of a love on Wyndimere you might get too distracted and that would get you killed.

"Neil and my friends in the service have always kept me abreast of your progress. You have impressed many with your knowledge, skills, dedication, and courage. Graduating at the top of your class at medical school while being so involved with your training, and making the rank of Captain were no mean feats, either. I apologize for using your life for my own purposes. Had I another choice, I would have taken it in a heartbeat. Your parents, your uncle, and I are pleased with you beyond anything we can express. You have freely given more than we've asked of you."

The image turned slightly and startled Kalen when it continued.

"Now, Kalen, I would like to address you. I did not reveal my relationship to the Santiagos on the night we talked, because I didn't know where your feelings lay, or what your father told you about the trouble between the families. It is my strongest hope that you and Quintin have already made your peace. Since you are here, I suspect you have done that

and more."

Mayla reached over and paused the projector. She squeezed Kalen's hand and smiled up at him.

"He was a good man, Mayla. Do you think he would be okay with us?"

"He would be pleased at the outcome." She restarted the vid.

"Kalen, I want you to know how much I regret having to leave you in stasis for the full twenty-five years. Your friends tried their best to clear your name, but no one could get to your father's data. You have a loyal friend in Cal, he's never stopped believing in you. I know you will have tried contacting your other friends after your recovery, but I have instructed them to ignore you. Once again, I wasn't trying to be cruel, but after Martin Santos' death, I think you understand the need to protect them. It must appear to our enemies you're alone and friendless. My hope is to make you disappear once Mayla contacted you, so you can investigate without interference. Neil has instructions to contact your friends once he feels it is safe, and explain your situation. You might want to catch up with some of them in the future."

The old man walked around a desk to a chair and sat down. He hesitated a moment, cleared his throat, then picked up a sheaf of papers and straightened them. After tapping them on the desk half a dozen times, he placed them on the corner, looked into the recorder and continued.

"Now I would like to address both of you. Mayla, I know you never voiced your concerns that my theories of a conspiracy might be groundless, but, as you got older, I could hear it in your questions and see it in your attitude. After we last spoke, prior to your graduation, I could sense your. . .growing resentment. I . . . I went back and read over some of my journals and my thoughts about Kalen and his trial. By now you must know I visited him the night before I sentenced him. I read and reread my entry about our meeting. The more I studied my journals, the more I thought about the two of you working together, and that has weighed heavily on my mind. I began to worry that I had forced you both into something you couldn't handle and that I might be responsible for one or both of your deaths. Then, as I started to record this, I received a strong impression the two of you would wind up good friends, or even more."

Richard R Draude

"See, I told you." Mayla whispered.

"I want to assure you, this is not an old man's manipulations, idle wishing, or daydreaming, but a genuine feeling the two of you belong together. I cannot explain why I feel this way, but it is something I feel to my very core."

Mayla nuzzled her head against Kalen's chest. A soft contented sigh rose in her throat.

"Kalen, not a day has gone by in the past twenty-five years that I have not thought about you and what you have sacrificed. Your courage in accepting my solution impressed those in the CCMF I have shared your story with. Your great-grandfather is not the only MacKenna this world should honor. When you and Mayla finally solve this mystery, I believe that both your names will stand large with your ancestors. Take care of each other and be careful.

"Bien viaje, Mayla Liana Santiago. May you find peace and content-ment along the road of life.

"Bien viaje, Kalen Shawn MacKenna. May the sweetness of a faithful love fill your heart and drive all bitterness of loss away."

The image faded.

Mayla turned her face into Kalen's shoulder and wept.

Lake Solana
North Of Santiago Estate

Chapter 8
Training Day

Dani Santiago had no sooner settled into her new flyer, than she heard the faint sound of Laney panting. She closed her eyes, took a deep breath, and let it out. "Caesar!" Her youngest brother didn't answer. She tapped the center console. Her door moved outward and tilted forward. Heading for the house to get her father, she stopped short when her mother stepped through the courtyard gate.

"He's hiding in your flyer again, isn't he?" Lily hurried toward her daughter.

"I locked it last night. How is he getting inside?"

"Thanks for not starting a fight with him." Lily patted her daughter on the shoulder. "Be patient. He just misses Kalen. I'll try and find out how he's getting past the locks, but don't hold your breath."

"All right, Mother." Dani rolled her eyes and huffed. "But we've got to make him stop."

"Caesar, come out here." Lilianna tapped her foot while counting loud enough for her youngest son to hear her. When she reached eight, Laney bolted from the flyer, stopped, and looked up at the two women, her ears against her head and her tail still. Lily reached down and patted the dog's head. "It's okay, girl, you're not in any trouble. Caesar, if I have to come and get you, it'll be a lot worse." The boy threw the blanket aside and crawled out of the back seat, his eyes glued to the ground. "What did I tell you about sneaking off?"

"But I want to see Kalen."

Dani swallowed her anger. *He really does care about Kalen.* She dropped onto one knee and lifted Caesar's chin. He fought her. In spite of his resistance, she managed to raise his face until their eyes met. "Caesar, Kalen will be back for mid-meal."

"But I want to go and see him now!"

"You can't go with me." She pulled him close and despite his continued resistance, she hugged Caesar and whispered, "I love you, little brother."

Caesar broke loose and ran. Over his shoulder he yelled, "I don't love you!"

"Caesar, come back here right now!" Lily said, but he never slowed down. When he disappeared into the courtyard, Lily turned to Dani. "He doesn't mean it."

"I know." Dani stood and hugged her mother. "It's okay. I have to go." She stepped over to her flyer and dropped into the pilot's seat. Closing the door, she started the anti-grav engine, lifted off, and headed north. *What a morning. First Grandmother and then Caesar.* A smile tugged at the corners of her mouth. Still miffed at her grandmother for making her agree to less than her goal of a two year break from school, she had won a small victory over her parents, nevertheless.

"Dani," her father had said, *"I'd rather you go right to school. Your education is important. In two periods you won't want to go back. Why this sudden urge to explore?"*

"Papa, I'm not ready to get trapped in classrooms again. Carmen and I want to get out and see our world."

"Zavier," Liana, her grandmother said. *"Give Dani the time off.*

She'll go back to school when she's done."

"But two years!" her parents said in unison.

"I didn't say two years." Liana touched Dani's shoulder. *"Dani, I think your father and mother will consider one year. That's plenty of time off before you return to school."*

"But Grandmother, Carmen and I want to take off for longer."

"You agree to a year now, we can see after that."

Knowing she could argue her case later, she gave in. *"Oh...all right."*

Dani peered out her side window. She passed over the northern boundary of the estate. The rugged taupe and dark brown of the natural Outlands landscape looked foreboding, a stark contrast to the family estate with its extensive green lawns and cultivated acreage.

My parents are so out of it. Dani pushed her speed past the limit her father set while she learned to fly on her own. Banking right, she flew out over the water and put her new flyer through a series of aerial maneuvers, looping, barrel rolling, and just enjoying her new-found freedom. After a few minutes, she realized she had reached the southern boundary of Kalen's land. She turned inland over the long rows of saplings Kalen and Mayla had already planted. Seeing the laser straight rows reminded her of another problem she faced. *I'll never agree to inherit the family's land holdings.* She turned toward a building north of the tilled land. "Let Lucas take care of them. Papa may love being an agriculturist, and Mother may find life as a botanist fulfilling, but that's not for me. I want more excitement out of life than watching plants grow."

She circled the house site and remembered Kalen negotiating to buy this land and contracting her grandfather to construct their new home. She laughed to herself now, when she thought of Kalen requesting the home be ready in time for the wedding, six months from now. *He has a lot to learn. He doesn't understand my Abuelo's meticulous attention to detail.*

She settled her flyer next to Kalen's, and giggled. *It won't be ready until well after the wedding.* Dani popped open the flyer's door, and inhaled. Taking a deep breath, she sighed when the scents of citrus trees, the foundation's opened earth, and fresh-cut timbers, flooded the cabin. *I love grandfather's work. It is always out of doors.*

From the back seat of her flyer, Dani pulled her new fighting staff, climbed the hill to the house site and gazed down on the deep blue waters of Lake Solana. She scanned the area for any signs of Mayla or Kalen, but she didn't see them. *They'll be in their new gym.*

A gentle breeze blew her long, raven black hair around her face. She dug into the pocket of her training robe and removed three leather cords, pulled her hair back, and tied it in three places, forming a loose tail that hung to her waist. She looked out at the lake again and spotted a black flyer performing aerial stunts over the water. *Is that Connor?*

Dani uttered a long, angst-filled sigh. *No, his flyer's a lot cleaner.* Turning toward the muted sounds, she recognized the clacks of staffs smacking together and headed for the large plasti-panel building further back from the home site. When she moved past the house's framed structure, the clacking sounds grew louder and quicker. *Kalen and Mayla's bout sounds heated.* She drew nearer the gym Kalen and her Uncle Jamie had built a few weeks ago and thought back to three days past.

"Aunt Mayla, could you teach me..." she had left the question unfinished.

Mayla and Kalen both smiled. Then Mayla handed her the two-meter long tapered pole she now carried.

"Thank you very much," she had whispered. *"How did you know?"*

"We could tell you were dying to try this just by the way you watched us, so Kalen made it for you."

Letting out a playful squeal when she remembered how it felt the first time she took the staff, Dani tossed it into the air. She caught it, let the staff slide in her hand, and stared at her name and the Santiago family crest carved into the head.

The door slid open with a soft hiss. She entered the gym in time to see Mayla leap into the air, avoiding Kalen's staff when he tried to sweep her legs out from under her. While she was still in the air, Mayla snapped her leg out. Her foot came within millimeters of his head.

Dodging the blow, he brought his staff up and caught Mayla behind her knees before she could get her feet on the floor, and flipped her over.

Dani's own body recoiled when Mayla landed on her stomach.

She rolled over and blocked Kalen's strike, spun around and kicked Kalen's legs out from under him with a powerful leg sweep.

Kalen dropped to the mats with a muted thud.

Mayla raised her legs, snapped them down, bounding to her feet. With a quick swipe, she brought her staff down to hit him in the chest.

Kalen rolled to his left and she missed. He sprang to his feet.

Now behind him, Mayla swung.

Kalen raised his staff over his head, blocked Mayla's strike, spun to face her and blocked her next swing. Then they spotted Dani and ended their match.

"Good morning–Dani." Kalen said, between breaths.

Mayla let her staff slide in her hand until one end rested on the ground, then leaned on it. "You're early this morning."

"I tried to leave early to avoid Caesar, but he was already hiding in my flyer. He always wants to come with me."

"You could bring him with you. I don't mind having him around," Kalen said.

"Mother doesn't want him up here. She says he needs to stop pestering you and Mayla."

"Maybe I can speak to him."

"Would you? Mother scolds him and Papa has confined him to his room, but it doesn't help."

"I'm not so sure I'll have much of an effect, but I'll talk to him after midday meal. Are you ready to spar?"

"You're not staying?" Dani looked at Mayla, panic in her blue eyes.

"No, not this morning. Your mother and I are going into So-lana."

"Aunt Mayla, I thought we would be practicing together?"

"You are going to spar, Dani." Mayla patted her back. "You'll be doing it with Kalen today."

The heat rising up her neck made her lower her eyes.

"Dani, he doesn't bite. He's better at staff fighting than I am. You'll learn more if he teaches you."

Dani turned her head to hide her blush when Mayla kissed Kalen. "I'll see you in a few minutes, after I've showered."

Backing off a couple of steps, Kalen snickered, "More like

thirty." He ducked when she swung her staff at him and then Mayla hurried away.

Watching the play between her aunt and Kalen made Dani long for attention. *I wish Connor would call or stop by.* She let out a heavy sigh, laid her staff on the floor and began her warm-up routine. She found her anxiety mounting, since in the past three days she had only faced Mayla. Though she stood as tall as Kalen, his strength and agility intimidated her. Worst of all, Dani always felt shy and nervous around men, except her father and grandfather. Of course there was one other male easy to talk with, and she couldn't stop the smile pulling at her mouth. Since he had appeared at the retreat when Kalen was lost, she hadn't thought much about Connor, at least not more than ten times a day. *Why hasn't he called me?* His silence bothered her, especially since they had gotten along so well while he stayed at the retreat. *If he thinks I'm going to chase after him, he's crazy.*

Kalen's voice brought her back to the present. "Dani. Dani, I'll be right back."

She looked up. Mayla had reentered the gym, her hair wrapped in a towel. She and Kalen left together.

Dani closed her eyes again and continued her warm-up. She tried to imagine feeling as Mayla had taught her, like water flowing from one position into another. While she practiced, her mind wandered back to a conversation with her aunt and a turning point in her life.

"Why do you want to learn this? You could wind up hurting someone."

The idea had startled Dani.

"Hurt someone? I don't want to hurt anyone!"
"Then why learn to fight?"
Between her sobs, she had swallowed her fear and explained. "It's not the fighting I want to learn. It's the way you move. Look at me, Aunt Mayla. When I turned eighteen, I thought I was as tall as I would get. In the past six months I've grown over twenty more centimeters. Now, I'm taller than almost everyone at school. The boys laugh at me and some girls even make fun of me. I'm constantly bump-

ing into things. I can't control my arms and legs. I don't get asked out much because I'm clumsy and stupid, and I'm not very pretty. I've watched you and you are so in control of yourself. You don't trip over your own feet. You're graceful like mother. I thought if you taught me how you move, I can be more like you and her."

Mayla slid down next to her. They sat for a few minutes, Dani's sniffles the only sound breaking the silence between them.

Mayla let out a long sigh. "I guess I forgot just how awkward being in your teens and being tall can be. Uncle Neil had me shipped off to the Marine training camp on my seventeenth natal day. I got over my clumsiness real fast. I am sorry I was so hasty, Dani, having a growth spurt like that is uncomfortable. I would love to help you. I do have a few conditions."

Her tears dried up. "Anything!"

"First, stop referring to yourself as stupid." Mayla reached over and squeezed her shoulder. "You have earned some of the highest grades in your class. Second, you're a very pretty young woman, stop thinking you're not. If you believe I'm just saying that because I'm your aunt and I have to, then ask Kalen. He has told me how much you look like your mother. Third, don't worry about your schoolmates. An intelligent woman intimidates them. You combine that with good looks and a good figure and you'll discover you frighten them. The only defense they have is to tease and laugh at you to hide their own insecurities. Children can be cruel, it isn't until they mature that it stops, and sometimes not even then. Consider it a great compliment to have them so jealous of you. Another thing I want you to do, stop slouching over to hide how tall you are."

Dani remembered blushing when she looked down at herself.

"When I do that I stick out."

Mayla had pulled her close and whispered.

"We all do, Dani. It's nothing to be ashamed of, in fact it's part of becoming a woman. Be glad you didn't wind up tall and flat-chested,

47

that's a pitiful combination. Now, do you think you can agree to the things I just told you?"

Dani could not stop her smile from spreading. She nodded. "Then we can get started."

"Aunt Mayla, why did you come looking for me when you already said no?"

"Because someone reminded me, I was being an idiot."

"Kalen?"

"Yes. He cares a lot about all of you." Mayla stood and said, "Oh, and another thing, don't expect results overnight. You will have to practice and be very patient."

A sudden thought struck Dani.

That's when I stopped resenting Kalen.

Finished with her routine, she opened her eyes and found Kalen smiling at her. "I'm not very good at it yet," she said, to cover the heat she felt rising in her neck again.

"Dani, I can tell you have kept up with your practice. You've come a long way in a short time."

"You can tell?"

"Of course, it shows in your movements."

"Do you really think so?"

"Can't you see a difference?" "Well, I feel different, but…"

"Still, you can't see yourself, so you don't really know, do you?"

"I want to believe I'm doing better, but…" Dani shook her head. "I just don't feel like I'm improving."

"Well, believe me. You've improved a great deal in the past six cycles."

Dani felt her face flush at the compliment. "Now let's see if we can make you even better."

Dani grimaced at the knot Kalen's grin put in her stomach.

Chapter 9
Attack

Outside the gym, Dani stood, aching, bruised, and showered, waiting for Kalen. She went over their training session. Once he had reinforced his basic instructions for using her staff, they sparred. Each round he pressed her a little harder. She had managed to win their last, but only after he dumped her six times.

Dani rubbed her outer thigh. Oh, that hurts." Other parts of her body, including her backside, hurt just as bad. Not just from their sparring, but because every time her attention wandered, he emphasized her need to keep a close eye on him by whacking any part of her anatomy she failed to protect.

While she waited for Kalen to finish his shower, she watched the same black flyer she'd seen earlier making loops over the lake. From this distance, she thought it might be Connor's, but when the pilot finished and flew closer to the shoreline, she realized this one looked nothing like his. The flyer glided toward her and hovered over the framed structure of Kalen's new house. The gym door slid back and Kalen stepped out. Dani turned to him and said, "Are you expecting anyone?"

"No. Why do you ask?"

"It's just that there's–" she pointed toward the house, "a flyer coming." However, when she looked again, the flyer was only a speck over the lake. "That's weird. It was right there a moment ago."

"Maybe they're lost." Kalen looked out over the water. "We'd better head back." He led the way to her flyer. "You did very well today, Dani. You've picked up the defensive moves quickly. That last leg sweep caught me off guard."

"I tried to combine the exercises Aunt Mayla taught me with the staff moves you showed me."

For a moment, Kalen looked startled. "Very good. You connected the two quickly. Mayla told me some people never make the connection."

They reached the flyer and Dani headed for the passenger side.

"Dani, this is your flyer, so fly us back. Your father tells me you're already quite a good pilot."

"Really? Papa said that? You don't mind?"

"Really. He did, and I don't. I still remember what it was like after I got my pilot's license and my father let me take the Lexicon out for short flights. Take us home."

Dani could not stop the grin pulling at her mouth. She hurried around the flyer, opened the doors, and slipped into the pilot's seat.

Kalen climbed in and secured his harness.

She took her time fastening her harness. Once she started the engine, Dani made a careful check of the power levels and the instruments, then fidgeted with the controls. She rechecked her harness, rechecked the reading, then fingered the throttle and played with the flight controls.

Covering her hand with his, Kalen said, "You're a good pilot, Dani. Stop fidgeting and take off. You'll do just fine."

Dani's cheeks warmed.

"Let's go." Kalen laid his head back.

She pushed the throttle forward and lifted off. The landing struts retracted, and she pointed the flyer south, then glanced over at Kalen. He still had his head back and he had closed his eyes.

"You see, nothing to it."

Dani's hands trembled as they flew south. She laughed to herself, remembering how her father had sat rigid and nervous, watching every move she made. The onboard computer's alto voice shattered the quiet, *"Vehicle approaching from the northeast, possible collision."*

Kalen sat up and scanned the starboard side while Dani looked around. Off to her port side she spotted a black flyer. "Kalen, that's the flyer I saw coming in from the lake."

The ship slowed its approach, but continued to close in. "What do they want? What should I do?"

"Dani, stay calm and continue toward home."

Kalen opened the comm and called, without an identifying pre-amble, "Hey Cal, you around?"

After a moment, to Dani's delight, instead of Cal, Connor respond-ed. "Cal's not on the hunt today, might I be of service?" His response confused her.

"That's too bad." Kalen looked out the rear window. "I thought he'd be interested in a bird we spotted over the lake."

"That he would. I'm in the area. Are you needin' me to come over and take a few shots of this bird?"

Dani gave Kalen a puzzled look and tried to speak, until Kalen put his fingers to his lips. She bit off her words, realized what the two men were doing, and listened to Connor, fascinated by his brogue, then disappointed he could be in the area and had not contacted her.

"Yes." Kalen looked out the rear window and scanned their surroundings again. "You'd best hurry, before it realizes we're interested and flies away."

"Headed toward home, are ya?"

"That we are."

"I'm thinkin' a wee bit of a detour is in order. Just ta see how curi-ous this bird is about ya."

Before Kalen even told her, Dani made a sweeping curve to port and headed farther out over the lake, then turned south again. The pursuing flyer turned with them and closed the gap.

"Good girl." Kalen squeezed her shoulder. "Careful, Dani. Now speed up and stay out ahead."

"Kalen, how far away is Connor?"

"I have no idea. I didn't even know he was in the area."

"Neither did I," she half whispered. *Why hasn't he called or come by to see me?* Dani flinched at Kalen's attempt to hide his smile.

She increased their speed and the other flyer fell behind. She glanced at her flyer's nav-computer, then took the opportunity to scan the air in hopes of spotting Connor.

Kalen twisted around and stared out the rear window at the pursuing vehicle. "Connor, how long before you get here?"

"I'll be there in two minutes."

"Kalen, that other flyer's getting closer. What do you want me to do?"

"Keep on this heading. I want to–"

The computer broke into their conversation. *"Vehicle approaching from the southwest."*

Kalen snapped his head around. "Dani, turn hard to port!" The second flyer closed the distance.

Dani accelerated, staying out ahead of the two ships, until the first pilot put on a sudden burst of speed.

"Climb, Dani, climb!"

Dani pulled on the yoke and the flyer shot skyward. A sudden burst of pulsar fire whizzed past the flyer on her side. For a moment, Dani's hands froze on the yoke, but she managed to put the flyer into an inside loop.

"Connor, get here quick! This bird has a friend. We're taking fire."

"I'll be right there."

At the top of the loop, Dani scanned the flyer's computer screen. She could see the other flyer closing in from the south, while the trailing flyer stayed right on her tail.

"Dani, roll out to starboard now!"

"Kalen, I can't fly like this!"

"Just do as I tell you, roll out to starboard!"

Dani tried to maneuver, but she couldn't get her flyer to respond. The other ship fired again and her flyer lurched. The control console blazed with red warning lights. Dani panicked and released the yoke.

She saw Kalen reach over and yank the yoke, then twist it to the right. The flyer shuddered, righted itself, then plunged toward the lake.

She stared at him. He shouted something, but his words didn't make sense.

Her flyer continued to plummet toward the water. She couldn't move her arms, they felt rooted to her lap. It didn't matter, she knew they were going to crash. Something made her cheek sting. She heard Kalen shout, "Snap out of it, Dani! Hold the flyer steady!"

"Kalen, I'm sorry." She grabbed the yoke, refocusing her attention on controlling the little ship.

Kalen released his grip on the yoke. His hands danced over the computer controls, and the flyer leveled out.

Despite her best efforts, they continued to lose altitude. The eastern shoreline loomed ahead.

"Dani, the main converter's damaged. The secondary's not keeping up and we're losing power. We have to land."

The pursuing flyer fired again, Dani twisted to port and the energy bolt whizzed by on their starboard side.

"Where?" She winced from the pain coursing through her stomach.

Kalen put his hand on hers. "Take it easy, Dani, you can do this. Now make for that grassy patch just beyond the shoreline." Dani slowed the flyer's descent, while Kalen spoke over the comm. "Connor, our main converter's damaged. Dani's going to land."

"I see ya. I'll be there directly."

Dani resisted the urge to look for him, and aimed the flyer at the beach. Just meters above the water, she held on as they closed in on land. They made the shoreline, then hit the ground, bounced, skidded, and turned sideways, sliding in the grass toward the trees. When it hit the bare ground, it came to an abrupt halt near the edge of the woods. Kalen slapped the door controls, and Dani released her harness. Kalen grabbed their staffs from the rear seat. Dani and Kalen scrambled out of the wreck.

Dani got a good look at her flyer. "Oh no, Papa's going to kill me!"

"Dani, forget the flyer!" Kalen grabbed her arm and dragged her into the woods, while energy bolts ripped the ground open behind them. At the edge of a wide ravine they halted.

She stared at her flyer now in flames.

"Dani! Snap out of it!" Kalen pushed her staff into her hands. "Hang onto this! Look!" He pointed toward the lake. The first flyer was almost on top of them. It fired again and set the trees to their right ablaze. Dani tried to spot the second flyer, but it was nowhere in sight.

"Quick, down into the ravine." Kalen gave her a firm push.

She dropped over the edge, and half slid, half tumbled down the steep embankment, just ahead of the dust cloud. She hit bottom and dashed south across the floor of the deep cut in the landscape. In the distance, she spotted the other flyer coming toward her, and turned to warn Kalen. He stood on the top of the ravine fighting with someone.

The flyer stopped and hovered above the ground about twenty meters away. A thin-boned man leapt out and ran at her. She backed away, her heart in her throat. Then, in her mind, she heard Mayla's voice. *Don't let fear control you. As long as you are free, you can defend yourself.*

Dani pushed her dread aside and raised the staff.

The man closed in. Still unsure of herself, she held the staff out vertical, but continued to back away. She knew he could read the fear in her eyes, because he laughed and raced straight at her. She swung at his head.

He ducked under her blow and dove at her legs.

Dani leapt into the air and over her attacker. The man skidded on his side, rolled over, and sprang to his feet. Before she landed, he kicked her legs out from under her. Dani tumbled to the ground. She cried out in pain when the hardpan and rocks bit into her back. She almost lost her grip on her staff.

The thin man reached for her.

Dani drove the heel of her boot into his right thigh, recovered her staff and hit him in the head.

"Yow, ya little bitch!" Limping, he staggered backwards, his hands clutching his right temple. Dani scrambled to her feet, charged, swung, and hit his head again. She turned to run, but another man tackled her.

"Not this time, deary. You're comin' wit' us."

They tumbled to the ground. Her staff flew from her hands. The second man lost his grip on her and she rolled away. Dani leapt to her feet and dodged the second man when he tried to grab her. Over his shoulder, she saw Kalen alone, sliding down the ravine wall. She spotted her staff just behind her opponent. When he lunged at her, she leapt into the air and he missed her. To her left, his companion staggered to his feet. Dani hit the ground, dove for her staff, grabbed it, and rolled back onto her feet in time to face the two men. She backed away from them. The first man grabbed for her, but howled in pain when she smashed his face with a blow from the heavy end of her weapon.

The second man lunged for her, when from out of nowhere Connor tackled him.

She took a deep breath then turned to face the first man, but he was busy fighting Kalen.

The first flyer dove at her. She flattened to the ground as it skimmed over her, the ping of its weapon so loud and close the flash almost blinded her. Under the bombardment, her two assailants broke away and fled. Kalen and Connor gave chase, but the airborne flyer fired again, stopping them in their tracks. The two men made it to their vehicle, took off. Then both flyers disappeared.

Dani sank to the ground, struggling to catch her breath. "Dani, are ya all right?" Connor rushed over to her.

She nodded her reply, her chest too tight to talk.

"Connor, Dani, let's not wait around here, in case they come back with more men." Kalen headed for Connor's flyer.

Connor extended his hand to Dani.

She grasped it and Connor pulled her to her feet. Exhausted from this unexpected struggle, she didn't resist when he slipped his arm around her waist to help her run. By the time they reached Connor's flyer, Dani felt stronger, but let him help her into the back seat. Once secure, Connor took off and they raced across the lake toward the estate.

Lake Solana
Santiago Estate

Chapter 10
Trapped?

Dani looked back toward the lake. "Oohhh noooo, my parents are going to kill me."

"Now, why would they be doin' that?" said Connor. "Didn't you see what I did to my new flyer?"

"It's all right, Dani." Kalen reached over the seat and took her hands in his. "It's over." When she wouldn't look at him, he lifted her chin until they were eye-to-eye. "Dani, forget the flyer. It's not your fault."

"How can I?" She turned her head away. "Papa warned me to take care of it."

"Because it's just a machine." Connor took a quick look over his shoulder. "They'll be glad no harm's come ta ya." He touched down at the edge of the south grove and opened the doors. He and Kalen climbed out. Liana reached the flyer first, and took her granddaughter's hands in her own. "Mi hija, are you all right?"

With her family close, emotions she'd held in check overwhelmed her and tears flooded Dani's eyes. She shook her head and trembled. "No, Abuela, I've never been so scared." Her hands and legs trembled, and she started weeping.

"Come, Dani, let's go inside." Liana stood, and extended her hand to Dani.

Dani tried to stand, but her legs wouldn't support her weight. Her grandmother stepped aside. Another pair of arms lifted her out of the vehicle. She looked up into her father's concern-filledeyes.

"Papa, I'm sorry. I didn't mean to–"

"Hush, Dani." Zavier pulled her close. "This wasn't your fault. A flyer I can replace. You, on the other hand, are one of a kind."

"I love you, Papa." Dani lay her head on her father's chest. "Dani, Dani!" Caesar came running up, and grabbed her hand. "I'm sorry."

She looked at her little brother, his face ashen and his eyes wide with fright. "I'm sorry, Dani. I do love you."

"I know, Caesar. I love you too."

The adults stepped aside as Zavier carried Dani to the house, Caesar clutching the cuff of her pant leg.

Catherine, Jamie, and Quintin gathered around Kalen and Connor. Quintin asked, "Kalen, how could this happen?"

Kalen turned his attention to the adults. "I'm not sure. Dani spotted a flyer earlier this morning, before she started her workout. She thought the pilot was practicing aerial maneuvers over the lake. When I came out from my shower, she told me that same flyer had approached the building site. When she turned around, it was far over the lake. I didn't think much about it at the time."

Zavier approached the group and placed his hand on Connor's shoulder. "I'm glad you were nearby, son."

"I wasn't close enough, Mister Santiago. Kalen and I were busy with the first attackers. Dani, I mean, Daniella kept those two men busy on her own. If it wasn't for her fighting them off, their plan might have succeeded."

"Let's go inside." Quintin slipped his arm around Liana's waist. "I've placed a call to Neil. He should be here late this afternoon. Until then, let's see if we can sort some of this out."

Dani looked up from her bed when her mother entered her room. She stood and Lily put her arm around her. "Connor and Kalen told us what happened. How are you feeling?"

"A little better." She laid her head on her mother's shoulder. "I was never so scared in my life."

"I can't imagine how terrifying that would be. Connor told Mayla how well you defended yourself."

The tone of her mother's voice changed with her last statement.

Dani lifted her head from her mother's shoulder so she could look at her. "Connor told you?"

"He sounded really impressed. He's quite taken with you, you know?"

The heat rising in her cheeks made her turn her head.

Her mother laughed, then held Dani at arm's length. "I know you want to rest, but Neil just landed. He's asked that you join us."

"Oh, Mother, do I have to?" She let out a long, breathy sigh.

Her mother ignored it and led Dani to the door. Reluctant to face anyone, she dragged herself down the stairs, perking up when she saw Connor seated with the other adults. Neil stood in the center of the west wing's large sitting room. She took a seat next to her mother, smiled at Connor, and listened while Kalen went over the events.

"Dani, did you recognize either of the men who attacked you?" Neil turned. His question startled her.

"I've–I've never seen either of them before." Dani pulled her eyes away from Connor. "Why–why were they after me?"

"I don't know, Dani." Neil came to her, knelt down, and covered her hands with his. "You can be sure we are going to find out." He turned to Connor. "Mister O'Dell, did you see any other activity in the area?"

The question caught Connor off guard. He sat up straight. "No–no, sir. I only saw the two flyers. Might 'ave been others, but I wouldn't 'ave noticed, though. I was too busy tryin' to get ta Miss Santiago and Kalen."

Despite the effect of the day's events, the sound of Connor calling her Miss Santiago put her on edge. *Why is he acting so formal?* Out of the corner of her eye she caught a smile pulling at the corners of her mother's mouth. *What's so funny?*

"How about you, Kalen?" Neil's question interrupted her thoughts. "Anything familiar about them?"

"No. I went over everything I could remember, but Jenna's crew was mostly women. None of those men were up at Brighten Meadow."

Quintin paced the floor behind Kalen and Mayla. "I've never heard of such a thing, attacks in broad daylight."

"But why Dani?" Lily gripped her daughter's shoulder. "What could they want with her?"

"I'm grateful Connor was nearby to help." Zavier looked over at the Verdean. "I will not forget this, young man. My wife and I are in your debt."

Connor's cheeks reddened. He glanced at her.

In his eyes Dani saw panic mixed with something more important. Her heart beat faster. He dropped his gaze and looked away.

Her mother nudged her and leaned closer. "Dani, pay attention to Neil. You can talk to Connor later."

Neil's words sounded distant while she stared at her mother. *How does she know what I'm thinking?* She turned her attention to Neil.

"Until I know what we are dealing with," Neil said, "I am going to insist that all of you have an escort whenever you leave here."

At Neil's declaration Dani groaned. *Any freedom I did have just evaporated.* The adults fell into discussion about the need for additional security and how they would protect all the children. Dani looked over at Connor. *Being stuck here could have advantages.* When their eyes met, she turned up her smile. *Why is he calling me Miss Santiago?*

Connor's eyes got wide and he looked away again.

"I'll close the house in Andalusia," Quintin said. "Our families will remain here until this crisis is over. I never intended for this home to become an armed encampment, but protecting all of you here will be easier. I will put one of my crews to work around the clock on Kalen and Mayla's new home until it is finished."

"What can we do to help?" Kalen took hold of Mayla's hand. "Mayla, Kalen, I'm sorry to push you like this, but Liana and

I want you to move up your wedding date. That will be one less thing that our enemies can interrupt."

Kalen squeezed Mayla's hand.

She leaned her head on his shoulder, her smile an unmistakable yes.

"I think we can live with that," Kalen said, his eyes alight. Neil turned to Dani. "Dani, I understand you and your friend

Carmen are scheduled to do a little exploring, now that you have finished school."

Yeah, you just killed that idea. Dani gave him a clipped nod and frowned.

"Instead of trapping Dani here." He spoke to Zavier and then Lily. "I think that is exactly what you should let her do."

Though he startled Dani, her mother bolted upright. "Neil, are you out of your mind? I'm not letting her go exploring alone and unprotected. There's no way to watch over her!"

"It seems that whoever is after Dani already knows her whereabouts and schedule." He stepped closer to Lily. "I would not endanger her life in any way. I will have Kalen put together an itinerary of places she can go that are within a long day's flight of here. He should have enough to keep them busy for about six cycles. After that, we will see. The only ones who will know where she is at any time will be our immediate family."

"Lily, Neil's right." Zavier slid forward in his seat. "Can you think of any better place to hide her?"

"No. I'm not sure I want her out there alone." Lily pressed her lips together and hugged Dani. "But that doesn't mean I won't worry."

"Dani."

"Yes, Papa."

"You and Carmen will stick to the route Kalen lays out." Zavier said. "No side trips on your own. Otherwise, we will bring you home, do you understand?"

"Yes, Papa." Dani could hardly believe her ears or her luck.

"I want you up at our gym every day until you leave," Mayla said. "Kalen and I will see to it your training is complete."

Dani's shakes disappeared. She sat up. "Mother, can I call Carmen and tell her we're going a little early?"

"Oh, all right." Lily brushed a stray strand of hair from Dani's face. "I still don't think this is a good idea, but go ahead."

"Oh, thank you!" Dani gave her mother a quick kiss on the cheek.

"Make sure you tell your friend to talk to no one about this." Neil walked over to her. "In fact, tell Carmen to act as if you have had to cancel your plans. Tell her to say she's coming here for a visit. And ask her parents to drop her off. I will speak to them."

Dani nodded and bolted from the room.

Kalen tried not to laugh when Lily leveled a cold, hard stare at Neil. "You should have discussed this with us first."

"Easy, Lily." Leaning forward, Neil checked the stairs. "I haven't lost my mind. She won't be out there alone. I intend to keep a close eye on her. I will have four men not far away. As long they think they are out on their own, we can let them enjoy themselves."

"Did you know about this?" Lily turned to Zavier with the same look in her eyes.

"It is news to me, but I have to agree." Zavier looked over his shoulder. "I don't relish the idea of trying to keep her cooped up here."

"Neither do I." Quintin's gaze shifted to the staircase. "I don't know who would be more miserable, her or us."

"Quintin!" Liana's indignant tone made Quintin wince. Zavier came to his father's defense. "You know it's true,

Mother! We'd all be miserable."

Liana huffed. "You don't have to be so blunt about it."

"Look at it this way, Lily," Catherine said, "she'll think she's out on her own, but we'll know exactly where she is and what she's doing. That's better than what you had a week ago. With Neil's men watching her, what could go wrong?"

Outlands
Santiago Estate

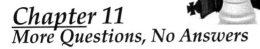

Chapter 11
More Questions, No Answers

Kalen looked around the corner. "Why is everyone looking at the stairs?"

The others laughed.

"What's so funny?" Kalen checked the stairs again. "I don't understand."

"Zavier, don't keep him in suspense." Mayla giggled. "Dani has a real knack for eavesdropping."

"You've caught her at it?"

Zavier peered over his shoulder. "So far, no one has." "Then how do you know she's doing it?"

"Because my granddaughter always knows too much." Liana glanced at the stairs.

"All right, enough." Quintin took a quick look over his shoulder. "Now that we've settled Dani's suspected foibles and her safety, Neil, what else can you tell us?"

"Sorry I have been away for so long." Neil took a seat opposite the family. "I know you are all anxious to learn what my investigation has uncovered, so I will get straight to it. We have completed the analysis of the compounds being pumped in the Verdes water supply by Maria and her people.

"Kalen, we found, among the files you copied, your father's journal entries on his discovery of the people pumping their poison into our waterways. It seems there is a naturally occurring element in the water of the Muro Verdes. By itself, it is harmless, but when mixed with the compound Maria and her people were injecting into the waters and then ingested, it causes sterility in men. As Mayla surmised, its effects are neither permanent, nor does it cause birth defects."

Mayla let out a sigh. "Shannan will be glad to have that confirmed."

"Why did they wait so long before they started in on the Barreras' waterways?" Kalen said.

"Because the Barreras receive their water from the ice harvests, the element does not occur naturally in these rivers and lakes." Neil rubbed the back of his neck, a wry smile on his long face. "From our tests it is highly unstable once removed from water. After it's extracted, they needed a process to keep it stable until they could combine the two elements and pump them into the waters in the Barreras. Only then could they start on this part of Arriesgado. It must have taken them all this time to get it to work."

"To what purpose?" Lily shook her head, her eyes wide with disbelief. "It hardly seems worth the effort and expense twenty-five periods of research and development would cost. Besides, none of it makes any sense, they never really stood a chance of taking over our world."

"What Maria Atwood's plans are, still has not become clear, but we now know she's the moving force behind all we've come up against. My father always felt that any action against this world by the Consortium was partially out of revenge for our success."

"That's absurd!" Zavier leaned forward and raised his hands, palms up. "No one carries a grudge for a hundred periods."

"Thank you, brother." Mayla narrowed her eyes, and turned her gaze on Neil. "That's exactly what I told him the night we left Wyndimere."

Keeping his face neutral, Kalen almost laughed at the silent standoff taking place between his fiancée and Neil.

"Do you believe there's something to your revenge theory?" Quintin said.

Breaking eye contact with Mayla, Neil turned his attention to his brother-in-law. "Without the rest of Russell MacKenna's records, I cannot confirm much of anything. What we do know is this. Kalen's father became aware of this group's activities. When he dug into what they were doing, whoever started this became aware of him. They had him and Jancee killed, and framed Kalen for the murders. What they did not count on was my father. Kalen, when he sentenced you to Cold-stasis, it put a large kink in their plan. The chance you would go looking for answers must have worried the original conspirators."

"Damn straight I'd look into their deaths." Kalen lifted his arm from Mayla's shoulder and stood. "But how could Maria Atwood be connected to all this? She's what, in her early thirties? That makes her between eight and fourteen when your father sentenced me. Neil, how could she be involved?"

"Her family is one of the oldest and most powerful in the consortium." Neil closed his eyes and pinched the bridge of his nose. "Her father and husband both hold prominent seats on the Governing Quorum, as did her grandfathers, going back eighteen generations. More than likely one of her family was there when Shawn and Arturo made their appearance."

"Is the Quorum getting involved again?" Quintin said. "Publicly the Governing Quorum has remained silent. My sources tell me that some of the members are demanding they enforce the 'Ordered Colonization' rules on all the colonies."

Connor slammed his fist into his open hand. "The Quorum and their precious theory! Even when they're proven wrong, they want ta continue to enforce it, puttin' a stranglehold on everythin'." His blue eyes narrowed. "The only people who benefit from enforcement are the Consortium and the Quorum."

"That's why they want it, Connor," Quintin said. "It's not about making things better, it's about control." He returned his attention to his brother-in-law. "Neil, what about Maria Atwood and Jenna? Do we have anything on them?"

"No. They have covered their tracks completely." Neil's bewilderment showed when he stood and walked to a window overlooking the courtyard. "We have no proof of their presence here. I have made discreet inquiries and Maria's husband and her father will only say that she has been under a doctor's care for the last six cycles, unable to leave her home. Jenna's identity, on the other hand, is a complete mystery. She is not in any of our databases. I cannot even find out her lastname."

Kalen took a deep breath. He let it out in a slow, quiet stream, and started pacing in front of Mayla. "Neil, we saw Maria! She knows who planted the bomb that killed my father and Jancee!"

"I know, Kalen, calm down." Neil turned away from the window. "You saw through her disguise, but you did not actually see her."

"No." Kalen clenched his fists, disgusted with himself for letting her and Jenna get away. "It was more of a desperate guess."

"I am afraid it is your word against hers." He walked over and put his hand on Kalen's shoulder. "Though all of us here know it is true, it will not hold up in court. An ex-stasis prisoner's and his fiancée's word are not legal reasons to spur an investigation into the life of such a prominent and powerful woman. We need to capture her on Arrisian soil to prosecute her."

"What about the other women in the camps?" Zavier almost jumped from his chair. "Can't we use them to prove her presence here?"

"Maria left nothing behind of a personal nature. Before escaping, she destroyed everything connected to her or Jenna."

"Uncle Neil, surely some of them can identify her!" Mayla said. "Cal's friend in Crystal Lake RPs worked up a complete description of Maria from the women they questioned." He removed a cube from his pocket and pressed into the large vid viewer on the wall over the fireplace. "To the last one, they all described her as an older woman with red hair, blue eyes, and a pock-marked face." An image of a woman appeared.

"That's damn close," said Kalen.

"Maria must have lived in disguise." Neil removed the cube. "Kalen, I am surprised you could see through her camouflage."

"Maria's arrogant and thought she had us. That overconfidence let me get close to her and Jenna." Through clenched teeth he said, "I should have hit Jenna harder. Another half second and I would have had her and the modules!" Kalen paused and scratched the back of his neck. "This is getting us nowhere. What did you find out about the Kliner Institute?"

Returning to the window, Neil clasped his hands behind his back. "When questioned, they told the RPs they don't use La Blanc model one cruisers, way too expensive for their needs. As for the ones you saw, they have no idea who registered them to their company and put their logo on the sides."

"How convenient," Kalen said, not hiding his disgust.

"I cannot press the investigation any further, since the service is not supposed to involve itself in local matters."

"Then they've managed to cover their tracks and this really isn't over?"

"No, Kalen, this is not over. We still do not know about the changes my father said he discovered would open the way for the Consortium to begin mining on Arrisian soil. With the Central Council suspending business, they have sealed away the documents spelling out changes in the laws up for a vote. A connection to the New Surrey Mining Company concerns me, and questions of the murders of your father, your wife, and my father are still unanswered. Since we cannot prove Maria's involvement, we have no way to clear your name, yet."

Neil paced in front of the window. "Cal's RP friends in the Crystal Lake region interviewed all the women taken in the raid. To a person they claim to come from a world they call Avalon, yet no such colony exists." He looked over at Quintin and said, "Since Kalen and Mayla know who Maria is and she knows they are still alive, I want to keep my contingent of men on guard. We do not want any further surprises. I will make sure they stay out of the way."

"They're not in the way," Quintin said. "Tell them to stop avoiding the estate. They're welcome here."

"I do not think they should–"

"Neil, if Maria or her people are watching, don't you think it will be better if your men appear as part of my work force, instead of a guard unit?"

"Of course." Neil paused for a moment, took a deep breath, then said, "Enough of this gloom and doom talk, life goes on." He turned from the window, a frown on his face. "Mister Mackenna. you have dragged my niece all over the Arrisian countryside without the benefit of a proper chaperone. When do you plan to make an honest woman of her?"

"Uncle Neil!" Mayla slid forward in her seat. "He's done no such thing!"

A mischievous smile crossed his long face. "Well, maybe so, but he has corrupted your speech."

"A necessary change." Mayla reached up, took hold of Kalen's hand. "And one I find rather pleasant.

"Kalen sat down, put his arm around her shoulder and pulled

her close. "I can assure you, speaking formal colonial wasn't wise. The change was necessary. As to our marriage, I would do it tomorrow, but in this house cooler heads prevail."

Mayla touched Kalen's cheek and said, "Kalen and I were to be married in four cycles, but you heard my father, it will be sooner."

Chapter 12
Revelation from the Past

Kalen returned to reviewing his father's data. Buried deep in those files he discovered the vid Neil mentioned. Transferring the file to an individual data module, he loaded it into the player, and activated it. A miniature image of his father appeared and spoke. Kalen listened, stunned by what his father said in this journal entry.

When it finished, Kalen removed the earpiece and went in search of his future bride. He found Mayla sitting in the west wing of the Santiago home in a whispered conference with her mother and two sisters-in-law. At his approach, the women fell silent. They began doing this the day Mayla announced their new wedding date. He'd expressed his annoyance to Zavier a few days earlier.

"Kalen, don't let it bother you. They're only discussing your wedding. My mother, Lily, and her mother, did the same thing to me. There's nothing secret. They're teasing you."

"They make me nervous."

"That's the idea." Zavier had laughed and slapped him on the back.

Approaching the four women, Kalen said, "If you ladies can spare Mayla for a bit, I would like her to listen to something."

Catherine, Jamie's wife, smiled, a twinkle in her pale blue eyes. Now, in the last weeks of her pregnancy, she seemed to take the chaos being wrought upon her body with a patience and grace Kalen's father once told him the gods reserved for women. "Must you? We were just getting to the good parts!"

Kalen could feel his face redden. Liana and Lily chuckled.

Mayla gave Catherine a playful nudge, stood and took Kalen's arm. "Have you found something to make sense of Cal's mother's prophecy?"

"No." Kalen pinched his lips together and shook his head. "Do you remember what your uncle told me about a vid that would interest Quintin and me?"

"Yes." Mayla pulled him closer. "Did you find it?"

"Yes, I did. Would you listen to it, and then tell me what you think we should do?"

When they entered the tech room, Kalen handed her a fresh earpiece. Mayla inserted it and he restarted the vid. While Mayla listened, Kalen stood back and observed his fiancée. Her thick hair reflected the late afternoon light flooding through the window. It revealed a myriad of dark red colors, that made up the deep luster of her auburn hair.

He leaned against the wall and watched as she chewed her lower lip, a nervous habit he was sure she wasn't aware of. They'd been together for more than a year now, yet he found something new to discover each day. Her lavender eyes fascinated him, always implying more than her words. The way her nose flared when she got angry, the smooth texture of her skin, and the warmth of her smile. When they'd been apart and she reentered the room, her presence filled him with wonder.

Mayla's eyes brimmed with tears as she listened to his father's voice. She looked up at him and smiled, her whole face alight with amazement. She removed her earpiece. "Kalen, this is incredible. It's as if you read your father's mind."

"What he says explains a lot. I just wanted to know if you think your father and mother would want to hear this alone or share it with your brothers and their wives?"

"You and I know the reason for the schism is dead and buried. I don't think my father cares who knows now. I believe he'd want all the family to hear this, even the younger children. It's something that we can all learn from."

"I felt the same way. We'll gather everyone tomorrow evening."

Caesar, sitting in Quintin's lap, lifted his head off of Quintin's chest. "Grandfather, who's Ramon?"

"He was my brother. A long time ago, my brother and Kalen's

father were once good friends, until Ramon did something terrible and he went to jail."

Jamie and Catherine sat captivated by this family history they were hearing for the first time. Cal, Shannan, and Neela sat on the floor next to Jamie and Catherine's children, just as eager to hear what Russell had to say. The children all asked questions and Kalen and Quintin reassured all of them the trouble was in the past and over.

Seven-year-old Caesar climbed down from his grandfather's lap and went to Kalen. "Kalen, are you mad at grandfather?"

Kalen looked into the boy's blue eyes. "No, Caesar, I'm not. Your grandfather, your father, and your Uncle Jamie are some of the finest men I know."

Caesar beamed and smiled at his father and uncle.

"They are my friends. They have welcomed me into your family. We are here because my father died before he could tell your family just what good people they are."

The boy ran back to Quintin, climbed into his lap and put his head against his grandfather's chest.

Kalen placed a data module in the viewer and Russell MacKenna coalesced into a large, semi-opaque image above the viewer.

"That's Grandfather Russell," Neela said. Shannan shushed her, as Russell started to speak.

> *"Kalen, there are some things about me past and our family's history I have kept from you. I have come to regret your mother and I did this. When you were young, you and Cal inquired many times about the scar on me back, how it got there, and about the Santiago family. The answer ta your first question is what drove a wedge between the Santiago and MacKenna families and is the real reason there is no contact between us to this day."*

Kalen looked into his father's face. He hadn't noticed it earlier, but now he could see just how much this weighed on him. Russell's face brightened as he spoke of Quintin's father.

"I want to tell you 'bout the family o't he man I admire, James Santiago. James is one o' the most honorable men I know, though if I'd let your grandfather Martin tell you 'bout him you'd think otherwise. James Santiago has two sons and a daughter. Quintin is the oldest of the three and his sister, Angelina, is the youngest. James' middle son, Ramon, was, at one time, me best friend.

"Ramon and I grew up great companions and as children we explored Mesa Escarza, the same way you and Cal explored Mesa Tyree. As we grew up, Ramon became smitten with Alannah, your mother. I also believed she felt the same way 'bout Ramon. Though I also felt strongly 'bout her, but livin' up in the Muro Verdes, I had limited personal contact with her."

Russell's right hand went out of frame for a moment. When it came into view again, he held a glass with amber liquid in it. He took a long drink, almost draining the glass. He placed it out of frame and continued.

"He used to tell me o' the grand life he planned for them. When Ramon and I graduated, we went away to separate schools. Ramon chose the Mesa Verde University and I took up geology at the Mesa Mardan College. Alannah would never tell us which school she'd chosen. Imagine me surprise when she showed up at Mesa Mardan, and we wound up in many of the same classes.

"When Ramon found out, he came to see her as often as he could. Alannah tried to tell him she didn't 'ave the same feelin's for him as he had for her. Then Alannah and I started seriously dating. Ramon congratulated me and stepped aside. When I asked your mother to marry me, Ramon seemed glad for us and gave us his whole-hearted support.

"'Bout a cycle before our weddin', he invited me to go huntin' with him in the Barreras. While we were on the trail o' a large mountain ram, he told me he would get out in front o' the animal, head it off, and drive it toward me. I agreed and continued stalkin' the ram.

"A few minutes passed. I heard a noise behind me, then a

burnin', tearin' pain in me shoulder made me scream."

Russell's voice grew thick and his eyes shone in the light with unshed tears. He paused and the vid went off for a moment. When it came on, he appeared more composed.

"Now, where was I? Oh, yes. When I came to, I found meself in a ravine below the trail, covered with dirt and debris. Me shoulder burned and I'd lost a lot of blood. I called to Ramon, but he didn't answer. I thought someone must have shot both o' us. I lost track of the number o' times I passed out in the process of draggin' meself up to the trail and finally made it after half a day. Once there, I stumbled around. In me weakened condition it took me hours to scour the surroundin' woods, searchin' for Ramon's body.

"When I couldn't locate him, I found a stream, drank and washed me wounds. In me backpack I found food unburned by the pulsar hit. I made a small meal, then fell asleep. I remained there for two days while regainin' a wee bit o' me strength."

Russell paused, took a deep breath, and then continued.

"Before startin' out, I found a large branch and made meself a staff ta support me weight and went in search of our flyer, but that was gone also. At the time, I thought whoever tried to kill me, had killed Ramon and stolen it. The only way home for me now was to make for Foxdown Pass.

"I headed west hopin' to come across another huntin' party, but the season was over and the campsites along the way were long since abandoned. I walked and rested, experimentin' with different berries and nuts for food. I got sick a couple o' times and that slowed me progress. In order to get to a lower elevation where it would be a little warmer at night, I turned southwest. I guess I was lucky, because I never ran into any Silvan wolves."

Mayla squeezed Kalen's hand, acknowledging his recent life and death struggle with the animals.

"When I was far enough south, I turned west and worked me way around the canyons and through the woods. Once I crossed the Andalusia River at Brighten Meadow the land flattened out, travel got a little easier, and I made better time. For a brief moment, I thought 'bout turnin' south at the meadow, but I didn't know how I'd get down the Central Barrera escarpment. I wanted to get home, to get help, and go back to find Ramon's body, so I continued west.

"I can remember nights when it felt like I would never see me home again, and there were many times I wanted to give up. Finally, after two cycles, I stumbled into the camp of a survey team. I had no idea how far west I'd come until they told me they were workin' two kilometers east of Foxdown Pass. I'd walked over six hundred and forty kilometers, according to them.

"They called in the Rovin' Patrol and a medi-flight. While the med team patched me up, I told the authorities 'bout the attempt on our lives.

After they contacted me Da and me Mother, they went in search o' Ramon's body, and the med team flew me to the medical facility on Mesa Jaldee. I thought me troubles were behind me. That is, until me Ma, Da and James showed up."

Again, Russell's voice grew thick. He paused, wiped his eyes, and then went on.

"I learned Ramon had returned home, then helped me father and James search for my body near Foxdown Pass. Later, he flew back to school to comfort Alannah.

"You can't imagine me shock when Da told me where Ramon had led them. I explained that we were huntin' below Hannigan's Pass. It only took me Da a nanosecond to put two and two together. Infuriated, he ran from my room, swearin' to kill Ramon.

"James followed, and only caught up with your grandfather after he found Ramon at the Santiago home on Mesa Escarza. James prevented Da from fulfillin' his oath to kill Ramon. Durin' the scuffle, Ramon escaped. Me father, in his rage, thought James helped his son get away. The next day James and

me Da returned to the hospital. James tried to assure me father he would see to it that he turned Ramon over to the authorities and his son would pay for what he'd done.

"Da was so incensed by Ramon's attempt on my life, he laid into James, callin' him names, and cursin' his whole family. Me mother tried to stop him, but once Da got started, his tongue was sharper and deadlier than any knife."

Russell's voice faltered and Kalen forced his own tears down. The vid flickered and the screen went blank for a moment. When it restarted, Russell's eyes were red and swollen. He took a deep breath, let it out, and continued.

"When Da finished, he ordered James out o' his sight. James left us and spent two days huntin' Ramon down. He tracked his son to Alannah's home. Ramon was tryin' to talk to her, but your mother had already learned what Ramon had done. James found Alannah in a rage o' her own. She had already slashed Ramon's left arm. James stopped her from killin' him usin' the knife she wielded. James and Alannah's father, Jason, captured Ramon and turned him over to Escarza Roving Patrol, then they brought Alannah over to Mesa Jaldee. My father would not believe James turned in his own son to stand trial. Alannah pleaded with him to stop blamin' his best friend, but Da refused to calm down. He shoved Alannah aside and demanded James leave and never return."

Pausing again, Russell gulped air, tears filled his eyes.

Lily leaned close to Zavier. She rubbed his arm and Kalen heard her whisper, "I'm so glad this is out in the open and over."

"Thanks for not prying, mi amor." Zavier patted her hand. "I couldn't have shared it with you."

Kalen returned his attention to the vid and his father.

"Even after Ramon's trial, me father refused to apologize to James. He forbid me to ever have contact with the family again. I had always obeyed him, but this is one time I wish I hadn't. Our families thought with the passage o' time he'd come around,

*but Da let his pride poison his mind until no one, not even me
mother could talk to him and we gave up.*

*"I always meant to go see James, and try to make amends for
my father's cruelty, but me own guilt and shame stopped me.
Now, time has slipped away like a dream. James is gone and I
don't know if I could ever make it up to Quintin and Angelina
for the pain me Da's words caused.*

*"Remember what I taught you about the destructiveness of
hatred. I have tried to instill in you respect for all people and
all life. Your mother and I decided not to let your grandfather
influence ya, because it's our hope that one day you'd meet the
Santiago family. No man should have to bear up under what me
Da said and did. I miss me friend Quintin. I always admired his
dedication to building the old way. He married a beautiful woman, Liana Elano. As I write this, Liana has given Quintin three
boys. Their names are Zavier, Abel, and Jamie."*

"Madre de los dioses," Liana said. "I wish he'd come to
us."

*"Kalen, I may never get the courage up to speak with Quin-
tin, so if the day comes that you have the opportunity to meet
this good man, I would 'ave you apologize for what transpired
between his father and mine. I don't know where he lives now,
but you might start by approachin' Quintin's oldest son, Zavier.
He farms the family's land holdings on the west central side o'
Mesa Escarza. He might be willin' to speak to his father on your
behalf and arrange a meetin'. Or he might tell you where he lives
and you can try and approach him on your own."*

Russell paused, swiped at his eyes and took another
deep breath.

*"Kalen, your grandfather was wrong to blame James, or
his family, for Ramon's treachery, but he could never admit
that. Your mother, me Ma, and I felt so strongly that my father
should never expose you to his rabid hatred, we forbade him to
ever speak to you o' the trouble. This angered and embittered
him even more. He died with his hatred intact and death took him
before his time. Me Da never understood that Ramon's treachery*

turned out to be a gift in disguise. It was because o' Ramon that I learned to survive on me own and to love the Barrera Mountains. All the skills I've taught you and Cal come from me struggles to survive during my trek out o' the mountains. "If I leave you with only one thing you remember, this is what I wouldhave you remember and pass on to your own children."

Russell's voice changed and he spoke with less of a brogue.

"Never allow hatred to rule you. If you allow that to happen, it will consume and wither you before your time.

"Kalen, if I don't accomplish this in me own lifetime, it falls to you to heal the wounds of these good people. It is a hard task, son, but somethin' I know you're capable of and one I know you can accomplish. Heal their wounds, son. Let Quintin know your mother, me Ma, and I never thought ill of him or his family."

Russell's image faded and the room fell silent. When Kalen turned to Quintin, he found him staring at the place where the image of Russell had just been. Not a person to show his emotions, he sat quiet and unmoving, his eyes brimming with unshed tears.

"All the wasted years of useless blame and anger." Quintin held his voice just above a whisper. "All those years of silence. I thought your family hated ours. When all the time Russell blamed his father for the division of our families."

"I guessed right when I said my grandfather's pride destroyed him." Kalen left his seat, and stepped to Quintin's side. "I apologized to you once when I guessed what my father might do. With his admonishment, I offer you my hand again, in proxy for his, and make his apology to you on behalf of my whole family."

Cal stood, walked over, and stopped next to Kalen. "I would join Kalen in his apology, sir. Though I am not his by birth, Russell treated me as his own."

Ceasar tugged on the leg of his grandfather's pants. Quintin looked down. "Are you okay, Grandfather?" Quintin gripped Ceasar's shoulder. "Why yes, Caesar, as a matter of fact I'm very happy."

"Good." A big smile filled his cherubic face.

"You knew nothing of this." Liana rose from her chair, moved to her husband's side, and took Quintin's free hand. "And yet you did exactly what your father wanted. Thank you, Kalen, you are indeed a rare man."

Kalen shrugged, grateful when the children started asking questions. While he and Quintin spent the next half hour answering all of them, Mayla came to Kalen's side and hooked her arm in his. After a while the children, their curiosity satisfied, found other interests and the room emptied. Quintin and Liana went for their evening stroll.

Cal patted Kalen on his shoulder. "I'm glad that is finally put to rest. Shannan and I need to get some sleep. We have to get back to Armagh tomorrow. The mines don't run themselves, you know. We'll be seeing you in the morning before we leave."

"Thanks, Cal. It meant a lot having you and Shannan here."

"Russell was a man of many secrets, I wonder what else we don't know?"

"No telling. I'll keep going through the records I have. Even with what Maria stole, I still have a lot to read."

"We'll talk in the morning. Good night." Cal and Shannan walked off.

"If we can be of any help, you have only to ask," Catherine said. "You know, Catherine, I've come across some technical work my father saved. I have no idea what it means. If you could look it over it would help."

"Just give me a copy and I'll start on it in a few days."

"Thanks."

Catherine and Jamie excused themselves, and went up to bed. Zavier and Lily remained talking with Mayla and Kalen.

Zavier wore a troubled expression on his face. "I wish Abel had been here. It would have done him good to see and hear this."

"Let your father deal with Abel." Lily took Zavier's hand. "I don't need you two butting heads again."

"I wish I knew what had made him so angry." Zavier's look grew more puzzled. "When he was younger, he was temperamental. Now, he doesn't see that my father is different. With his dark heart, he refuses to see or understand the changes, much less accept them."

"Let it go, Zavier." Mayla touched his arm "We may learn something tomorrow when he returns."

"Don't remind me." Zavier rolled his eyes and his perplexed look remained on his face.

"Enough, Zavier Quintin Santiago!" Lily turned her husband so he faced her. "Your father wore that look long enough. I will not share my bed with a man who walks around with a look of doom fixed on his face."

Zavier cringed, then grinned at Kalen. "I had better leave Abel to work out his own problems." In a half whisper he said, "When Lily uses my full name, I'd better listen. I hate sleeping alone in the guest room."

Kalen and Mayla laughed when Lily delivered a solid, playful punch to Zavier's arm. The big man flinched and then wrapped his arm around her waist.

Kalen couldn't help smiling at the playful spirit this couple had between them.

Zavier and Lily excused themselves, leaving Mayla and Kalen alone.

"You have quite a gift for brightening an evening."

Kalen extended his hand to Mayla. "Let's see if I can brighten your evening with a little stroll in the moonlight. Your mother has kept you so busy we've hardly had any time alone."

"What do you have in mind?" Mayla pulled him closer.

"Just some time with my fiancée, so we can talk and you can tell me about our wedding plans. So far, you've kept me in the dark."

"Your part is simple, sweetheart." An impish smile filled Mayla's face. "You dress up, show up, and say yes."

Chapter 13
The Middle Child

The drone of a flyer's anti-grav engine drew Kalen's attention away from his work on the Lexicon. He looked up and saw Mayla approaching. Behind her, a new model flyer he'd not seen before settled down on the edge of the south grove. The blue iridescent skin changed colors, accentuating the curves of the sleek body. "Who's that?"

'That?" Mayla stopped next to the Lexicon and rolled her eyes. "That is my brother Abel, and his new SMS flyer, model seven-two-four."

"SMS?" Kalen closed the Lexicon's engine compartment and put his tools in the pod. "That's not made locally, is it?"

"No, it's not. He imported it all the way from the Selwyn colony. He's been bragging about it to Jamie for more than a cycle."

The pilot's door rotated forward and dark-haired Abel Santiago exited the vehicle. He stepped around it and waited for his wife to exit. Georgina Santiago slid her long thin frame out. She stood almost as tall as Lily, but her slim figure made her look more gaunt than athletic. The expression on her face appeared pained and her blue-gray, deep-set eyes mirrored the same. She looked around and let out an annoyed huff through her thin, aquiline nose. Abel stopped to inspect his flyer, buffing a spot with the sleeve of his shirt. The couple approached Quintin and Liana, who had just emerged from the courtyard.

"Abel, Georgina, how good to see you." Liana held out her arms.

"Mother, Father, how are you?" said Abel, looking over his

shoulder at the flyer.

Abel's question sounded, to Kalen, insincere. Hand in hand, Kalen and Mayla approached the couple. Abel kissed his mother on the cheek and Georgina did the same. A look of disdain crossed Abel's and Georgina's faces when Kalen and Mayla joined Quintin and Liana.

"Georgina, Abel." Quintin placed a hand on Kalen's shoulder. "This is Mayla's fiancé, Kalen MacKenna."

Kalen extended his hand. "Georgina, Abel, it's good to meet you both."

Georgina gave Mayla a curt nod, but did not offer her hand or make eye contact with Kalen.

"Mayla," Abel said, gripping her shoulders and kissing her on the right cheek. "How are you?" He took Kalen's hand in a quick, limp-wristed shake, then turned, and stared past his parents at the house. "It looks as if the repairs are coming along quite nicely." His attempt to sound aristocratic, mixed with his Outlands accent, came across as aloof and comical.

"We're almost done." An amused smile filled Quintin's face. "How did your meetings turn out?"

"Very well. I have signed contracts to build four homes in La Huerta."

"Seems you are well on your way," Jamie said, joining them. "I hope you're not planning to haul any material up there yourself. You do remember the Hannity job?"

"I seem to recall someone telling me the hauler's load was secured." Abel shot his brother a blistering look.

"That's enough." Quintin tried, but failed, to suppress his widening smile. "We all learned a valuable lesson about checking our cargo before traveling."

Georgina glared at Jamie, then locked her arm in Abel's. "Abel, dearest, take me inside." She pulled Abel toward the house. "The heat here is simply beastly." She and Abel hurried through the courtyard gate.

Quintin and the others followed.

Kalen kept an eye on Quintin's face, surprised by the continued amused look he saw there.

They crossed the courtyard, and once inside the mansion,

Georgina and Abel headed toward the kitchen. Abel stopped in the middle of the room, turned and faced his father. "In order to fulfil my contracts, I will have to have access to our mill. I want my share of our lumber to build my homes."

His fists clenched, Jamie stared at Abel, his face turning red. "What do you mean our–"

Jamie fell silent when Quintin placed his hand on his youngest son's shoulder.

"Abel, I've already explained this to you." Quintin stepped closer to his son. "I am under contract to build nine homes in the Verdes and we start as soon as the weather turns. Once the snows melt, I will need the mill's full capacity. You must find your own resources."

Jamie smirked at his father's refusal.

"I will not be able to fulfill my contracts without access to our mill!"

"Abel, have I not warned you about not thinking a problem through? You're well aware of our workload. It hasn't changed. Albert and the men are working long days to get my materials ready. They'll be working even longer in a few months."

Abel shot Kalen a blistering look, and then paced the floor. "You're deliberately doing this, just so I cannot make it on my own!"

"No, Abel, you know me better than that," Quintin's voice remained flat. "I told you the situation when you announced you were going out on your own. Nothing has changed."

Hooking her arm in Abel's, Georgina made a faint huffing sound.

Liana shot her a hard look.

"The men can work a few extra hours on my materials, after they finish with yours."

"When would they rest, or spend time with their families?" Jamie shoved his face in Abel's. "You're always willing to tell other men how hard they should work to fulfil your needs!"

"They are our employees!" Abel leveled a hate-filled look at his brother. "They owe me–I mean us! We pay them well to do what they're told!"

"What do you mean, owe you?" Jamie backed away from Abel.

They owe you nothing!" He unclenched his fists. "Excuse me, Papa, I'm going outside. This room has developed a particularly foul odor."

Abel's face twisted in anger and he glared at his younger brother.

Ignoring him, Jamie turned and stormed out of the kitchen. Mayla tapped Kalen on the arm. They withdrew, following Jamie into the courtyard. Before they exited the house, they heard Abel raise his voice. "You cannot deny me access to the mill. I'm your son, it's my right! I want–"

Kalen closed the door and joined Mayla and her brother. "Jamie, are you all right?"

"I'm sorry, Kalen." Jamie stared at the house. He took a deep breath. "It's hard to believe he's my brother, that the same parents raised us. He's always been one to feel he's better than those who work for us. He forgets many of our employees worked for my father all of their lives. They sometimes worked and waited for their wages in order to help my father succeed. We live a comfortable life because of their loyalty. Though my father always remembers how we've succeeded, Abel seems to put all his effort into forgetting that fact."

Jamie turned and walked to the center of the courtyard. He stopped in front of the fountain and sat down.

"Zavier and I received our educations here, as did our wives, and all our parents. Here on our world. That wasn't good enough for my brother. Noooo, not Abel. He insisted on going off-world to get his education. He came back with that Selwynian snob he calls a wife, an intense case of elitism, and little else."

"Would Papa give in to him?" Mayla glanced back at the house, a worried look on her face.

"I hope not. It would overwork the men and throw us too far behind." Jamie scratched his chin. "No...he'll let Abel argue until he realizes it's useless."

"Why did he feel it–"

The door flew open and Abel stormed out of the house, his outburst interrupting Kalen. "Never mind, *Father*! I know why you are acting like this! You're right, and I have thought this through! I know how to solve my problem!"

He stomped across the courtyard, without seeing Kalen, Mayla or Jamie. A few seconds later, Georgina appeared and chased after him.

"I wonder what he means by that?" Mayla took hold of Kalen's hand. "Maybe he's coming to his senses."

"Abel? Give up that quickly?" Jamie rubbed the back of his neck and stared at his brother's back. "No, I think he's lost his mind! Kalen, what were you going to ask?"

"Never mind, Jamie." Kalen winced from the knot forming in the pit of his stomach. "Never mind." Kalen's neck hair prickled at the steel in Abel's voice.

Chapter 14
Pride and Revenge

A sweet-scented breeze wafted through the courtyard as Kalen left the house. He roamed alone through the courtyard, lost in thought. The atmosphere at the estate had become oppressive since Abel and Georgina arrived. He drew a deep breath in hopes the fresh air would clear his head and then meandered out into the citrus grove in search of a quiet place to think. Every time he and Abel made eye contact over the past two days, Kalen felt as if Abel looked right through him. *I'll talk to Abel tomorrow.* A noise to his left distracted him. He looked around, but saw nothing out of the ordinary. *Whatever's bothering Abel, I'll settle it with him before the wedding.*

The trees stirred and the sweet fragrance of citrus floated all around him. He walked deeper into the grove. The Lexicon sat in the clearing where he'd moved it, away from the house, to get it out of the way. He approached the vehicle, folded his arms, leaned on the roof and stared heavenwards. The stars pulsated in the warm, rare moonless sky, but he found no pleasure in the soft evening. Abel's actions puzzled him. He stood, deep in thought. The first moon peered over the eastern mountain peaks. He broke out of his thoughts and stepped back. "Computer, vehicle access," then repeated his password. The interior light came on, the door locks clicked, and the passenger wing door rose.

He bent over and reached in to retrieve his staff. A sudden sense of danger made the hair on the back of his neck prickle. In the same instant, movement in his peripheral vision caught his attention. He jerked away from his vehicle just as something metallic flicked past his face. With a quick twist, he side-stepped and found himself facing Abel. Kalen scrambled back. "Abel, what are you doing?"

"Big man." The long, slim-bladed knife in Abel's right hand glinted in the moonlight. He wove the knife through the air. "Do you think you could use my sister, live off our wealth and make our family crawl to you for the rest of our lives?" His voice, thick with contempt, sent a chill skittering up Kalen's spine. "It's because of you my father refuses me access to the mill!" He slashed at the air. "I will kill you before I let your name mix with ours and destroy my family!"

Abel lunged and cut Kalen off before he could get the Lexicon between them.

"Abel, what are you talking about?" Kalen avoided Abel's next swipe at his chest. "I'm not here to cause your family any grief."

"Liar! Do you think I'm stupid?" He pointed toward the estate with his free hand. "Just look at the destruction that follows you!" He lunged again, but tripped over something in the dark, and stumbled to his knees.

Kalen moved in to disarm him, but the enraged man swiped his knife through the air, then scrambled back to his feet.

"Abel, stop. You're wrong." Kalen retreated a few steps, circled Abel, looking for an opening.

Mayla's brother juggled the knife from hand to hand. "What will you do now, pendejo?" Abel sneered at Kalen. "What will you do when I spill your guts on the ground?" He lunged, swiping the air.

Kalen backed away.

"Who will be begging then?" Abel rushed him.

Kalen side-stepped, but he felt the blade slice across the flesh of his left side just below his ribs. Before Abel could pull it back, Kalen looped his left arm around Abel's outstretched arm. With his right arm trapped, Abel tried to hit Kalen with his left fist, but Kalen pushed upward against Abel's elbow.

"Let go of me, Mazy-boy!" Abel clung to his knife.

Kalen ignored the insult and forced Abel's arm and elbow higher.

"Oohh, my arm!" Abel screamed, but still clung to his knife.

Kalen forced Abel's arm up as high as he could, making him cry out and the blade fell to the ground with a dull thud. Kalen released Abel's arm, snapped his right arm out, and drove his open hand into the dark-haired man's chest. The blow drove the air from Abel's lungs. He grunted and doubled over.

Kalen's side burned, and his shirt felt warm and wet. He reached down, snatched the knife from the ground and backed away.

Hunched over, Mayla's brother staggered backward, while trying to catch his breath.

Kalen reached across his chest with his right hand, and probed his abdomen through the cut in his shirt. When he pulled his hand back, it had blood on it.

"What now—*pendejo?* Will you kill me—in retaliation—or drag me to my father and make him beg for your forgiveness for this attack?" Tossing the knife behind him into the trees, Kalen stepped back and kept a wary eye on Abel. He heard hurried footsteps approaching and took two steps back, ready for trouble.

Out of the darkness Mayla appeared. "Abel, what's going on?" She stared at her brother, then at Kalen. "I heard shouting."

Abel's face twisted in rage, he stepped away from his sister. "I will not let you marry this murderer and ruin our parents' lives!"

"What?" Confusion clouding her face, Mayla stared at her brother. "What are you talking about?"

"Your brother thinks I'm here to humiliate your father because of your uncle." Kalen took a deep breath and turned so Mayla couldn't see his wound. "He doesn't believe your father and I settled the matter."

"Abel, Kalen and Papa settled the family schism cycles ago." Abel turned to his sister, hatred filling his eyes. "¡Puta!"

Mayla recoiled at the insult.

Despite the pain in his side, Kalen charged Abel and hit him, closed-fisted, in the mouth.

The shorter man staggered away and fell backwards, blood oozing from his split lower lip.

Before he could recover, Kalen dropped, knees first, onto the stunned man's chest, using his weight to pin Abel down. When he tried to buck him off, Kalen drove his right fist into Abel's face. His head snapped to the left. He stopped struggling.

"She must have been very pleasing." Abel took a deep breath and squirmed under Kalen's weight. "Now you come, pretend to forgive our father so you can marry into a rich family and glut yourself off of our family's hard work!"

"Kalen, you're bleeding!" Mayla reached for him.

He pushed her away, then hit Abel again when he struggled to free himself.

Mayla tried to pull Kalen off her brother.

Pushing Mayla away again, Kalen grabbed Abel by the collar of his shirt with his right hand and twisted until Abel choked. "First, you foul-mouthed fool, your sister was not sent to soften me up! I don't know what you think you know, but your father and I settled our families' differences, and it didn't require begging by anybody."

"Liar!"

"You use that word pretty freely." Kalen twisted his collar a little tighter.

Abel gagged and struggled to breathe. "Because, I know–I know the real–reason you've come here!" Abel grabbed Kalen's wrist to break his grip.

"Suppose you tell me why you think I'm here!" Kalen twisted Abel's collar until he choked again and ceased fighting.

His voice hoarse, Abel said, "You've come to demand that my father beg you to forgive our family for my uncle trying to kill your father!"

"Why do you think Kalen would make Papa beg?" Zavier's voice sounded out of the darkness. Mayla's oldest brother stepped out of the shadows.

Surprised the big man could be so light on his feet, Kalen loosened his grip on Abel's shirt. In the moonlight, the anger on Zavier's face made Kalen lean back. Zavier reached the two men and pulled Kalen off of Abel as if he were little more than a child. "Mayla, see to him." When Abel tried to scramble to his feet, Zavier brought his large, booted foot down in the center of his brother's chest and drove him flat, eliciting a loud scream of pain from him and he ceased struggling.

While Mayla settled Kalen on the ground, Zavier dragged Abel to his feet.

Abel beat on Zavier's muscled forearms, until the big man delivered a vicious open-handed slap to the side of his brother's face. The power in the blow caused Mayla to jump and startled Kalen.

Abel staggered backwards, landing against the Lexicon and cried out in pain.

"If you ever call our sister that again." Zavier planted his left hand in the middle of his brother's chest and pinned him against the Lexicon. "I'll cut your tongue out in front of your wife, and shove it down your throat."

Kalen's neck hair prickled at the steel in Zavier's soft-spoken voice.

Abel's eyes bulged. He twisted and beat on his older brother's forearm to free himself.

In his quiet voice, Zavier demanded, "Now, tell me how you know about Uncle Ramon?"

Mayla removed Kalen's shirt and gasped.

Recoiling from the pain, Kalen closed his eyes against his light-heartedness.

Abel remained defiant, and silent.

"This is going to require surgery." Mayla wadded up Kalen's shirt and pressed it against the wound. "I'm going to have to make sure Abel didn't cut anything vital. Kalen, hold this."

With his open hand, Kalen applied pressure to the wadded-up shirt, and Mayla left his side. Kalen heard her searching the flyer and turned his attention to Zavier.

Mayla returned as Zavier raised his hand again. "Zavier, stop!"

"Stay out of this, Mayla." He backhanded his brother and Abel's whole body reverberated from the blow. "Now tell me where you got these twisted ideas!" Zavier raised his hand a third time.

"I have known about this pig for many years." Abel blurted out, raising his hands to shield his face. "I heard father and grandfather talking about Uncle Ramon, a few days before grandfather died. I heard what Uncle Ramon did and why. I know the things this pig's grandfather called our grandfather and our family. I will not let this—this fortune-seeking murderer marry into this family!"

Zavier's face tightened with anger. He grabbed his brother by the throat and lifted him until his legs flailed in the air.

91

"Zavier, please stop! You'll kill him."

Zavier hesitated, as if considering the alternative to Mayla's plea, then released his brother.

Abel dropped against the flyer. He coughed, gasped, and refilled his lungs in quick gulps.

"My younger brother. Big mouth, small ears! As usual, you never get the whole story. You only pay attention to the parts that feed your twisted logic. Kalen knew nothing of Uncle Ramon or his treachery, his father never told him. But when he learned of it, he understood better than any of us where the problem lay. He settled the family quarrel months ago, while he stayed at our house." Zavier shook his brother. "He and father had a long talk. Kalen has apologized to Papa for the insults of his grandfather. If you had bothered to join our family two nights ago, you would have heard Kalen's own father make the same apology from his journal. You have worked with Papa since that time. If you had taken the time to look and listen, you would have seen he has changed, he is a different man."

"I saw how he is acting." He looked at Kalen, hatred filling his eyes. Despite Zavier's restraint he leaned toward Kalen and shouted in Outlands. "You've stolen my sister's honor and disgraced her!"

"You are the one who disgraces this family." Zavier grabbed Abel by the throat. "As usual, you don't look or listen. You have let your anger twist your heart until you cannot recognize the truth!"

"I need no one to teach me the truth about him! I will not see him marry into this family, and glut himself on our family's wealth!"

"Who are you to decide who will marry into this family? And just so you know, Kalen doesn't need our family's wealth to live well. Cal has seen to it that he is well off. I don't think you want to know just how well off."

Some of Abel's bluster vanished. "I, I don't believe you."

"I don't care what you believe, I-don't-lie! What I do care about is our parents. Think what you have just done with your anger and blindness. Mother's heart will be broken. How will Papa face Kalen now? How are our parents going to live with this, knowing you tried to murder the man our sister loves, under our roof?"

Kalen shook himself out of his stupor. "They are not going...to find out."

"Kalen, I've stopped the bleeding for now." Mayla turned

Kalen's head. "But this is no minor cut. I cannot hide this with a skin patch. I will need to close it up and you have already lost a lot of blood! We will not be able to hide this from my parents!"

"Don't try to hide it." Kalen closed his eyes to ease his nausea. The world rotated around him. "We'll tell them I got hurt working on the Lexicon."

"Kalen, we won't lie to our parents!" Zavier pulled Abel back when he tried to move away.

"Would you rather have them suffer all over again because of your brother's ignorance and anger?" Kalen worked up some saliva to moisten his mouth. "If you can't do that, then tell them you found me out here injured while working on my flyer. That much, at least some of that, is the truth and I will confirm it! Then we'll avoid any further explanations. Please, do it for your parents' sake."

Zavier turned and pulled Abel to him. "Look at him. Is that the voice of a man bent on injuring our parents? He kneels there, bleeding because of your anger and stupidity, and still he shows more concern for our mother and father than you have!"

Abel hung his head, his face a play of conflicting emotions.

"Go back to the house." Zavier shoved Abel away. "Stay with your wife and keep your mouth shut! Change your clothes and don't let anyone see Kalen's blood. You'll let your sister and me handle this, if you know what's good for you." He gave Abel another hard shove and turned back to Kalen.

Abel stumbled away. After a few steps he ran, disappearing into the darkness.

"Take it easy, Kalen." Zavier stood beside him. "As soon as Mayla's ready, we'll get you to the house."

"Zavier, in the flyer you will find some water and my medical equipment." Mayla pulled the shirt away from Kalen's side. "Good, you're not bleeding anymore."

Mayla's and Zavier's voices sounded far off and tinny. The night had a fuzzy edge.

Zavier rose and disappeared for a moment, then returned. Kalen felt Mayla pull the makeshift bandage away and pour the cool water down his ribs, rinsing the blood away. "We can move him now. Just let me tie off this bandage."

Richard R Draude

While she worked on his side, Kalen pulled Zavier to him. "In the rear compartment, find the pod with tools and parts. Scatter some of the tools around near the front of the Lexicon, then open the front compartment."

Zavier left Kalen's side.

"Whatever happens, don't tell your parents about Abel." Kalen reached for Mayla. "Patch me up and then let me deal with your brother."

When Mayla shook her head, Kalen put his hand on her face. "Promise me."

"All right, Kalen, all right, I promise. Now hold still so I can make sure it is safe to move you into the house."

"You're the doctor." The night grew darker. "I think I just need a little sleep."

"No, Kalen, stay with us!" Mayla slapped his face.

Kalen tried to focus but it was getting difficult. He coughed and hacked. A ripping pain tore at his side.

The hollow echo of Mayla's voice sounded in his ears. "Zavier, he's torn something open, he's bleeding again, worse this time. We have to get him in the house, now!"

Chapter 15
Death and Life

Second moon's silver white light spread a path between the trees. The glow raised shadows, helping Mayla avoid stumbling on the debris littering the ground from the recent harvest. She raced alongside Zavier, carrying her medical kit, and keeping Kalen's wadded-up shirt pressed over his wound.

Reaching the courtyard gate, Zavier stopped, his breath coming in quick gasps.

Mayla's medical case hit the ground with a thud. She shoved the gate open, grabbed the case again, and hurried in alongside her brother. She and Zavier stepped into the light. "Let me do the talking, Zavier. The less said the better."

"I don't like this."

"Would you like to see Abel dead?"

"If Kalen dies, I will–" Zavier inhaled. "I will see to that personally!"

Mayla's heart thumped in her chest when she stepped into the lighted courtyard and spotted the family. From near the fountain Dani jumped to her feet and screamed. "Papa, what's happened to Kalen?"

Quintin bolted from his seat and almost dropped his book and Jamie's youngest child, Caitlin. "What's happened?"

"I found him out by his flyer, injured," Mayla turned her attention to Jamie. "Jamie, in Kalen's flyer is the rest of my medical equipment. Get it!"

Without a word, Jamie rushed off.

"Mother, I need a place to work on him or he'll bleed to death!"

"The kitchen!" Liana darted ahead, and Mayla and Zavier followed.

The rest of the family started toward the door.

Mayla grabbed one of the maids and placed her hand on Kalen's wadded-up shirt. "Gina, keep the pressure on his side." She pushed Zavier ahead and turned in the doorway. "Please, Papa, keep everyone outside. They'll just get in the way."

"All right, children, do as Mayla asks." Quintin lifted Caitlin. As the children gathered around him, Mayla's eyes met her father's and she couldn't hide her fear.

Tapping the activator, the entry door slid closed. She hurried down the hall and into the kitchen. Liana had already covered one of the kitchen tables with a white sheet, and Zavier laid Kalen on top of it. Isabella and some of the staff gathered around the edge of the room.

"Mother, I'll need hot water after I've finished."

"I'll take care of it." Isabella ran to the food prep area.

"Zavier, here." Mayla opened her med-kit, and handed him a device. "Use this laser cutter to remove his clothes, then cover him with another sheet. I need to clean up." She headed to the sink with her op-sterilizer. "Mother, point this at my hands while I scrub."

"Mayla!"

Mayla spun and faced her brother.

"Kalen is bleeding so badly we can't get his clothes off and keep pressure on his wound at the same time."

"Here, Zavier, I'll help." Lily rushed into the room. "Gina and I will hold the bandage while you finish."

Mayla took a deep breath and returned to her scrubbing. "Sis, where do you want these?" Jamie burst into the room.

"Set them on the closest table and open all three," Mayla said, without looking up.

When she returned to the table, Jamie had her equipment cases open and on the second table where she could get to them. Zavier and Lily finished stripping Kalen, and covered him from the waist down. The sheet under Kalen held a frightening quantity of his blood, and his color had turned ashen.

"Hang on, my love. Mother, point the sterilizer toward Kalen's wound."

Liana came to her daughter's side.

"Jamie, set up this support stand. Attach the sterilizer Mother's holding to it."

Jamie did as Mayla asked, while she attached a container of solution to Kalen's right arm.

"What will these do?" Liana said, while Mayla clamped the container in place.

"The beam will keep a sterile field around Kalen's wound, and prevent contamination. You must keep it pointed at his wound, no matter how I move him. The liquid is enriched plasma and will replace some of the blood he's lost."

"Sis, do you need me for anything else?"

"No, Jamie. Go and tell the others he will be all right."

"He's a good man, Sis." Jamie passed close behind Mayla. "Please, keep him with us."

Mayla nodded, without taking her eyes off Kalen, and Jamie left the room.

"Zavier, go around to the other side and hold his arm out of the way. Try to keep him from moving. Lily, when I tell you, remove his shirt from his wound."

Mayla pulled out her hypo, loaded it and administered an anesthetic to Kalen, then lifted another instrument and placed it on his chest. The little box flickered to life and Kalen's vital signs appeared. Mayla scanned the reading, tightened her jaw, and grabbed a container of sterile water from her kit. "Zavier, keep an eye on Kalen's readings. Tell me if they drop any lower."

Checking the transfusion's progress, she then poured the sterile water over his wound. Lily pulled the makeshift bandage away. Blood flowed from the deep gash in Kalen's side. Only a thin layer of muscle lay between her and Kalen's intestines.

"Oh, mi hija." Liana's gasp shattered the silence. "Can you save him?"

"He is not going to die, Mother."

Mayla probed the wound until she found the source of the bleeding. "Ah, here it is." She lengthened the gash with her laser scalpel, and continued to probe, dabbing and wiping blood as it drained down Kalen's side. She turned to her medical kit to retrieve supplies to repair the damage.

"Mayla!" Zavier's voice sounded near panic. "He doesn't have a pulse!"

"Zavier, let go of him and step back!" Zavier released Kalen.

Pressing the center of the instrument on Kalen's chest, two small probes extended from the sides and pierced Kalen's chest near his heart. The device emitted a strong pulse. Kalen's back arched. Mayla checked the instrument, pressed the center again and the device emitted another, stronger pulse. Kalen's entire body convulsed. Mayla grabbed Kalen's wrist. "He has a weak pulse. Zavier, quick, pull his arm out of the way."

Zavier's hands shook when he took hold of Kalen's arm and pulled it out of Mayla's way.

Mayla checked the fluid being pumped into Kalen and raised the rate. "Zavier, he's going to be all right."

Zavier nodded, but his eyes still held doubt, and she wondered herself if she could pull Kalen through this. She worked with speed and precision and sealed the damaged vein. "Lily, in my kit you will find a blood analyzer, get it, please."

"What does it look like?" Lily turned to the kit.

"Silver box, fifteen centimeters square. The label reads Bio-metra- con."

After a moment Lily said, "I found it!"

"Bring it here."

Lily appeared at her side.

"Quick, open it and dip the orange probe into Kalen's blood." Lily fumbled with the analyzer.

Mayla took her eyes off Kalen and assisted her sister-in-law. The silver case flipped open, and lights on the instrument flashed. "Take that orange probe, dip it here in Kalen's blood. I need to know what his blood type is."

Lily's hand shook as she moved the probe toward Kalen's side. Mayla looked up at her, took hold of her wrist, and guided the probe into a puddle of Kalen's blood. Lily withdrew the probe. "So much lood, how can he still be alive?"

The analyzer flashed, displaying Kalen's blood type on the readout. Lily extended it so Mayla could see the results.

She scanned his side for any additional leakage, then pulled her eyes from Kalen, surprised when she read the analyzer. "Type Two, negative three, the same as mine. Lily, deactivate the orange probe. I need you to take the analyzer outside and use that green probe to test the family and staff. I will need at least three other people, besides myself, to give Kalen blood."

"How do I do that?" Lily twisted the base of the green probe.

Mayla heard the faint click and the instrument activated.

"Just press the sensor pad against their necks, here." She touched the base of Lily's neck and pressed on the carotid artery. "Hold it there until you get the readout. Test the adults first, then the older children. When you find three with the same reading as Kalen's, ask them if they will help."

"What if no one matches?"

"Anyone with type fifteen, negative two is a universal donor. We can use their blood."

To test it, Lily, pressed the probe against her own neck. When it beeped, she checked the reading. "Sorry, I don't match." She reached over Kalen and tested Zavier. He watched his wife with a hopeful look in his eyes. Lily shook her head. "Sorry, mi amor, you don't match either." She turned to leave, but Isabella blocked her way. "Lily, test us."

"Thank you, Isabella." Lily tested each of them. "Sorry, Isabella, you don't, but Gina you do. Will you help Kalen?"

"Yes, it would be an honor."

"Thank you, Gina. Mayla will tell you what to do." Lily left the room.

"Thank you, Isabella," Mayla whispered. "Thank you, Gina."

Mayla rechecked her work. After watching the exposed area for a few minutes, she washed the wound and continued to probe Kalen's side for other damage. "All right." She let her breath out. "I can close him up." She removed a silver cylinder from her case. Pinching the skin together, she placed it over the gash in his side.

"What is that, Sis?" Zavier leaned closer.

"It's called an Adherative. It saves me the tedious work of closing the wound manually." Mayla triggered the device. It made a low- pitched sound and pulled itself the length of the gash. When it reached the other end, Mayla removed it.

"That's amazing, Sis." Zavier stared at Kalen's wound. "The

skin's pulled so tight you can hardly see the scar line."

"There shouldn't be a scar." She cleaned and replaced the Adherative in her case, removed a roll of skin patch, and covered the wound. Placing her fingers on Kalen's neck, she frowned. "His pulse is weak and thready. Zavier, you can let go now. Mother, would you get Kalen's room ready, please?"

"Will you need anything special?"

"Some extra pillows, and blankets."

"I'll see that it's ready." Liana hurried away with two of her staff. Isabella and Gina carried the heated water over and set it on the table. As the woman set the water close to Kalen, Mayla said, "Thank you, Isabella. I will tell Kalen of your concern."

"He is a kind man, Miss Santiago." A warm smile filled Isabella's face, lighting her brown eyes. "We all like him."

Swallowing the lump in her throat, Mayla looked down at Kalen's still form. *You have that effect on almost everyone.* She turned to the stack of sheets lying on the table, grabbed one and tore it into pieces. When she turned back to her patient, she caught a glimpse of her brother, the color had drained from his face. "Zavier, are you all right?"

"It's the smell!" He took a shallow breath and blanched. "How can you work so close to all that blood?"

"You get used to it. Lift Kalen. I'll remove the sheet and we'll scrub the table. That should take some of the smell away."

"What if I tear his wound again?"

"The Adherative's binding is flexible. Don't worry."

Zavier slipped his arms under Kalen and lifted.

Mayla removed the blood-soaked sheet from the table, while Isabella pulled the sheet covering Kalen. Tearing another sheet into pieces, Isabella scrubbed Kalen's blood from the table's polished stone surface, while Mayla bathed Kalen's back and sides, dropping each bloody piece into a nearby waste container one of the other kitchen staff brought to her. When she finished, Isabella helped her spread out a fresh sheet and Zavier lowered Kalen onto it.

To another maid, Isabella said, "Have one of the men burn those."

The woman nodded and left.

"Zavier, open the door and let in some fresh air."

Her brother made a beeline to the far wall and flung the old-style double doors wide open. Mayla heard him taking deep breaths. A warm breeze reached her. The smell of citrus refreshed the room and drove the foul, iron smell away. She removed the hypo-spray and the vial of nano-biotics. "Oh damn!"

In an instant, Zavier stood at her side. "What is it?"

"I'm going to need more nanos to speed up his healing." She rechecked the vial. "This will have to do for now."

After injecting Kalen with the remaining drug, she tore the left sleeve of her blouse and removed two more devices from her case. Securing one device onto her arm, she did the same with the other on Kalen's arm, replacing the plasma injection unit.

"Zavier, I need a chair to sit in while I transfuse him." She hooked a long tube from the device on Kalen's arm to the one on hers. After Mayla filled and purged the line, she activated the transfuser.

Her brother retrieved a chair from a nearby room and set it close to Kalen.

Mayla settled in and sat chewing on her lower lip while she watched her blood flow to Kalen. After a few minutes, Mayla said, "Zavier, the instrument on Kalen's chest, what do the numbers on the lower right side read?"

He studied the readings. "Ninety-nine and sixty-three."

"Keep an eye on them. Tell me if they start to go lower." She closed her eyes, laid her head back, tried to relax, and willed herself to believe her skills would pull Kalen through. After a few minutes, someone touched her arm. She opened her eyes. Lily stood at her side.

"Mayla, Dani and Lucas are universal donors. Mariah has the right blood type. They would like to help."

Mayla smiled at the children.

Lucas looked from Mayla's blood-stained clothes toward Kalen. "Is he going to die?"

"If he was going to die, Lucas, Aunt Mayla wouldn't need our blood!" Mariah rolled her eyes.

Lucas' face reddened at his cousin's rebuke.

On the verge of tears, Dani stared at Kalen, then put her hand on her younger brother's shoulder and squeezed.

"Thank you." Mayla took Lucas' hands in hers. "With your help, Kalen will be fine."

Wide-eyed, Lucas returned her smile.

"Please, go into grandfather's library and read. I'll come get you."

The children nodded and moved off to the library in the east wing.

"Lily." Mayla signaled her sister-in-law to come closer. "Mayla, what's going on? This was no accident." The tall brunette bent over, and lowered her voice. "I know a knife wound when I see one, and Abel would not let me test him or Georgina."

Not surprised by Lily's revelation, Mayla looked over to Zavier. He checked Kalen's blood pressure then returned to the door to take deep breaths. "Why don't you and Zavier scrub up and change clothes? Take my brother for a walk. He could use it. I'll let him explain what's going on."

"Are you going to be all right?" Lily looked toward her husband. "How will you get Kalen to his room?"

"It'll take at least an hour to finish these transfusions and stabilize him. By then you and Zavier should be through with your walk and he can help move Kalen."

Lily went to her husband's side, and whispered something to him. He looked back at Mayla and she nodded. Zavier and Lily left the room.

Mayla stood and checked Kalen's readings again. *Take it easy, mi amor. You're going to make it.*

Mayla laid her head back, her gaze locked onto the rise and fall of Kalen's chest. His color remained pale, his breathing shallow but steady. *How can life deal one gentle man so many cruel blows?*

The transfuser's signal drew Mayla out of her thoughts. She put the machine on standby, removed the device and swiped her arm with a chemical swab, sealing the vein. She kept an eye on Kalen while she installed a fresh interface. At least his color's improved.

She finished with the transfuser, and checked his readings. His blood pressure had not improved much though. Mayla looked up and found Gina waiting. She attached the transfuser to the maid's arm and had her sit. "Close your eyes and relax, Gina. This will take a while."

"Yes, Miss." The dark-haired woman nodded and laid her head back.

Zavier and Lily returned. "How's he doing, Sis?" Zavier stood over Kalen's still form and checked the monitor on his chest.

"Better. Now go. Take a walk."

Grasping Lily by the hand, the couple stepped through the open door and disappeared into the darkness.

Mayla busied herself cleaning her equipment and packing her med cases. When the transfuser signaled, Mayla checked Kalen, then turned to remove the device from Gina's arm. Her face had turned pale. Mayla stopped her from standing. "Isabella."

Isabella came to her side.

"Please give Gina a couple glasses of juice and something sweet to eat. Gina, I need you to lie down. Isabella, I don't want her working, she could get dizzy, fall, and hurt herself."

"I understand, Miss. I'll see to it she does what you say." Isabella helped Gina stand and guided her out of the room.

Mayla went to the library and leaned through the door. "Lucas, would you like to be next?"

Lucas blanched, but nodded, his face filled with concern. He rose from his chair and followed Mayla out of the library. "Is this going to hurt?"

"Not at all. Remember when you and Caesar got stung by those Klanneth Wasps?"

A pain-filled look replaced the concern in the boy's eyes. Lucas nodded.

"You are just going to feel one little sting, that's all." She sat Lucas down and cleaned a spot near the joint in his right arm. "Good veins."

"Really?"

"Yes, this is going to be easy. Now just look away while I put this on your arm."

Lucas turned his head and after a moment he said, in a nervous voice, "Okay, I...I'm ready."

"I'm all done."

Lucas turned back and stared at the tube carrying his blood to Kalen. "Awesome!"

"Now sit back and relax. This should take about ten minutes."

Lake Solana
Santiago Estate

Chapter 16
Brothers' Confrontation

Her arm hooked in Zavier's, Lily pulled herself closer to her husband's side. The couple moved along the north side of the big house, their footsteps muffled by the thick grass. Once out of earshot of the estate, Lily stopped. "Zavier, what happened to Kalen? Mayla said you'd explain."

"My stupid brother, Abel." Zavier lowered his eyes. "He attacked Kalen!"

"What!" Lily looked back at the house. "Why would he do that?"

"He's convinced Kalen is here to embarrass my father, because of Uncle Ramon."

"How can that be? Kalen and your father made their peace. Abel must've seen the changes in your father! Everyone else has noticed a difference."

"My brother only sees what he wants to see! He still believes Kalen is guilty."

"Guilty? Guilty of what? You mean, of murdering his wife and his father?"

A pained look filled Zavier's face and he nodded.

Lily felt the muscles in Zavier's arm tense. "Mi amor, there's more isn't there?"

"Abel believes my grandfather and my parents sent Mayla as a gift, to placate Kalen so he wouldn't harass our family. He accused his own sister of being a..." Zavier flinched, his sentence left unfinished.

"How could he think that?" Lily stroked Zavier's arm. "Is he out of his mind?"

"No, he's not crazy. I believe I know where the idea came from."
He turned his head and looked toward the house.

"Where?"

"The same place the idea Kalen is marrying Mayla just to make
my father crawl to him. The same place he wants to live off our family's wealth. That lying *perra*, Georgina!"

"Zavier! She's family."

Zavier's eyes hardened. "Not as far as I'm concerned."

"But, why would she do that?"

"I don't know. Why else would he accuse Kalen of being the
reason my father is refusing to allow him access to the mill? He
knows it's always in full use. That selfish harpy he married has
changed him. He won't listen to anyone other than her."

"Maybe that's the reason he wouldn't let me test him or Georgina
for their blood types!"

"He withheld his help?" He stepped away from Lily. "He
refused to allow me anywhere near either of them." Zavier pulled
Lily's hand off his arm.

"Zavier, where are you going?"

"Go back to the house, Lily."

"Zavier, please, stop." Lily stepped in front of her husband.
"You shouldn't confront Abel, not while you're angry. Wait until
tomorrow. After you've calmed down, then you can talk to him."

"I can't believe he refused to help Kalen after he caused the
damage! I have to make him see how wrong he is." Zavier stepped
around her and headed toward the house.

Lily hesitated, torn between stopping her husband before he did
something rash, and letting him deal with this family matter. After
battling her indecision, she went after Zavier.

"Look! Look at the destruction he's already brought upon our
family!" Lily heard Abel shouting and headed toward the voices.
From between the trees, she spotted Zavier dragging his brother
toward the far western edge of the nut grove. She almost laughed
at the sight of Abel running to keep up with her husband's long
strides. *Please, mi amor, don't do anything we'll regret.*

"How–how can you–" Abel gulped air while struggling to free

himself. "How can you defend him?"

Stopping, Zavier used Abel's momentum to launch his brother toward the edge of the grove. "How can you blame Kalen for your problems?"

"He's a murderer!" Abel stumbled backwards, but avoided falling by grabbing hold of a low-hanging branch. He straightened up and glared at his brother. "It's because of him I won't be able to fulfill my contracts."

Lily moved closer so she could keep an eye on her husband.

"You should have used those tiny ears of yours to listen to Grandfather Elano also." Zavier tried to grab his brother, but Abel scurried backwards. "Do you think he would have jeopardized his career to spare Kalen's life? Or asked our mother to send her only daughter away? Kalen's innocent! The people trying to kill him are not out to avenge his father's death, and he's already helped Uncle Neil destroy one threat to our world."

"I don't believe you!" Abel squared his shoulders and stuck out his chest. "I won't stand here and listen to you make up reasons to defend him!"

"Well, I will defend him. And how is it his fault that you can't fulfill the promises you made?"

"Because father will have to support him and Mayla!"

"I told you Kalen doesn't need our wealth. He's well enough off."

"Sure, sure, his friend gave him a few thousand credits out of friendship to tide him over!" Abel swept his hand through his dark hair. "He'll run out of that soon enough, then Papa will have to support him. His bloodline is from those mountain people. He is just as lazy as the rest of them."

"How dare you bring that racist attitude into this house? Kalen has worked hard, helping to repair the damage, and asked for nothing."

Lily gasped when in a sudden move, Zavier grabbed for his brother. *Please, Zavier, please, don't hurt him.* She tensed, ready to interfere, but Zavier missed. He continued to chastise his brother.

"As for Cal, he is more than Kalen's friend. Russell MacKenna helped raise him. They're like brothers." Zavier paused, a wicked grin spread across his face. "And as far as what Cal gave Kalen, it's more like many millions of credits!"

Richard R Draude

Abel stared, his mouth agape. "You're lying!" His eyes darted around. He avoided making eye contact with his brother. "I–I don't believe you."

"The only person around here who lies is Georgina."

Abel looked like he would explode.

"The only person who believes lies, is you." Zavier grinned. "Cal put aside credits for Kalen from his mining operations. Kalen has no need of our wealth."

Abel's mouth moved, but no sound came out.

"That puts a kink in your reasoning or should I say Georgina's. What excuse will the two of you come up with now?"

"Leave my wife out of this!" Abel glared at Zavier and backed away. "I won't stay here any longer!"

A cheerless laugh came from Zavier. "Really, what are you going to do?"

"I'll take Georgina and leave here. As long as he is here, I will not return. I will not be part of this farce. I cannot believe all of you are still willing to appease him! It's bad enough Papa allowed that Mazy-boy to use our sister so shamefully. Now he will let this murderer—"

Even in the dim moonlight, the rage Lily saw flash in Zavier's eyes frightened her.

Zavier moved so quick, Lily gasped when he reached out and grabbed his younger brother by the neck before he could turn to run. He spun Abel around and cocked his massive arm.

No, Zavier, you can't! Lily darted from the shadows. Crossing the gap between her and her husband, she forced herself between the two men before Zavier could strike. "No!" She took hold of Zavier's arm and pulled. He lost his grip on his brother. "Zavier, let him be!"

Abel scrambled backwards.

"Lily, stay out of this!" Zavier's rage-filled stare riveted on his brother.

He never raises his voice to me, or to anyone. "No!" When she failed to distract him, she lowered her voice. "I will not have the man I love, the father of our children, in jail for doing something stupid!" *I've never seen him this angry.*

With scarce control of her own emotions, she pivoted. Her back

108

to Zavier, she leaned against him and pushed him away, while glaring at her brother-in-law. "The only person who will destroy this family is you, or should I say that wife of yours! Her blind ignorance, prejudice, and pride will get you killed! If you wish to believe the lies she's conjured up, then do so, but get out of my sight before I lose my husband because of your stupidity!"

Abel's face contorted with more rage than Lily thought possible. "You'd defend MacKenna too?"

In spite of his resistance, Lily managed to back her husband away from Abel. Then she felt Zavier try to move around her. "No, mi amor!" Turning away from the smaller man without answering, she reached up and palmed Zavier's cheek. "Mi amor, calm down."

Zavier's breathing slowed. The anger drained from his eyes, his taut muscles relaxed.

Lily turned his head until their eyes met. "Mi amor, is he worth destroying all our lives?"

Zavier covered his wife's hand with his and closed his eyes. "No. I'm sorry, mi querida. You're right."

Lily hooked her arm in Zavier's. She moved her husband away, leaving Abel to stew in his own anger and unanswered accusations.

Lake Solana
Santiago Estate

Chapter 17
Aftermath

Finished with Lucas, Mayla repeated the process with Mariah. For all her bravado, the strawberry-blond teen appeared more frightened and nervous than her younger cousin. She sat with her blue eyes squeezed shut while Mayla applied the transfusion cuff. As her blood flowed to Kalen, she blanched and slumped in the chair.

"You'll be fine, Mariah. This won't take long." Mayla busied herself cleaning and storing her equipment. She checked Kalen's blood pressure. *That's better, and your color has improved too.*

When the transfuser signaled, Catherine came and stood beside her daughter. "Mariah, I know doing this frightened you, but you're helping to save Kalen's life. Thank you."

"I like him, Mother." Mariah looked over at Kalen's prone figure. A smile lit her thin face. "He's funny and always talks with us."

"I'll let him know how you feel." Mayla brushed her niece's hair out of her eyes. She instructed the staff to give her extra juice.

While Catherine escorted her daughter out of the kitchen, Dani came and sat down without being called. She stared at Kalen, her eyes filled with unshed tears. "Aunt Mayla, is he really going to be all right?"

"Yes, Dani, he is. With the blood you are giving Kalen, his volume will be close to normal. Are you all right?"

"Not really." The raven-haired girl brushed away her tears. "When I saw Papa carrying Kalen, and all that blood, I thought he was dead. I can see why you love him, Aunt Mayla, he's very easy to be around. Besides Grandfather, Papa, and Uncle Jamie, he's one of the few men I can talk to without feeling self-conscious."

"Kalen thinks you're pretty special, too." Mayla stroked Dani's dark hair with her hand. "There is another you can talk to though, isn't there?"

Dani blushed, then looked at Kalen lying on the table. "I'm glad I could give him my blood. Now it really makes us family."

Swallowing to ease the lump in her throat, Mayla touched Dani's cheek before attaching the transfuser to her left arm, then finished cleaning and packing her instruments. When the machine signaled the end of the transfusion, Mayla removed the device and took her niece's hand. "Thanks for caring. Kalen's going to be fine."

"We all love him, Aunt Mayla."

Mayla hugged Dani. "I know you do." She checked Kalen's vital signs again, then sat and waited for Zavier and Lily to return.

Mayla looked up when her oldest brother stepped through the double doors.

"Mayla, are you ready to move Kalen?"

"Zavier, where have you been? I thought you two had..." She spotted the look on her brother's face and glanced at Lily.

Her sister-in-law shook her head.

Zavier stepped over to the now-clean table. He slipped his arms under Kalen. With great care and little effort, he lifted Kalen and carried him out of the kitchen.

"Lily, where have you two been?" Mayla gripped her sister-in-law's arm. "Did something else happen? Zavier seems a bit... subdued."

"Yes. I'll tell you about it later."

The women followed Zavier into Kalen's room. After laying him on the bed, Zavier started to leave. Mayla put her hand on his arm. "Thanks for caring."

"Sis, I feel the same way Jamie does. He's a good man, and the right man for you. I'm glad you kept him with us." Turning to his wife he said, "Lily, I'll be upstairs."

Lily cupped Zavier's cheek and kissed him. "I'll be up as soon as we're done here." She leaned in closer and lowered her voice. "I love you."

Zavier blushed and left.

Lily turned and helped Mayla arrange the blankets and pillows to make Kalen comfortable. While they worked, she filled Mayla in on Zavier's latest confrontation with Abel.

"I'd better go check on my husband." Lily moved toward the door. "He's probably upstairs beating himself up for losing his temper."

"Does he do that often?"

"Zavier? Lose his temper? No, Mayla, he's the gentlest man I know. He never raises his voice. I've never seen him so upset. I really believe that if I hadn't gotten between those two, he could've killed Abel."

"Lily, what are we going to do about Abel?"

"He's threatened to leave." Lily tapped the activation panel. While the door slid open, she looked over her shoulder. "For all our sakes we can only hope he makes good on his threat and takes Georgina with him."

Mayla stared open-mouthed at Lily.

The tall brunette said, "I'd better go. Zavier will need some extra attention tonight." As she left the room, Isabella stepped in. "Miss Santiago, what about the kitchen? What do you want us to do?"

"It needs to be cleaned and sterilized. Isabella, I know it's late, but it should be scrubbed from top to bottom right away."

"I will see to it, Miss Santiago."

"Isabella, please, call me Mayla."

"Very well, Mayla. The staff and I will see to the kitchen."

"Isabella, is Gina resting?"

"I made her lie down. Call me if you need anything."

"I will."

After the door slid closed, Mayla rechecked her work, then began her vigil.

The house burned with intense heat, but he tore his gaze from the flames and looked across the road toward the space between houses. Ignoring the twisting flittering shadows, he searched for the eyes. They materialized and glared at him, their red-rimmed hatred flaying his soul open. He pointed at the figure and shouted, but no sound came out and no one paid any attention to him. An intense pair of green eyes materialized next to the hate-filled ones and their appearance froze his heart. He quit trying to get his

113

neighbor's attention and leaned closer, as if it would help him get a better look. In the dancing firelight, he could see tears glistening in the disembodied orbs. His vain effort to connect them to a face failed. The eyes vanished. The house burned with intense heat—

Kalen forced his eyes open and tried to sit up. His body ached and when someone placed a hand on his chest, stopping him, he decided not to resist. Looking up to see who owned the hand, he stared into Lily's eyes and warm smile.

"Easy, Kalen, you're still weak."

"Water." Kalen swallowed, trying to moisten his throat. "Please, Lily."

Reaching behind her, she picked up a full glass from the nightstand. Lifting his head, she pressed the glass to his lips.

"Thanks." Kalen drained the glass and laid his head back. "How long have I been out? What time is it?"

"It's five in the morning." Lily adjusted the pillow cushioning his side. "You've been unconscious for three days."

"I feel exhausted." He closed his eyes, rubbed his face with his left hand, and stretched. "What have I been doing while I was unconscious?"

"Do you remember any of your dreams?" Lily straightened the covers and refilled the glass.

"No, I don't. Was it bad?"

"It wasn't good. You were screaming and tossing around." Lily brushed the hair out of his eyes. "Mayla worried you'd injure yourself, so she gave you a powerful sedative. You've been resting quietly since late yesterday."

"Mayla, where is she?"

"She's sleeping. We made her go to bed a few hours ago."

"I have to speak to her."

"It can wait. You're too weak to do anything right now and you both need rest."

"I really need to talk to her. It's important."

"Not as important as your health. You're both exhausted." Lily pulled the covers up and sat down in the chair opposite the bed.

Kalen gave up. He could already feel himself sliding toward sleep. Closing his eyes, he let the darkness claim him.

Chapter 18
Concerned

The muffled splatter of heavy rain sounded in Kalen's ears drawing him from sleep. He opened his eyes and stared at the wispy, gray light of the late day filtering through the window's curtains and wondered how long he'd slept. He tried to sit, but found himself too weak. From his position he scanned the room and spotted Caesar asleep in a chair opposite the foot of his bed.

When he stirred again, Laney, lying on the floor out of his line of sight, barked. Caesar's eyes popped open. He looked into Kalen's eyes. "You woke up!" The boy forced a smile, and then slid out of the chair. Reaching Kalen's side, he stopped next to the bed, his expression, one of grave concern.

Raising up on her hind legs, Laney put her front paws on the bed.

When she dropped her head across Kalen's thighs, he patted her head. "Hello, Caesar, have you been here long?"

"Mother wouldn't let me come in." For a brief instant Caesar's eyes lit up. "But I sneaked in anyway." His look turned serious. "I wanted to see you. Kalen, please don't die."

The boy's genuine anxiety touched Kalen. "I think your Aunt Mayla made sure I'll be around." He reached over and tousled Caesar's blond hair. "I promise, I'll be here for a long time." He gave Caesar a big smile and pulled him close. "Okay?"

"Okay." The worried expression didn't leave the child's face.

The room door slid open and Mayla entered. Caesar's expression turned to panic.

"Oh, you're awake. I thought–" She spotted Caesar and Laney. The dog lowered her head and managed to look guilty, while Caesar shrank down behind Kalen. Mayla came around the bed and stroked Laney's back. "It's okay, girl." She squatted down in front of Caesar, reached out and squeezed his shoulder. "I'm glad to see you're awake."

"I'm sorry, Aunt Mayla, but I wanted to see Kalen."

"It is all right, we're all worried about him. Do you feel better now that you've talked to him?"

"Yes." Caesar stared down at his feet. "Are you going to tell Mother I was in here?"

"Tell you what, I'm going to tell your mother I said you could visit. Okay?"

Caesar's eyes lit up. "'Wow! Thank you, Aunt Mayla!" He jumped into her arms, almost knocking her over. "I love you." He wrapped his arms around her neck and kissed her on the cheek.

Mayla regained her balance and returned his hug. She stood, took Caesar's hand, led him to the door and pretended to check the hallway. "Okay, the way is clear."

"Can I come back and see Kalen again?"

"Of course. How about just before you go to bed?"

"See you later, Kalen." Caesar smiled and waved. "Thank you, Aunt Mayla." He peeked out of the room, then he and Laney disappeared.

"Poor little guy." Mayla watched Caesar for a moment, then turned back to Kalen. "I don't think he's slept well since this happened. Did he wake you?"

"No. He was sound asleep in the chair. When I moved, Laney barked, and that woke him. How long was he sitting there?"

"Over two hours. He's been so worried. He kept trying to see you. I finally told Lily to leave him alone, it couldn't hurt to have him in here. How are you feeling?"

Kalen tried to shift onto his right side. "Like someone has been plowing under my ribs." He laughed and wrapped his arms across his abdomen. "Why does my whole body ache? My muscles feel like they did after my bout with post-stasis shock."

116

"You have to lie still." Mayla brushed his hair away from his eyes. "Abel's knife cut deeper than I thought. I had to open you up farther-to repair the damage and stop the bleeding. Your nightmares had you thrashing around."

"Lily told me."

"Do you remember any of your dream?"

Lowering his eyes, he hesitated. "Mmm—no—I don't." He lifted his eyes and could tell by the look on her face she didn't believe him, but said nothing.

"How long will I be laid up this time?"

"You'll need to remain still and rest for at least another five days. I didn't have sufficient nano-biotics, so it is going to take you longer to recover."

He moved and winced at the pain. "Why does it feel like someone tied every muscle in my body into knots?"

Mayla stopped brushing his hair with her hand. "Your heart stopped and I had to shock you to restart it."

"You mean I–"

"Yes, you were dead for a few seconds."

Mouth agape, Kalen stared at her. "What does one do for someone he owes his life to?"

"Nothing." Mayla reached out and pushed up on his chin. "Just get better and promise to stay out of trouble."

"I can try, but I can't promise. What did you tell your parents about Abel?"

"We've said nothing. Zavier and I told them we found you injured out by your flyer."

"Did they believe you?"

"It's hard to say." Mayla adjusted his covers. "With all that is happening, I think they're too busy to think too hard about it. I don't like lying to them, Kalen, neither does Zavier. I can't look my father in the eye, and he may have figured out something is wrong. He has asked to speak to you."

"I'm going to have to be the one to tell him what happened." Kalen closed his eyes and shook his head. "For now, just let him know I'm asleep."

"No! Abel started this. He needs to take responsibility for his blind stupidity and own up to what he's done. He should be the one to tell my father he tried to kill you! He must apologize!"

"Will you be the one to start it this time?"

"What do you mean? I have started nothing. My brother did."
"My Outlands may be very poor, but I know what he called you."
Mayla turned her back to him and her shoulders began to tremble.
"Mayla, I can't imagine how that hurt."

"How could he think that I would– that my parents would–that I
would allow myself to be used like that! Oh, Kalen, that did hurt and
then I was so–scared I couldn't save you."

Mayla turned and Kalen held his right arm up. She crawled up
onto the bed and laid her head on his chest. He held her while she
wept, glad they were alone. Despite his father's lectures on self-con-
trol, the sight of Mayla so distressed made him want to wrap his
hands around Abel's throat. He stroked her hair and let her cry,
while fending off his own exhaustion. When she calmed down and
pulled her face from his chest, her nose was red, and her eyes puffy
and swollen.

"Now I'm a mess."

"It's okay. You're still beautiful."

"You're a terrible liar." Mayla kissed him. "Thanks for letting me
get that out of my system."

"That's what I'm here for," Kalen said, "to comfort and cheer."
"Among other things." Mayla snickered, leaned over and kissed him
again, pulled back, and turned serious. "My father wants to speak to
you. I told him he could see you tomorrow, that you're too tired right
now. What are you going to tell him?"

"I'm not sure. I'll come up with something."

"I still think Abel needs to admit to my father what he's done."
"And how likely do you think that is?"

"He doesn't seem capable of owning up to his mistakes, does he?"
"Not really." Kalen settled back, dropping his head on the pillow.

"Will I see you later?"

"I'll be back to check on you after I fly into Andalusia to replenish
my medical supplies."

"Please don't do anything rash. I can deal with Abel."

Mayla glanced down at Kalen's side. She took hold of his hand
and squeezed it. "He and Georgina are going to leave. Don't confront
him for both our sakes. I don't want any more trouble."

Chapter 19
A House Divided

Kalen woke, and turned over. He checked his side and could tell his wound had closed, it didn't ache as much. *Mayla's wrong, the nanos worked.* His gaze strayed to the window. From the lack of shadows in the courtyard, he knew it was near midday. *I feel much better after another night's rest.* He pushed himself into a sitting position, rotated his body until his legs dangled off the bed. Lowering his feet to the floor, he attempted to stand. The act required all his strength. Using the wall for support, he hobbled off to the attached bathroom to clean himself up. After a hot shower and a shave, he felt stronger. He straightened his bed and had just climbed in when he heard a soft knock on the door.

"Come in."

The door slid open and Quintin stuck his head in. "I was hoping you were awake."

"I am, sir. Please come in."

"How are you feeling?" Quintin stopped at the foot of the bed.

"Much better." The look in Mayla's father's eyes made Kalen lower his. *He knows.*

"Are you up to talking?"

Not really. I should have thought this through. What do I tell him? He knew he couldn't put Quintin off any longer. "Of course, sir." "I want to know how you were injured." Quintin pointed to his side.

Damn, straight to the point. Remembering the tools he'd told Zavier to spread around the Lexicon, he plunged ahead. "I had a problem with the converters on the Lexicon and wanted to look at them. After I finished working, I was pulling myself out of the compartment and tore my side open on something sharp."

"Wasn't it rather hard working alone, out there in the dark?"

Kalen kept his face neutral. "It wasn't one of my brighter ideas." He knew how weak his hasty explanation sounded.

"I looked around the area." Quintin turned and faced the window. "I didn't find any blood near the front of the Lexicon." From his back- pocket Quintin pulled something out wrapped in a rag. "Do you have any idea how this got out in my grove? None of our help lost it. It's not used for harvesting the fruit." He unwrapped the object, faced Kalen and held out Abel's bloody knife.

Kalen tried but failed to maintain his neutral gaze while he viewed the weapon.

"Am I right to assume this is your blood, and this is what caused your wound?"

Lowering his eyes, Kalen nodded.

"Who tried to kill you? Was it one of my sons? Why would one of them want you dead?"

"Quintin, please. This is a personal matter. Let me handle it."
"Kalen, this is my home. I want to know who tried to kill you."

"I won't tell you, sir. Please, this is my problem, let me take care of it."

"If you won't tell me, then I'll find out for myself!" Mayla's father stormed out of the room.

The shame he felt brought another of his father's lectures to mind. Then, as now, he had been caught in a lie, and had compounded it by withholding the truth. He lay there for another minute, but knew what he had to do. Swinging his legs over the edge of the bed, he forced himself onto his feet.

While he dressed, another knock sounded. He pulled on his shirt, crossed the room and slapped the activation panel, hoping to see Quintin. Instead he faced Mayla.

"What are you doing up?"

"Your father came to see me." Kalen tucked his shirt in.

"And, what happened?"

"He found Abel's knife in the grove. Now he knows one of your brothers did this. He left here angry because I wouldn't tell him who is responsible."

"We have to find him before he does something we'll all regret." Mayla turned, and Kalen followed her up the hall toward the sitting room. As they entered the small room in the west wing, they found Liana in a whispered conversation with Lily and Catherine.

"Mother, we need to find Papa." Mayla said.

"Your father called your brothers upstairs to our sitting room."
"Well, he called Zavier and Jamie," Lily said. "He stopped Abel from leaving and dragged him upstairs."

The furrows in Liana's forehead deepened. "I've never seen him so angry." She looked at Kalen. "He asked you about your wound, didn't he?"

Kalen could only nod.

"My husband didn't believe you injured yourself, Kalen. He thinks one of our sons is responsible."

"Any bets as to who it is?" Catherine whispered. "We know which two it isn't," said Lily.

The five adults headed down the hallway. Despite his weakened state and the pain in his side, Kalen bounded up the stairs two at a time and came out opposite the doorway leading to Quintin and Liana's suite. He took a dozen quick steps and reached the door in time to hear Mayla's father shout, "I will have the truth of this, now! I want to know which one of you has brought this shame upon my name and into my home!"

He spoke his last words so loud Kalen figured the whole house heard it, but the hallway remained void of any younger prying eyes. Mayla, Liana, Catherine, and Lily made it to the top of the stairs as Kalen pushed the huge double doors open and surveyed the room.

To his left, Zavier and Jamie sat. Jamie's eyes had a bewildered look in them, and Zavier kept his downcast. To his right, across the room, Abel stood, his expression hard. Between them stood their father, his back to Kalen.

At the sound of their entry, Quintin spun, his face contorted with rage. When he saw Kalen, his eyes widened and he approached him. "It seems old wounds never heal. Our family's malice and hate lives on. Kalen, I will get to the bottom of this, then—"

121

"No! Father, do not lower yourself to this pig."

Kalen cringed, and wished Abel had kept his mouth shut.

Quintin caught Kalen's look, turned and stared at Abel. "It was you! I knew it! I should've known better than to drag your brothers into this." Quintin lunged toward Abel.

Liana screamed, "Quintin, no!"

"Zavier, stop him." Lily stepped around her mother-in-law.

"Jamie, your father," Catherine reached out as if trying to grab Quintin.

Zavier and Jamie jumped from their seats to intercept their father.

Springing forward, Kalen shoved Quintin, knocking him off balance and into Zavier's arms. Kalen tumbled to the floor, as pain seared through his left side. He staggered to his feet and stood in front of Abel, while Zavier and Jamie restrained their father.

"Zavier, let me go." Quintin tried to free himself from his oldest son's grip.

"Quintin, stop!" Liana came to her husband. "Is this how you want your grandchildren to see you?"

Quintin ceased struggling, but Zavier continued to hold his father. Quintin glared at Abel. "If I hadn't stopped you from leaving, you would've skulked away from here and never said a word!"

Abel clenched his jaw, stared at his father, and remained silent.

Jamie crossed the room and closed the double doors. "Zavier, let go of me!"

"Not until you come to your senses. I won't let you do something we'll all regret."

"There's been enough bloodshed." Jamie returned and stood in front of his father. "Kalen's right, please stop."

"Your brother must answer for his cowardice!" Quintin strained against Zavier's restraint. "After we've made our peace, under my roof, he tried to murder Kalen!"

"Would you do that?" Kalen adjusted his stance to ease the throbbing in his side. "Kill your son, and widow his wife for the sake of a misunderstanding?"

"Stinking pig!" Abel pushed Kalen from behind. "There's no misunderstanding. I don't need you to defend me."

Kalen spun, took one step, and drove his right fist into Abel's face.

Abel staggered backwards, tripped over the chair behind him, and landed hard on his back.

No one moved.

"You really should learn to keep that sewer you call a mouth shut." Kalen grimaced, while rubbing his knuckles.

Abel glared at Kalen, scrambled to his feet, and rushed him.

Mayla took two steps past Kalen, snapped her right leg out and up. She caught her brother under his jaw with the heel of her boot. His head snapped back and he flew sideways, hit the floor and slid until he slammed into the side table with a loud crash.

The room grew still.

Mayla went to her brother and dragged him to his feet. With her left foot she tipped the chair upright and then shoved him into it. Bending close, she spoke in a voice just above a whisper. Kalen heard her say to the dazed man, "If you ever call me a whore again or attack Kalen, *mi estimado hermano*, I will snap your neck like a dry twig and save your wife the humiliation of having to crawl in bed next to you, and save our father the trouble of dirtying his hands."

Abel shrank under Mayla's verbal assault.

She raised her voice a notch. "The only pig in the room, *mi estimado hermano*, is you! Now sit there and keep your filthy mouth shut! Otherwise I will call the RPs and have you arrested for the attempted murder of my fiancé!"

Mayla's expression shifted from anger to pain, and her eyes filled with tears. She straightened up, crossed the room to her mother's side, lowered her head onto Liana's shoulder and wept.

Liana encircled her daughter with her arms and stroked her hair. Her own eyes brimmed with tears.

Mayla's gentle weeping, now the only sound in the room, tore at Kalen's heart.

Quintin's shoulders sagged and Zavier released him. Quintin, Zavier, Lily, Catherine and Jamie gathered around Mayla and Liana.

"Is this what you want?" Kalen wanted to comfort Mayla, but he turned to Abel instead. "Your family fighting with each other over something you don't understand?"

"I understand everything! My grandfather sent his own son to prison to make up for what Uncle Ramon did. Your grandfather's hatred would not allow him to forgive my grandfather. Then your grandfather shamed mine with his words. Now you come, and use my sister to worm your way into a life of laziness."

"How did you learn of these things?" Quintin turned toward his son. "The only one I've ever spoken to about my brother Ramon is Zavier."

"The same way you did." Zavier answered when Abel remained silent. "He overheard you and grandfather talking a few days before James died."

"Quintin?" Kalen turned and faced Mayla's father. "Did you ever tell your father you'd overheard him and my grandfather arguing?"

"No."

"And you let it eat at you all those years. When your father placed the burden of mending the rift between our families on you, your own resentment of my grandfather was already deeply rooted, wasn't it?"

Quintin's eyes widened. "I never considered my own resentment of Martin."

"Abel's done the same thing." Kalen shifted his position to ease the growing pain in his side. "He's convinced himself the only reason the grandson of the man who insulted his family would come here is to seek further vengeance. He believes that you and your father-in-law sent Mayla as a gift...to placate me."

Mayla's weeping became louder.

Kalen stepped closer to Jamie. "In the computer room you'll find my father's journal and the player. Would you get them?"

"Good idea." He hurried from the room.

Kalen's side ached, but he took a deep breath, faced Abel and repeated his previous conversation with Quintin. His family staring at him forced Abel to sit and listen, but his defiant expression never wavered. When Jamie returned, he placed the projector on the table and turned it on. Abel sat stone-faced while Russell spoke.

When the recording finished, Kalen said, "I'm sorry, Abel. I'm sorry my grandfather caused your family so much grief. I don't know of any way to convince you, except to tell you that although he had a good life, he died a bitter man. As my father just said, it was because he could not bring himself to swallow his pride and apologize for the terrible things he said to your grandfather, a man he once called a friend."

"Abel, Kalen speaks the truth!" Quintin stepped closer to his son. "Have I not been telling you this, these past cycles? Abel, I'm not angry. Kalen's apology made me see I had to let go, too. Let go of the past, son. Let go of your bitterness."

Abel's eyes darted from his father to his brothers, then to Mayla and his mother, but his expression remained bitter. He bolted out of the chair and glared at Kalen. "All this means nothing. You murdered your own family! My parents' and my brothers' families' lives were put in danger. Zavier's home is wrecked, and our family home here is almost destroyed! Now, after using my sister, you want to weasel your way into our family!" He turned a hate-filled glare on his father. "I know he is the reason you have withheld your help from me. He's poisoned your hearts against me! Until he either leaves or is dead, I won't be part of this family!"

"No, Abel, please!" Liana released Mayla. "Don't do this!"

"You're wrong about Kalen." Quintin reached out and put his hand on his middle son's shoulder. "This world and our way of life are in danger. Kalen helped expose one of those threats."

"You've all lost your minds!" Abel shrugged his father's hand off. "No one is threatening our world!" He stabbed a finger at Kalen. "He's the only threat. I won't stand here and listen to any more of these lies!" He yanked the door open and bolted from the room.

"I'll stop him." When Zavier started after his brother, Lily placed her hand on his arm. "Don't, mi amor."

"Let him be, Zavier." Quintin shook his head. "Arguing will not change his mind." He took Liana into his arms and held her as she wept along with Mayla.

Kalen hung his head. Just when life was settling down for him and his friends, another schism threatened to rip Mayla's family apart. *I can't remain here.* He turned away from the family and winced from the pain in his side. *I've caused these problems.* He looked down at his shirt, then moved his arm to cover the spreading blood stain. A spasm of pain threatened to double him over. *I'll find Abel and assure him I'll be gone by tomorrow.* He took a deep breath and moved toward the door. *I won't stand by and see this good family destroyed.*

Kalen stopped when he felt a hand on his shoulder. "I won't have you blaming yourself for Abel's attitude."

"Quintin, who else is to blame?" Kalen didn't turn when he spoke. "My presence here has caused your son to turn his back on his family!"

"Abel was always a stubborn child." Zavier moved closer. "He has become more so as a man. Don't let his lies and prejudices divide us further."

"But if he leaves now, this could wind up the same way we ended up." Kalen's side ached, but he wouldn't let it show. "You might never speak to him again."

Mayla left her mother's side, and took Kalen's hand. "Mi amor, don't try and take the blame for Abel's pride." She swiped at her remaining tears. "We know everything he said is a lie."

"My presence is the reason he is acting like this!"

"No! It's not your fault." Liana sniffed back her tears, her voice filled with iron when she spoke. "You've done nothing to bring on his anger. He's known from childhood why we sent Mayla away."

Jamie spoke up. "You're part of our family now. If you weren't here, he would find another reason to fight with us. He can't get his way, so it's easier to blame you than to admit his own mistakes."

With every heartbeat Kalen's side throbbed. His strength drained from his efforts of the past few minutes and he swayed on his feet.

"Kalen," Lily said. "Don't let Abel's twisted logic poison your heart. Your coming to us is like a breath of fresh air and has healed many old wounds. Our families started out together. Your father's greatest wish was for our families to stand united. Your marriage to Mayla makes that possible in a way your father never imagined. Let Abel go."

"Don't let his anger destroy yours and Mayla's happiness," said Catherine. "I cannot imagine our family without you being here. Neither can our children."

Liana's voice grew more determined. "He has to realize his mistakes. When he's had time to think, he'll come back."

"And if he doesn't?"

"We'll cross that river when we come to it," said Quintin.

Kalen relented, nodded, then lifted his left arm. The red spots had spread. Until now he had kept them hidden, but he couldn't conceal the blood any longer.

"Kalen!" Mayla's face paled. "You're bleeding again."

"S–sorry." His legs gave out.

Wrapping her arm around his chest, Mayla helped him sit down, then tore his shirt open. She examined his side. "It's not too serious. Zavier, please help Kalen back to his room."

"I can walk."

He attempted to stand, but Zavier took hold of his right arm. "Not today." Jamie grabbed his left. The two men pulled Kalen to his feet, and headed toward the door. The rest of the adults followed.

Once in his room, Mayla came in with her med-kit and worked to close his wound.

"Kalen, I won't have you blaming yourself for this." Quintin's voice hardened. "Abel has always acted as if he were better than

others. That Selwynian witch he married–" "Quintin!" Liana pulled on her husband's arm.

"No, Liana." With a gentle push, Quintin brushed her hand away. "I won't remain quiet. You know I speak the truth. We've both seen the way she treats our family, like she's better than any of us. She acts like it is a burden being part of our family. She looks down on Catherine and Lily as if being pregnant and having children is a disease. I love my son, but I can't sit by and allow him to make excuses and blame others for all his poor decisions, including his marriage. Mayla, do you have the bleeding under control?"

"Yes. Why?"

"I will speak with Kalen, alone."

Mayla looked as if she were about to object.

"Alone."

The look her father gave her squelched her protest. She took another quick look at Kalen's side, then she and the rest of the family left.

When the door closed, Quintin turned to Kalen. "Your father, when he was older, but before the trouble between him and Ramon, would show up unannounced at our home. He never had to ask about stopping by. My parents looked on him like another son. When he arrived, he'd pitch in with the chores and help on any project. If he arrived at meal time, which was most of the time, he would fix his own plate, sit down, and join in the family conversation. He was as much a part of our family as Ramon was part of his." Quintin paused and rubbed the back of his neck. "One thing I know about your father, he never ran from a problem. I expect no less from the son he raised. Now I want you to answer me and I want you to do so truthfully."

Kalen cringed.

Quintin placed his hands on the dark wood rail of the footboard and leaned in. "*Son*, why didn't you tell me Abel tried to kill you?"

"There's been enough bad blood between our families." Kalen lowered his eyes. Quintin's use of the word, *son*, redoubled his guilt. "I wanted to avoid hurting you and Liana again."

"Admirable, but foolish. You think having you and my children lie to us isn't painful?"

"I'm sorry, Quintin." He looked up at Mayla's father. "Mayla and Zavier did that at my insistence. I thought, given some time, I could talk with Abel and reason this out. I had hoped we'd become friends."

Quintin snorted. "After listening to him, do you still believe that's possible?"

"No, I don't think he's going to change his mind." Kalen clenched his fists. "Not in the near future, anyway."

"Abel was always difficult even as a child." Quintin stood up straight, but continued to grip the top rail of the foot board. "Learning about the conflict between Ramon and your father didn't help, but it doesn't justify his hostility toward you."

"He's convinced himself you sent Mayla as a gift to turn my anger away. When we were out in the grove, he shouted 'Puta' at her."

A pained look flashed across Quintin's rugged face. He closed his eyes, and took a deep breath. He released his white-knuckle grip on the top rail of the footboard, let his breath out, and continued. "There is no excuse for his thinking I would stoop to using my daughter as a shield. When he returned from school, married to Georgina, he started acting aloof." Quintin shook his head. "At first I thought it amusing, the way the two of them put on airs. Then Catherine announced her latest pregnancy. I overheard Georgina tell Abel, when she thought no one else was around, that Catherine was little more than a common brood mare to fill the Santiago stables." Quintin paused and stared into Kalen's eyes. "You're still considering leaving here, aren't you?"

"How can I remain? My presence will be a constant reminder of the trouble between our families."

"What about Mayla?"

"We'll have to postpone things for a while." Kalen lowered his eyes and stared at his lap.

"Maybe you don't love her as much as you claim?"

"That's not true!" Kalen snapped his head up. "I can't begin to tell you what she means to me. The thought of not having her in my life is unbearable."

"Then be the man I know your father raised." Quintin circled the bed and placed his hand on Kalen's shoulder. "Don't attempt to placate Abel and Georgina by leaving. He believes you are trying to live off of our family's wealth. We both know that isn't true. I cannot give him access to the mill. I wouldn't, even if we weren't so busy. He wanted out on his own, he must fend for himself. If I thought for a minute it would help, I'd send you away, but that won't change his attitude."

Quintin released Kalen's shoulder and stepped back. "Jamie's right, if you leave, he'd find something else to complain about. You haven't been with us long, but you're already a part of our family. I understand you wanting to withhold the truth from me, but don't ever do it again. Now, do you stay of your own accord or do I put my people to watching you all the time?"

"You're right." Kalen took a deep breath and rubbed the back of his neck. "I won't run from him. Appeasing a bully only emboldens him. I'll stay, but you must promise me something."

"What?" Quintin narrowed his eyes.

Kalen sat up and returned his future father-in-law's gaze. "I will stay as long as you and Liana don't blame yourselves. This is no more yours and Liana's fault, than it is mine or Mayla's."

A smile filled Quintin's face. "You have my word." Quintin offered his hand, and the two men shook. "Good, now I'll get Mayla." He crossed the room and activated the door.

Mayla stood just outside with her mother and two sisters-in-law. "Your fiancé needs your attention. Where are your brothers?"

"They went looking for Abel." Lily pointed down the hall.

"Good, I have a few words for him before he leaves." Quintin stepped through the door and disappeared. "Mayla, do you need our help?"

"No, Mother, I can take care of Kalen."

"Good. I'll take Lily and Catherine upstairs. I don't want to be close by when your father lays into Abel this time." Liana headed down the hallway. Lily and Catherine followed. By the expression on their faces, Kalen could see both women had a tight rein on their emotions.

"What did you and Papa talk about?" Mayla stepped into the room and closed the door.

"Mostly he talked and I listened. He wanted to make sure I wasn't still considering leaving."

"Are you?" Mayla went to work on his side.

He could read the concern and worry in her eyes. "I had thought it a good idea, but your father's right." He reached out, placed his hand under her chin and raised her face until their eyes met. "I love you more than I can express. I'll not give in to Abel. It won't change his mind or his attitude."

"Good. I'm glad you've come to your senses." Mayla kissed him, and then examined his side.

When she'd finished, he said, "I'm sorry, mi amor, I couldn't just lie here."

"I know. But now you need rest." She placed her hypo against Kalen's neck.

"What's in that?"

"The same mild sedative I've given you before."

"I think I can sleep without it."

"You need to rest. This will assure your doctor you will do just that."

The hypo hissed and the world faded.

Lake Solana
Santiago Estate

Chapter 20
Culls

First light crept into the room giving shape to the shadowy forms. Groggy and disoriented, Kalen blinked several times, stretched, then wondered why he felt so much better than the night before. His thoughts shifted to Abel, and despite Quintin's admonition, he wondered if he should stay.

He realized his side didn't ache and let go of his concern for Abel's opinion. *I'm not going to let him get to me.* Lifting his shirt, he stared at the place where his bandaged wound should be. To his surprise, the covering was gone and the slice had healed over, only a thin, reddish line remained. He pulled back the covers, slipped his legs over the side of the bed, and stood. His right hand strayed to his face. He rubbed his cheek, surprised that his beard felt thicker than one night's growth. He padded off to the bathroom to shower and clean up.

Dressed and feeling better, he crossed the room and tapped the door activation panel. The solid slab slid open and on the other side stood Mayla's brother Jamie. He had his usual grin plastered on his face. "I see you're up. How are you feeling?"

"Better." Kalen rubbed his face. "Jamie, how long have I been asleep?"

"Why do you ask?"

"Well, my wound's healed and I just scraped off two or three

Richard R Draude

days growth of beard."

"Let's see." Jamie stared at the ceiling, a look of mock concentration on his face. "I'd say a few hours over two days."

"Over two days! How could I possibly have slept that long?"

"Mayla kept you out."

"She did *what*?" He stared at Jamie. "How?"

"After patching you up, again, she left here, flew over to Andalusia, and spent a few hours replacing her medical supplies. When she returned, she injected you with additional nano-biotics, and added a stronger sedative into the mix. She said it was the only way to slow you down long enough to let your side heal. Once you were down, it didn't take that much to keep you under. Until last evening, she had you attached to a piece of medical equipment to keep fluids in you and prevent dehydration."

"I don't remember any of that."

"She said you wouldn't. You were too exhausted. You really haven't been sleeping well, have you?"

Kalen shook his head.

"I didn't think so." Jamie grinned again. "You woke the entire house up last week."

"Er, sorry." Kalen cringed. "I still have a little trouble with my dreams."

"Not this time." Jamie's grin widened.

"That's absolutely the last time I let her near me with that hypo of hers!"

Jamie raised his eyebrows.

"What, you don't believe me?"

"Oh, of course I do." He patted Kalen's shoulder while shaking his head. "Absolutely."

Kalen laughed. "Where's Mayla now?"

"She's upstairs with Catherine and Lily, they are making her wedding dress."

Jamie's revelation aroused Kalen's curiosity. He grinned at his future brother-in-law.

"Oh, no you don't." The smile faded from Jamie's face. "I won't get involved in that stupid game. I haven't seen her dress, and if I did, I wouldn't tell you about it. Catherine may be small and petite, but I value my hide right where it is." His grin returned. "Mayla told

132

mother you'd be hungry. We have first meal waiting."

"I could do with a bite to eat."

Kalen and Jamie headed up the west hallway, toward the kitchen. This house continued to awe Kalen, though he had trouble thinking of it as an ordinary house. He'd taken to wandering the estate and found the upper floor held over forty large bedrooms, ten or more in each wing. At each end of a wing, between the bedroom groupings, sitting rooms provided a homey atmosphere for visiting. The first floor held guest bedrooms, sitting rooms and the computer center. The kitchen took up almost the entire north wing. An enormous formal dining room and library occupied the east wing.

The furniture, all handmade of dark Acajou wood from the Arrisian forests, by Quintin and his sons, filled the rooms with more warmth.

The two men reached the kitchen, though to Kalen it resembled more a dining hall. The gleaming polished stone counter tops sat on top of dark wood cabinets. On the counters, sat baskets holding fresh fruit, picked from the groves surrounding the estate. The counters ringed the cooking area forming a 'U' with a piece cut out of one side. In the midst of the 'U' stood a large island where the staff prepared the day's meals. The refrigerated storage units built into the west wall at the top of the 'U' stored at least a full cycle of food. The enticing smell of fresh baked Mossia wafted through the air and made his stomach growl.

Quintin and Liana sat together and smiled when he and Jamie entered.

"Well, finally." Liana pointed to a spot across from them. "Come, sit down, first meal is ready."

Kalen took the indicated place across from Liana and Quintin.

Jamie sat next to him.

Quintin asked, "How are you feeling?"

"Rested, recuperated, and ravenous." Kalen grinned.

"Good." Liana signaled to the staff. "Isabella, please bring Kalen his meal."

In front of Kalen, Isabella set a plate of fresh picked fruit, sliced and arranged around the rim. "It's good to see you up and well, Mister MacKenna."

"Thank you, Isabella." He reached out and touched her arm.

"Mayla told me how you and the other staff offered to help when I was injured. I want you to know I'm grateful. Please convey my thanks to the other women, especially Gina. Oh, and my name is Kalen. My father was Mister MacKenna."

"Good enough...Kalen." A broad smile lit Isabella's face. "I will convey your thanks to the others." She turned and went back to work.

Kalen paused before taking his first bite, reached across the table and took hold of Liana's hands. "Are we good?"

"Abel has chosen his course." Liana looked into his eyes and smiled. "We will not vary from ours. Whatever lies my son and Georgina choose to believe, so be it. You're part of our family now. As Lily said, your marriage to Mayla will bind our families together in a way no one could have foreseen." She slid her hands loose, reached across the table and palmed Kalen's cheek. "Quintin and I have no regrets."

A comfortable silence filled the room. Kalen nodded, lifted his fork and tasted the fresh fruit. "I didn't realize I could be this hungry." Between bites Kalen said, "Quintin, I'm sorry I didn't tell you the truth about Abel."

"I understand why you did it."

"That still doesn't make it right. My father raised me to know better. I promise you I'll always give you a straight answer from now on."

"Good, then drop it."

"Thank you, sir." Kalen turned his full attention to his meal. He downed half the fruit on the plate and paused. "What are you up to today, Jamie?"

"The women have an entire shopping list that needs filling." Jamie clapped Kalen on his shoulder. "I think you should come with me when I fly into Solana."

Kalen swallowed the last bit of melon. "What does my doctor say?"

"She's the one who suggested it. She seems to think it will ease the temptation to cheat."

"On that note." Liana stood. "I'll go and see how the girls are coming with Mayla's dress.

Kalen gave her a quick glance and took another bite of food.

"That's a wise decision, young man." Liana's eyes narrowed.

Kalen put on his most innocent smile and sliced off a large piece of the breaded Cassyin Isabella had just set in front of him. "The men caught this in the lake this morning."

"It's one of my favorites, Isabella."

Liana's gaze turned on Quintin for a moment.

He flinched, then she left the room.

"I'm surprised at you, Kalen." Quintin recovered from his wife's withering stare and chuckled. "You should know better. The last person in this world you want to try and play the Arrisian wedding game with is the bride's mother. Liana is the reason my sons always lost. Even if you managed to win, remember, it's never wise to start one's married life with your wife or mother-in-law, or both, mad at you."

"You sound as if you speak from experience." Kalen paused. "Did you play the game?"

When Quintin cringed again, Jamie chuckled. "Papa, don't tell me you actually got a look at Mother's dress before your wedding!"

"If you remember, Jamie, your mother and I eloped the year Ramon went to prison. My family was still trying to recover from his betrayal. Liana and I wanted to get married. We felt it inappropriate to speak about a wedding at the time, but we didn't want to wait either. We ran away. Before we went to the magistrate, I paid the porter at the inn to get a picture of Liana in her dress before she came down. I don't know how she managed to do it, but the porter brought it to me. I thought myself quite clever to have won the game."

A look of amusement played across Quintin's face.

"After a few minutes, I felt terrible." The smile faded. "I tucked the picture away, and forgot about it. A few years later Liana found the stupid picture. She laughs about it now, but she never lets me forget it. So, go right ahead and play the game, Kalen, but remember, even if you manage to win, you lose."

"So that's why Mother is so good at this!" Jamie laughed.

"After she saw that picture, she swore no man would ever get past her. I've heard all about how stupid the wedding game is, but she plays it well. Your mother made sure you and Zavier failed and she'll do so for our granddaughters, and our grandsons' wives."

Kalen turned to Jamie. "So, you did play the game."

"I tried." Jamie's cheeks reddened. "And Cat didn't need my mother's help. She told me in no uncertain terms what would happen

Richard R Draude

if she ever found out I peeked."

Kalen and Quintin had a good laugh at Jamie's expense. Kalen finished his breakfast, returned to his room, and grabbed his staff. Following Jamie out to the north edge of the citrus grove that served as the family parking area, his future brother-in-law looked him over. "You don't look like you're up to piloting yet, so let's take my flyer into Solana." They walked over to a large, muted silver vehicle.

"Nice. What model is this?"

"It's last season's Lexicon Imperial Ten series. They're not as maneuverable or as fast as their Imperial Flyer series, but it carries my family comfortably, without the kids killing each other."

"I can't imagine your children fighting."

"You haven't been cooped up with them for five hours or more." He snorted, and stepped up to the pilot's door. "Computer, vehicle access." The two front doors rotated forward and Jamie pulled his wiry frame into the pilot's seat.

Kalen spotted another staff in the back, tossed his on the middle row of seats next to it then climbed into the passenger seat. "You use a staff?"

"I've trained a bit."

"We should spar sometime."

"I'll pass." Jamie shook his head. "I've watched you and Mayla go at it. No, thank you."

The doors closed. Jamie lifted off and headed for Solana. They were in the air about a minute when Jamie asked, "Why so quiet, Kalen? You getting nervous?"

"About our wedding, no. I was just wondering."

"About what?"

"About what happened after your father left my room to confront your brother. What did he say to Abel and Georgina?"

"Oh, that. I wish you could have been there." Jamie laughed so hard it took him a minute to calm down before he could continue.

"We knew Papa would want one last word with our dear brother and his wife. Zavier and I stopped them from leaving until Papa showed up. He laid into Abel and Georgina and let them know their attitudes aren't welcome in our home. You should have seen Georgina's perfect porcelain face. I thought it would crack when Papa told her that his daughters-in-law are precious

136

members of our family, not brood mares. Nor were his grand-children horses filling a stable. He let them know he loves them both and they were welcome here when they want to be part of our family. He made sure Abel understood why he couldn't have access to the mill, it's because we're too busy. He also told Abel that, poor or wealthy, you are part of this family. Then he let Abel know just how much Cal saved for you while you were in stasis. You should have seen him, Kalen, I swear I could hear the hot air leaking out of his head. When he left, he looked like a deflated Karchen ball."

Jamie and Kalen burst into laughter and Jamie almost lost control of the flyer. After they recovered, Kalen said, "You're okay with Abel walking out?"

"I'm good." A smirk slid across Jamie's face. "Besides, you for Abel, I can live with the trade-off." Jamie made another course adjustment. "How about we continue working on your use of the hunter's language?"

"Good idea. I've watched you and Quintin use it so you don't have to shout at each other when working on the estate roof. I've picked up some of the short phrases and simpler gestures, but I still don't have the knack of the more intricate finger movements." He tried making a sentence up.

"Well—" Jamie cringed and laughed. "That'll work...if you're trying to proposition a woman, but I wouldn't try that one on Mayla."

"What did I say?"

"Never mind. Let's not reinforce bad habits. I think what you meant was this." Jamie fluttered his fingers in slow motion so Kalen could catch each motion.

Kalen watched, then repeated the movements.

Jamie signed again.

"You're right, I can read your signs better than I can talk. Let's keep working on it, I think it will be useful for me to know."

They arrived on the outskirts of Solana, and Jamie slipped into the busy sky lanes. Maneuvering through traffic, he set down across from a cluster of shops, and secured his flyer. The two men crossed the street and headed down the walkway, past the open store fronts.

Kalen liked the Outlands style, with their goods on display.

It made the street more like an open-air marketplace and shopping more enjoyable. Kalen and Jamie moved past the displays, examining shoes, clothing, and household items. Kalen stopped at a store handling hiking and camping equipment. He just finished his examination of a new style climbing harness, when two men stumbled out of an alley. The older of the two ran headlong into Jamie and him. He shoved Kalen. "Hey, git out o' me way!"

Kalen stepped aside. "I'm sorry."

The men, dressed in crude, thread-bare clothes, eyed Kalen and laughed. The older of the two stepped closer to Kalen, looked him up and down, getting within a few centimeters of Kalen's face. "Lookee here, Flin. It looks ta me like we got us a Mazy-boy."

Kalen rankled at the insult, then almost gagged on the stench of the man's breath, his filthy clothing, and his unwashed body. He stood about Jamie's height. When he spoke, Kalen could see he had several missing teeth. His dark greasy hair lay pasted against his head. The stubbled beard, dirty hands, and watery brown eyes completed a grim picture of a man on the skids.

The blond-haired Flin moved closer. The sight of his dirty clothes, unwashed shaggy blond hair and rail-thin body made Kalen grateful for Cal's undying friendship. *I could've wound up like these two.*

Flin's brow furrowed as he moved alongside Kalen. "Michael, what ya think a Mazy-boy's doin' down here in the Barreras?"

Jamie grabbed Michael, pushed him away from Kalen, and then pointed toward the street. "Why don't you two gentlemen move along right now, before I'm forced to call those nice RPs over here."

Michael's gaze followed Jamie's arm and his eyes popped open. He grabbed his youthful companion by the collar and yanked. Flin resisted.

Michael gave the boy a kick in his rump, then pointed. "Don't be a bigger fool then ya are, Flin Devlin! We'll not be wantin' any run-ins with the law this day."

Flin's eyes widened as if he just remembered something important. "Ya, ya, Michael. Best we be movin' on."

"We'll be catchin' you another time, Mazy-boy." The two men turned, hurried down the walkway and ducked into another alley.

"Who or what was that?" Kalen sniffed to clear his sinuses.

"A new plague in these mountains." Jamie wiped his hands on

his pant leg.

"What?" Kalen gave him a puzzled look. "A new plague? What do you mean?"

"That's right, you wouldn't know about any of this, would you? Two and a half years ago, the Central Council changed the laws concerning the inheritance of land. Our founders created the law so a person who had no direct heirs to pass their farmland to, could will it to distant relations, close friends, or even his employees. Some group sued, claiming the law was unconstitutional." Jamie huffed in disgust. "The CC changed the law so a farmstead under those conditions must go to auction."

"How can the CC do that?"

"Beats me. Now, most of the land coming up for auction is bought by a small group of business women. I know several men who lost out because they couldn't raise the funds needed to make a successful bid. At first, no one thought much of it, but that same outfit has bought many of the smaller landholders out. Now they hold almost all of the land between Mesa Alcon and Mesa Verde."

He pointed north toward the mountains.

"Men who stood to inherit land find themselves on the outs. Those that can't find work in the cities wind up taking refuge in the Barrera wilds. Some have turned to wood cutting and we buy a lot of our hardwoods from one group that organized their own guild. Some have sunk to thievery and others to kidnapping."

"Kidnapping?" Kalen stared at Jamie, wide-eyed.

"We're not supposed to know it's happening." Jamie made a sour face. "Recently eight young women have disappeared from here and the surrounding towns. I also heard a rumor that it's happened in the valleys and in the north country."

"And they've never been found?"

"No." Jamie shook his head. "Rumor has it that the authorities suspect some of these men."

"What about ransom?" Women disappearing without a trace made Kalen shudder with the thought of what might be happening to them. "Can't they follow whoever picks up the ransom?"

"I wouldn't know. I learned about this by accident. All I do know is they've disappeared. The logger's guild we deal with has taken to calling the worst of these outcasts, culls." Jamie hitched his left thumb over his shoulder. "Like Flin and Michael."

"A man would have to sink pretty low to be considered worthless."

"Forget those two. We need to get started on Lily and Catherine's list." Jamie pulled his hand held out of his work vest, tapped the screen, and handed it to Kalen.

"Just a short list." Kalen whistled. "Shouldn't take more than the rest of the day."

"That's the idea."

Kalen made a face and looked over his shoulder.

"Forget those two." Jamie patted Kalen on the back "They're more trouble than they're worth. Those two are harmless."

Chapter 21
Caught In The Act

"Gimmish! I hope that didn't break." Kalen squatted to pick up a package he dropped in the grass bordering the landing area. "This is our third trip. Are you sure the women need all of this stuff?"

"Probably not." Jamie readjusted his grip on a large box he carried and laughed. "But it keeps us from being underfoot and in trouble." As they approached Jamie's flyer, Kalen spotted two men concealed in the shadows of half a dozen large willows across the street. The woman with them looked distressed. He pulled Jamie behind a parked cruiser.

"Kalen, what are you–"

Kalen put his finger to his lips, then pointed across the street. "Isn't that Michael and Flin, the guys we ran into earlier today?"

"It sure is, and that doesn't look good." He grabbed Kalen's bundles. "Keep an eye on those two. I'll put this stuff in the flyer and be right back." Jamie hurried away.

When Michael craned his neck to scan the area, Kalen moved closer and took cover behind a cruiser.

Close to a shop, Michael and Flin had taken up refuge in the shade, amidst the trees, near the opening between two buildings. The location kept them out of sight of the casual glance of most pedestrians.

Michael said something to the woman.

She shook her head and backed away.

Michael grabbed her arms, spun her around, and then Flin cuffed her, open-handed, across the cheek.

Her head snapped to one side

Kalen winced and clenched his fists.

Michael covered her mouth, then the two men pulled her between the shops, and disappeared down the alley.

Jamie came up alongside Kalen, carrying their staffs. "You sure you know how to use that?" Kalen grabbed his.

"I wasn't always the gentle soul you see before you. You do realize that if you tear your side open again, Mayla will skin both of us without benefit of anesthesia."

"So we just let those two clowns go."

"Not in this lifetime." Jamie grinned. "Just thought I'd warn you."

"Like I need a warning. Let's go, they must have a transport of me kind they'll use to get away behind those stores."

Kalen and Jamie darted out from behind the flyer, past an elderly couple, startling them.

"Call the Roving Patrol!" Jamie pointed. "Send them down that alley."

They continued at a dead run. Crossing the street, the two men dashed between the buildings. Reaching the far end of the alley, they spotted Michael and Flin dragging the dazed woman down the hill toward an old, beat-up cruiser.

Michael looked over his shoulder, spotted Kalen and Jamie, and sped up. Dragging the woman, he slammed her into the old vehicle. "Hey, cull, let the lady go." Kalen stepped away from the buildings.

Michael stopped short and turned. "What did ja call me?"

"You heard him, cull." Jamie took a couple of steps away from Kalen. "Let her go and move along."

Michael released his grip on the woman's arms, and forced her to kneel. "Try runnin' and I'll kill ya meself."

The woman lowered her head and cowered.

Michael's hand went to his side and he pulled a knife from a sheath Kalen hadn't noticed before.

"Doesn't anyone ever just give up?" Kalen rolled his eyes.

"What is it with guys like them?" Jamie shook his head and huffed in disgust. "They always have a knife or some other nasty weapon, yet can't afford to bathe or buy decent clothes."

"You'll be findin' out, directly." Michael charged, knife gripped in his fist.

When he moved within a meter, Kalen sidestepped, dodging Michael's knife swipe. He grabbed Michael's outstretched arm above the wrist and yanked. With the added momentum, the would- be kidnapper flew past him.

Jamie gave him a sharp rap on the back with his staff.

The sour-smelling man stumbled, crashed face first in the gravel and dirt, then skidded to a stop. Before Kalen could pin him down with his staff, he moved with unexpected agility, rolled to his left and jumped to his feet.

"You're a wee bit slow, Mazy-boy."

Kalen ignored the insult and backed away. "I've got this one, Jamie."

"I'll see to the kid." Jamie went after Flin.

"Hey, Mazy-boy. I'm gonna gut ja!"

With more caution this time, Michael approached Kalen. He darted in and swiped his knife at Kalen's face.

Kalen deflected the blade with his staff, danced out of Michael's reach, and circled so he could see Jamie. He fended off Michael's next clumsy attack with a sharp rap to Michael's shoulder.

"Ya bloody knacker!" Michael backed off, rubbing his shoulder. Slashing at Jamie with all the inexperience of youth, Flin rushed Mayla's brother. Jamie turned his thrusts aside and jabbed Flin hard in the solar plexus.

Flin staggered backwards.

Michael swiped at Kalen again. "I'm gonna teach you 'bout interferin' in me business, Mazy-boy."

The insult refocused Kalen's full attention on the sour-smelling man.

Michael ran at him.

Dodging another arching swipe, Kalen rapped Michael on the side of his skull.

Staring open-mouthed at Kalen, Michael shook off the blow. "Time to pay up, Mazy-boy."

"I'm right here." Kalen danced backwards, moving closer to the cowering woman.

"Yer gonna die!" Michael bolted toward Kalen at full speed.

Kalen swung his staff, cracking the would-be kidnapper in the face.

The greasy-haired man howled, veered away, and shook his head. With his free hand he probed the inside of his cheek, then spit out blood and a piece of broken tooth. His eyes narrowed. "I'll kill ya!"

"I'm waiting." Kalen chuckled and danced closer to the woman. "I'll cut that smile right off your pretty face!" Michael charged again, his knife held low.

Hooking Michael's arm, Kalen parried the thrust, knocking him off-balance. The force spun Michael around. Kalen jammed his staff into his left kidney.

Dropping to one knee, Michael bellowed in a mixture of pain and frustration. He jumped up, spun around, and charged again.

Time to end this. Kalen feigned a step left and Michael followed, leaving himself open. At the last second, Kalen sidestepped to his right, thrust his staff below Michael's knife arm, and drove the heavy end of his staff deep into Michael's abdomen.

Air burst from Michael's lungs. The blow halted his forward momentum. He sank to his knees, his face turned bright red and his knife arm extended. Kalen slammed his staff down on Michael's wrist.

The knife flew from his hand. "Me arm! Ya broke me arm!" Michael grabbed his wrist. "Ya busted me wrist!"

"Make up your mind." Kalen kicked Michael's knife away. "Did I break your arm or your wrist?" He turned in time to see Jamie jam his staff deep into Flin's gut. The youth staggered backwards, crumpled in a heap on the ground, close to Michael, moaning and gasping for air.

Kalen lowered his staff, stepped over to the young woman, and extended his hand. "You're safe now, Miss."

She took Kalen's hand, stood, moved close to him and sniffled back her tears. "Thank–thank you."

As he placed himself between her and her would-be assailants, a voice called out, "Jamie, what's going on here?" Kalen looked around and spotted two uniformed officers emerge from the alley.

"It figures, they'd show after all the work's done." Jamie turned toward the men and put on a big smile. "Eli! You're just in time." He pointed at the men. "These two culls tried to kidnap this woman."

The two officers drew their weapons. They reached Kalen's side and the first officer took hold of Michael and dragged the man to his feet.

"Me wrist!" Michael writhed in pain. "He busted me wrist!"

The second officer moved past Kalen and the woman, grabbed Flin and dragged him to his feet.

"Jamie, what are you doing here?" The officer looked from Michael to Flin.

"We spotted these two arguing with this young lady." Jamie moved closer to Eli and pointed. "Flin there struck her and then the two of them dragged her down here. We followed, invited them to move on, but of course, they refused."

"Michael pulled that knife and rushed us." Kalen pointed at the weapon with his staff.

"Flin tried the same thing."

While the second officer grabbed Michael, Eli scooped up the weapon, then turned his attention to the woman still clinging to Kalen. He removed a mini recorder from his belt. "I'm Officer Eli Marcos. What's your name, Miss?"

"Julia. My name is Julia Davenport."

"Can you give me an account of the incident?"

"I...I just finished shopping." She paused, wiped the tears from her blue eyes, then took a deep breath to get control of herself. "I headed back to my cruiser. These two men approached me in the parking area and asked me for the time. After I told them, they blocked my way when I tried to get to my vehicle. That one," she pointed to Michael, "grabbed me. The other one hit me when I tried to yell for help."

"All right, Miss Davenport, we'll get you over to the Med Center and then see about getting you home." Officer Marcos stopped. "Davenport. Now why does that name sound familiar?"

"My uncle's a detective at the Andalusia east station."

"Mel Davenport?"

The woman nodded.

Officer Marcos reached over, grabbed Flin and shoved him next to Michael. "Hombres, you're in a lot of trouble! Kidnapping's stupid, but you two dummies tried to steal a member of an RP officer's family!"

145

Jamie asked. "Eli, will you need us to stay?"

The officer seemed unaffected by the use of his first name. "If you wouldn't mind, Jamie. Al can start questioning them while I take yours and Miss Davenport's statements. I'll have Al book these two when we're done here, and then contact my superiors."

Kalen kept watching Michael, who, despite the pain in his wrist, seemed preoccupied with the old cruiser. "Officer Marcos, it might be a good idea if you took a look in their cruiser right away."

Eli stared at Michael, who diverted his eyes from the battered vehicle, his face covered with a guilty, frightened look.

"Check it out, Al. I'll keep an eye on these two."

Al moved toward the vehicle, his weapon at the ready. He circled the cruiser and looked into the windows. "Damn!"

All eyes snapped in his direction. "Mister Santiago, please come help me!"

When Al activated the driver's wing door, Jamie went to aid the officer. Al forced it up and reached inside. The rear hatch released with a soft click. "Woman– in the back."

Jamie reached in and pulled a female out, hooded and bound. When he removed the hood, he cried out, "Makayla!" He removed the gag from her mouth, untied the girl's hands, and wiped the tears running down her cheeks.

Jamie placed her in Al's arms. Rage filled his eyes as he bent down, grabbed Flin's knife off the ground, and started toward the prisoners.

"Jamie, don't!" Eli yelled and raised his weapon.

"Do you know who that child is?" Jamie didn't halt.

"No," Officer Marcos said. The RP officer reached Jamie's side, and took hold of his arm. "It doesn't matter!"

"The hell it doesn't!" Jamie shrugged off Eli's hand. "That's Albert and Isabella Shanahan's youngest child. Albert runs our mill. His wife, Isabella, oversees the staff at our estate. They're our friends!"

Eli tried to turn Jamie away. "Jamie, I said it doesn't matter because it's still kidnapping. The crime carries the death penalty. We'll handle it! Put the knife down!"

"Jamie, stop," Kalen said. "They're not worth it. Officer Marcos is right. They've been caught red-handed. There is no way they're getting off!"

Jamie ignored Kalen. He moved closer to the prisoners. "What about the rest of the girls these people have taken?"

His eyes riveted on Jamie, Officer Marcos said, "How do you know about that?"

"Come on, Eli, you know nothing stays a secret around here!" Jamie held the knife up. "Now do we pry some information out of these two or wait until some Bar Rep shuts them up?"

Eli took hold of Flin and pushed Michael toward Jamie.

Mayla's youngest brother lowered the knife and pressed the point into Michael's lower abdomen.

Julia gagged and turned her face away. Over behind the men, Makayla said, "Please, Mister Santiago, stop. I don't want you to go to jail." When Jamie didn't listen, her weeping grew louder.

Jamie undid Michael's rope belt and yanked it out.

"Stop it!" Michael grabbed the waistband of his pants before they slipped off his hips.

"Look at that, Kalen. I guess his wrist isn't busted after all. That should keep your hands busy!" Jamie lowered his voice. "You've got one chance to talk before I fix it so you'll sing falsetto all the way to the chamber."

"Ya—ya can't be doin' this!" Terror filled Michael's eyes. "I got me rights!"

"So do those missing girls. Now talk or live out what's left of your days as a eunuch."

"I ain't telling you nothin'." Michael's gaze darted to the RP officers. "Ain't ya gonna stop him?"

"Have it your way." Jamie slit his pants open. "Stop!" Michael screeched.

"Where are they?"

"They're up in the eastern arm." Flin's wavering voice answered just above a whisper.

"Flin, you'll be shuttin' your mealy mouth!" Michael clamped the waistband of his pants with one hand and tried to get at Flin.

Jamie pressed the knife against Michael's abdomen, halting the smelly man's advance.

Eli turned his attention to the younger man. "Where? Where were you taking them?"

"It's supposed to be about five hundred kilometers from here, up at the end of the old North Ford Highway."

"How many of your people are up there?" "Flin, shut ya stupid—"

Jamie grabbed Michael's shirt, pulled him close, and brought his knee up.

Michael grunted and his eyes popped open. He sank to his knees, coughing, sucking air through clenched teeth. He stopped threatening Flin.

Kalen cringed, his own groin muscles clenched.

"Good." Julia whispered.

Officer Marcos turned back to Flin. "You were saying."

"I don't know the location." Flin looked at his wheezing companion and winced. "We were told ta grab two girls and meet a man at the inn in Avila. He was supposed to show us the way."

"Why are you doing this?" Kalen wrapped his arm around Julia. "We heard there's a woman there, paying for young women to be brought to her." "Why?" Eli said.

"I–I don't know why." Flin shrugged and stared at the ground. "We were gettin' desperate. Michael said we could make enough wafers ta be livin' easy."

Eli pulled his comm from his belt. "Barracks, this is Officer Marcos."

"This is Corporal Higgins."

"Corporal, I need you to send a transport to pick up a couple of prisoners. We're in the rear parking area of the furrier's shop on Solana Avenue. I want them over here ASAP. Then call Lieutenant Castellano and tell him we have a lead in the kidnapping case. Marcos out."

Jamie pulled Eli aside. "Do you believe him?" "I don't know. That was a good bluff though."

"Was I bluffing?"

"I certainly hope so. Anyway, that kid's too frightened to lie, but I think he knows more. It's for sure Michael won't tell us much." Eli looked around, then said, "I'll call the Med Center. Could you and your friend take Miss Davenport and the girl over there so a doctor can examine them? I'll need that report to fill out mine."

"We'll wait there for you." Jamie went to Makayla.

She let go of Al and latched onto him. "Come on, Makayla, on the way to the Med Center, we'll call your parents."

"Oh, please, Mister Santiago, do we have ta?"

"Yes." Jamie pulled her close. "We can't keep this from them."

Chapter 22
A Vague Plan

While Kalen and Jamie headed toward the flyer, Makayla continued to weep. "Me Da's goin'–goin' ta kill me."

"Why?" Jamie stroked the girl's hair.

"Because Da and Mother warned me ta be stayin' with me friends. I wasn't supposed ta be wanderin' around alone."

"They'll be more relieved to know you're safe." "Who are you?" Julia looked over at Jamie.

"Just some concerned neighbors." The group reached the flyer. "Vehicle access," said Jamie. The doors rotated open.

"Well, concerned neighbors, thank you for being so alert. I thought they were going to kill me." Julia looked up at Kalen. "Thanks for coming after us."

"You're welcome." Kalen helped Julia into the flyer.

Jamie made sure Makayla secured herself and then circled the flyer. Climbing in, he lifted off, and while en route, he called his father and explained what had happened.

"Mayla, your mother, and I will leave immediately," Quintin said. "We'll bring Albert and Isabella with us."

"Make sure they understand she's with us and she's safe and unharmed."

"I'll do that."

Jamie made the short hop to the Solana Med Center and entered the waiting room.

"May I help you?" said the admitting clerk. "Yes, Officer Marcos
151

sent us."

"Ah yes, the mugging victims. I was told to expect." He looked around, spotted another employee and said, "Miss Aberdeen, please take these women to exam rooms seven and eight so Doctor Reyes can examine them."

The med tech led Julie and Makayla away. Kalen and Jamie settled into a couple of dark blue overstuffed chairs in the lobby to wait.

Kalen tapped Jamie's shoulder when a woman in a medical uniform approached them. "We should get some answers now." Both men stood.

"Which one of you is Mister Santiago?"

"I am."

"I'm Doctor Reyes. I've been examining the two young women you brought in."

"How are they?"

"They're both fine. Miss Davenport is going to have a bruised cheek from the slap she received and bruising where the men grabbed her."

"What about the girl?" Kalen could see Jamie growing tense.

"Is the girl a relative?"

"Her parents are in my father's employ, but they are more like family. Is she all right?"

"She was roughed up a bit and drugged, but she is otherwise untouched. I'll explain in more detail to her parents."

"Thank you, Doctor." Jamie let out an explosive breath.

"They're both getting dressed. I'll need to speak with Miss Shanahan's parents. When will they be here?"

"They're on their way. They should arrive shortly. I'll make sure they find you as soon as they get here."

"Thank you." Doctor Reyes returned to her work.

Makayla emerged from the examining area and attached herself to Jamie. He enfolded her in his arms and she wept while they waited for her parents to arrive.

Officer Marcos came into the lobby and spent some time taking their statements.

"Makayla, this is Kalen." Jamie said. "Stay with him while I talk to this officer."

The girl sniffled. "I know who he is. He's the one your brother stabbed. He's engaged to your sister."

When she slid over next to Kalen, he shot Jamie a questioning look and mouthed the words, "She knows?"

Jamie shrugged. "She's friends with Mariah. I told you nothing stays a secret around here." He stood to talk with the officer. "Eli, is there any way you can keep our names out of this?"

"Not really." Eli rubbed his chin. "It could be kinda difficult, but I can try."

"When you make your report out, just say you spotted the trouble and followed them. If our names have to come up, just say you pressed us into service or anything else you need to say. That way you get the credit. That should impress your superiors."

"It certainly wouldn't hurt Al or myself."

"Thanks, Eli. By the way, this is my good friend Kalen. Kalen, this is Eli Marcos. His brother and I went to school together."

The two men shook hands.

"Do you always carry this pole around?" Eli picked up Kalen's staff leaning against the chair and examined it.

"I recently discovered I shouldn't leave home without it." Kalen tapped the staff.

"Eli, what about the other women?" Jamie said, when the officer finished examining the staff.

"I tried to contact Lieutenant Castellano, he's in charge of the task force looking into the kidnappings." Eli leaned Kalen's staff against the chair. "I could only reach his assistant. She said they'll send someone over to check out these guys. According to her, they don't think those two know enough to lead them to the missing girls."

"What!" Jamie's jaw dropped. "They practically told us the location of the kidnappers! I would think they'd come flying over there!"

"Lieutenant Castellano's admin told me his people are spread pretty thin. She said they'll get here as soon as they can. If you'll excuse me, I want to check on Miss Davenport."

"Of course you do." Jamie grinned and winked. "Here she comes now."

Eli turned as Julia emerged from the exam room. "Miss Davenport, how are you feeling?"

"Better. Thank you for asking, Office Marcos."

"Please, call me Eli. Where do you live?"

"I'm staying with my parents. Their home is on the east side of Solana, in Las Haciendas del Cañón de Cobre."

"Have you contacted them?"

"No, they're visiting family in Andalusia. I don't want my mother worrying. I'll explain everything when they get home."

"If the doctor's released you, I'd be glad to fly you there."

"I'd like to pick up my cruiser and take it home." She smiled at Eli. "I would feel safer with an escort."

"A Roving Patrol escort it is then."

Julia started toward the exit, but stopped and looked at Kalen "Thank you again. I'm pretty sure you two saved our lives today."

"You're welcome." Kalen put on his warmest smile. "I'm glad we were nearby. Look, Miss Davenport, we'd appreciate it if you would give Officer Marcos and his partner the credit though."

"Are you sure?" A puzzled look crossed Julia's face. "My parents and uncle will want to know what really happened."

"We're sure," Jaime said. "My friend and I like to keep a low profile, that's all."

"All right, but thanks again, both of you." Eli escorted Julia from the lobby.

Jamie sat down with Kalen and Makayla to wait. "You know my sister may still skin us both for getting in the middle of this."

Kalen grimaced and let out a long sigh.

Jamie laughed. "I see you're beginning to grasp the idea of what it means to marry a Santiago woman."

"I figured that out after I met your mother." Kalen glanced toward the entrance, dreading Mayla's appearance.

At the sound of hurried footsteps Kalen looked up as Quintin, Liana and Mayla arrived with Albert and Isabella. Makayla's parents rushed into the waiting room and their daughter let go of Jamie and ran to her mother.

While Liana and Isabella comforted Makayla, Jamie took Albert aside. "Albert, Makayla's fine."

"How did those men get her?"

"You know kids. She strayed away from her friends. Go easy on her. I don't think you'll ever have to tell her again to stay with a group."

"Jamie, do you know if those men–if they–"

"Doctor Reyes told me they drugged her." Jamie gripped Albert's shoulder. "When we found her, she was bound, gagged, and had a hood over her head. These men were desperate for money."

The tension left Albert's face. "Thank you, Jamie. We owe you and Mister MacKenna a lot."

"You owe us nothing, Albert." Jamie patted Albert's back. "Just see Doctor Reyes, then go take care of your family."

Albert squeezed Jamie's shoulder. "Thanks." He left to join his wife and daughter. Jamie went and stood by Quintin, Mayla and Kalen to give the family some privacy.

"I can't tell you what that child means to them." Quintin glanced over at his foreman. "Isabella tried for years to have another child. After four miscarriages she finally carried Makayla to term. If they'd lost her, I don't how we could've consoled them and their other children."

"Just can't stay out of trouble, can you?" Mayla put her arm around Kalen's waist. "Are you all right?"

"I'm fine. Nothing a little enforced sleep didn't cure."

"I had to do something to keep you inactive."

I'm glad you did, my love, otherwise I wouldn't have been here to help Jamie."

Albert approached them. "The doctor says we can take Makayla home. Quintin, if you're busy, we can hire a public transport."

"You'll do no such thing." Liana turned to face Albert. "Take Isabella and Makayla to the flyer, we'll be along in a minute."

"Albert, I want you to take a couple of days off," Quintin said. "Your daughter will need the two of you at home."

"But sir, what about that load for the first Crosskey job? We need to get it completed and loaded."

"Calm down, Albert." Quintin gripped his foreman's shoulder. "Dom can handle the men. I don't need either you or Isabella trying to work with your mind on your daughter. One tragedy's been averted, let's not tempt fate."

"That goes for you too, Isabella," Liana said. "Gina and the other women can take care of things for a couple of days."

"Thank you, Liana, and thank you, Jamie, and, you too, Kalen."

Isabella pulled her daughter close to her side. "Makayla told us that you two are the ones that found her."

"Isabella," said Jamie, "Kalen and I would appreciate it if you, Albert, and Makayla would forget about us. If anyone asks, just say Officer Marcos' good police work saved your daughter."

"If you say so, Jamie." Albert put his arms around his daughter and his wife and left the lobby.

Liana hooked her arm in Quintin's. "What are you two going to do now?"

"We're going to get out of here." Jamie scratched his head. "I don't know how I'll explain this to Cat."

"Mayla, did you come in the Lexicon?" Kalen said.

"Of course. It's faster and easier to fly than that freight hauler of Papa's."

"I'll have you know, young lady, that's a very expensive freight hauler." Quintin managed to keep a straight face and look offended.

"Sorry, Papa." Mayla laughed, then looked at Kalen. "Why do you ask?"

"You're going to think I'm crazy, but I feel we need to go and look for that camp. I have the strangest feeling about this whole business."

"What do you mean?" Jamie said.

"Normally I can think of only two reasons for stealing people. One, kidnappers want ransom. Two, for slaves. Neither of these reasons makes any sense. I don't know about the ransom angle, but what would you use female slaves for on Arriesgado?"

Mayla put her hand to her mouth and coughed. "I can think of one other reason men kidnap women."

"That's another kind of slavery. That could explain why a woman would be offering to buy other women. Still, I don't believe that's the reason."

"What are you thinking?" Quintin said.

"I know it doesn't make sense, but somehow I feel Maria Atwood's hands all over this. Since the police are short-handed and they're going to take their time getting here, we should lend a hand and see if we can find this camp."

"Kalen, the end of the North Ford Highway is some pretty rough country." Jamie gripped Kalen's shoulder. "You should know better than anyone how bad it is."

"I know, Jamie. There are thousands of small canyons cutting into the eastern arm. We could search for cycles and never find them, but I have an idea. We'll need your police friend's cooperation, some additional information from Flin, if he'll cooperate, and Mayla as bait."

"You want to use my daughter as what?" Liana glared at Kalen.

City of Solana
Roving Patrol Barracks

Chapter 23
Everything but the Girl

Cringing under Liana's intense stare, Kalen hurried to explain. "We'll need a female to attract the kidnappers' attention. Mayla is capable of defending herself and Jamie and I will be there to protect her."

"I think I understand what he wants to do, Mother. If Maria is behind this, then we should go after her before she comes looking for us."

Lowering her voice to a whisper, Liana said, "I don't like this." "I don't like it either, but Mayla's right." Quintin pulled his wife closer. "Jamie and Kalen have stumbled onto something important. Let them go after her."

Kalen rubbed the back of his neck. "Quintin, we'll need you to take Jamie's flyer and leave the Lexicon."

"Of course. Jamie, when we get home, I'll tell Catherine you were delayed in town. No use her worrying all night."

"No, I'll call her myself. I'll tell her what happened and what we're up to." He looked at Kalen. "By the way, just what are we up to?"

"Let's head over to the RP barracks, and I'll explain on the way."

The evening turned dark and cool. A soft, moist breeze stirred the air when Kalen, Mayla, and Jamie walked into the Solana RP barracks. Jamie approached the desk officer.

"Can I help you?" the sergeant said. "We'd like to see Officer Eli Marcos."

The desk officer tapped his comm. "Yes, Sergeant?"

"There are some people here to see you."

"Who is it?"

"Tell him Jamie Santiago," Jamie whispered. The sergeant repeated the name.

"Send them back, Sergeant."

The officer pointed. "Straight back. At the end of the hallway take a right, then straight ahead."

"Thank you." Jamie led the way deeper into the building and the trio approached Eli's office.

Kalen glanced around, a strange urgency to flee tugged at him.

Eli looked up from his desk. "Jamie, I didn't think I'd be seeing you again. To what do I owe the honor of this visit?"

"I'll tell you in a minute. First, how did you do with Miss Davenport?"

Lowering his eyes, a tight, sheepish smile spread across his face. "So, you asked her out? Did she say yes?"

"She did, but never mind that, why are the three of you here?"

"We've come to ask a favor."

"What can I do for you?" Eli leaned forward and rested his arms on the grey metal desk.

"We'd like to talk to Flin," said Jamie.

"I thought you wanted to stay out of this."

"We've changed our minds. Could you clear it so we can talk to him?"

"Jamie, you know I can't do that." Eli rearranged some papers on his desk. "I've already let you stretch the rules. I could be accused of interrogating him without legal representation. Anything we get from him would be inadmissible, and they might use it to try and get him off."

"Eli, those two culls came close to making two young women disappear today. I don't know what's going on, but word about missing women is circulating around Solana. If Flin can give us any information, maybe we can help find them."

"Why would you be interested?"

Kalen stepped next to Jamie. "You have to admit, Officer Marcos, something strange is going on. If we could talk to Flin, we might be able to find who is behind this."

Eli sat up, his dark eyes narrowed. "If you have any information concerning these disappearances, I need it."

"We don't have any real information, Officer." Mayla stepped forward. "Three months ago Kalen and my niece, Zavier Santiago's daughter, were attacked and four men tried to grab her."

"And who are you?"

"Eli, this is Kalen's fiancée, Mayla Santiago."

A curious look spread across Eli's face. "Is she related to you?"

"She's my sister. Before you say anything, it's a long story and I'll share it with you, but not today."

"Pleased to meet you...Jamie's sister." Eli stood and extended his hand. While they shook, Eli asked, "Jamie, why haven't I heard about this attack before now?"

"We didn't report the incident because my father, under advice from a friend, decided to keep it quiet. Look, Eli, Kalen has a hunch and we would like the chance to follow it."

"Kalen told me that one of the men you captured is not much more than a boy." Mayla leaned on Eli's desk. "If we get him to talk, you could tell the prosecutor he cooperated, and then you could see if you can help him."

"I doubt you'll get anywhere with him, but you can try." Eli grabbed his key card from the desk drawer. Kalen, Mayla, and Jamie followed him back into the cell area.

Again, Kalen's stomach went queasy on him.

"You've got company, kid." Eli unlocked the cell door and stepped back.

Kalen and Mayla entered, but Jamie held back. "I should stay out here. I'm not sure I won't hit that filthy little marlet."

Flin moved to the furthest corner, a frightened look on his face. "We're not going to hurt you." Mayla sat down on the bunk. "We just want you to tell us what you know about the kidnapping."

Flin flinched and stared at his feet. "Why?"

"Because if you cooperate, we might be able to help you."

"I don't know, Miss. Michael said ta keep me mouth shut."

"Thata be right." Michael yelled from his cell across the aisle. "We got rights and we ain't sayin' nuthin' without a bar rep present. And I ain't seen one yet."

Mayla ignored Michael's outburst. "There are parents out there who have lost children. Think how you might help them."

"Can you help me stay out of da chamber?"

"Sorry, I can't promise anything, but Officer Marcos will try."

"It don't make no difference." Flin shrugged. "Look, all I know, we was supposed ta go ta the town of Avila."

"Flin, shut yer snivelin' trap!" Michael jumped up from his rack. "You stop yer yammerin' this minute!"

The youth pushed himself against the cell bars and cowered. Looking at Eli, Jamie tilted his head toward Michael.

The officer nodded, opened Michael's cell, and with a none-too-gentle tug, yanked the smelly man out. "After I've hosed you down, there are some nice accommodations on the lower level. I think you'll be safer downstairs, just in case word gets out about you two." As Eli pulled Michael through the rear door, the greasy-haired man yelled, "Keep your whinin' trap—" The door to the room slammed closed and guillotined Michael's words.

With Michael gone, Flin's backbone stiffened. "I told Michael 'twas a bad idea. I wanted ta go work with the loggers guild up north."

"You tried to get work with Niles Montoya's guild?" Jamie said.

"Yeah. I think he'd have hired me on, but he didn't want Michael around."

"That's understandable." Mayla's brother shook his head. "You should have cut him loose."

Flin shrugged. "I didn't feel right 'bout doin' that."

"I'm sorry you didn't get hired on." Jamie shook his head. "Niles is a good man."

"Won't change nothin' now."

"What can you tell us about the missing women?" Kalen said. "Near the southern edge of town, ya need ta be lookin' fer a roadhouse called the *Mesón De la Caída*." Flin leaned against the cell bars and folded his arms across his chest. "Ask fer a man named Skylar, he's the buyer. He wants the women ta be brought ta him in twos. Talk only ta Skylar."

"Why?"

"I don't know why, Miss." Flin shrugged again. "That's what we was told."

"You don't know anything else about these people?"

Flin shook his head. "Michael jest heard a rumor, that's all. He

162

wouldn't tell me much, jest said we'd be livin' easy if we could get in an' sell the two women we caught."

"Why?" Jamie stepped closer to the cell door. "Why get involved at all?"

"I already told ya." Flin looked at Jamie. "We was desperate and we thought we could be makin' a few easy wafers."

"That's not what I meant. Why did you get involved in kidnapping a child and terrifying her and her parents?"

"I guess I wasn't lookin' at it that way." Flin stared at the floor. "Me parents died when I was still a lad. Me uncle, that's me Ma's brother, took me in. He was supposed ta come in ta some land, but the farm wound up goin' ta auction. The new owners got rid of all the old employees and me and me uncle went our separate ways lookin' fer work. A few months back I ran in ta Michael. Since then, things haven't been too good, but he's kept me fed and I've 'ad a place ta sleep. Won't 'ave much ta worry about now, will I?"

"That's still no excuse." Jamie shook his head.

Flin didn't answer. He hung his head and dropped onto the far end of his bunk.

Mayla stood.

Kalen turned and she followed him out of Flin's cell.

The trio returned to Eli's office. He looked up from some paperwork. "Was he of any help?"

"I think he's told us all he knows." Kalen dropped into a chair across from the officer's desk.

"Isn't there anything you can do for him?" Mayla chewed her lower lip.

Kalen reached up and took hold of her hand.

"You caught them in the act of kidnapping those women." Eli shook his head. "The law doesn't allow for much leeway. I'll make sure the prosecutor knows he cooperated. That's about all I can do. What are your plans now?"

"Well, I was going to suggest we take their old cruiser, go to Avila, and see what we can uncover." Kalen ran the fingers of his free hand through his hair. "But, Flin said whoever is behind this wants the women brought to him in pairs. We have everything we need, everything but the girl."

"So, unless you've got someone willing to get trussed up and carted off to Avila," said Jamie, "I guess we'll head home."

"What if you had another woman to go along?" Eli slid forward in his chair. "Would you be willing to continue looking into this?"

"Why?" Jamie furrowed his brow. "What do you have in mind?" Tapping the comm unit on his desk, Eli spoke. "Officer Nolan, would you please come to my office?"

"Yes sir," a female voice answered.

In a few seconds a slim woman entered Eli's office. Officer Nolan stood about one hundred and eighty centimeters tall. She wore her chestnut hair pulled into the standard knot behind her head as required for female RP officers. She scanned the room then stopped in front of Eli's desk.

"Officer Nolan, this is Jamie, Kalen, and Mayla. This is Mandi Nolan." After exchanging handshakes, Eli said, "Officer Nolan, Jamie is an old friend. Would you be willing to work with these people on a plan they're putting together to investigate the recent rash of kidnappings?"

"What's involved, sir?"

"I'm not sure." Eli turned to Jamie. "Just what is involved?"

"This is Kalen's show." Jamie stepped back. "I'll let him explain."

Kalen slid forward. "It's simple, really. Jamie and I show up with you two tied up in the back of our vehicle. We offer to sell you to this Skylar and join their organization."

Officer Nolan's eyes showed doubt. "You're going to use us as bait?"

"Well, we can't very well stroll in there empty-handed. We need something to offer."

"If things go wrong, how do we defend ourselves?" "You'll be armed."

She asked Mayla. "You're okay with this?"

"I'm not sure it'll work, but I am willing to try. We've run into the people behind this before. They won't stop unless someone steps in and puts an end to this."

Officer Nolan looked at Eli. "Is there some reason you're letting civilians start their own investigation?"

"Call it a hunch. We have a couple of good suspects right here in our jail. I don't like the idea of being blown off because Lieutenant Castellano claims he is too busy. This is the best break in the case I've heard about and these two men are the reason we have it."

"I'm not convinced this plan will work, but I'll go along if there's a chance we can find out who's behind these kidnappings. I do have a couple of suggestions."

By the time they finished preparing, Jamie said, "It's too late to do anything tonight. Let's get some sleep and get a fresh start in the morning."

"Mayla, why don't you stay with me?" Officer Nolan offered. "Are you sure it's not an imposition?"

"Not at all. We'll let these two spend the night sleeping here. At least we can get a good night's sleep. And you can fill me in on how it is you're willing to go along with this."

"When do you get off duty?"

Officer Nolan's gaze shifted to Eli. "I believe I'm off duty as of now."

"I do believe you are, Officer." Eli grinned.

"All right." Mayla pulled Kalen to his feet. "Just give us a minute." Kalen and Mayla stepped away to say good night, then the women left.

Jamie called Catherine. After his long conversation with his wife, Kalen heard him coming up behind him. Kalen continued working on a computer station, checking on the Central Council's activity.

"Kalen, what are you searching for?" Jamie looked over his shoulder.

"You said eight women have vanished. I've been searching for some mention of women or girls disappearing. I can only find a report from up in Escarza of a young woman, an Asilyn Ryan. This report states two women shot her with a tranq-gun. Miss Ryan's friends stopped their attempt to kidnap her. "

"I remember that. She's Dani's friend. Dani was there the night those women shot the young lady with a tranq-dart."

"How come I didn't hear about this?"

"It happened while you and Mayla were hiding out somewhere. By the time you arrived home, we'd forgotten all about it."

"Jamie, a kidnapping is news, yet there is nothing online about that or any other incident. I only found this reference in the girl's mother's complaint on one of the info feeds, and it's buried. What is going on with law enforcement?"

"We may find out when we go to Avila."

"I've been thinking about our trip. We're going to look out of place if we show up dressed like this. We'll just put this Skylar on alert, or scare him off altogether."

"What would you suggest?"

"I have an idea. Let's go into town again."

Later, Kalen and Jamie settled into an unlocked cell at the barracks for the night. Kalen tried the door several times to make sure it would open.

Jamie put his hand on Kalen's shoulder. "Don't worry, brother, it'll open in the morning."

"It will if your friend doesn't dig into my past." Kalen dropped onto his bunk and stared at the door.

Chapter 24
Contact

Kalen pulled Jamie out of sight when he spotted Mayla and Officer Nolan returning to the barracks in the early morning gloom and rain.

Mayla shook her coat out and moved through the front desk.

Kalen stepped out from behind the partition wall. "What do you think?"

Mayla did a double take and stared at him. "Where did you find that getup?"

"Jamie and I did a little shopping last night. You like?"

Mayla put her hand to her mouth and giggled. "In those outfits you two look like a couple of ancient road agents."

"Good, we're supposed to." Dressed in a black shirt and pants, Kalen also wore mid-calf boots, with his pant legs tucked inside. Over his outfit he wore a muted green collarless leather duster that hung down below his boot tops. On his head he wore a brimmed green hat. A small leather lanyard circled the front of the hat, passed through the brim, the two ends tied together, hung behind his head. The hat sat cocked on his head at a jaunty angle.

Jamie laughed. "We couldn't stroll into this looking like a couple of constructioneers." Dressed similar to Kalen, Jamie wore a dark brown outfit. They carried sidearms and both had their staffs.

Kalen looked Mayla over and smiled. "I definitely like Milady's outfit."

"Why, thank you, kind sir." Mayla pirouetted, showing off her black, one-piece jumpsuit. "It's what all the stylish ladies are wearing to a kidnapping these days." Mandi arrived dressed in a light gray outfit of the same style. Both women had changed into stylish, serviceable boots.

Mayla completed her exhibition. "Are we taking the Lexicon?"

"No. The Lexicon is a bit ostentatious for a couple of men on the run. We considered using Michael's cruiser, but it stinks and I don't think it will make the trip." Kalen led Mayla and Mandi outside. "While we were shopping, Jamie took me to a friend of his. I purchased this older cruiser from him. It doesn't look like much, but the propulsion system's in top shape."

"What about the Lexicon?" Mayla looked around. "Its speed and weapons might come in handy."

"They will, and it'll be nearby. Eli and Al took the day off, and I've given Eli and Al instructions on flying it. They've already flown ahead, ready to render assistance if we need help. If someone does spot the Lexicon and checks it out, being a civilian registered vehicle, it won't raise suspicions." Kalen opened the door to the cruiser. "Let's get moving, at this rate we won't make Avila until past midday."

The sun floated overhead in the midday sky when Kalen slowed the cruiser and stared at the windswept, towering grey-black hills of the Barreras' eastern arm. "This place always looks depressing." The contrast between land and sky made a stark backdrop for the town of Avila, squatting on the upper portion of the Eastern Barreras' second eco-tier.

"Everything here is so stark and brown here."

"That's because the natural vegetation at this elevation consists of small, gnarled trees, like that Pillion over there."

"Where do the people draw their water from?" Mandi leaned forward and peered over Jamie's shoulder.

"Waterways in this area tend to disappear underground." Kalen continued toward the town. "The last time I traveled here, the town survived by drawing all their water from wells drilled as deep as four hundred meters."

Jamie keyed their portable RP comm unit. "Eli, we're approaching Avila, where are you?"

"Eli here. Hovering over the town." Eli paused, but the comm remained open. "This is a really sweet rig, Mister MacKenna."

Kalen grinned, imagining the two officers experimenting with his flyer. "You can thank Jamie's family for that."

"Really? Okay. Anyway, while you make contact, Al and I are going to scout ahead. We might be able to spot some activity from the air."

"Sounds good, just don't wander too far in case we need you." Jamie shut the comm off, and tucked the powerful police unit under his seat.

Ten kilometers outside the town limits, Kalen stopped the cruiser. Jamie exited the vehicle. With the binocs they brought along, he scoured the surrounding landscape for anyone watching. "All right, ladies, it looks clear. This is where you get in the back."

The women climbed out into the raw midday air.

"This is the Outlands. How can it be so cold this close to the Wastelands?" Mandi shivered and pulled her coat tight around herself.

Kalen turned and scanned the Barreras' peaks. "This close to the Eastern Arm, there's a continual stream of cold air pouring down from those ice-covered peaks. Avila is never really warm except at mid-year, then look out."

The sun slipped from behind a thick layer of clouds floating out from the Eastern Arm. It did little to warm the day. Mayla and Mandi shivered while Kalen bound their wrists and ankles. Jamie pulled hoods over their heads, then laid the women in the rear compartment, and covered them with the blankets they brought along. Hidden in their clothing, the women each had a knife to cut the slack bonds and a button pulsar for protection.

Kalen guided the cruiser into the western edge of Avila, slowed to a moderate pace, and glided along the main road. They passed some occupied buildings in need of repair. Other homes and shops stood abandoned, their windows and doors either boarded up or broken out. A few cruisers navigated the streets, but they passed a number of disabled or wrecked vehicles, many stripped to worthless hulks. Along the walkway, massive withered tree trunks looked like dead sentinels guarding the now dirty and untidy streets. The condition of the town shocked Kalen. "Jamie, what's happened to this town?

I traveled here with my father. Back then the townspeople cared for their homes. Most had lawns with trees. I remember the town council planted those Satinwood trees to shade pedestrians from the day's heat. Avila wasn't the best town in the Outlands, but now it's a slum."

Jamie watched an old man limping along the walkway. "Just another sign the Central Council isn't upholding its oath of office. Avila once supplied a big portion of Arriesgado's copper needs."

Kalen moved to the middle of the road to avoid a dead animal. "I remember. There is a good-sized copper mining operation nearby. It's the reason the town existed."

"Was, Kalen, was. When the ore played out, the owners wanted to move the mining operation. The Central Council waited until they reclaimed the land, then yanked their temporary permit granted to open a new area. Some dissatisfied jerk pointed out a minor infraction of the law from years ago. The CC treated it like a recent, major violation. The council members said mining destroyed the environment. They voted and ruled the mine unnecessary. The company went belly-up, the town dried up, and most of the residents left. Those few that remain here scratch out an existence somehow." Jamie pointed. "Take the next right."

Kalen turned at the corner and drove south along another main road. "They can't do that! By law, successful operations are granted new permits when they've complied with the environmental and restoration laws."

"Ha! The Central Council doesn't listen to reason anymore."

They traveled southward and passed a few pedestrians who eyed the cruiser with suspicion. The buildings thinned toward the town's limits. Jamie scanned both sides of the road and pointed. "There's the inn."

Kalen pulled up to the ramshackle building, well beyond any other homes or places of business. The three-story structure, set back from the road, squatted on a large plot of land surrounded by withered vegetation and wilted and dying trees.

Kalen parked close to the inn, but away from the other vehicles in the lot. "Okay, we're getting out."

"Leave the heater on low," Mayla said, "or we will freeze before you get back."

Kalen shut the cruiser down then set the temperature control on auto. "Just remember," Kalen whispered, "If we pull Mayla out first, act aggressive, otherwise act submissive. Flin wasn't sure what they are looking for."

"Kalen, we know what to do, just hurry."

Kalen and Jamie grabbed their staffs, set the locks and strolled toward the building. A deep covered porch surrounded the inn on three sides. The steep pitched roof needed repair. In a number of places the stone facade had fallen away and revealed the green color of the old plasti-panels beneath. The sun-faded brown paint had peeled and exposed the wood trim to the elements. Broken sheets of the cheap material covered two windows in the south wall and the other windows looked as if they had not been washed in years. At one time this building probably looked typical of the type of work Quintin referred to as 'prefab boxes'.

Sprawled on chairs out of the wind, two men dozed. Kalen and Jamie mounted the porch and walked past the two drunks. To their left, two other men, coats pulled tightly around their bodies, leaned against the railing, and kept a wary eye on them.

Rounding the corner to the west side, a sudden knot cramped Kalen's stomach. "Jamie, I'm getting a bad feeling. Let's make this fast. If we don't get any attention in half an hour, we head home."

"Agreed. How's your Outlands?" Jamie whispered.

"Poor at best." Kalen shrugged.

"I'd better do the talking."

"Whatever you want. Don't forget our names are Ajan and Daric." Kalen said. "And try to speak different. You're on the run, not a prosperous Andalusian."

"If you do have to speak, you gonna talk like Connor?"

"I do it the best." Kalen grinned and pulled the door open.

They entered the inn's foyer. The smell of stale food and unwashed bodies permeated the air. They strolled past the desk and into the attached pub, made their way to a table, took a seat, and waited. The floor looked as if it had been cleaned about the same time as the windows. After a few minutes an older, weather beaten man wandered over.

"Can I git you two gents someting ta drink?" the man said in accented Colonial.

"Is this yer place?" Jamie looked around.

The man nodded.

"We ain't eaten in a while," Jamie said. "How's yer food?"

The man raised his eyebrows. "Depends. How hungry are ya?"

"We're hungry."

"What can I git you?"

"Bring us two prime cuts, fried tubers and white maize on the cob."

The innkeeper stared at Jamie.

Kalen could read the man's suspicions behind his light gray eyes, as he scanned them. *Looks like these disguises might just work.*

The innkeeper then ran his fingers through his thinning gray-streaked brown hair. "Have ya got the credits ta pay for a meal like that?"

"We've enough." Jamie laid several gold wafers on the table, then lowered his voice and continued in a conspiratorial tone. "We'll have plenty more of these, once we unload our cargo."

The owner shrugged and reached for the wafers.

Kalen slammed his hand over the gold. "Here now, you'll be bringin' our food first."

The man snatched his empty hand back and grinned. "Be a couple of minutes." The innkeeper headed toward the back, but stopped at a table off in the deep shadows. He spoke to a couple of men seated there.

Kalen nudged Jamie with his leg. "I think we've already caught someone's attention."

Without raising his head, Jamie looked over to where Kalen indicated and saw the owner and two men huddled close together. After a brief conversation, the owner moved away and a short stocky man got up and headed outside.

Chapter 25
Betrayal

Jamie placed his hand on Kalen's arm. "Easy, Kalen. The cruiser's locked. Let him satisfy his curiosity."

Kalen kept an eye on the entrance. A quarter hour later the man returned. He went straight over to his companion and the two men held another whispered conversation.

The innkeeper returned with two plates and set them on the table.

Kalen took one look at the unappealing meals and his stomach rebelled. The meat looked overcooked, the tubers lay in a puddle of grease and the maize amounted to mush on the cob. Kalen stared at the plate and whispered, "Geeze, your little Sonia could fix a better meal!" He took a bite and grimaced. "In fact, she has."

Jamie choked, trying to keep a straight face.

He and Kalen pushed their food around the plate, until footsteps approached. Looking up, Kalen saw the second man coming toward them. The dim light made it difficult for Kalen to see him in any detail. When he stopped at their table, Kalen didn't like the look of him. The barrel-chested man stood a little less than two meters tall. He had narrow hips, and long dark, greasy hair clinging to his neck. It spilled down over his forehead, covering his eyes. Kalen thought he didn't look much older than Jamie, but the man's weathered face told of too much time in the sun. His eyes were dark and brooding like storm clouds over the Barreras, his mouth tightly drawn, reminded him of a skinflint's purse. When he spoke, his voice came out in a raspy whisper. *"Buenas tardes, señors."*

Jamie stared at the man. "*Buenas tardes.*"

He said something else in Outlands Kalen didn't understand. Jamie answered. "*Mi amigo no habla de Outlands. El habla Colonial.*"

"Sorry." The man shrugged. "Where are ya two from?" He continued without a pause, his Outlands' accent pronounced.

"My friend here is from the Seventh Mesa," Jamie said, referring to Mesa Tyree in Outland terms. "I once lived on Fourth Mesa."

"What brings ya to Avila?"

"We've heard a man could earn decent wafers fer the right cargo."

"Dat yer silver cruiser parked outside? The one close ta da building?"

Jamie narrowed his eyes and stared at the man. He took a drink, and then nodded.

The man scratched his chin. "I seem ta recall a similar cruiser belongin' ta a different pair of men, I saw hanging around here."

"That one 'twas in a wee bit more disreputable shape,"Kalen said. "As 'twere the two unfortunate souls who owned it."

"What do you mean, unfortunate? Who are ya talking about?"

Kalen scratched his head. "Now what are the names of those two?"

Jamie swallowed his food. "Would ya be speaking of Michael and Flin?"

"Older man, younger kid," the man said.

"That's them. That's names they gave when the Solana RPs picked them up." Jamie grinned and took another bite of his prime cut.

"They got themselves in a wee bit of trouble with the law, they did." Kalen chuckled.

"And how did ya wind up here instead of dem?"

Jamie chewed the meat, making the stranger wait. He swallowed and took another drink. "We was talkin' to them a few days before the RPs pinched 'em. They told us they'd come across a sweet setup. When the Solana authorities grabbed them, they needed funds so they could hire a bar rep. We paid 'em a bit fer this location, grabbed some cargo and headed out here."

"What did dey get hauled in fer?"

"Don't know, don't care," Kalen said. "We were needin' a new location. Seein's how this place fit the bill, and the price bein' right, we paid 'em, no questions asked."

"Mato," the greasy-haired man said, hiking his thumb over his shoulder to indicate the owner of the roadhouse, "tells me yer cargo's fer sale?"

Jamie looked the man over, shoveled in a mouthful of food and chewed. After he swallowed, he said, "Might be." He took a drink. "Who's asking?"

"Someone who's interested."

"That someone got a name?" said Jamie. "Skylar."

"You him?"

The man shook his head. "No, but I'm authorized ta speak fer him, and I can make ya a fair offer."

Jamie filled his mouth again and chewed while he eyed the dark-haired man. He set his fork down, wiped his mouth, and dropped his napkin. His fingers danced while trying to catch the gray cloth.

Kalen understood and knew something wasn't right.

Jamie picked the napkin off the table, finished chewing, and swallowed. He stared at the greasy-haired man. "Well."

He narrowed his eyes and remained quiet. "We're waiting. Let's hear what yer offering!"

"I ain't seen da merchandise yet," the man said, stroking his chin. "What are dey like?"

"What's Skylar looking fer?"

"It ain't what Skylar's looking fer," the man said. "It's what his customer wants, young, docile, and easy ta manipulate. Can't have too much fire."

"Well then, we got just what he wants. These two didn't struggle at all when we invited them along fer the ride."

"I'll still need ta see 'em."

"Suit yourself. You got a name?" "I'm Marcus."

"What about yer friend over there?" Kalen nodded toward the man who had checked the cruiser.

"His name is Sully. You two got names?" "I'm Ajan, and his name's Daric. "

"Good enough. Now how 'bout we take a look at yer cargo?"

Jamie slipped a wafer onto the table. He and Kalen stood, grabbed their staffs and the four men exited the inn. The men who occupied the porch earlier were gone. Walking to the cruiser, Jamie opened the rear hatch.

Kalen stepped next to him, and reached for Mandi. Jamie signed. <I don't like the feel of this>

Kalen flashed. <Me either>

They pulled Mandi into a standing position, then Mayla, helping them to balance on their bound feet.

Kalen pulled the hood off Mandi's head.

Marcus whistled. "Nice."

"Please, what's going on?" Mandi whined on cue. "Please, let me go."

"Keep yer mouth shut." Kalen had a role to play, but he hated speaking to any woman in such harsh tones.

Marcus moved around her, examining Mandi like one would inspect cattle.

Kalen could feel Mandi's muscles tense under her clothes, and his own dislike of this man grew. He checked Sully and noticed his eyes darting from Kalen to Jamie, then to their surroundings.

Marcus looked Mayla over.

Jamie whispered, "Keep yer mouth shut!" Then he yanked her hood off.

Mayla blinked in the light, looked at the four men, cringed, and lowered her eyes, while the dark-haired man examined her. He reached for Mayla and pulled her face up to get a better look.

"Nice eyes."

"So, do we got a deal? You can tell this Skylar my friend and I can get more like this, but we need a place ta hide out. Things are gettin' a bit warm in the cities. Otherwise, we'll head ta the Muro Verdes. I hear we can get a better deal fer these goods up there."

"Like I said earlier, I don't know either of ya. I'll have to check ya out before I talk ta Skylar."

"And just how do ya intend doin' that?" Kalen forced a laugh. "Call the authorities in Solana or Andalusia and go about askin' fer our references?"

Marcus rankled at Kalen's rebuff. "I have my sources."

"Come on, Daric." Jamie looked at Kalen. "We're wastin' our time here." He slipped Mayla's hood over her head.

Kalen did the same to Mandi. "I should have listened ta you and gone north. We're not going ta make any profit here."

They laid the women inside and turned to head for the front of the cruiser. Kalen made a quick gesture with his fingers, hoping Jamie would understand his warning.

"I don't think you'll be goin' anywhere," Marcus said.

Jamie spun.

The greasy-haired man reached around behind him. Before Marcus' hand made it all the way, Jamie jabbed him in the chest with his staff.

Kalen rushed Sully and caught the startled man on the side of his head with his staff. The resounding crack reverberated up the shaft.

Sully's eyes crossed and he dropped to the ground.

Jamie brought his staff down on Marcus' shoulder.

Kalen scooped up Sully's weapon and turned to see Marcus down, and Jamie's staff in the hollow of his throat.

Loud applause made Kalen jump.

"Very good, gentlemen, very good," a male voice from behind them said.

Kalen turned and stared at a tall, whip-thin man, standing on the roadhouse porch.

As they backed away from Marcus and Sully, Kalen said, "And who might ya be?"

The man stepped off the porch. "I am Skylar Covington." His nasally voice came with a strange accent. "You two have just saved me from making a very grave error. I've been watching these two men for weeks trying to figure out if they would fit into my organization."

Jamie pointed his staff at Marcus. "He told us they work fer ya."

Skylar laughed, the sound raked Kalen's nerves like nails across slate. "Not these two culls, but they might have been, had they not just revealed their true colors." He signaled with a wave of his hand and four men emerged from the side of the building and came toward them.

Kalen and Jamie backed away and stood ready for a fight. "Easy, gentlemen." Skylar held up his hands, both his palms toward Jamie and Kalen. "Take it easy."

The four men stopped short of Kalen and Jamie, took hold of Marcus and Sully and dragged the stunned men to their feet.

Kalen watched Marcus and Sully being led away, his stomach in knots.

"I see you two can handle yourselves," Skylar said. "I can use a couple of good men. I heard you say you need a place the law cannot find. Since I have already seen your cargo, there is no need to examine the goods again. Please, follow me and my men if you wish to avoid any legal entanglements."

"Why should we trust you?" Jamie held his staff at the ready. "Are you about to get a better offer?" Skylar looked around. "Of course not. You could stay here and explain your two guests to the authorities when they show up here."

"And why would they be doin' that?" said Kalen, an uneasy feeling growing.

"Because the authorities are watching this place. The Roving Patrol checks in here quite regularly. I don't believe the owner is entirely trustworthy." Skylar pointed to Marcus and Sully. "Why, it wouldn't surprise me if those two aren't police officers themselves."

Kalen flashed Jamie a quick glance and saw Jamie's jaw tighten.

"Those two are the law?" Jamie covered his shock with a scowl. "What are you going ta do with them?"

"My men will take care of them. Now this place is getting a little too well-known. I think it would be wise for all of us to leave." Skylar turned and walked to a fifth man standing a short distance off to his left. After a brief whispered conversation, the man nodded and headed for the cruiser.

"What's he doin'?" Jamie said.

"If you're coming with us, then I must insist that Asa ride with you for security reasons."

They'd stumbled into something bigger than they anticipated, and now two undercover RP officers' lives stood in jeopardy. Kalen's mind raced. *We've got to do something.*

Jamie looked to Kalen, his fingers moving in small rapid movements.

Kalen caught Jamie's idea and nodded. The two men moved toward the rear of the cruiser, while Skylar's man climbed into the vehicle.

"What are you doing?" Skylar's voice edged toward indignant. Sauntering to the cruiser's rear, Jamie lifted the rear hatch. "Just checkin' our cargo. I wouldn't do fer them to be getting' hurt or bruised, now would it?"

"No. We do want them in good condition, don't we?" Skylar's comment sent a chill up Kalen's back. He waited while Jamie readjusted the women's hoods and pretended to check their bindings. When Skylar walked to the open cruiser door and spoke with his man, Kalen reached over and pulled Mayla's hood.

Jamie's fingers circled in a blur of rapid moves.

Mayla nodded and Kalen pulled her hood down and closed the hatch.

Climbing into the cruiser, Kalen flashed a friendly smile at Skylar's man, who had already installed himself in the rear seat.

In response, Asa scowled, pulled out his pistol, and placed it across his lap.

While Jamie settled into the front seat, Kalen saw another cruiser heading south with Marcus and Sully in it. His mind in a panic, he pulled away from the inn.

"Look, Asa, there's no need fer that pistol," Jamie said. "Mister Covington likes his people ready fer trouble. Now, go north 'til we reach da main road, then head east." Jamie turned and looked at Asa. "How far is it?"

"You've got a few hours of drivin'. It's easier if I tell ya what ta do."

Kalen jerked the cruiser to a stop. "We'll not be goin' anywhere unless we know where you're takin' us."

Asa shrugged, making him look like a giant Sea Mydas tucking its head into its shell. "Have it yer way. Follow da old highway road east fer three hundred kilometers until ya reach da foothills. You'll come ta a fork in da road, turn right and continue another fifty kilometers south. We come ta da mouth of a canyon. We go up the canyon fer eight kilometers, 'til we reach da end."

"After that?" Jamie said.

"You'll find out," Asa held up his hand. "'Til we get there, that's all I can say."

A cold lump settled in the pit of Kalen's stomach. "Yer expectin' me and me partner, ta go into a blind canyon with only yer say so?"

"Dats how it is. It's not dat I don't trust you two, it's jest da way things are handled."

Richard R Draude

Moving through streets, Kalen made a left turn, and headed east on the main road. As they left the town behind, a cold unnerving silence settled over the cruiser.

They moved into the barren land beyond the city limits. After a few minutes Jamie turned to face Asa, a feigned, startled look on his face. "Watch out!"

Eastern Outlands
East Of Avila

Chapter 26
Secret's Out

Kalen jerked the cruiser to a stop. Mayla clamped her arms around Asa's thick neck

Kalen and Jamie made a show of fighting her off, but their actions prevented him from breaking her choke hold.

Asa's eyes bulged. He struggled for another moment, then passed out.

Mayla let him go. "Kalen, Jamie, what's going on?"

Kalen held up his hand.

Jamie pulled the police comm from under the seat and turned it on. "Eli, this is Jamie, come in!"

"This is Eli. Where have you two–?"

"No time to explain. Two police officers' lives are in danger!" He gave Eli a quick explanation of what they had run into. "There's a light brown cruiser heading south away from Avila, stop it al all costs. Also, Skylar has one of his men riding with us, so we won't be able to contact you after this, but as far as we know, here's where we'll be." He gave Eli the directions. "We'll be somewhere up where the canyon ends."

"What's up there?"

"We don't know yet. Right now you need to get after that cruiser. We'll contact you when we can."

"We're on our way. Al out."

Jamie cut the comm. "Quick, let's get Mayla and Mandi tied up, before this slug comes to and starts more trouble."

Kalen pulled the manual release, and the back hatch opened. The men circled to the vehicle's rear.

Mayla and Mandi climbed out of the cruiser.

"Kalen, are you sure you want to go through with this?" Mandi looked around.

"I don't like the feel of this, but there may be young women out there wondering if anyone cares enough to search for them. If it looks like it's going bad, one of us will say something about the weather. Get yourselves loose and take Asa out again. For now let's see what happens."

"Jamie, what are you going to tell him?"

"The truth, Sis. You got loose. After he passed out, we subdued you."

"Kalen, do you think he'll believe you?" Mandi retied her feet.

"I don't know." Kalen picked up the poly cord. "He's already suspicious. It's either that or dump him here, then turn and run. It's up to you two."

"For the missing women's sakes, let's see this through." Mandi slid back into the cruiser and raised her arms.

"I agree with Mandi," Mayla said.

"Okay, then let's get the stage set." Kalen retied Mandi's hands. Jamie retied Mayla's hands and feet, then laid her next to Mandi.

When they finished, Jamie closed the rear hatch, circled the cruiser, and hid the police comm. He took a deep breath, then pulled Asa into a sitting position. "Hey! Hey, are you all right? Come on, wake up!"

Asa opened his eyes and bolted upright. "What happened?"

"One of the women got loose and tried ta kill you."

"Which one was it?" Asa turned and glared at the bound women, his fist clenched.

"Why?" Kalen dropped into the driver's seat, turned, grabbed Asa's shoulder and pulled him into his seat.

"Because no woman does that ta me!" He shrugged off Kalen's hand, pushed Jamie aside, and tried to get out of the cruiser.

Kalen reattached himself to Asa's shoulder and yanked him back into his seat again.

Asa glared at Kalen, shoved his hand away, and tried to get out.

Kalen forced him into the seat a third time. "I can't be lettin' you do anythin' ta 'em. Ya might be hurtin' her and ruinin' her value. Leave 'em be 'til after we get our business done. You owe us that much, after all, we jest saved yer life. Now you'll be settlin' down 'til we've made our sale. After that you can be talkin' ta Skylar. Maybe he'll let you get a wee bit o' revenge."

Asa rubbed his neck. "Are dey secure this time?"

"We retied the one that got loose and checked the other one's bindin's." Jamie patted his chest. "They won't be causin' us any more trouble."

Asa glanced behind him one more time, adjusted his weapon in his lap, then settled back into the seat.

Kalen restarted the cruiser and continued east.

Jamie kept a close eye on their passenger to make sure he didn't try anything.

Kalen took a deep breath and kept his face neutral. He could feel Asa's stare burning into the back of his head. He turned his thoughts to Eli and Al. With his left hand he signed. <Hope Eli saved the two officers>

<I'm sure Eli made it in time> Jamie replied, his hands in his lap.

The old highway veered southeast and the nav-guide dropped out.

Kalen tried to re-engage it.

After his fourth attempt, Asa laughed. "Give it up. Yer CC ain't made road repairs this fer south in years."

In manual mode the old cruiser became awkward and hard to steer.

Out ahead, Kalen could see a fork in the road. "How much farther?"

"Just keep drivin', we're gettin' close."

Kalen veered to the right, taking them deeper into the Barreras' first Eco-tier. After an hour, the road entered the rocky foothills. The country turned barren with little vegetation to break up the monotony of the rugged landscape.

Craning his neck, Kalen looked up and saw thunderheads building above the mountain peaks. His memory of this corner of the Barreras was of a dry, parched land that received little or no rain. When infrequent rains managed to hit the ground, it did so in torrents, sweeping through the desiccated landscape in flash floods.

Still over four hundred kilometers away, the vast Southern Wastelands simmered in the distance. To their left, the lifeless gray- black hills making up this part of the eastern arm rose in sharp contrast to the flat lands behind them. The road grew rough, full of holes and waterworn ruts. The anti-grav engine struggled to maintain an even, smooth ride. After another hour, the track faded and the ride grew rougher.

The sun slipped westward, chased by heavy, wide-spaced clouds. An oppressive air hung over the land, and Kalen's nerves tightened. The further into this desolation they drove, the calmer Asa got. Kalen looked at Jamie.

Jamie flashed a signal. <Something is not right>

Kalen signed. <You feel it too>

<Need diversion>

Kalen made a deliberate hard swerve, distracting Asa.

"Can't ya drive any better?"

Jamie slipped his hand to his side.

Asa straightened in his seat and tugged at his harness.

"Sorry." Kalen waited a second then swerved again.

Jamie withdrew his weapon.

Kalen clenched his left hand into a fist. He was ready to stop and toss Skylar's man out, when Asa said, "This is the canyon, turn here."

The dull, dark gray, weather-eroded rock of the narrow canyon walls rose skyward at a steep angle. Devoid of plant life, the rock-strewn canyon floor looked impassable. Kalen pushed the old cruiser's power to maximum.

The anti-grav engine whined in protest, inching the cruiser upwards.

Kalen dodged and maneuvered around the larger rocks, scraping the cruiser's bottom on some. Twenty minutes of nerve-jarring bumps moved them deep into the oppressive canyon and brought them to a place where the bottom cleared. A sand and gravel dry-water course lay before them.

Kalen leaned forward and studied the overcast sky. "Bad place ta get caught in a rain storm."

"It rarely rains here," said Asa. "But when it does, ya don't want to be down here, now keep goin'."

Kalen sped up, moving deeper into the bleak landscape. As he maneuvered their way east, his gut knotted, and the look on Jamie's face showed his anxiety. Daylight dimmed and Kalen craned his neck, he stared at the patch of sky he could see above the canyon walls. Thick clouds gathered overhead, blotting out the blue.

Jamie followed Kalen's gaze, frowning. "I thought ya said it doesn't rain up here. I don't like the looks of those storm clouds."

"I said, it don't rain often, but it does rain."

They came around a sharp turn. Up ahead the canyon came to a dead end. Kalen brought the cruiser to a halt. "What are we supposed to do now?"

"Well, Mister MacKenna." Asa raised his pistol. "This is da end of the line fer ya. Yer gonna die."

Eastern Arm Barrera Mountains
Unnamed Canyon

Chapter 27
Flight and Fight

Kalen and Jamie turned, grinning at Asa. The look on his face changed from puzzlement to shock when Mandi pressed her button pulsar against his temple. "Drop it!"

Asa let out a string of expletives.

Jamie disarmed Asa and handed the weapon to Mandi. "Watch your mouth, there are ladies present."

"I shoulda checked yer bindings!"

"You'd have died trying," Mandi whispered.

Kalen grabbed Asa. "How did you know who I am?" The man refused to answer.

"Skylar Covington. Now that's a very unconventional name for an Arrisian." Mayla leaned forward. "Sounds more like someone's surname from Kaladon's Crossing or the Selwyn colony. I wonder if this could have anything to do with him working for Maria Atwood?"

Asa scowled.

"Gimmish!" Jamie scanned the canyon walls. "Kalen, get us out of here!"

"Yeah, like five minutes ago." Kalen spun the cruiser about.

Three energy bolts exploded on the canyon wall. Pieces of the canyon walls pelted the cruiser.

Asa laughed when Kalen tried to maneuver back down the narrow canyon. "Ya can't git away, MacKenna. Ya were a dead man da moment Mister Covington recognized ya, so drop the phony accents."

Kalen moved the power level up. He maneuvered close to the canyon wall and headed west.

"There's an opening in the north wall." Mayla pointed. "We can take cover in there!"

Kalen headed for the gap. Thirty meters from the opening a large explosion rocked the cruiser, the white-hot burst blinded him. He lost control of the vehicle, careened into the canyon wall and came to a bone-jarring halt. Kalen rubbed his eyes with his fingers. "I can't see!"

Two more pulsar bursts hit the ground behind them and rocked the vehicle.

"Your friends don't seem to care if they kill you!" Jamie glared at Asa.

"That's why they ain't hit the cruiser. Go 'head, MacKenna, try runnin'."

Someone grabbed Kalen's arm and dragged him from the disabled vehicle.

"I've got the comm!" Jamie said, shouting over the commotion. "Where's Asa?" Kalen hit the ground and felt his way along the vehicle.

"Mandi's got hold of him." Mayla pulled him behind the cruiser. "Now keep your eyes closed, I'll guide you." Half a dozen blasts pinged off the cruiser rocking the old vehicle.

"We've got to find better cover!" Mandi yelled over another series of blasts. "What should I do with our friend here?"

Kalen heard a dull thud above the ping of weapons' fire. "Let him sleep this one out." He turned and through blurred eyes he saw Asa slump to the ground, Jamie kneeling beside him.

"Good idea." Kalen blinked several times and found the blast's effects fading.

"Here, hang onto this." Mayla shoved his staff into his hand. "Mandi, guide Kalen!" Jamie and Mayla returned fire over the top of the cruiser. "Jamie and I will cover you. We should be able to find cover once we get around that bend in the canyon!"

"I can see well enough now to follow." Kalen slipped his arm out of Mandi's grip.

More pulsar fire blasted the canyon walls and splattered against the cruiser.

186

"These pistols are useless!" Jamie fired another half a dozen times. "Skylar's men are out of range. They're using pulsar rifles. If we don't get out of here, they'll pick us off one at a time. "

Rubbing his eyes, Kalen's vision remained blurry, but he could make out his companions. Another volley sprayed the area and a chunk of the flyer's left side disappeared. "What do you suggest we do?"

Mayla fired over the vehicle's roof. "Wait for the next lull and then pour it on. We won't hit anyone, but we can make them duck for cover. Once they're down, we run. Head for the opening in the canyon wall."

"We better do it now," Mandi said, waving Asa's pistol. "We can't stay here much longer."

"On one," Mayla said. The four prepared to fire.

At the next lull Mayla counted down, "Three-two-one!"

Opening fire, the quartet bathed the area across the canyon with a heavy, steady barrage. When the return fire stopped, they sprinted away. Several explosions erupted behind them. Racing down the canyon, Jamie took the lead. Mayla and Mandi followed.

Kalen brought up the rear, firing over his shoulder. The rocks and canyon walls came back into focus after they turned the bend. The weapons' fire splattered against the rock wall, now shielding them.

Jamie tried the comm. Loud static issued from the speaker. "There's too much iron in these canyon walls." Kalen pointed to the opposite wall. "The signal's being deflected and bounced in all directions."

"We better seek higher ground." Jamie shut off the comm. "Let's hope Eli's close by!"

Continuing west, the foursome hugged the rugged rock face until they came to the opening Mayla spotted earlier, leading into a narrow side canyon. Kalen knelt down, scooped up a handful of the material at his feet. He blinked several times to clear his vision, then studied the sand and smooth gravel in his hand. "This way." He led them in. The floor of the narrow opening pointed due north and angled upward.

"Kalen, this could be a dead end!" Mayla said.

"I don't think it is. The floor and walls of this wash are worn down. I think the water runs out here for this section of the canyon.

We should be able to get to the top by following it."

The sounds of angry voices grew closer.

The foursome ran until they came to a steep rock face blocking the way. Kalen scanned the walls and spotted the water course in the worn rocks on the far wall. Pointing, he said, "We'll have to start climbing, the east side looks the easiest."

While Kalen kept lookout, Mandi helped Mayla get a foothold, then Jamie helped Mandi up. The shouts of their pursuers grew louder. From behind the rocks, a man charged Kalen and Jamie. Kalen tossed Jamie Asa's pistol. "Get up with them and cover me!" Without waiting for Jamie's answer, he rushed to meet their attacker.

The man skidded to a halt and raised his weapon.

Kalen continued his charge, closed the gap, stabbed his staff into the ground, and vaulted into his opponent before the man could fire. Kalen's feet slammed into his chest. His weapon flew from his hands and he sailed backwards. Kalen dropped to the ground. Both men scrambled to their feet.

The man charged again, but twisted sideways and flew backward, a blackened hole in his chest from Jamie's pistol.

Kalen snatched the man's pulsar rifle from the ground and a pistol from his holster, then ran to join the others. He tossed the additional pistol and his staff to Jamie.

Behind him Kalen heard a man's voice shout, "They're up there!"

Mandi and Mayla opened fire.

Jamie reached out, grabbed Kalen's outstretched arm and dragged him the rest of the way. Kalen and Jamie covered the women while they continued to worm their way upward. When a new group of five men charged into the open, Jamie killed their leader. The remainder scattered for cover and continued to fire.

"We can't stay here!" Jamie shouted, while taking out another man trying to flank them. "They'll pin us down."

Kalen acknowledged him and kept shooting, while scanning the area for better cover. High up on the west face, he spotted a slide of earth and boulders perched precariously against a rock ledge. "Jamie, fire at that rockslide. If we can bring it down it will buy us some time."

Jamie concentrated his fire at the base of a large rock holding the slide in place.

Kalen kept their enemies dodging for cover. Farther down the wash he spotted more men moving toward them. He turned his weapon on Jamie's target and fired. The additional detonations caused the ledge to explode and collapse, breaking the slide loose. Dust spread outward and cut visibility to zero. The slide spilled into the wash. Pain-filled screams split the air while boulders and rocks crushed and buried the men.

The dust cloud billowed upward, engulfing the foursome. The women scrambled up the rocks, Kalen and Jamie on their heels. The ground leveled out. Kalen found the dry-water course, and continued leading the way northwest. Behind them, the shouting and screams grew fainter. They continued northward until the path came to an abrupt end, blocked by a sheer rock wall.

Eastern Arm Barrera Mountains
Unnamed Canyon

Chapter 28
A Tight Squeeze

Jamie, Mayla, and Mandi took up defensive positions in front of the impassable wall.

"I thought you said this went somewhere." Jamie glanced down the canyon. "What now?"

Kalen scanned the sheer wall of black granite. "The rock face is too smooth to climb. There aren't any signs of water wear." He turned his attention to the ground and to his left at the base of the wall, he spotted an opening covered by weeds and brush. Dropping to his knees, he tore the foliage away, and found a waterworn opening under the wall. Leaning over, he stared into the dark cave. "Jamie, look."

Mayla's brother came to his side. "What did you find down there?"

"Even with limited rain fall, the water's bored a tunnel under this stone wall." Kalen dropped flat on his chest, and spotted daylight on the other side. "We go under!"

"You've got to be kidding me! Kalen, that's a bit tight."

"It's gonna get a lot tighter if we get pinned in here."

"No argument there." Jamie glanced over his shoulder, knelt down, and wiggled in. While Mayla kept a lookout, Mandi followed. When the police officer's feet disappeared, Kalen turned to Mayla, her eyes already wide with panic.

191

"I'm sorry, mi amor, but it's the only way out."

"Kalen, you know how I feel about enclosed spaces. This is worse than the shaft we had to climb up in the cave."

Kalen pulled her to him. "I'm going to go through feet first. I want you to close your eyes and grab my hands. I'll guide you through."

Mayla looked into his eyes.

He could read her fear and pulled her close. "We'll make it through this together." Kalen bent over and tossed his staff, then the rifle, into the opening. He shinnied in feet first, and waited for Mayla to lay down.

Gripping his hands, she looked into his eyes. "Does anything frighten you?"

"Yeah, losing you."

Mayla looked behind her. "They're getting close, move!"

Kalen crawled backwards.

Mayla groaned, squeezed his hands and entered the opening. Face to face, they inched their way through the narrow tunnel. When Kalen's feet touched his staff and the rifle, he stopped and shoved them behind him, then shinnied a little further.

The tunnel widened and the floor dropped away. Movement became easier. About to tell Mayla she could move on her own, he stopped when the light behind her dimmed. Kalen released her hands. "Mayla, roll to your left, someone's coming."

Mayla removed her pistol, handed it to Kalen, then rolled, and pressed herself against the east wall of the tunnel. Kalen rolled to the opposite side. He could hear faint voices and shouting. Then he heard the grating sound of someone crawling over the sand and loose gravel. After a moment he saw a weapon, then the man's head. When their pursuer came onto view, his head turned toward Mayla first. Kalen raised his weapon and pressed it to the back of the man's neck. "Move a muscle and it will be your last," he whispered.

The man cursed and dropped his pistol. Mayla grabbed the weapon.

"Now keep crawling. When you reach the other end, stay on your belly or she'll kill you before you can get your feet under you, do you understand me?"

The man scowled and crawled toward the far end of the tunnel. "Mayla, can you make it from here alone?"

Her weak voice issued from the darkness, "No, but I'll have to now."

Kalen waited until she was well behind him, then continued his backwards crawl until he felt a touch on his legs. At the far end of the tunnel, Kalen spotted someone in the entrance. He took the rifle, fired three shots straight at the opening, then fired four times at the chamber's roof. The ceiling shattered, dropping the broken rock into the passageway, blocking the tunnel.

Kalen scrambled to his feet and found Mandi and Jamie standing over their prisoner. Kalen looked around. They stood in an extension of the canyon, but here the wall tapered inward higher up. In the narrow opening far above, he could see the thickening storm clouds. He turned his attention to their prisoner. "How many people are behind us?"

The man refused to answer. He glared at Kalen, defiance in his eyes.

Jamie dragged the man to his feet, and shoved him back toward the tunnel opening. With a sweep of his staff, Jamie knocked the man's legs out from under him and he hit the ground with a dull thud. "You can answer me or we bury you alive. Now, how many people are with you?"

"Ya won't kill me in cold blood," the man said, his tone arrogant. "Besides, killing me won't save any of ya."

Retrieving his staff, Kalen twirled it once and caught the man under his jaw. His head snapped back and he crumpled, unconscious. "This conversation was getting boring," he said to his startled companions. "We're wasting time and the weather is turning nasty." Pointing to the canyon walls, he added, "If it starts raining, it looks like the water backs up against this rock and gets two or three meters deep in here. I don't feel like swimming. We have to get to higher ground!" He looked up. "It never rains up here!" He took hold of Mayla's arm. "Are you all right?"

"No. Yes. Please, keep us out of places like that."

A sound caught Kalen's attention. In the confines of the narrow water course the wind whistled across the opening overhead as the storm moved in. "We'd better get moving." He took the lead and hurried up the canyon. The rock walls turned a powdery black. The water course rose and the sound of the wind grew louder. They neared the canyon's mouth and the walls grew farther apart.

"There's no sign of pursuit, so far," Mandi said. She glanced over her shoulder. "I don't like this! They wouldn't have given up so easily."

"We're pretty far out in the wilds," said Jamie between breaths. "They might think they can leave us out here to die."

"They won't chance leaving Kalen alive." Mayla glanced over her shoulder. "We know what Skylar looks like now and he knows we'll report this to the authorities. If he's working for Maria, she'll kill him for letting us get away."

"She's right." Kalen slowed his pace. "Keep your eyes open, they can't be far behind us."

"Or they've gotten ahead of us." Jamie craned his neck to see farther up the canyon.

Pointing overhead, Mayla said, "We're closer to the top. Jamie, try the comm again."

Jamie slipped the comm unit out of his pocket, and called, "Eli, this is Jamie, come in." They waited, but only static issued from the unit. "We have to get clear of these walls."

Continuing northward, they reached an open area. In front of them, the wash spread out and branched in five directions. The storm rolled in and broke. The first stinging drops of rain pelted them.

Jamie keyed the comm. "Eli, this is Jamie, come in."

The comm remained silent for a moment, then Eli's voice broke through. "This is Eli, Jamie. Where are you?"

"North of the canyon we told you about. We need help, there are at least a dozen people after us."

"We know. We spotted the cruiser burning. It looks like someone kicked open a Kafler colony. You four really know how to stir up trouble. How do we find you?"

Kalen signaled and Jamie handed him the comm. "Eli, this is Kalen. About a hundred meters west of the cruiser on the north side is a narrow side canyon. Follow it to where it widens, and branches into five washes, we'll be going up the extreme west wash. Hurry, the rain is getting heavier and this area will be flooded soon! Kalen out. Jamie, we've got to find higher ground before the water rises and we get swept downstream!"

They took off, running through the puddles already forming on the ground. In the lead, Kalen headed up the western-most branch, looking for a way to scale the wash's high walls. As they entered the western wash, the ground erupted in a spray of mud and rocks.

Mandi screamed, grabbed her left arm and stumbled to her knees.

More weapons' fire hit the ground.

Kalen scanned the sky for the source of the pulsar fire and spotted a flyer coming in from the northeast. Off to the east, jagged bolts of lightning split the leaden sky. A loud thunderclap exploded, the sound rolling overhead. The clouds opened in a torrential downpour. The puddles increased in size, connected, and started to flow.

The flyer circled around and came at them again, this time from the east. Kalen and Mayla returned fire, while Jamie helped Mandi to stand, a bloody gash on her left forearm. Plumes of brown water, mud and rocks leapt into the air. The flyer streaked overhead.

Kalen and Mayla flanked Jamie and Mandi. Kalen spotted the flyer making a run at them from the north, straight down the wash. Water swirled around them and they struggled to move against the now ankle-deep flow.

The small ship dove and fired again. Plumes of brown water exploded all around them. Kalen and Mayla fired in rapid succession at the fast-moving vehicle.

Mayla landed a solid shot on the flyer's belly. The little ship wobbled and veered away.

Kalen raised his captured rifle, spun and fired twice. A plume of smoke issued from the ship and it nosed downward. He tossed the rifle away, linked arms with Mayla and pulled her along, while he scanned the canyon walls for some way out. He spotted a ledge jutting out from the west bank of the wash. "Over there!"

Struggling through the knee-deep water, the four stopped and stood under the ledge. Kalen boosted Mayla up, then both men lifted Mandi. Mayla grabbed her arm and dragged her onto the ledge.

The rain beat down in a stinging torrent, and the water rose to Kalen's waist.

Jamie and Kalen tossed their staffs up to the women. Jamie tossed the comm up on the shelf, then Kalen locked his fingers together. Jamie stepped into the cradle and scrambled over the edge, spun around, and extended his arms to Kalen. "Kalen, grab my arm!"

Fighting the pressure from the rising flow, Kalen reached up and locked his fingers around Jamie's wrist.

Jamie struggled to pull Kalen up, while the water tore at his body.

Kalen tried to ball himself up to get out of the muddy stream, but a sudden surge ripped his hand from Jamie's grip and the muddy waters carried him under the ledge.

Eastern Arm
Barrera Del Sur Mountains
Unnamed Canyon

Chapter 29
Along for the Ride

"Kalen!" Mayla took two quick steps and leapt off the ledge, sailed through the air and landed feet first near Kalen's hand. His head popped up for a moment then disappeared again. A couple of quick strokes brought her close enough to grab his hand when it appeared above the muddy water. A quick yank and Kalen surfaced. He coughed up a mouthful of slime, recovered from the shock of seeing her, and locked arms with her.

The churning water pulled at their bodies while they struggled to keep their heads above the gritty guck. The water's swift flow carried them across the confluence of the washes. The converging flows threatened to pull them under.

The raging flood continued south, reentering the narrow canyon they had just escaped from. The current pushed them close to the west canyon wall. Kalen and Mayla kicked and swam to keep from slamming into the sides. The muddy waters, now high up on the black walls, carried them farther downstream.

Out ahead of them, Mayla spotted a fast-approaching jagged protrusion.

Kalen wrapped his arms around her, wrenched their bodies around, thrust his legs out and pushed off at the last possible instant. They continued downstream until their rapid pace ceased. The waters slowed and rose higher in the narrow canyon, forming a muddy lake.

Kalen pushed Mayla toward the west wall. "The water has no place to go."

"You blocked the only outlet."

Thunder cracked overhead in a deafening boom.

"We've got to get out," Kalen shouted, while spitting out the brown water. "That blockage won't hold for long, not against this much pressure."

Struggling through the muddy soup, Kalen and Mayla searched for a way out. Mayla expected the blockage to give way at any moment.

"Mayla, look, there's a cave entrance." Kalen pointed to an opening ten meters below the top on the east side, farther down the narrow canyon. He pushed her toward the center of the canyon, then together they swam to the east wall.

Floating in place below the mouth of the cavern, they waited for the level to rise. Within arm's reach of the opening, Mayla tried to grab the lip. Her wet fingers could not maintain a grip on the rock.

"The water stopped rising. Mayla, we have to get out now!" Positioning himself behind her, Kalen took hold of her waist.

With his help she pushed upward and grabbed the lip of the opening, then clawed her way into the cave. Spinning around on her stomach, she extended her arms to him.

Kalen grabbed her wrists and tried pulling himself from the slimy brown soup. Downstream a muffled rumble echoed off the canyon walls. A roar drew their attention. Behind Kalen a whirlpool formed.

Mayla tightened her grip on Kalen's wrists. "Hurry before you get pulled in!" She could feel her wet clothes slip on the cavern floor and jammed her feet against the walls while Kalen struggled and kicked against the current.

Another rumble shook the ground. The water level dropped, leaving Kalen suspended with two meters of air between him and the swirling waters. He wiggled and kicked until he managed to get his waist over the lip, then Mayla yanked him the rest of the way into the opening.

Kalen turned over and let his pent-up breath explode from his lungs. "Geeze, what else can go wrong?"

Below them the sound of air being sucked into the brown vortex became a deafening roar. They lay on their backs, panting from the exertion. Lightning flashes clawed at the sky, thunder boomed, while the relentless downpour continued.

When he regained some of his strength, Kalen stood and looked out at the swirling waters and the steady downpour.

"I don't understand, Mayla. Something's changed in the last twenty-five periods. The Outlands are never this wet."

"The weather satellites must have a lot to do with it."

"The satellites can push a storm cell south, so the high mountain passes can relieve some of that pressure when a storm slips through. The closest one is Silk Pass but we're too far east. Arrisian storm systems travel west to east or south to north. This one came straight out of the east, I'm sure of it. No, Mayla, there's something else in play here."

"You can't solve the weather problems right now. How are we going to get back to Mandi and Jamie?"

Kalen turned and stared into the black depths of the cave. After another flash of lightning illuminated the tunnel, he picked up a loose stone and tossed it into the darkness. It hit the floor, echoing while bouncing away in the dark. "We'd better wait until it stops raining, then we can try to climb up. If we can't go that way, we'll have to see if this goes anywhere." He took hold of Mayla's arms and turned her so she faced him. "What kind of fool stunt was that anyway? We might have both wound up dead!"

"I guess I realized that what frightens me the most is the thought of losing you."

"Please don't risk your life like that again." Kalen enfolded her in his arms.

"Please don't get yourself into any more situations like that." Kalen held her and they stared out in the canyon, listening to the storm, and above that the roar of the water draining out of the canyon.

Mayla stared out into the muddy waters. "Jamie and Mandi probably think we're dead."

Eastern Arm
Barrera Del Sur Mountains
Unnamed Canyon

Chapter 30
From Grief to Hope

"Mayla!" Jamie tried to wrap his arms around her waist, but missed. Mandi grabbed his belt in time to stop him from sliding off the ledge. His throat constricted with grief, while he watched his sister and Kalen get carried away by the muddy waters. He pushed himself upright and stared into the raging flow, unable to believe what had just happened.

Mandi's hand touched his shoulder. "I'm so sorry, Jamie."

"Thanks." Jamie covered her hand with his. The water level rose, lapping at their feet. Mandi jumped back. Still in shock, it took Jamie a moment longer to realize what it meant. He looked up to the top of the bank. "You're going to have to stand on my shoulders to reach the top!"

"You'll have to go first, I won't be able to pull you up with this bad arm, but I can boost you."

"All right." Jamie stared up at the top of the wash. "Let's get moving."

Interlocking her fingers, Mandi leaned against the bank of the wash and squatted. "Quick, the water's eroding the ledge."

Jamie put his left foot in Mandi's hands and sprang upward. His fingers grabbed hold of the top of the bank. He kicked clear, disappeared over the edge, then reappeared, and reached down. Mandi tossed the comm, the two staffs and their other weapons up. Jamie extended his staff over the side and Mandi grabbed it. The water continued to rise, pulling at Mandi's feet. She slipped, lost her grip and almost fell into the brown soup.

"Mandi, jump, the ledge is almost gone!"

Mandi bent her knees, leapt up, and grabbed the staff midway from the bottom, then slipped downward. Below her, the ledge crumbled and disappeared into the muddy waters.

Mandi tightened her grip, then pulled herself upward until she touched Jamie's hands. She locked her right hand onto his left wrist.

Jamie released the staff. It disappeared, carried away by the waters lapping at Mandi's feet.

She swung about in a wild arc.

Jamie could feel her slipping. "Grab my other wrist."

Mandi grimaced and swung her injured arm up and grabbed Jamie's hand, but her wet fingers could not maintain her grip.

Shinnying forward, Jamie extended his arm as far as he could. "Mandi, grab my wrist, not my hand." Straining, he pulled her closer.

Mandi managed to lock her fingers around his wrist. Stable in his grip, she kicked at the rain-softened bank, and dug out a foot-hold with the toe of her boot. With her new footing she kicked out another toe-hold above the first and climbed higher. The water rose and continued to lap at the soles of her boots. She kicked out two more toe-holds, then Jamie dragged her over the edge. Panting from their efforts, they lay in the rain, oblivious to the downpour.

"Is–is your arm okay?"

Cradling her arm, Mandi panted and nodded. "Where—where's the comm?" she said, between labored breaths.

Still too winded to move, Jamie pointed toward his feet.

Mandi dragged herself to the comm, lifted it to her mouth and keyed the unit. "Mandi to—to Eli, come in."

"This is Eli, we're on our way."

"Hurry!" Mandi dropped the comm, and sat in the mud, cradling her arm.

Jamie lay his head back and listened to the water's roar while it sped by in the wash. A thought came to him. He staggered to his feet, walked to the edge of the wash, stared downstream at the water level, and recalled Kalen's warning. *'If it starts raining, it looks like the water backs up against this rock and gets two or three meters deep in here.'*

"Mandi, how deep would you say the water in that canyon is?"

Mandi rolled to her feet, came to Jamie's side, and looked downstream. "Eight, maybe ten meters, why?"

"Remember what Kalen said about the water depth in the canyon, if it started raining?"

"'The water might get two or three—'" She looked downstream again, then grabbed Jamie's shoulder. "When Kalen blasted the tunnel, he sealed off the only outlet!"

"If they can stay afloat, they could get out. They may still be alive!"

"As high as the waters have risen, they could find somewhere to climb out. We should go search for them!"

"No." Jamie gazed south, expecting to see the Lexicon. "We have to stay put and wait for Eli. We stand a better chance of spotting them from the air. Besides, your arm needs attention."

"Is that Eli?" Mandi pointed to the south.

Jamie squinted and recognized Kalen's vehicle. "Yeah, it sure is." He raised his arm and waved.

The flyer sped up a nd closed the gap. Jamie stepped to the flyer after Eli set down next to them. The wing door lifted.

"We've got to get back!" Eli shouted. "Those men have our officers pinned down and we're out-gunned." He looked around. "Where are Mayla and Kalen?" He spotted Mandi cradling her arm. "Are you all right?"

"I'm fine. What is going on?" "How bad is it?" Jamie said.

"We've got one officer dead and two others wounded already." Another thought came to Jamie. He helped Mandi into the flyer, then scoured the floor and found an empty black waterproof bag from Mayla's medical supplies. Dropping the comm in it, he ran back to the bank, grabbed Kalen's staff, and laid it on the

ground, the tapered end pointing south. He pressed it into the softened ground, gathered up loose rocks, and stacked them so the staff's tapered end pointed to the mound, then ran back to the flyer.

"Eli, you better let me fly."

The men switched places, then Jamie took off. He flew low over the canyon and searched the water below.

"I hope you still have your weapons," Eli said. "We're going to need all the fire power we can muster."

"Better than that." Jamie looked at Eli, grinned, then reached across the console and activated the Lexicon's weapons.

Eli's eyes widened when the targeting computer came on. "I'm not even going to ask."

"I don't see any sign of them," Mandi said. "I hope they got out before that started!"

Jamie looked down at the swirling vortex. "They're alive. I know they are." He pushed the Lexicon's throttle forward. "Let's go help your people, then get back here and find my sister and Kalen."

Barrera Del Sur Mountains
Eastern Arm
Canyon Cavern

Chapter 31
Discoveries

Kalen released Mayla, sat down, and removed his boots. He emptied the water, then cleaned out most of the grit.

Mayla removed her boots and did the same.

The thunder faded into distant rumbles. The tunnel grew quiet and the sound of flowing water echoed from within the cavern. Kalen tugged his boots on, then walked deeper into the opening.

The echo grew louder.

"There may be a place we can rinse off farther in," Mayla said.

She limped up behind Kalen.

"We should try and get back to Jamie and Mandi." He looked back toward the cavern's mouth. "What's wrong with your leg?"

"I twisted my ankle, I'll be fine. Do you think we can climb up the face of the canyon walls?"

Kalen closed his eyes and tried to picture the walls in his mind. "We might if we had the proper equipment. I think the walls are too smooth and sheer to attempt a free climb, and with your ankle it's out of the question. This cave may lead to a way out."

"And it may just lead to a dead end."

"Either way, we are going to have to get some of the grit off if we are going to do any walking, and that water sounds inviting." Mayla leaned on Kalen and took the weight off her ankle.

"You're right." Kalen started down the dark shaft, moving slow to allow time for their eyes to adjust. The air grew cooler, and then the shaft opened up into a high roofed chamber. On the east wall a translucent glow from above revealed water cascading over the rocks, forming a large pool at the bottom of the cavern. They picked their way down and across the chamber floor to the near-edge of the water. Kalen knelt down, dipped his hand in the water, scooped some to his lips, and grimaced at the taste.

"Kalen, what's wrong? Are you all right?"

"Yeah, the water is loaded with dissolved iron." Kalen wiped his mouth. "It's okay to drink, it just tastes bad."

"Is that all?" Mayla leaned over and scooped a handful to her mouth. "I have drunk worse."

Kalen didn't bother to ask where she might have tasted nastier water. They drank, then rinsed off the grit from their mud bath.

"Let me have a look at your foot." Mayla sat down on a nearby rock.

Kalen lifted her foot and removed her boot. He examined her leg and massaged her ankle.

"I hope Jamie and Mandi are all right. Mmm," Mayla said, while Kalen massaged her ankle. "Under more favorable circumstances this could be very pleas–, ouch!"

"Sorry." Kalen cradled her foot. "I don't see any cuts, but you're going to be tender for a couple of days."

"Say, you're quite handy, soldier." Mayla pulled Kalen to her. "I should keep you around."

"Play your cards right, Captain Santiago, and I might marry you."

"Sorry, but it is not wise for officers to fraternize with civilian personnel." She drew him close and kissed him. "Mm-mm, I think for you I could make an exception." Mayla shivered in the cool air.

Kalen wrapped his arm around her to help her keep warm. "Let's see if we can find a way up the canyon wall or back down. I don't like trying to pick our way through a labyrinth."

Returning to the opening, Kalen leaned out and studied the cliff face above them. Then he looked down. Muddy water still flowed in the narrow canyon. He turned to Mayla. "The face is too sheer and the canyon floor won't be passable for days. Looks like we'll have to try the cave."

"What are the chances of there being a way out?"

"I don't know, but feel that air being drawn in here. There has to be an outlet somewhere. It's just a matter of finding our way underground and hoping that outlet is big enough to get through."

Moving back down the tunnel, Mayla stopped at the pool to get one last drink before they continued on.

Kalen scanned the cavern in the dim light and spotted two openings on the opposite wall. They crossed the cavern and stood before the two tunnels.

Mayla asked, "Which one?"

Stooping over, Kalen gathered up a handful of dirt, and tossed it into the air. The air flow drew the dust down the right-hand tunnel. "That way. Stay close and watch your footing." Kalen hooked his left arm with Mayla's. With his right hand on the wall, he moved into the dark tunnel and proceeded at a slow pace. The floor sloped downward at a shallow angle. The passage twisted and turned, until Kalen lost all sense of direction. He could feel the steady flow of air moving around them.

Mayla cried out and stumbled.

Kalen tightened his grip and kept her from falling. He pulled her close. "You all right?"

"I think so." Mayla shifted her weight, taking the pressure off her leg. "Let's take it slower."

Moving forward, Kalen slid his feet to better detect any obstructions. Echoes of running water filled the passageway.

Mayla said, "I thought you said there is no water on the lower elevations?"

"I said there's no water on the surface. Water sinks below the land on the lower levels. The wells at Avila are sunk down four to six hundred meters to reach the water table."

"Where does all the water go that flows out of the mountains?"

"I never really thought about it." Kalen paused their progress. "I guess I just assumed that the towns used most of it. I wonder if that's why Dad spent so much time alone down here drilling core samples."

The tunnel leveled out and made a sharp right. Ahead, a faint glow coming from the far end illuminated the shaft. Mayla released Kalen's arm. "That light's not natural."

"You're right, it's not."

Drawing nearer the glow, echoes of whispered voices reached them. Then a scream reverberated through the cave.

Barrera Del Sure Mountains
Eastern Arm
Under the Mountain

Chapter 32
More Discoveries

Kalen and Mayla pressed themselves against the cavern walls. "What was that?" Mayla whispered.

"It wasn't an animal. That was definitely human."

"And female."

Kalen signed for Mayla to follow, then they headed down the tunnel. In the distance, echoes from shouting bounced off the cavern walls, distorting the words. Though the sounds grew louder, Kalen couldn't distinguish any of the conversations. To him their tone sounded angry and urgent.

The light grew stronger. Moving along the stone corridor became easier. Kalen and Mayla came to another tunnel branching off to their right. Kalen looked in. While ahead the light grew brighter, this tunnel was pitch black. He took a couple of steps in. The floor sloped downward at a steeper angle. He could hear the same noise and voices echoing in this tunnel.

"Anything useful?" said Mayla.

"I can't tell where this goes." He stepped back. "Let's see what's up ahead."

Turning another corner, they approached the tunnel's end and faced a sheer drop off into a large, well-lit chamber. Just below them, a flyer and two large transports sat one behind the other. Equipment pods and crates lay scattered all around. Far below, men scrambled to and from the ships, loading equipment. A thin man appeared, dragging a woman toward the lead ship. In spite of her struggles, he shoved her through the door, then shouted to another man. This time Kalen could understand him.

"Hurry! Get all the women loaded, then we'll hide this transport in the wastelands until things die down."

"We've stumbled onto the kidnappers' hideout!" Kalen whispered.

The man turned and Mayla pointed. "Is that Skylar?"

Kalen leaned out to listen. "That's him, all right. There's no mistaking that voice."

"Or that strange accent," said Mayla.

"We can't let the local authorities catch us here." Skylar scanned the cavern. "Haru, get everyone else aboard the other transport, we'll use it as a decoy. Anyone not onboard in twenty minutes gets buried."

"Look." Mayla pointed to the far side of the cave.

High in the walls, three men in anti-grav belts hovered, setting devices on the rocks.

"Those look like the same kind Jenna placed around the cavern to bury us. They're planning to create another implosion. We can't let him take those women off world."

"Can you fly that big transport?"

Mayla looked down at the ship. "Shouldn't be a problem. How do we get down there in less than five minutes without being spotted? This is at least a ten-meter drop."

"That shaft I looked into. I think it leads down. I could hear their noise in it."

Turning away from the lit cavern, they made their way back to the side tunnel. Kalen slipped into the darkness and started downward. The passageway narrowed, slowing their progress.

"If this gets any tighter–," Mayla grunted, her clothes rasping against the wall. "–we could be in trouble."

"Just a minute." Kalen stopped. Stepping back, he kicked at the wall, After the third kick, he dislodged three large bulges from the wall. "That's better. Watch your step."

The floor of the passage grew steeper, twisting first to the left then back to the right. Noise and voices from the cavern grew louder and more distinct. With one final step, Kalen's foot hit flat ground.

Emerging in a small side chamber, he stepped aside, let Mayla out, then moved behind a stack of cargo pods for cover. Footsteps at the chamber's entrance made them duck behind the stack.

Two men entered. One of them grabbed a container near the entrance, pulled the top open, and removed three items. He handed them to his companion, then grabbed three more.

"Shouldn't we take all of them?" the other man said, juggling his load.

"No, there's no time." He steadied his companion. "Careful with those! We'll leave the rest to enhance the explosion in this part of the cavern. The boss wants to make sure this stuff is destroyed." The two hurried away.

Kalen and Mayla moved into the chamber. Kalen peered out into the main cavern.

Mayla examined the container near the entrance. "More sapper mines."

"It looks like they've finished loading the women on the lead transport."

Mayla came up beside Kalen. "Good, then we can steal it." She handed him a canister. "Attach these to the second transport."

"How do you set this thing?"

"Pull the cap off and set the timer like this." Mayla removed the top of the long cylinder. She fingered the keypad until the digital timer showed ten minutes. "You push this blue button to activate it." Kalen copied her movements. Peering out into the main chamber, he spotted a stack of long wooden poles leaning against the wall. He grabbed two and handed one to Mayla. "I don't know what these are doing here, but we may need them."

Mayla took one and hefted it.

Slipping out of the chamber, Kalen and Mayla took cover in a shallow pit near the lead ship, and waited for activity around the transports to slow. The men finished and hurried to get aboard. Kalen took the mine from Mayla. "Get on board that transport. I'll set these on the hull, then join you."

"Hurry, those charges go off in less than ten minutes." Mayla headed for the lead ship.

Chapter 33
Escape

Kalen approached the second transport. To his right, he heard footsteps. He dove behind a tumbled stack of cargo pods. A man rounded the ship's bow, made a quick inspection of the hull, then hurried and climbed aboard the ship.

Kalen scanned the cavern, laid his new staff near the pods, ducked under the transport, and crawled to the nearest forward landing strut. He shoved the cylinder into the recess, then crawled to the farthest strut and did the same. He froze at the sound of footsteps at the transport's hatch. Another man emerged from an opening in the chamber's far wall. From above him Kalen heard Skylar say, "Is everyone on-board?"

"Yeah. Should I start the timers?"

"No. Give it another two minutes. They still haven't found MacKenna or the people with him. I'm taking the flyer. I'll find them and make sure they don't talk to anyone." Skylar stomped down the ramp, heading toward the first transport.

The other man remained on the ramp forcing Kalen to wait until he reentered the ship. When he did, Kalen tapped the mine, then hurried to the other strut, and started the other timer. Scrambling out from under the ship, he grabbed his staff and raced to help Mayla. The lights went out, and from all around the chamber, the devices' timers flashed to life. Red eyes blinking their death count.

Mayla ran along the lead transport's far side. Pressing herself against the ship's hull, she crept forward. Stopping opposite the hatch on the far side, she bent over and peered under the ship. Someone walked toward the ship. When their footsteps echoed off the metal ramp, Mayla crawled under the transport and halted again when another pair of legs hurried past the ramp and toward the flyer. A deep rumble filled the cavern. The front wall slid back and the flyer disappeared down a dark tunnel.

Mayla crossed under the transport and stopped beneath the ramp when two men ran from the ship, crossed the chamber, and returned with two more prisoners in tow. The women struggled and screamed, but the men managed to drag them onto the ship. Mayla waited until the two men exited the ship and ran to the second ship. She scrambled out from under the transport and up the ramp.

Inside the hatchway another man stood with his back to her. He turned and Mayla caught him under the chin with her staff. He let out a startled cry as he flew backwards, landing in the aisle. She swung her staff in a tight arch, hitting him on the side of his head. His eyes rolled back and his body went slack. Behind her, Mayla heard voices and concealed herself in a recess across the aisle.

Two men entered and spotted their companion on the deck. "Matthews, what happened?" One man knelt down to help him.

Mayla stepped out and jabbed the standing man in the side of the head, then kicked the other man in the face. Both men went down, the first stunned. The second man rolled, came to his feet, and reached for his weapon.

Taking a step back, Mayla tilted her head, grinned, and pointed.

Gaping at her for a moment, he turned.

Kalen jabbed him in the throat.

Skylar's man crumpled to the deck, gasping for air.

"Matthews, close the hatch." A voice ordered over the transport's comm. "We're ready to lift off."

Kalen searched for the activator. He found it, and slapped the panel. The hatch hissed, slammed shut, and the transport lifted off.

Kalen hit the gasping man in the forehead, knocking him out. He bent over, pulled the men's weapons from their holsters and handed one to Mayla.

"We had better get to the pilot." She tucked the pistol into her waistband.

The two headed forward, stopped and reached the closed bridge hatch. Kalen tapped on the metal slab. When the door mech hissed, he drew his weapon.

The hatch slid open and the emerging crewman's jaw dropped. Kalen grabbed his shirt and yanked him out of the cabin.

Mayla rushed in, knocked the pilot from his seat, while shutting the comm off with her foot.

The ship lurched sideways, scraping the cavern wall.

Grabbing the yoke, Mayla steadied the transport. She dodged the pilot's next roundhouse swing, and punched him in the jaw, staggering him. He pulled away. Mayla kicked him in the inner thigh and then in the stomach.

Kalen grabbed the pilot in a bear hug.

Mayla kicked him in his jaw, his head snapped back and Kalen released him. He collapsed in a heap at their feet. Dropping into the seat, Mayla steadied the ship, and turned the comm on.

"....s going on over there?" an angry voice shouted.

Kalen leaned close to the comm. "Someone let a full- grown Kye lizard get on-board, it startled us."

Silence followed Kalen's answer.

On the pilot's view screens Kalen saw the red eyes of the explosives continue their deadly countdown. Ahead the wall of the cavern slid back.

The man on the other ship asked, "Who is this?"

"It's Matthews," Kalen said.

"You don't sound like Matthews and you don't belong up with Kyto! Who's back with the women?"

"They're locked in the cargo hold, quit worrying."

Mayla moved the ship forward.

A new voice came over the comm. "Kyto, what's going on over there? Turn on your viewer!"

Mayla guided the transport down the narrow tunnel.

The ship lurched.

"Mayla, they're firing on us! Get us outta here!"

Mayla shoved the throttle forward.

The ship's hull scraped the cavern wall when the second transport hit them with another round. Mayla centered the ship, held it steady until they cleared the cavern walls. When they broke out into the open, she pulled back on the yoke.

While the bulky ship waddled skyward, Kalen activated the ship's rearview screens.

Mayla dodged two more volleys from the pursuing transport. "Kalen, how long before those devices go off? I can't get far enough ahead of them to get us out of this."

"Any second now. They should go off just after the cave does." Mayla circled in an effort to elude the weapons' fire. Another shot hit the ship, it lurched, and lost altitude. Then, far below, they saw in the rear-view screen a cloud of dirt and rock blast skyward.

Kalen adjusted the viewer for a closer look. The mouth of the cavern belched fire, dirt, and rocks. Large chunks of the mountain shot skyward.

Mayla continued to evade the second transport's weapons. The pursuing ship accelerated toward them. She banked to starboard and headed north. The ship fired again, hitting them on the port side. "I can't evade them for much longer." Mayla pulled the nose level. "This ship was never meant to maneuver like this. Sooner or later they are going to hit something vital. How long did you set the timers for?"

Kalen checked the viewers. Behind them the mountain continued to throw boulders into the air. The dust cloud billowed upward. "That's just about long enough." He activated the ship's vid. When the screen flared to life, Kalen recognized Asa.

"MacKenna!" Asa shouted. "Ram them!"

Someone off screen, "Are you crazy? You'll kill all of us."

"I don't care what happens, ram them!" Asa reached off screen and the transport closed the gap.

Mayla pushed forward on the yoke. The bulky ship nosed down, and sped up. The other transport matched her moves.

"I'll see you dead." Asa shook his meaty fist at the viewer.

Kalen grinned, clicked his tongue, and winked at Asa. "I'm really sorry you won't be able to stick around and make that happen."

Asa's rage turned to puzzlement. "What the hell–" The vid-screen flared white and went dark.

On the exterior viewers Kalen and Mayla watched the nose of the second transport erupt in a fireball. The ship plummeted downward and disappeared, swallowed by the cloud of fire and dust rising from the mountain tearing itself apart. The shock wave from the explosion rocked their transport.

Mayla increased their speed and the ship settled out. "Kalen, I'll try and raise Jamie and Mandi. You go release the women."

"Right after I secure these two."

Kalen grabbed the pilot, turned him onto his stomach, and pulled his shirt out. He tore off a long strip of cloth, and tied the pilot's hands behind his back. After he secured the pilot, he tied up the other crewman. "Mayla, maybe you should go and release the women. If I try, they are liable to attack me before I can explain who I am."

"Do you think you can fly this?"

"Without the others shooting at us, I think I can handle it." Kalen climbed in the co-pilot's seat and grabbed the yoke. "I'll call Jamie."

Mayla slipped out of the pilot's seat. On her way aft, she stopped and secured the other three crewmen, then dragged them into the empty passenger compartment. She moved to the rear bulkhead, opened the hatch, and sidestepped when a tall woman lunged at her.

Another smaller woman grabbed her. She eyed Mayla with distrust. "Who are you?"

A sudden violent lurch threw Mayla against the bulkhead. The transport heeled over to starboard. "I'll explain later. All of you get into the passenger compartment and strap in! Get those three men on the deck into seats and secure them. We need them alive so we can turn them over to the RPs. All of you get strapped in. We might be in for a rough landing."

The ship bucked and nosed downward. Mayla grabbed hold of the seat backs and worked her way toward the cockpit. She hit the activator panel. The ship pitched forward and threw her into the hatch. When it slid back, Mayla grabbed the hatchway lip to keep from falling into the cabin.

Kalen struggled with the controls. The instrument panel flashed almost solid orange.

Mayla dropped into the cabin, pulled herself into the pilot's seat, and grabbed the yoke. Warning lights on the control panel blinked non-stop. "What happened?" She scanned the console.

"I think one of the hits we–took did some real damage, I can't keep the ship level."

Working together, they brought the nose up and leveled out. The transport continued to buck and fight their efforts for control. Mayla scanned the console again. "It looks like they hit the steering controls, we're going to have to land now!"

Kalen studied the view screens. "Does that look familiar?" He pointed to the forward viewer.

Mayla recognized the wash they had been swept down earlier. "We're right back where we started from!"

A muffled explosion rocked the transport and the fire warning light blinked on.

Mayla scanned the console. "Now there's a fire in the engineering bay. We have to land!"

Kalen pointed to the forward view screen. "On the west bank of the wash. We can land there." While Kalen aimed the transport toward the flat area, Mayla released the yoke and strapped into her harness.

The ground rushed up to meet them, and they braced for impact. The ship hit hard, bounced twice, then skidded on its belly. The cabin went dark and the vid-screens turned black. Terrified screams reverberated from the passenger compartment. The transport plowed deep into the rain- softened ground, then rotated sideways and came to a jarring halt.

Mayla and Kalen released their harnesses, then raced to help the women. She reached the outside hatch and hit the release, but it did not move. "Kalen! The hatch is jammed!"

"Get the women up here!" He yanked a panel open and pumped the emergency hydraulic override. The pressure gauge pegged past max, but the hatch remained closed. He gave the handle three more pumps, grunting from the effort. The metal slab slid back enough for Kalen to wedge his arm in the opening. Grunting from the effort, he forced the door open halfway.

One at a time, Mayla hustled the women outside. Smoke billowed through the ship, filling the compartments. She grabbed the woman who stopped her from being cold-cocked, by the arm. "Get them into that wash for cover, the ship may blow! And keep an eye on those three." The women dragged the half-conscious men outside.

When the last of the women darted through the hatchway, Kalen yelled, "We can't leave the pilot and other crewman here to die!"

A muffled detonation in the engineering bay rocked the ship. Kalen and Mayla raced forward, pulled the men to their feet, and then dragged them through the smoke and flames. Reaching the hatchway, Kalen pushed the men outside, then he and Mayla jumped. They dragged the stunned men to their feet, then the four ran toward the wash.

Another explosion spewed flames skyward. The shockwave threw Mayla, Kalen and their prisoners to the ground, sending them tumbling over the edge of the wash and into the women's laps.

Kalen grabbed Mayla and pressed her against the bank of the wash.

Another explosion shook the ground. A wall of flame swept over their heads. Large pieces of debris embedded themselves in the wash's opposite bank.

Barrera Del Sur Mountains
Eastern Arm

Chapter 34
Cleanup

Fires drove back the night. Shadows jumped and danced on the opposite bank. Eerie moans and pops from the burning wreckage drowned out all other sounds. While the women remained huddled together for warmth, Kalen peered over the lip of the wash. Remains of the ship's shattered hull lay scattered over a wide area. Clawing his way up the bank with Mayla's help, he looked around. "I think it's safe." He reached down and pulled Mayla up and out.

"Kalen, let's see if we can find Jamie and Mandi." Mayla scanned their surroundings. "We have to let them know we're alive."

"Let's see to these women first."

Flickering light from the burning fuselage, made the rocks appear to dance. The wind picked up, washing the air clean of the rank odor from burning wiring, electronics, and the ship's plasti components.

Mayla helped the petite brunette from earlier climb out of the wash.

"I don't know who you are, but thanks for saving us." She stuck out her hand. "I'm Regina del Largo."

Mayla shook her hand and pointed to a tall female. "You're the one I need to thank. You kept her from bashing my brains in."

The woman looked up from the wash and cringed. "We thought you were the men coming back and we decided to try and escape."

"I'm Mayla Santiago and this is Kalen MacKenna."

"How did you find us?" said Regina.

"That's a long story. We'll tell you about it later. Right now, there are some friends we must find. Will you see to the other women?"

"Consider it done." Regina turned her attention to the women still in the wash, huddled together against the cold.

"Mayla, the place we last saw Jamie and Mandi is south of here." Kalen pointed. He grabbed two long, thin pieces of the flaming wreckage to use as torches. They headed along the bank of the wash. Kalen and Mayla walked for more than a kilometer, before splitting up. When they neared the last place they saw Jamie and Mandi, they slowed their pace and scoured the bank of the wash.

"Over here!" Mayla called out. Kalen raced to the spot where the bank showed signs of Jamie and Mandi's struggle to escape the rising water. He stabbed his torch into the rain-softened ground and cupped his hands around his mouth. "Jamie! Mandi!" The night remained silent. He looked around for any sign of them. A short distance from the wash, he spotted his staff on the ground, pressed into the soil, the tapered end pointed south. Half a meter from the staff's end lay a fresh pile of rocks. "Their footprints end here."

"Eli must have come up during the storm and pulled Jamie and Mandi out." Mayla caught up with Kalen, and stared at the staff. "Jamie must believe we're dead. He left your staff behind."

"No...I don't think that's why it's here. Look."

Mayla held her torch up as Kalen stepped over the pile of stones. He knelt down, started moving rocks aside, and revealed a black plastic sack.

"What's that?" Mayla leaned closer and peered over his shoulder. Kalen pushed the rest of the rocks away and lifted the black bag. "It's one of your medical sacks you left in the Lexicon." He opened ii and pulled out the comm unit.

"Why would they leave that behind?"

Turning the comm over in his hand, Kalen stood and walked to the edge of the wash.

Mayla followed, lighting the ground.

"The water must have backed up well beyond this point." Kalen stared south toward the canyon, invisible now in the dark. He pointed at the wash. "See, the ledge we were standing on is gone.

Jamie or Mandi realized what that meant and figured if we were still alive, we might get out. He couldn't be sure, but he took the chance and left the comm behind in case we made it back."

"Do you think they're looking for us?"

"Only one way to find out." Kalen keyed the comm. "Kalen to Jamie, come in."

The comm sputtered with static, then Jamie's voice answered, "You are alive! Is Mayla okay?"

"Muddy and bruised, but standing right next to me. Jamie, what's going on?"

"I was about to ask you the same thing. Do you know anything about the explosions we heard a little while ago?"

"More than we care to admit. What's all the noise? Is that the Lexicon's weapons I hear?"

"It is. We're just about to finish with this bunch. What happened to you two?"

"We'll tell you about it when we see you. Let Eli know we found some of the missing women. He'll need to send a couple of transports up here and a medical team, ASAP."

"You found the women! How many?" Mayla answered. "We rescued fourteen."

"Where are you?"

"You can't miss us. Look for the burning wreckage a kilometer north of where you and Mandi crawled out of the wash."

"As soon as we finish helping the RPs, we'll be on our way."

"Hurry, it's late, and we're cold."

Kalen picked up his staff, then he and Mayla headed back. Arriving at the wreckage, they found Regina had organized the women into four small groups. The women managed to pull four pieces of burning wreckage away from the ship. Each group huddled around the fires for warmth. Behind the women, the five men lay bound, on the damp ground.

One of the young women looked up at Mayla. "When can we go home?"

Another asked, "How will we get out of here?"

Kalen searched the faces of these strangers, all younger than Mayla. Their clothes were in poor shape and none were without bruises and other signs of abuse. Some huddled close to others, their eyes downcast. A few glared at the bound men with naked hatred. When Kalen made eye contact with any of the women, they looked away.

Mayla squatted down near the woman who spoke first. "The authorities are on their way."

"How do you know?"

"We just spoke to our friends, several of them are RPs, and they're making the arrangements. You'll all be going home soon."

"Thank you." The woman shivered, then huddled closer to the fire.

Mayla touched Kalen's arm and whispered, "Keep an eye on our prisoners while I tell the others what's going on."

"Yeah, that's probably a good idea." Kalen scanned the women's faces again. "I think they'll have an easier time talking to you if I step away." He pulled his weapon from the waistband of his pants and walked over to where the five men lay on the damp ground. Turning his back on the women, he bent down and checked the men's bindings again.

While Mayla moved between the groups speaking to them she kept glancing southward, looking for Jamie and the Lexicon. She became aware of a faint humming coming from behind her. It grew louder. Scanning the night sky, Mayla wondered how Jamie could miss the fires. *Why is Jamie bringing the Lexicon in from the east?*

The night sky blazed with sudden light and the ground near the bound men exploded. Kalen drew his weapon, covering their prisoners while searching for the source of the attack, but the women's terrified screams made it impossible to hear.

A flyer leapt out of the darkness, its weapons blazed, strafing the ground, and passing so low anyone in its path flattened on the ground.

Mayla dove to her left, rolled and came up on one knee. Her weapon pinged in rapid succession, blasting the retreating ship's underbelly, but without success. The flyer melted into the darkness.

Kalen regained his feet and raced to cover the women cowering in a knot near the burning pieces of wreckage. "Get away from the fire!"

The women stared at him.

He yanked two of them out of the firelight, then the others scrambled to follow. Regina herded the women farther away from the fires. Mayla and Kalen turned in time to see the flyer's silhouette appear in the northern sky and dive toward the bound men. They raced to cover them, but the flyer's weapons pinged before they could reach their prisoners. Two of the men managed to roll away, but the other three were too slow. Their broken bodies flew through the air.

Mayla fired, then dove out of the way. "That looks like Skylar's flyer!"

"It is and I think he's been taking lessons from Jenna!" Kalen released a half-dozen energy bolts, but missed. Skylar's flyer turned in a tight arc and dove again. Mayla and Kalen fired, flattening on the ground. The flyer passed low enough, Kalen could feel the pressure of the anti-grav wave. By the time they regained their footing, Skylar's ship had disappeared in the darkness.

Kalen examined the surviving men and found one wounded, but the other untouched. He searched the night sky. "Come on, Jamie, where are you?" He took Mayla's weapon and covered her while she examined the wounded man. He scanned the sky and spotted the flyer in another dive. "Mayla, look out! Skylar's making another run!"

Chapter 35
Homeward Bound

Skylar's flyer dove at a steep angle. Unmistakable above the women's screams, the whine of its approach rent the air. Bursts from the flyer's pulsars tore the ground open. Kalen stood firm, blasting the ship amidst the storm of dirt and rocks filling the air around him. Fire raced across the flyer's bow and pieces of the skin disappeared. Skylar leveled out, made another tight climbing turn. At the top of his arc, he dove again. This time Kalen held his fire, waiting until the ship passed overhead. He fell backwards and fired both weapons at the flyer's belly, blowing a large hole in the ship's underside. The vessel bucked and twisted. From behind Kalen, additional pulsar fire slammed into the ship.

Skylar veered away and flew north.

The Lexicon streaked overhead and took up the chase.

The night sky filled with the light of multiple energy bursts. Kalen turned his attention to Mayla. "Are you all right?"

"I'm good."

"What about our prisoners?"

She finished her exam and looked up at him. "This one's dead, too."

Kalen yanked the uninjured man to his feet. "Looks like Skylar decided you and your friends are expendable."

The prisoner remained silent, fear and confusion filling his eyes. Pulling away from Kalen, he stared off in the direction of the midair battle. Kalen shoved him toward the fires while tracking the flashes of the Lexicon's weapons. The firing stopped, and a few seconds later a fireball lit the landscape. *I hope that was Skylar.*

Regina ran toward him, pointing. "It's coming back!"

227

His prisoner dove for cover when Kalen turned and aimed. He grinned and lowered his weapons. "It's okay, they're with us."

The Lexicon passed overhead, then stopped, hovering south of the wreckage.

Mayla took the comm from Kalen and keyed it. "Jamie."

"Where are you?"

Kalen and Mayla stepped closer to a piece of burning wreckage. "Fifty meters to your left."

Jamie swung around and moved closer. The passenger wing door rose, and Mandi leaned out. "It's good to see you two alive."

"It's good to be alive." Mayla moved closer to the flyer. "How is your arm?"

"It's just a gash. I'll be all right."

"Where are Eli and Al?"

"They're down with the task force." Jamie grinned. "They're closing up the can of crawlers we opened." He glanced at the smoldering wreckage. "What happened here?"

"We'll explain later," Mayla said. "Are the authorities sending transports for these women?"

"I called for them myself." Mandi craned her neck to get a better view of the women returning to the fires. "They're coming from Solana, should be here in two hours."

"Mandi, as the only official here," Kalen pushed their prisoner toward Mandi. "You should take charge of him."

"You managed to capture one of them?" Mandi arched her eyebrows. "Lieutenant Castellano won't be able to complain now."

Mayla pointed to the four bodies. "We had five, but Skylar managed to kill those four before you arrived and chased him away."

"He won't be killing anyone else." Jamie pointed to Mandi. "She saw to that. Looks like you two will have to wait awhile to take a bath." Jamie waved them away. "I'd better set this down."

Mayla and Kalen stepped back while Jamie landed the Lexicon. "Kalen, can you keep an eye on the prisoner?" Mandi climbed out of the Lexicon. "I want to talk with the victims."

"Sure, you won't cause any trouble, will you?"

The man shook his head and dropped, butt-first on the ground.

"Mayla, help me?"

"Sure." The two women walked away, stopping at the closest group of women gathering around the fires for warmth.

Jamie looked around. "Where did you find them, and what the heck happened up here? I thought we were having a quake!"

"We found them in a cavern a little way southeast of here." Kalen handed one of the pistols to Jamie. "Take this, you might need it if that guy causes any trouble. We should have a lot of company soon. Every geo-survey team south of Crystal Lake will be up to find out what caused the disturbance." He squirmed in his clothes. "I hope those transports show up soon, I do need a bath."

They waited for over two hours before Eli and Al showed up ahead of the transports. Eli pulled Mayla, Kalen, and Jamie aside. "I want the three of you out of here and take Mandi with you. I don't know how I'll explain all of this. Not being part of the task force, I am way out of my jurisdiction."

"Eli, are you sure we can't help?"

"Jamie, if I need anything, I'll contact you."

Mandi joined the group, her prisoner in tow. "I should stay."

"No. I asked you to get involved. If there's any fallout from this little dust-up, I don't want your job in jeopardy."

"But you'll need my report."

"And I expect you to make one. I don't want you here when Lieutenant Castellano arrives. I'll take the heat for this. After things settle down, I'll make sure we include your involvement."

"Are you sure I shouldn't stay?"

"Yes." Eli gave Jamie a push toward the flyer. "Right now, I want the four of you to take that fancy rig and get out of here."

Jamie, Kalen, and Mayla shook hands with Eli. Al took charge of the prisoner, and the foursome headed for the Lexicon.

"Kalen, do you want to take over?" Jamie said.

"I don't have the strength to hold the yoke." He raised his hand, and shook his head. "If you're not too tired, you can fly us home."

Jamie grinned. "I'm never too tired for that."

The women climbed into the back and Kalen dropped into the front passenger seat. Jamie took the flyer straight up and headed west.

"You'd better veer north for a bit." Mandi leaned forward between the seats. "We don't want to run into those transports or their escorts. One of them might be Lieutenant Castellano, and he'll demand we stop so he can check us out."

"Good idea." Jamie turned the flyer north and increased their speed. He held the course for ten minutes than resumed the westward heading.

Through half-closed eyes, Kalen watched his future brother-in-law pilot the Lexicon, smiling every time Jamie nudged the speed up when he thought no one was looking. He sat up, reached across the console, and engaged the inertia dampers. "Jamie, stop fooling around and open her up!"

A sheepish smile spread across Jamie's face. He increased the power and the flyer shot westward. "Wow! This is really something!" He maneuvered the vehicle, playing with the controls, performing some basic loops and rolls. "Your father did a fantastic job with the power plant, Kalen."

Mayla watched her brother for a few minutes, then said, "Jamie, if you're through being impressed with Kalen's toy, would you mind telling us what happened to you after Kalen and I went swimming?"

"Right. Let's see. Eli and Al managed to rescue those two task force officers we interfered with, and they wanted our heads." Jamie slid the throttle back and set the navigator. "They weren't going to settle for anything less, until Eli told the detectives we sent Al and him after them. They turned Skylar's men over to another RP unit, then came looking for us. When he and Al saw the cruiser burning, they thought we were dead, until he spotted the men running around like a freshly disturbed Kafler colony. The task force has had this area under surveillance for about a month. Eli and Al took cover and called for backup. The task force tried to move in with a small contingent, but they didn't have enough men and the fight turned nasty."

Jamie glanced at the navigator, then continued.

"Eli dropped Al and the two other officers off when he heard from us, and flew north. He found Mandi and me, then got a call for backup. Mandi and I realized you blocked the only outlet and you could float to the top. I knew if you got out of the canyon, you'd come back to look for us, so I left your staff and the comm. I'm glad we returned when we did."

Kalen slid down in his seat. "You were almost too late. Skylar was piloting that flyer and he had a bead on Mayla and me."

"If you hadn't driven him away," Mayla said, "his next shot would have killed us and the women."

"You can thank Mandi." Jamie grinned and hiked his thumb over his shoulder. "She practically cut his flyer in half, the long way."

"No big deal." Mandi shrugged. "Jamie, could you take me to my apartment before you head home?"

"You're not going home." Mayla took hold of Mandi's wounded arm. "You're coming with us. It's been a long day and your arm needs looking after. The last thing you need after a day like this is to sit home alone and worry."

"I really couldn't impose."

"Mandi, don't argue with her." Kalen sat up and turned. "She'll drug you and you'll wake up at the estate anyway."

"I insist, and you are not imposing." Mayla hit Kalen on his shoulder. "Jamie, just take us home."

Jamie adjusted the Lexicon's course.

"Really, I couldn't impose."

Jamie laughed. "I've learned over the years, whether by birth or marriage, you don't argue with a Santiago woman."

"All right, it does hurt." Mandi settled back and closed her eyes. "Thanks, I really didn't want to be alone tonight."

Lake Solana
Santiago Estate

Chapter 36
I Should Explain

"Ah, home at last." Jamie pointed at the light across the lake. "And it only took two hours. Your flyer is fast." Jamie dropped to a lower altitude and let out a long sigh.

"What's wrong?" said Kalen, sitting up. "I hope Catherine is still talking to me."

"What do you mean? Why would she be mad at you?"

"She gets upset when I take chances on a building site. When she finds out what we've been doing she'll go hyper-sonic."

"You don't have to tell her everything, do you?"

Jamie pointed to the back seat then signed, <*You think those two will keep quiet?*>

Kalen rolled his eyes and shook his head. He looked out the side window while they crossed the lake. "Jamie, hover over the water near the shoreline for a moment." Kalen slipped off his boots.

"What? You can't wait to take a shower?"

"No. If I don't get this grit off me now, I'll go crazy. Besides, I don't want to drag all this grime into your mother's clean house."

"Oh, don't worry, none of us will get anywhere near the house." Jamie grinned. "Mother will make us hose off in the courtyard." Jamie hovered five meters from the shoreline.

"I'll take a bath in the lake first." He opened the wing door. "I'll see you later. Please have Zavier bring some towels down." Kalen rolled out of the seat and dropped, feet first, from sight. He hit the water and surfaced in time to see the Lexicon setting down on the edge of the citrus grove. Swimming closer to shore, he stripped off his clothes, and tossed them on a boulder jutting out into the water. By the time Zavier appeared, he had most of the dirt and grime rinsed away.

"Are you about done with your moonlight swim?" Zavier stopped at the shoreline.

"I've rinsed off most of the grime and sand." Kalen stepped out of the water. "Now I'm ready for a long, hot shower."

"What have you four been up to? Jamie said something about you and Mayla taking a mud bath."

"I don't think you want to know." Kalen took a towel from Zavier and wrapped it around himself. He grabbed a second one and dried off.

"Nothing Mayla does would surprise me."

"Don't bet on it." He slipped into the robe Zavier brought, then gathered up his wet clothes. "Thanks." Heading up to the house, Kalen remained quiet, waiting for Zavier to ask the obvious question.

"All right, Kalen, out with it. What did my sister do I wouldn't believe?"

"Okay, but don't say I didn't warn you." The men headed for the mansion, and Kalen gave Zavier a detailed explanation of what the last two days had turned into. When he got to the part about Mayla jumping in the muddy waters after him, Zavier stopped short.

"I can't believe she did that!"

"I said you really didn't want to know. Imagine my shock I felt my hand grabbed. I was yanked back to the surface and found myself staring at her."

Zavier paused at the gate to the courtyard. "You'd have jumped in after her, wouldn't you?"

"Yeah, I'd have done the same thing."

"So, she's not the only crazy one in this relationship?"

"No, I'd have to go after her. I can't imagine my life without her." He changed the subject. "How's Catherine? Jamie seemed worried about her reaction to our little adventure."

"If I were you, I might want to avoid your future sister-in-law for a day or two."

"Is she really upset?" Kalen pushed the courtyard gate open and looked up at Zavier.

"You don't know Catherine very well yet." Zavier laughed. "Let's just say, my little brother is going to be treading lightly for a few days."

"Maybe I should talk to her. After all, Jamie followed my suggestion."

"Go right ahead," Zavier said, shrugging his shoulders. "After all, it's your funeral."

They crossed the courtyard. Reaching the front door, Kalen hesitated. "Is she really upset?"

"Go talk to her and find out."

"Maybe I will wait a couple of days."

"Wise decision, brother." Zavier patted him on the back. "Wise decision."

Since Jamie and Catherine's room was on the second level, he could avoid running into her. Kalen made his way to his room, took a long, hot shower, and settled in for the night.

Chapter 37
Unwanted Meeting

Light streamed through the window of the bedroom Dani and Carmen, her best friend, shared, adding to the bright mood the two girls were in already. Dani tapped one of the campsites marked on Kalen's map he laid out for them. "I know Kalen has our route planned, east to west, but you're right, Carmen. We should begin farthest from here and work our way toward home."

"Do you think your father will get upset?" Carmen twisted a lock of her hair around her left index finger. "For us making these last minute changes?"

"Don't worry about Papa." She tore her gaze from the map and looked at her friend. "I can't believe we're finally going."

"Yeah, but we're not going anywhere if you don't get moving."

"I could get done a lot faster if you came along."

"Shopping for camping gear is sooooo boring. "The petite brunette giggled. "Besides I already helped. I placed most of the order online, didn't I?" Carmen glanced over at the time. She bolted upright and pointed at the chronometer on the dresser. "Dani, get moving. You still need to pick up your clothes, buy the rest of the equipment, and get back here, so Kalen can check everything out before we pack and leave in the morning."

"Oh gimmish, it's almost midday. How did it get so late?" She grabbed Kalen's list, jumped off the bed and flew out the door.

237

Dani handed two pair of monoculars, as a last-minute addition to the equipment on Kalen's list, to the shop owner. "I think that's all, Mister Sandoval."

"That's a lot of camping gear, Miss Santiago. I appreciate you coming here." Art Sandoval scanned the monocs, adding them to the total. "That'll be fifteen hundred and thirty-seven credits."

"My grandfather and father always tell me to shop with the local merchants." Dani paid for her purchases, scooped up some of her equipment, and headed for the door.

Art followed her out, his arms loaded with the rest of her supplies and gear. He packed it into the cargo compartment of her new flyer and stepped back.

"Thanks, Mister Sandoval."

"You're welcome, Dani. Where are you going to do your exploring?"

A warning voice went off in her head and she remembered Neil's admonition. "My friend and I will be spending our time in the western Verdes around Crystal Lake."

"Really? Make sure you check out the Carlin caves."

"Caves? What are the Carlin Caves?"

"They're at the north end of the lake, in the hillside by Pointer's Cove. You can't miss 'em, the entrance and path are clearly marked. There are some fascinating formations down there. I think you'll enjoy it. My sons and daughters always do."

"Thanks. We'll be sure and check them out."

"Enjoy your trip." Art smiled, stepped away and waved.

Dani lifted off. She flew to the outskirts of the city, landed in the Solana West Inn's parking lot, and sat for a moment, admiring her replacement flyer. She patted the console. "Don't worry, I'll take extra special care of you." She stepped out of the flyer and headed for their specialty shop to pick up clothes they had tailored to fit her.

Entering the store, she inhaled. The scent of new clothes mingled with the aroma drifting in from the inn's restaurant, gave the shop a unique, inviting aroma. She leaned against a circular rack of new blouses and waited while the owner finished with a client. When the customer left, Dani stepped to the counter. "Hi, Gabrielle."

"Hi, Dani. You're here to pick up your clothes, aren't you?"

"Yes. Are they ready?"

"I'm real sorry, Dani, the alterations aren't finished yet. Katy's working on them right now. They should be ready in an hour."

"All right. I'll be in the restaurant, having my midday. I'll come back in an hour."

About to key in the payment for her meal, the hair on the back of Dani's neck prickled. She looked around for the reason and spotted Abel and Georgina approaching. *What are they doing here?* Inserting her iden-disc in the receiver, she tried to punch in her payment and stand, but the couple reached her table before she could complete the transaction. *I'm not in the mood to put up with their antics.*

"Dani, how good to see you," Abel said, an insincere smile plastered on his face.

In spite of her feelings, she suppressed her anger, and remained civil. "Aunt Georgina, Uncle Abel, this is uh...a surprise."

"We were hoping to find you here." Georgina moved closer and patted her arm.

"Really. How did you know I would be at the inn?"

"I know you buy some of your clothes here, Dani." Georgina's mouth pulled into one of her cheerless smiles. "They have styles and sizes to fit those long legs of yours."

Without being asked, Abel pulled out a chair for Georgina and they sat down.

"Why did you come looking for me?"

"We have something important to share with–"

"Abel, my love." Georgina said, touching Abel's arm. "Before we get into all the boring stuff, I simply must use the facilities." She stood and looked at Dani. "Daniella, would you mind?"

Dani pinched her lips between her teeth to keep from being rude. She stood, and dropped her shoulder bag on the table.

"Abel, be a dear and order us some drinks. Mind you, nothing too strong for our niece. We wouldn't want Lilianna and Zavier upset with us."

"Of course, my love."

Dani clamped her jaw tight to keep from gagging. Following behind Georgina, they headed toward the back of the restaurant to the lavatory. She wagged her head and said under her breath, "Abel my love, I simply must use the facilities." *Gimmish, I hope I don't throw up.* Dani waited, making sure her foot tapping echoed off the tile walls while her aunt relieved herself.

Georgina washed her hands, fussed with her makeup, and primped. "I do so admire you. Living outdoors is so crude. Tell me, Dani, where are you and your friend going on this grand adventure?"

The hair on the back of Dani's neck prickled again. *I have no use for the way she walks around with her nose in the air. Or the way she treats my family.* "Carmen and I decided to spend the first few cycles up around Crystal Lake."

Georgina finished with her makeup, turned and smiled at Dani. "Really? I heard Kalen laid out an itinerary for the Barrera wilds. Horrid place."

How does she know where we're going? Dani tried not to stare at Georgina. *She and Abel weren't around when Kalen gave me the maps and travel schedules.* "We changed our minds. Being in the Barreras leaves us too close to home and I'm afraid Papa will come and check on us."

"Oh, my dear, your father isn't that bad." Georgina laughed. "He wouldn't do that, would he?"

Dani turned away and washed her hands so she wouldn't have to look at her aunt. "You really don't know my father at all, do you?"

The muscles in Georgina's face tensed.

I guess you do. He doesn't like you either.

"We should get back to Abel." Georgina gave Dani a quick sideways glance. "He'll be wondering what has become of us."

Returning to the table, Dani saw Abel had their drinks ordered. Georgina took her seat.

"Please, join us, Dani," said Abel.

Dani reached for her shoulder bag and realized it had been moved. She remained standing and shook her head. "I really don't have time to talk, Uncle Abel. My clothes are ready and I need to pick them up. I have to get back so Carmen and I can finish packing."

Abel looked at Georgina, his eyes pleading for help.

"Please, Dani. We only need a few minutes." Georgina patted the table top.

"No. I don't want to talk with either of you. I know what Abel did to Kalen and I willingly gave him my blood."

Abel's face clouded over. His mask of civility cracked, and he glared at her.

"Yes, Uncle Abel, he is part of our family. I heard you tell grandfather you're not anymore, so stop pretending."

Abel shot up from his seat. "You sit down right now, and don't speak to us in that tone of voice!"

"Don't let her upset you, dear." Georgina put her hand on Abel's arm. "She is just a spoiled, petulant child."

"I'm not a child anymore!" Dani calmed herself, took a deep breath and said, "I don't have to do as you tell me. If you're upset that I'm being rude, why not have a long chat with my father. In fact, I'll tell him you came to see me."

Abel blanched and dropped into his seat.

Dani turned and left Abel with his mouth hanging open. *I'll have to tell Papa everything, including what Georgina knows.* She made her way through the restaurant. *I shouldn't have been so abrupt.* Outside, Dani stopped near the entrance and leaned against a column. *I wonder what they wanted.* She took a deep breath and shook her head. *No telling. Not worth worrying about.*

She closed her eyes and centered herself. *Thank you, Aunt Mayla. This really helps.* Dani returned to the clothier, picked up her outfits, and headed to her flyer. Weaving her way through the cluster of cruisers, she pulled up short, and stared. Georgina stood next to her flyer waiting for her. Dani activated her remote and the rear hatch popped up. She riveted her gaze on the equipment and said, "Aunt Georgina, I'm really not in the mood to talk."

"Then get in the mood." She leaned in close. "I don't like the way you spoke to your uncle."

"You don't like?" Dani laid her purchases out on top of the equipment, and slammed the hatch closed. She turned and glared at her aunt. "You don't like? I don't like the way you treat my family. I don't like my uncle trying to kill someone we all love. I don't like you and I don't have to listen to either of you!"

Footsteps behind Dani caught her attention. Two women took up positions, close to her, preventing Dani from getting into her vehicle. A chill ran through her entire body. "What do you want, Aunt Georgina?" Daniella heard the familiar sound of Connor's flyer before Georgina could answer. She looked around, spotted him, and let out a sigh.

He landed a few spaces over and jumped out of his vehicle. "Dani, I'm glad I caught you before you left." He looked at the three women and asked, "Is everything all right?"

"Hi, Connor, I'm glad to see you." Dani stepped away from Georgina. She hooked her arm in his and glared at her aunt. "Everything is fine. My aunt was just....*leaving.*"

Georgina backed away, turned, and made a beeline toward the inn. The other women took off in different directions.

"Who was that?" Connor pulled Dani closer. "What did she want?"

"That," Dani said, pointing toward the inn, "is my Uncle Abel's wife, Georgina. She's angry because of the way I treated my uncle."

"What about the other women?"

"I don't know. Don't worry about it. What's up?"

"Have you had your midday yet?"

"I just finished, why?"

"Cal is sending me up to Erias. I thought you might let me treat you before I left. "

"My meal was interrupted." Dani hugged his arm. "I haven't had dessert, yet."

Connor wrapped his arm around her waist. "What did you have in mind?" He grinned.

"Connor!" She pushed him away, shook her head, and took his hand. "You can treat me to a large slice of Verdes Chocolate Supreme." *I'll have time to find out if Abel put something in my bag.*

Lake Solana
Santiago Estate

Chapter 38
Letting Go

Eyes, revealed by *a mask of light amid the black night, disappeared. They reappeared, but they had changed shape and color.*

Eyes. Two strange pairs, yet both somehow familiar.

Eyes, staring, appalled by the destruction one moment, taking pleasure in the blaze the next.

Eyes, changing color, moving from shadow to light.

A face half seen.

The silhouette morphed in size and shape, became grotesque, shimmering in the dancing firelight. Between him and the nightmarish creature a chasm opened, seething with blistering hatred. The ground under him tilted upward. He slid toward the abyss' gaping maw. The grotesque silhouette moved closer, grinned, and entered the light. The face—he could almost—

Kalen bolted upright, swallowing his last scream before it escaped his throat. Soaked in sweat, he untangled himself from the bed covers, sat up, and tried to catch his breath. When his panting slowed, he listened. The house remained quiet. *I haven't awakened anyone.*

He squeezed his eyes shut and tried to retain the bloated, grotesque image in his mind. He couldn't tell if it belonged to a man or a woman or if it were human at all. The harder he tried to match the silhouette to anything familiar, the more vague and unrecognizable it became. Now the eyes looked different and their color shifted.

A soft knock sounded on his door.

Kalen stood, grabbed one of his twisted covers, shook it out, and then wrapped himself in it. He padded across the room and tapped the activation panel. The door slid open and he stared into the concern-filled face of his fiancée. "Mayla, what are you doing up at this hour?"

"I'm worried about you." Mayla stepped into the room and tapped the panel. When the door closed, she stepped closer and took his hand. "I know you haven't been sleeping."

He stepped away from the door. "How did you know?"

"I've heard your screams three times tonight alone." Mayla reached out, took his hands, and squeezed.

When he realized he had awakened the household, he rubbed the back of his neck and stared at the floor. "I'm sorry. I thought I muffled them."

"Not really. I came here to see what I can do."

"I appreciate that, sweetheart." He looked down at himself. "I wouldn't want to explain to your parents what you're doing in my room at this hour."

Mayla released his hand and put her arms around his neck, "No one will question my being here. They know I'm concerned. Mi amor, tell me about your dreams."

He shuddered, removed her hands from his neck and turned way. *How can I share the madness of my nightmares with her?*

Life whirled around him at a dizzying pace. An uncertain future lay ahead, but the past made his heart ache and threatened to shatter his resolve to move forward. He felt torn, afraid of betraying what was, by embracing what could be. In difficult times like this he would have turned to his father for help in working through any problem. He missed Russell and tried to recall some of his wisdom. Right now, though, he couldn't remember anything his father might have said to guide him on this night.

Mayla crossed the room and settled on the bed.

He stared into the moonlight streaking through the window. Then, echoing in his mind as if his mother sat next to him, he heard Alannah's voice. *"Son, don't go wasting your existence grieving for me. You've a lifetime ahead of you and many things that need doing. Let go of the past."*

Kalen squeezed his eyes shut, brought Jancee's face into focus, and for one final moment he felt her with him. He stood staring upward, suspended in the moment. Time seemed to freeze. Then her face faded into the recesses of his mind. *Goodbye, Jancee.*

"Kalen, are you all right?"

He turned and faced Mayla. "I'm sorry, what were you saying?"

"I asked you what you were thinking about." She lowered her voice.

"Where did you go?"

Kalen rubbed his eyes. "Off fleece-gathering I'm afraid. Sorry."

"Tell me where you went just now." Mayla took hold of his hand.

For a moment Kalen wondered how she would react if she knew Jancee remained in his thoughts. He released Mayla's hand, took a deep breath and stepped back. "The eyes in my dreams have returned."

"The same way as before?" Mayla sat up straight.

"The same."

"Come, sit down." She patted the bed next to her. "Are there any changes?"

"Some, but they don't make sense." He shook his head and started to pace.

"What are they?" She leaned forward. "The details can be important."

"The shadow of the person I see grows more grotesque with every dream. Now it looks hunch-backed, as if it's not human at all. Then there are the eyes. They change shape and color."

"Do you still see the fire pit?"

"Yeah, that hasn't changed."

Mayla pinched her lower lip between her teeth, then said, "Kalen, who hated you so much they'd kill your father and wife and frame you for their murders?"

"I can only think of one man and he's dead."

"Are you sure?"

He nodded, fell silent, and continued to pace.

"Kalen, talk to me, please." Mayla reached out to him. "Who was this person?"

He stopped and let out a deep sigh. "Remember up at Half Moon

Richard R Draude

Canyon, when I told you how Jancee and I met. You said you thought that there was more to the story?"

"Of course I do."

"After Jancee and I were married two months, the company I worked for won a contract to engineer raw land north of Crystal Lake. I still had half a cycle to wait before the job started. Jancee and I grabbed the opportunity to get away. Dad was off with some other geologists, so I called Cal and borrowed his flyer.

Kalen slid under the covers and spooned Jancee.

She reached up, took hold of his hand and pulled it over her stomach. "Thanks for takin' the time off ta come up here, Luv. I do so love this place." Kalen slid back and she rolled over to face him. "Kalen, I want ta start—"

Jancee's eyes opened wide with fear. "Carlos!"

Kalen tried to turn, but someone dragged him feet first out of the tent, yanked him to his feet and drove a fist deep into his gut. His breath burst from his lungs. He retched and screamed in pain. His knees buckled and he doubled over, but never hit the ground. Someone yanked him upright.

"You're drunk, Carlos! The three of ya!" Jancee screamed. "Stop it! Leave Kalen alone!"

Kalen saw Carlos restraining Jancee in a choke-hold, and struggled to free himself, but a third man hit him again. She screamed and twisted, while the third man proceeded to pummel him, alternating between his face and gut.

"This'll teach ya ta screw up my life, MacKenna." Carlos yelled, "Hit 'em in the jewels, Danny, in-the-jewels!"

Danny laughed and drove a vicious blow into Kalen's groin. The world and Jancee disappeared.

Kalen clawed his way toward consciousness, the rising sun at his back. Rolling over he faced the warmth, forced his eyes open, and tried to stand. His body screamed in protest, and his legs refused to support him. On his belly, he clawed his way toward the stream. The sun had moved higher in the sky by the time he reached the water. Washing the dirt and dried blood from his face, Kalen quenched his thirst, and then forced himself into a sitting position.

Despite his muscles' firm objections, Kalen struggled to his feet and staggered back to their campsite. He pulled out two meal bars, crammed

246

one into his mouth, grabbed his staff, a water container, and the flyer's remote. Stopping at the stream he took another drink, refilled the container, then headed to the flyer he had borrowed from Cal. Reaching the vehicle, he could see where someone attempted to tamper with the flyer's locks. They'd never pry the code from Jancee. "I'm coming, Luv."

Kalen lifted off and followed the trail of destroyed vegetation the drunks' cruiser left behind. He crisscrossed the land searching for their trail on the hard rock surface. The sun stood almost overhead when he spotted a cruiser parked above a shallow canyon less than ten kilometers from his and Jancee's campsite. He set down among the same rocks, grabbed his staff and snuck up on the cruiser. The vehicle sat there wide open. Leaning in, Kalen reached under the forward console, yanked three wire harnesses loose and then attempted to start the cruiser, nothing happened. He worked his way among the rocks until he reached the campsite. Out of sight of the men, he listened to his enemy's rant.

Carlos paced with long, exaggerated strides. "—and with Mackenna out of the way, Jancee will give me a chance to show her how I feel."

Kalen couldn't believe what he was hearing. "Carlos, you're a dozen circuits short of a hyper drive."

Danny, the man who had beaten him, said, "We should go back and hide MacKenna's body. His Da is sure ta come lookin' for him."

"Cal will come up for sure," the third man said.

"Danny, Miguel, shut up! Leave MacKenna where he is. Let the wolves take care of him."

"Hey, Carlos, bring Jancee out to join the party." Carlos' companions laughed.

"Why not, Miguel? She might as well get used to us."

Carlos turned, stepped behind a rock and disappeared into a opening in the cliff face. Kalen held his breath when he heard Jancee scream. "Get your bloody hands offa me, ya crazy bastard!"

The sound of fear in her voice erased all Kalen's pain. He stepped out from his hiding place and moved up behind the two men.

Danny turned and his mouth dropped open.

Kalen hit him in the jaw with the heavy end of his staff and felt bone crunch. Danny flew backwards and landed hard, spitting blood and teeth.

Miguel turned at the sound.

Kalen drove the narrow end of his staff into the dark-haired man's abdomen, trying to push it through him. When Miguel doubled over,

Richard R Draude

Kalen slammed his staff into Miguel's head. Miguel hit the ground and didn't move.

"Kalen!"

Kalen spun and faced Jancee and his enemy.

Carlos held her in a tight choke-hold. "Why couldn't you just have died, Mackenna!"

"It's over! Let my wife go, Carlos."

Jancee struggled, but couldn't break his hold.

"No, it's not. If I can't have her, no one will!"

Kalen took a step toward them.

"Come any closer, MacKenna, and I break her neck!" Carlos looked around, then backed toward the trail leading up to his cruiser.

Kalen kept pace, but didn't close the gap. The path rose with a rock wall to Kalen's left and the sheer drop-off to his right. "Let her go, you can't get away."

"Stop where you are, MacKenna, or I swear I will push her over the side." Carlos looked behind himself.

Kalen scooped a rock from the ground and looked into Jancee's eyes.

She nodded, and then pushed backwards.

Carlos loosened his grip to keep his balance and Jancee broke his hold.

She dropped to her knees and Kalen let the rock fly, hitting Carlos in the center of his forehead.

He screamed, fell backwards, slipped between the rocks, but grabbed Jancee's right ankle and dragged her with him.

"Kalen!" Jancee cried out.

Kalen bounded forward and Jancee grabbed his staff. It jammed across the opening, stopping their fall. Kalen jumped over his wife and tried to drag Carlos to safety. "Give me your free hand and I'll pull you up."

"To hell with you, MacKenna!" Carlos bounced and twisted, making Jancee scream. "I'm taking her with me."

"Wanna bet?" Kalen reared his right foot back, then jammed the heel of his boot square in the center of Carlos' face.

Carlos screamed, lost his hold on Jancee's ankle and disappeared.

Kalen scrambled over the rocks and pulled his wife to her feet. "It's over, Jancee. He's gone." He wrapped his arms around her and stroked her long, red hair while she sobbed into his shoulder.

When she calmed down he started toward, the flyer and came face-to-face with Miguel. He pushed Jancee behind him, ready to fight.

"Where's Carlos?"

"He took a nose dive." Kalen pointed to the opening between the rocks. "It's over for all of you."

"You're crazy, MacKenna." He pushed past them, leaving his friend in the ravine, bleeding."

Kalen ignored Miguel and Danny, led Jancee to their flyer and called the Roving Patrol.

While they waited, he took water from the flyer and attempted to bathe Jancee's face.

"No Kalen, let the RPs see what they did ta me."

"What happened to the men and Carlos?" Mayla said.

"Two rangers arrived ten minutes after I placed the call. One of them grabbed Miguel, while he tried to fix his disabled vehicle. They took one look at us, then Danny, and called in a medical team. While we waited, we told them our story. Miguel tried to convince the patrol I started the trouble, but the two officers weren't buying his story, not with Jancee standing right there, all bruised and calling them bold-faced liars. I led them to where Carlos went over the side. We scanned the area, but couldn't find any trace of him. Jancee and I filed a complaint and the RPs issued a warrant for his arrest on charges of kidnapping, assault, attempted rape, and attempted murder. The medical team treated Danny, then Jancee and me. The Roving Patrol officers followed us back to our campsite to check out the rest of our story.

"Carlos' brutality shattered Jancee." Kalen turned and faced Mayla. "We stayed up there trying to recover a little before we went home. I didn't count on Dad getting concerned when we didn't return on time. He called Cal and the next day they came looking for us. Dad took one look at the damage done to us and went hyper- sonic. He knew assistant council member Farren, Carlos' father. Dad had Cal take us home, while he flew to Mesa Verde to have it out with Shay Farren."

"How was Jancee after that?"

"Different. I've never seen anyone so frightened and withdrawn. About two months after it happened, I suggested a trip up to the meadow. She said she couldn't go back there right away, but she did want to get away, so I took her to Half Moon Canyon. She spent the first night apprehensive and jittery, any noise sent her into a full- blown panic. I told her we could go home, but she insisted we stay. We spent two more days camping. On our last night we lay together, looking up at the stars until she drifted off and remained asleep all night. I think it helped, but I was never sure. When we returned home, she grew sullen. I needed to return to work so I took her to stay with her parents. After we testified at Carlos' trial, I thought she would recover, but I think she held a lot back."

"How did Carlos survive the fall? Where did the RPs find him?"

"He survived because he fell onto a ledge a few meters below the cliff. With the alert put out, he didn't get far. The RPs picked him upon the road leading to Foxdown Pass."

Mayla tapped her lower lip with her index finger. "You and your father have had similar experiences with your wives."

"I'm not sure I follow you?"

"Both of you married women who had other men wanting to possess them. Alannah had my uncle and Jancee had Carlos. Though under different circumstances, both men tried to kill their rivals and both failed. Both women died before their time."

The similarities had never occurred to him. Kalen drew Mayla close and kissed her. When their lips parted, he asked, "I don't have to worry about some rival coming from Wyndimere to try and claim you, do I?"

"I already told you, Uncle Neil kept me so busy with training, I had little time left for a social life." Mayla kissed him again. "Besides, mi novio, you have no rivals."

"That's good to know."

"Kalen, after the trial, what happened to Carlos?"

"Shay Farren hired a doctor who convinced the judge of Carlos' mental instability and his need of psychiatric help. The court sentenced him to a mental facility on Selwyn. He died while trying to escape. After his death Shay Farren cornered my father and blamed me for Carlos' death. Dad told me Shay was pretty torn up."

"And you can't think of anyone else who might have wanted your father dead?"

"No one else comes to mind. If I could only identify the eyes in my dreams."

"Try and let it go. The more you concentrate on them, the harder it will be to find an answer."

"If there is an answer. Maybe it's just my imagination. Maybe I'm suffering from post-stasis paranoia."

Mayla turned Kalen's face so they were eye-to-eye. "Kalen, you're not crazy! You saw something that night. Something your subconscious mind is trying to help you recall, but your conscious mind refuses to acknowledge. When we find the answers, you'd better be prepared for it."

"Now you sound similar to that vid of my mother. Don't tell me you're starting to believe that!"

"What I said had nothing to do with that vid. I've done some research. When someone has a recurring, vivid dream like yours, the conscious mind is usually trying to block the truth because it's too unbelievable or too painful."

"I hadn't thought of that." Kalen thought about it and nodded. "I guess you're right."

"Of course I am."

Kalen laughed and realized in spite of all their time together, he knew so little about this incredible woman. He couldn't bear the thought of another loss, but he also knew he could not endure living without her. The thought of facing his future without Mayla caused him to cringe, as if from some actual, physical pain.

He still scoffed at the idea of some unseen force reaching out to touch Shannan's mother and forewarn of future danger through her. But it didn't matter now whether he believed it or not, many others did. He had two choices. Run and hide, or face up to the challenge. With Cal's gift, he could take Mayla, disappear and live out of public attention. He thought about that prospect and for a brief moment found it attractive. Then his father's words intruded into his thoughts. *'Kalen, a MacKenna doesn't run from trouble, we stand and face up to it.'* Besides, he knew Mayla would never stand for living her life in hiding. Kalen touched the scar on his side.

But, they can sure cause it. What a grand mess you made of things, Martin MacKenna! All this trouble and pain you caused both of our families. All because you refused to swallow your stubborn pride.

Then Mayla snuggled closer and the irony of the whole situation hit him.

Richard R Draude

It is because you're so obstinate, Martin MacKenna, that I have these people to stand by me now. I love you, in spite of your pride.

Kalen held Mayla at arm's length. "I just thought of something. In spite of what my grandfather did, I'm grateful it happened."

"You're glad your grandfather insulted my family?"

"No, Mayla, I wish he hadn't been so cruel, but if he hadn't, I would be all alone right now, struggling to stay alive. I might even be dead, and the whole plot to sterilize Arrisian males would be going on right now. Because of him, I have your family standing with me, and you to share a future with. Otherwise, I wouldn't have a future, at least not one I am willing to contemplate."

"You mean you think all this was all meant to happen?"

"I–I guess when you look at the whole picture." Kalen blinked and stared at Mayla. "It does sorta look that way, doesn't it?"

"Now that puts Shannan's mother's experience in a different light." Mayla arched her eyebrows and gave him a coy smile.

"Well—yes, I guess it does. So what do we do about it?"

"We can go over it in the morning. Right now, I would appreciate it if my fiancé would pay a little more attention to me."

Kalen drew her close and kissed her. "Whatever Milady desires."

They lingered in each other's arms until the chirps and buzz of night critters ceased with a sudden finality. The quiet became profound, and a chill raced up Kalen's back.

Lake Solana
Santiago Estate
First Light

Chapter 39
Sneak Attack

Kalen stepped to the window and leaned out, staring at the citrus grove south of the estate.

Mayla came and stood beside him. "Kalen, what's wrong?"

He put his finger to his lips, closed his eyes and concentrated. *There's someone at the near edge of the grove.* The muffled sounds played another chorus on his nerves. *I don't like this.*

"Kalen, what is it?"

He pulled her close and whispered, "We've got company. Wake everyone. Tell Cal to meet me near the courtyard gate."

"Are you sure?"

"Yes. Whoever is out there doesn't want us to know." Mayla kissed his cheek and slipped out of the room.

Kalen dressed, and grabbed his staff. Leaving the room, he raced to the front door and slipped outside. Moving along the west porch, he made it to the gate without tripping the light sensors, and waited in the shadows, listening for movement. A minute later, hurried footsteps came up behind him, and Cal appeared at his side.

"What's going on?" He pressed a pistol into Kalen's hand. Cal had his weapon in one hand and his staff in the other.

Kalen peered into the darkness. "I'm not sure, but there's someone's out there and I don't think they're here for a friendly visit."

The breeze dropped off, and the stillness intensified the silence. Sweat ran down the sides of his face and Kalen held his breath. A dull pop sounded from the grove, then behind them a flash shattered the darkness. The explosion tore through the roof of the east wing. A second explosion ripped a crater in the courtyard. The concussion knocked Kalen and Cal to the ground. Silence from the house confirmed Mayla had already alerted the family.

Half a dozen figures dressed in black clothing bolted from among the citrus trees.

Kalen and Cal scrambled to their feet.

"They're launching the explosives from the orchard," Kalen said. "Should we go after them?"

"No." Cal fired at a black-clothed figure. "That will leave this way wide open. On your left."

Kalen fired, taking out the attacker closest to him. Cal and Kalen both fired and two attackers screamed in unison. Four more attackers rushed out of the trees.

Waiting until the assailants were on top of him, Kalen stepped out of the shadows, swung his staff and caught the nearest aggressor in the side. The person screamed and crumpled to the ground. Another figure, behind the first, raised a weapon.

Cal swung his staff low, sweeping the person's legs out from under their assailant. The weapon discharged, its blast flashed close to Kalen's ear and he recoiled from the heat. The wild shot sent chunks of the block wall flying in all directions. Kalen and Cal dove to the ground. The flying debris took out two attackers close to Kalen.

Cal fired while Kalen scrambled to his feet. "Cal, pull off their masks."

Cal bent over while Kalen provided cover. "They're both women! Kalen, you really pissed Maria off!" Cal fired at another attacker charging across the open land between the gate and the orchard.

"Where are the commander's troops?" Kalen jabbed the tip of his staff into the ground and vaulted into another female. The woman flew backwards and hit the ground. He landed near her, scrambled to his feet, and kicked the stunned woman in her left temple. She grunted and collapsed.

Another explosion rocked the house.

"Kalen, we better get inside." Cal fired at a woman reaching for her pistol, killing her.

"Let's go." Kalen hit the woman at his feet in the head with his staff, turned. and bolted through the gate, Cal on his heels. They raced across the courtyard. At the front door, Kalen skidded to a halt and shoved Cal through the opening. He turned and fired at two figures coming through the courtyard entrance. The attackers dropped and the two friends flooded the gateway with additional weapons' fire. They could not see anyone else in the flashes.

"They'll think twice about rushing through there!" Cal said. "Let's find our families."

"Cal, keep an eye on the gate, while I get everyone together!" "What about the other doors?"

"They're all locked. You'll hear them if they break in. I'll bring everyone down the main staircase, that way you can keep an eye on the gate and cover us."

"Hurry!" Cal fired again. The energy bolts exploding against the outside walls left no doubt the gate was being rushed again.

Turning, Kalen bolted up the stairs, running headlong into Lily and Liana. Quintin came down the dark hallway herding Jamie's children in front of him. Zavier brought up the rear, Shannan and Neela in front of him.

"Kalen, who's attacking us?" Zavier pulled Neela close.

"Maria. Keep an eye out for Jenna and get everyone downstairs. Where's Mayla?"

"She's with Catherine." Liana pointed toward the west wing.

The blasts and flashes grew in frequency and intensity. The children clung to the adults' legs.

"I'll help Cal and clear the way!" Zavier grabbed Kalen's pistol.
"Zavier, be careful!" Lily called to her husband.

"I will." Zavier disappeared down the dark staircase. Kalen hit the light switch in the hall.

Another explosion thundered through the house and part of the ceiling behind them collapsed. The children screamed and hugged Lily's, Quintin's, and Liana's legs tighter.

Lily moved the twins and Sonia in front of her. "Oh gimmish, where's Caesar?"

"I'll find him, Lily." Kalen grabbed Lily to stop her from going to search. "Get everyone else downstairs," he said, shouting over another explosion.

Lily tried to pull away.

Quintin took hold of her arm. "We have to go."

"No! I won't leave without Caesar!" Lily wrenched loose, turned and started into the smoke, but Quintin grabbed her arm and pulled her back. "Lily, Kalen will find him," he said, herding her and the children toward the stairs. When she resisted, Quintin lifted Sonia, grabbed Lily's hand and pulled her after him.

Shannan scooped Kaitlin into her arms, then pushed Neela ahead of her.

"Where's Mandi?" Kalen said.

"We haven't seen her." Shannan called out from the staircase. Liana led Mariah and the other children clinging to her nightgown.

Another explosion shook the upper level. Dust and smoke mingled in the air, making it hard to breathe.

Lily's heart-wrenching calls to Caesar spurred Kalen on. He plunged into the smoke and dust choked hallway, bypassing Catherine and Jamie's room. *I've got to find Caesar first.*

When he reached the junction to the west wing, he could see the night sky through a gaping hole in the roof. He climbed over a pile of rubble. Heading down the hall, he heard Laney's agitated barking and peered into the murk. *That's not coming from Caesar's room.*

He ran into the dust and smoke, heading toward the sound. A dull thump behind him made him pull up short and turn. A woman in dark clothing stood, her back to him, detaching a rope from a rappelling harness. The line went up through the roof. Kalen charged while she was still unaware of him. He swung his staff, and hit her on the side of her head. She went down with a heavy thud. He looked up and spotted another figure descending on a second line. He backed away and waited until her legs were within reach. He stepped out of the shadows and swung the heavy top of his staff with vicious precision at the attacker's right shin. Over the combined noise of another explosion and pulsar fire, he felt the crunch of bone and heard the woman's screams of agony. Swinging at her other leg, his blow shattered the shin bone. She dangled from her rope, screaming.

Three more lines dropped from above.

Kalen took off, following the sound of Laney's barking. Beyond the next pile of rubble, he spotted Mandi, her back to him and her arms wrapped around a beam fallen across the door to Abel and Georgina's bedroom.

At the noise of his approach, Mandi grabbed a smaller timber and spun around.

"Whoa, Mandi, I'm on your side."

She dropped her weapon. "Caesar's trapped in there!"

Kalen leaned his staff against the wall and grabbed the beam.

Another explosion rocked the far side of the house. "What's going on?"

"Remember that little operation we derailed?"

"Yes."

"This is payback! Let's find Caesar and get out of here!" Kalen wrapped his arms around the beam, and together they moved it away. Laney's barking became more agitated.

Kalen grabbed his staff and tried the door, but it would not budge. He leaned back and kicked the door with his foot, to no avail. Caesar screamed and Kalen threw his full weight against the unyielding slab.

"Mandi, on the count of three!"

Counting down together, they reached zero and slammed into the door. The lower part of the center panel shattered. He kicked it out. In the middle of the room he spotted Caesar standing, paralyzed, staring at something out of Kalen's line of sight. He could hear Laney's barking, but he could not see her either.

Scrambling through the opening, Kalen dashed into the room. Laney backed out of a connecting room, barking and growling at the shadow of another person. When he grabbed Caesar, the boy screamed. "Easy, Caesar, it's me, Kalen."

Caesar wrapped his arms around Kalen's neck. "Where's Mommy?"

A dark hooded figure entered the room.

Kalen passed Caesar to Mandi, and Laney circled around behind the officer.

The woman leveled her rifle at Kalen's chest, and shouted, "Where's the girl?"

Kalen raised his arms, his staff still in his right hand. "What girl?"

"Don't get smart with me! I want the Santiago g–"

Laney took two steps and leaped into the air.

The woman screamed in terror and pain when the dog's powerful jaws clamped down on her forearm. Laney's weight knocked the woman off balance and she tumbled to the floor. Her weapon flew from her hands and discharged with a loud crack. The shot went wild, blowing a large hole in the outer wall.

Mandi bolted from the room.

Kalen swung his staff at the aggressor's head and missed. In spite of Laney tearing at her arm, she dodged Kalen's swing and tried to kick his legs out from under him. He jumped over the woman's leg sweep, brought his staff down, hitting her in the center of her forehead. She ceased struggling. "That's the only girl you're getting today! Come on, Laney."

"Kalen! Help!"

He spun and darted back to the door. In the hall, Mandi struggled with a woman, while protecting Caesar. Using his staff as a battering ram he charged, caught the woman in the mid-section and shoved her though the porch door. The panes shattered and glass shards flew over the balcony along with the woman. Kalen made a quick scan of the courtyard. People dressed in black ran across the court-yard toward the front door. He grabbed Mandi's arm and pulled her down the hallway. "Come on, Laney."

The dog followed them down the south wing hallway. When they neared the turn, Kalen glanced over his shoulder and spotted three more black-clothed figures coming after them. He pushed Mandi into a large bedroom used for furniture storage.

Mandi slapped the activator panel. The door slid shut, and Kalen smashed the activator panel with his staff, then reached into the control box and yanked the connection loose, rendering the door inoperative.

Mandi put Caesar down and he burst into tears. She helped Kalen turn a big table on end, and pushed it so it blocked the doorway, then gathered the frightened child in her arms. "It's okay, Caesar, I'll take you to your mother."

He hugged her, but continued to cry.

Kalen ran to the far wall and looked out the window at a scene of complete chaos. He saw Zavier dragging Lily and the twins toward their flyer. Somehow, they got clear of the house. He smashed the window out. "Mandi, I've got to get you and Caesar out this way."

Zavier looked up and pointed.

Kalen cleared the frame of broken glass with his staff and looked below him. He signed to Zavier. <Caesar with us> To the frightened boy, he said, "We have to go out this window, Caesar. You're going to have to be brave."

Caesar nodded, trying to hold back his tears. "Where's Mommy?"

"Mandi is going to take you to her. Mandi, climb out the window and I'll lower you as far as I can. As soon as you hit the ground, I'll lower Caesar to you."

Mandi put Caesar on the floor and climbed into the window opening. Another explosion ripped through the house and she almost lost her balance. Kalen grabbed her arm and steadied her, while Caesar clamped onto his leg. The smell of smoke permeated the air. *The fires are getting worse.*

Someone started banging on the door.

Laney responded with bared teeth and a growl. "Easy girl, stay here."

Kalen grabbed Mandi's wrists. She slipped out the window and climbed down the side of the house. When she yelled, Kalen released her hands and she dropped to the ground, rolled, and stood. Across the room, Kalen saw the door giving way. He grabbed Caesar, thrust the terrified child through the window, lowered the boy as far as he could.

Lily stood next to Mandi.

Kalen released Caesar. The boy screamed and fell into the women's arms.

At the sound of splintering wood, Kalen turned and faced the door. The upper panel shattered and the attackers struggled to move the table aside. The first person cleared the blockage and tried to fire. Laney, out of sight of the woman, leapt into the air and clamped onto her jacket sleeve. She screamed and her weapon pinged, blasting the wall. Kalen turned, raised his staff and charged the door. Catching the second woman off guard, he slammed into her, ramming her backward into the third person.

Another explosion ripped through the wall of the house. The second floor swayed, throwing everyone off balance. Part of the ceiling caved in. The first assailant reached for her weapon. A heavy beam crashed into the center of the room and onto her hand, trapping her.

Kalen ignored her screams of agony, grabbed Laney, and dragged the snarling animal to the window. Outside, he spotted Mandi, with Caesar and Lily, running to the family's flyer. Cal, in the Lexicon, covered their retreat while pulling in close to the house. Kalen turned his attention to the two remaining assailants.

Another explosion ripped the wall open and the women climbed over the debris, weapons raised. "Drop your weapon and tell us where the girl is!" one of them shouted.

Outside the window Kalen could hear the Lexicon's engine. "Anything you want, ladies." He smiled, then dove sideways. The women stared, frozen in place. The Lexicon's pulsars fired, the sound drowning out the women's screams, while obliterating part of the wall. The house groaned. Another section of the roof caved in, filling the room with dust and smoke.

Grabbing Laney's collar, Kalen dragged her close to the window. Turning the flyer around, Cal raised the wing door. He moved the Lexicon into position, and then he called to the dog. Laney leapt into the flyer. Cal grabbed his weapon off the console. "Down!"

Kalen flattened on the floor.

Cal's weapon pinged half a dozen times. "Kalen, get out of there!" Bounding to his feet, Kalen dove through the window. Behind him, weapons' fire blasted the outside wall. Pieces of the house pelted the Lexicon.

Cal dropped to ground level.

Above the sound of the battle Kalen shouted, "Did Mayla get out with Catherine?"

"I haven't seen either of them."

More pulsar blasts hit the Lexicon. Cal spun the ship around and fired at three women shooting at them from the ground, killing two. The other dove for cover behind the house's east wall.

"I have to go back inside. Mayla was helping Catherine. They may still be in there. Take me around to the west wing."

"Hang on!" Cal maneuvered the flyer along the south side of the house, then turned the corner. When they neared the southwest corner, he stopped. "Get on the front."

Kalen grabbed Cal's weapon, jumped out of the Lexicon's wing door and onto the flyer's front deck. "Take her up. I think it's the third window from the corner."

Positioning the flyer under the window, Cal increased the power and hovered below the opening. Kalen gripped the sill and peered into the dark room. Amid the scattered debris he spotted Mayla hovering over Catherine. She looked to be in a great deal of pain. Kalen took a quick look back at Cal and nodded. When he peered into the window again, he spotted Jenna coming into the ruined bedroom, followed by three other women. Jenna remained in the doorway while the other women spread out.

Using hand signals, Kalen directed Cal to reposition the flyer, then signed <Fifteen count then fire>

Cal acknowledged him with a thumbs up.

Kalen started a mental count, turned and fired twice, shattering the window. He sprang off the front of the Lexicon, tumbled over, and came up firing, killing the woman closest to Mayla.

"MacKenna!" Jenna shouted, her eyes wide when she saw him. "Kill him. Forget the girl, kill all of them!" Using one of the injured women as a shield, she fired at Kalen, then bolted from the room.

He sprang to Mayla's side. "We've got to get out of here!" He looked to the doorway and fired again. "I'll help you get Catherine up."

"No, we can't move her, she's in labor."

Jenna's accomplices reentered the room. Kalen fired, finished his mental count, shoved Mayla to the floor, and covered Catherine with his own body.

Cal unleashed the Lexicon's weapons, obliterating the women along with part of the bedroom wall. The whole structure groaned and shook. Loose debris rained down.

Kalen threw off the chunks of plaster, and wood splinters, bolted to the ruined door and checked the hall. In the smoke and dust, he saw Jenna down and dazed, struggling to her feet. It was the first time he had gotten up close to her.

Taking aim, Kalen, took a deep breath. Ready to squeeze the trigger, he froze when she turned and he saw her profile. In the dancing firelight he saw something familiar about her face. *She looks familiar, almost like–*

The house groaned and shook. Smoke from the fires drifted into the room. Kalen blinked to clear his eyes, and the moment passed.

Jenna stumbled and lost her balance.

I've got to get answers. He aimed at her legs and fired. Another tremor shook the house, and he missed.

Jenna jumped, turned, fired at him, then glanced at something off to her right and bolted down the hallway.

Kalen gave chase, fired again and missed.

Chapter 40
Loss is Not an Option

Flames licked the estate's walls and ceilings. The heat, dust, and smoke choked Kalen as he chased Jenna along the west corridor. Flashes of pulsar fire illuminated the thick smoke. Kalen dove into a doorway as three energy bolts slammed into the wall to his left, showering him with plaster and other debris.

Peering out from his cover through the smoke and haze, Kalen saw Jenna stop, hook onto a line extending up through the hole blasted in the roof. Firing twice into the bodies of the women he had disabled, he heard her shout, "Get me outta here!"

You're not getting away this time. He bolted to his feet, raced up the hallway, skidded to a halt, and fired upward at the flyer pulling her through a hole in the roof. Noise from the house's lower level distracted him, causing him to miss his target. Taking cover behind a pile of debris, he fired once, and checked the weapon's power cell. Seventy-eight percent. He prepared to fend off the next wave of attackers.

"Mister MacKenna, stand down," a voice called out.

"Who are you?" Kalen raised his pistol to the ready.

"I'm Lieutenant Commander Cooper. Commander Elano sent us."

"Show yourself." Kalen shifted his position to get a better view of the staircase, and peered over the wreckage. Squinting, he recognized the Marine officer's uniform when a stray air current stirred and thinned the haze.

"Mister MacKenna, we've routed the attackers," the officer said. "Where are Captain Santiago and her sister-in-law? They're the only two still unaccounted for."

A pain-filled moan cut through the din.

"Kalen, Catherine's labor is farther along than I thought. I need help now!"

The urgency in Mayla's voice made Kalen scramble to his feet. He raced toward Catherine and Jamie's room. Over his shoulder he shouted, "Captain Santiago needs medical assistance to help Catherine!"

"You three," the Lieutenant Commander ordered," follow Mister MacKenna. The rest of you get these fires out. We'll have to use this building temporarily."

Kalen skidded to a stop in the room.

Mayla glanced over her shoulder. "Kalen, what is going on?" She stroked Catherine's forehead. "Hang on, Cat."

Smoke and dust poured out of the hole Cal blasted in the outer wall, keeping the air clear around Mayla and Catherine. "Neil's troops arrived, the attach's over. What do we need to do for Catherine?"

"Get my medical equipment. I may have to operate."

"We can't stay here, there's too much smoke and there are fires on this floor."

"Kalen, just get my med kits."

Kalen rushed to the gaping hole in the wall, and waved Cal closer. Leaning through the flyer's open door, he said, "Mayla needs her medical equipment, it's in the rear compartment!"

"Right away." Cal spun the Lexicon a hundred and eighty degrees, backed up to the house and popped open the cargo hatch cover.

Kalen yanked the first case out.

Lieutenant Commander Cooper pulled it from his hand. Removing the remaining cases, other Marines took them from Kalen. When he turned, he saw Mayla arguing with a blonde female officer. Looking closer, he recognized Sandra St. James, his rehab nurse from the prison.

"You can't open her up here, Captain!"

"Then what would you suggest, Lieutenant?"

"We're setting up an emergency hospital in the kitchen." Sandra pointed toward the door. "It's the most stable part of the house. The fires in the south and west wings will be out shortly. It's the only place you can operate on her. The servants' quarters are full. We don't need the children seeing your sister-in-law like this and we don't want them seeing the other wounded. It's the best we can do. It'll be a couple of hours before the men have the temp med center set up."

"How do you propose we get her down there? The child is already in the birth canal. She can't be moved down the stairs, they're too dangerous."

"The Lexicon!" Kalen pointed toward the hole in the wall. "We can use the Lexicon. We'll move her on the mattress and bring her around the side of the house. That hole is big enough."

Mayla glanced at the opening. "Do it! You two, follow me," she ordered the two men holding her equipment cases. Mayla, Sandra and the two Marines hurried out of the room.

Lieutenant Commander Cooper kicked out half a dozen loose blocks from the outer wall, enlarging the hole.

Kalen signaled Cal to move in closer. Following Kalen's hand signals, Cal positioned the Lexicon's nose against the wall.

Cooper signaled two more soldiers to help. "I want her lifted as gently as possible, and make it quick."

The four men lifted Catherine on the mattress, crossed the room, and slid it onto the flyer's front deck.

"Here, sir, cover her with this," one of the Marines said, yanking a small package from a pocket on his pants leg. The soldier tore open the pouch and handed the contents to Kalen. He shook out a survival blanket, stepped out next to Catherine, and spread the cover over her. "Cal, get us to the kitchen door, now!" Kalen turned his attention to Catherine. "We're taking you downstairs so Mayla can help you."

Catherine nodded, grimaced, and let out another weak moan. Her pale, sweaty complexion sent a shiver through his body. "Cal, hurry!"

The ping of pulsar fire and sparks jumping from the Lexicon's roof jarred Kalen. He dropped to his knees and put himself in front of Catherine. "We're being ambushed!" He crouched over Catherine.

Two Marines leaned out and returned fire.

"Sergeant Melendez," Cooper shouted over his comm, "We're taking fire on the west side. We need cover, now. MacKenna!"

Kalen looked over his shoulder and the officer tossed him a pistol. He snatched the weapon out of mid-air, aimed and fired, hitting one woman. The others disappeared around the corner of the house.

"Cal, go!"

Cal dropped the flyer to ground level, while Kalen and the Marines kept the assailants pinned down. Blasts from other weapons lit the southwest corner, forcing the women into the open as Marines on the ground closed in on them.

Using the Lexicon's rear pulsar, Cal fired twice, ending their resistance. Maneuvering along the side of the house, he turned the corner. Out of the line of fire, Kalen returned his full attention to his future sister-in-law. "Take it easy, Catherine, we'll be with Mayla in a few seconds."

No sooner had Cal set the flyer down, then the kitchen doors flew open. The same four soldiers from upstairs, grabbed the mattress and whisked Catherine away. Leaving the flyer, Cal and Kalen entered the kitchen. The lightless room had already been cleaned and readied. Four Marines carried a large power unit in and set it on the floor in the far corner. The operator started the generator and adjusted the transmission frequency. Overhead the lights burst to life. The men transferred Catherine to the table Mayla stood next to. Two of the men dragged the mattress outside.

Lieutenant Saint James attached Mayla's computer probes to Catherine's abdomen. The screen came to life. The officer studied the image, then pulled another man in a naval uniform close and whispered something to him. The man nodded, went to Mayla, busy cleaning up over the sink. Reaching her side, he whispered to her.

Mayla finished scrubbing and went to Catherine. She studied the screen and said, "Thank you, corpsman."

"There's something wrong–," Catherine moaned and clutched at her belly, "–with my baby isn't there?"

"Catherine, you're having twins, and we will have to operate right away." Mayla glanced at the screen of the fetal computer. "The first child is a breech. Sandra, Catherine's too weak to try and turn it.

If I don't get them out, we could lose her and both babies."

"We have to slow her labor down," Sandra said.

"Gentlemen, all non-essential personnel clear the area." Lieutenant Commander Cooper pointed toward the hallway. "On the double, there are wounded to attend to and fires to put out."

The room emptied.

Cal closed the outer doors, then he and Kalen followed the other Marines out of the room, and headed for the courtyard.

Lily and Liana rushed through the gaping hole that used to be the front door. "Kalen, where's Catherine?" Liana said, her face and voice strained.

"Mayla's with her in the kitchen."

Without another word both women hurried away.

"Lily, she's in labor," Kalen said to the women's backs. "Mayla's going to operate, she said one of the babies is breech." The two men hurried across the debris-strewn courtyard. "Cal, Quintin is pretty busy, we'd better contact Jamie. I don't want him hearing about this from anyone else."

"That's a good idea. When he gets here, don't let him near the house. I don't think he could take seeing her right now."

Kalen and Cal circled the house. While Kalen moved the Lexicon, Cal put a call into Jamie.

Santiago Estate
Lake Solana
Post Attack Kitchen

Chapter 41
Life

Mayla turned away from Catherine. Lowering her voice, she said, "Lieutenant, find the hypo in my medical case."

The lieutenant removed the device. "Captain, what drug do you want?"

"Anused."

Sorting through the drug case, the officer loaded a vial into the hypo and handed it to Mayla.

She raised it to the light, set the dosage to ten cc's, then pressed it to Catherine's neck. A faint hiss followed and Catherine's body relaxed.

"Captain, shouldn't you change clothes before we begin?" Sandra checked Catherine's pulse.

Mayla looked down at herself, handed the hypo back and raised her arms. "Laser scalpel, Lieutenant, cut it off."

Lieutenant Saint James grabbed the scalpel and cut away Mayla's filthy blouse. She set the instrument down, picked up a container of sterile water and poured the liquid over Mayla's hands and arms. Footsteps sounded behind the Lieutenant. "Mother, Lily, get ready, we need your help." Mayla lifted the hypo from the table.

"Mayla, thank the stars you're here," Lily said.

Mayla examined the fetal monitor. "Mother, I need clean sheets, and blankets for the babies. Bring everything you can find. And see if you can find me something to wear."

Liana ran from the room, the Lieutenant close behind.

Mayla started to cut Catherine's clothes off. "Lily, where's Mandi?"

"She's helping Zavier and Quintin get Shannan and the children settled in the staff housing. She'll be here shortly."

"Is Shannan all right?"

"She's fine. Mayla, what are you going to do?"

"Catherine's having twins, the first baby is breech. She is too weak to turn the child for delivery. I have to open her up and take the babies."

"Here's a blouse." Liana said, dropping the sheets on the table and swiping at her eyes. "Two babies?"

Following close behind, the lieutenant dropped some towels and other sheets next to Liana's.

"Yes, Mother, twins. Please finish undressing Catherine, then drape her with the sheets." Mayla ejected the used vial from the hypo and inserted another. She bent over to get close to Catherine. "I am going to put you to sleep, Sis, so I can operate."

"Please, Mayla, save my babies."

Fighting to suppress her own tears, she brushed Catherine's pale blonde hair out of her eyes. "You'll be holding both of them. . .before you know it." Mayla forced a smile and pressed the hypo against Catherine's neck. Her eyes closed and her breathing slowed. Mayla placed an instrument on Catherine's chest, checked the readings and called Liana to her side. While she slipped into the clean blouse she said, "Mother, I need you to set up the sterile field generator, the way we did for Kalen."

Liana went to the instrument case, removed and assembled the stand, then mounted the generator, turned it on, and aimed it at Catherine's swollen abdomen.

"Good. Now I need you to watch her blood pressure. If it starts to drop, tell me."

"Lily, you and the Lieutenant need to scrub up." Lily followed the officer to the kitchen sink.

Liana brushed Catherine's hair to one side. "You stay with us, sweet girl. Our family needs you here." She kissed Catherine's fore-head, then turned her attention to the readings and her daughter-in-law's breathing.

When Lily and the Lieutenant returned, Mayla instructed Lily. "Keep this pointed at Catherine's abdomen. It will maintain a sterile field around our hands and her incision. Mother, I'm going to start now, keep a close eye on her readings. Lieutenant, I'll need those blankets to wrap the babies in."

Mayla placed her laser scalpel against the lower part of Catherine's abdomen and began to cut. She made several passes, cutting through the layers of skin and muscle. The smell of seared flesh drifted through the room.

Lily inhaled a sharp breath when Mayla opened Catherine's womb and a dark, green fluid gushed from her womb. "Is she all right?"

"It happens when the mother and baby are under stress," Lieutenant Saint James said. "That's the reason we have to get the babies out now." The officer stayed close to Mayla, responding to each request for another instrument or help.

While stroking Catherine's forehead, Liana kept her eyes glued to the readings.

"Lieutenant Saint James, what's your first name?"

"Sandra, Captain."

"Sandra, I need you to widen the incision so I can remove the first child."

Lily winced when Sandra inserted her hands in the incision and pulled.

Mayla slipped both hands inside her sister-in-law, and drew forth a small pinkish-blue child. Turning the child on its side, she cleared its mouth and the baby started to cry, filling its lungs for the first time. "I know you can hear me, Cat. It's a boy. He's beautiful." Mayla tied off and cut the umbilical cord. "Lily's going to take good care of him."

Lily took the child.

"Mother, how are her readings?"

"They drop, but then return to normal."

"Good girl, Cat, you stay with us." Mayla turned and reached inside Catherine again. She pulled and drew the second child out, tied, and cut the cord. The baby remained limp and quiet. Mayla passed the child to Lily.

Lily called to the child, shaking and rubbing the baby. "Mayla, he's not responding."

Sandra moved to Lily's side. "You've got to wake him up." She grabbed the boy by his ankles, raised him up and smacked his buttocks. The child remained unresponsive.

"Is that necessary, Sandra?" Lily said.

"Normally no." Sandra prodded and slapped the child again. "But this is an emergency." She smacked the child's rump a third time. He gave a stuttering gasp, let out an indignant scream and turned pink.

"At last," Lily said. She took the baby and Sandra returned to Mayla's side.

"Another boy, Catherine." Mayla sniffed back her tears. "You've done good, Sis. Just hang in there a little longer."

"How is she?" Sandra said.

Mayla probed Catherine's abdominal cavity, feeling her abdomen with her bare hands. "I don't like what I'm feeling." Reattaching the fetal monitor, she adjusted the view, studied the readings and shook her head.

"Mayla, what's wrong?" Liana took her eyes off the vitals monitor. "She's–she's going to be all right, isn't she?"

"Her uterus is paper thin and badly damaged. If it ruptures, she'll bleed out. I should've been monitoring her."

"She was afraid you'd tell the baby's sex," Liana said. "We all thought she was doing fine."

"That's no excuse. I should have insisted."

Sandra asked, "What are you going to do?"

"I'm going to have to remove her uterus."

Liana and Lily's faces blanched when Mayla made her pronouncement.

Pushing thoughts of Catherine's reaction to the back of her mind, Mayla steeled herself and went to work.

Mandi entered the room. "How can I help?"

"Please search the house." Mayla set her laser scalpel down. "See if you can find a clean, warm nightgown for Catherine."

"Be careful upstairs," Sandra said. "The second floor is weak."

"I know." Mandi left the kitchen.

"How is she?" Liana stroked her daughter-in-law's forehead.

"She's going to be sore and weak for a while, but she'll be with us for a long time."

While Liana kept her eyes glued to the instrument, calling out Catherine's readings every few minutes, Mayla and Sandra worked. Behind her, Mayla could hear the two babies crying, and held back her own tears.

"How long, Lieutenant?" Mayla looked up after closing the incision. "Three hours and twenty-seven minutes."

"Lily, how are the babies doing?" Mayla wiped her hands.

"They're healthy and strong, but they're hungry."

"First things first." Using a large container of hot water supplied by the men, Mayla bathed Catherine to remove the blood and fluids. When she finished she checked Catherine's readings. "Lily, go and see if Jamie is here yet. Let Lieutenant Commander Cooper know Catherine can be moved. Sandra, tell the corpsman to bring in the wounded."

Chapter 42
New Life

An hour past sun's rise, the heavy scent of burning wood and debris hung like a pall over the groves and the ruined house. While Kalen and Cal shimmed the legs of the table taken from the kitchen to make it level, Kalen looked up, tapped Cal on the shoulder, and pointed north. "Jamie's here."

"He got here a lot sooner than I expected." Cal finished his task and the two friends hurried to the landing area on the citrus grove's northern edge. "He must have flown all night."

"This is Jamie we're talking about," Kalen said. "Catherine and the children were in danger. What did you expect?"

"Nothing less, brother." A smile pulled at the corners of his mouth. "Nothing less."

Jamie's flyer circled the house then came in for a landing. When the door rotated open, he looked frightened and haggard.

Kalen and Cal rushed to meet him. "Where's Catherine?"

Kalen touched his shoulder. "Mayla's with her."

"I don't like that look, Kalen. Where is she? What's happened to her?"

"Catherine went into labor during the attack. Mayla had to operate."

"Operate! Why? Is she all right?"

Cal shook his head. "We don't know anything right now."

"I've got to see her." Jamie started toward the house.

"No, Jamie." Kalen grabbed hold of his arm. It took both men to restrain him. "You can't go in."

"I need to be with her." Jamie looked toward the ruined mansion, anguish written on his face. "I want to know what's going on!"

"Mayla's with her," Cal said. "She's in good hands. I wouldn't want anyone else to operate on Shannan if she were in this position."

"It's not Shannan in there, Cal. It's Catherine. It's my wife! I want to know what's happening to her! Kalen, who else is with Mayla?"

"One of Neil's officers. Lily and your mother were also there when we left. Officer Ryan went in later."

"Mandi is still here?"

"Yeah, she's still on suspension," said Kalen. "How long have they been in there?"

"It's been about four hours," Cal said.

"Where are my children?"

"Your father, Zavier, and Shannan have them in the staff's quarters." Kalen patted Jamie's shoulder. "Jenna's crew didn't seem interested in the staff."

"What happened to Uncle Neil's men?" Jamie stared at the destruction, his face pale, his hands shaking. "They were supposed to guard against an attack!"

"Easy, Jamie," Neil said, coming up behind the three men. "No one could have foreseen this attack."

Jamie spun and faced his uncle. "Neil, where are the men you had guarding the estate?"

"Dead."

"They are all dead?" Cal stared, wide-eyed.

A pained expression filled Neil's face and he nodded. "Dead!" Cal repeated. "How?"

"They were ambushed. The women took out my Marines just before the attack. Whoever did this is more skilled than we thought, or they have someone on the inside watching this place. The only reason we got troops here at all is because Corporal Zane managed to kill one of the attackers and warn us before they killed him. I have men scouring the area. If you were being watched, we'll find their nest."

Jamie broke from the group.

Kalen and Cal tried to stop him, but he slipped past them and headed for the house. They saw Lily approaching, and all three men followed Jamie.

"Lily, is Catherine all right?" Jamie grabbed his sister-in-law's arm.

"Under the circumstances, she is doing well." Lily wiped her eyes, nodded and took Jamie's hands. "Mayla has her ready to move."

"What do you mean, under the circumstances?"

"I should let Mayla explain."

"No, Lily! You tell me. You tell me right now!"

"Jamie, her uterus was badly damaged. Mayla had to remove it."

Jamie stood frozen for a moment. "What about the baby? How's the baby?"

"Your sons are fine."

Jamie stared at Lily, a blank expression on his face. "Did...did you say sons?"

"Didn't any of you tell him?" Lily stared hard at the three men behind Jamie.

"He just got here," Cal said. "It's been a wee bit hard to talk to him."

"Catherine was carrying twins." She touched Jamie's shoulder. "You have two healthy sons."

Jaime's bewildered look turned into his usual toothy grin. "Lily, can I see Catherine?"

"Not yet, Jamie, she's still unconscious, the sedative hasn't worn off yet." Lily put her arm around his shoulders. "Neil, Mayla sent me to tell you she is ready to move Catherine to the staff housing. We need some way to transport her, and she said to tell you the front of the Lexicon won't do this time."

"The Lexicon?" Neil glanced at Kalen.

"We'll explain later."

Neil signaled to one of the Marines standing close by. The soldier approached and saluted.

"Sergeant Miller, how is the med center coming?"

"We finished setting it up ten minutes ago. Captain Santiago just started treating the wounded there."

"Well done. Sergeant, this is Lily Santiago. Take some men with a transport. Report to Captain Santiago. She has a patient to move to the staff quarters. This is a very special lady. Take extra care and get all the help you need."

"Yes, sir, I'll see to it." He turned to Lily. "Please come with me, Miss."

"Miss?" Lily giggled. "Neil, I like this man." She turned and followed the sergeant.

Kalen put his hand on Jamie's shoulder. "Congratulations, Jamie. Now, go see your children. I'm sure they're frightened and are wondering what's become of their parents. You can tell them their mother's all right and you'll be there when the men bring Catherine over."

"Two. Two sons." The dazed look stayed on Jamie's face. "I have two new sons!" He hurried away.

Kalen glanced at the smoldering house. "I wonder what Quintin will do?"

"Knowing my brother-in-law," Neil said, "he won't be frightened off. He'll rebuild, and the next time we'll be ready."

Chapter 43
Digging Out

Kalen and Cal busied themselves with the task of setting up the table and chairs for the meeting Quintin had called. While they worked, Kalen asked, "Cal, how did you and Zavier manage to get everyone out past the attackers?"

"Zavier's quick thinking." A sly grin slid across Cal's face. "He led us to the utility closet in the south wing. We blew a hole in the southeast corner, escaped through it. We used the grove as cover, putting us behind most of the attackers. By the way, don't ever get Lily mad at you."

"Why?"

"One of the attackers spotted Mariah and tried to take her. She didn't see Lily coming up behind her. Your future sister-in-law grabbed the woman and damn near twisted her head off."

"Lily! Really?"

"Yeah. I never saw anyone move so fast."

About mid-morning, Quintin and Liana emerged from the staff housing to survey the wreckage. Liana and the staff began salvaging household items, furniture, and personal belongings. Quintin issued orders to Albert, Jamie, and Zavier.

Although loathe to leave Catherine, Jamie flew north to recruit help from among their camps of men in the Barrera mountains. Albert took his crew, went to the mill and began working on the materials Quintin specified.

Zavier sent word to his foreman to prepare some of his terra forming equipment for transport. He spent a few hours seeing to his family's needs before flying north to assist his foreman.

Completing instructions to his sons and the staff, Quintin, along with Neil, Kalen, and Cal sat down at the large kitchen table. Quintin started the discussion. "It's a good thing you and Mayla were restless last night. Otherwise we would all be dead."

"And just what were you two doing up at that hour?" Cal grinned.

"I was having trouble sleeping. I woke Mayla and some of you. She came to see if I was all right. We were talking when I heard someone moving in the grove. That's when it all hit the fan."

"Did you recognize anyone?" Neil said.

Cal answered. "I didn't."

Kalen hesitated, confused by what he had noticed in his brief look at Jenna's face. He shook it off and said, "I did."

Neil asked, "Who?"

"Our old friend, Jenna. She was the one I was chasing when your troops showed up. A flyer hovering over the roof pulled her out. Neil, I take it your people didn't have any luck bringing it down?"

"No," Neil said. "By the time my Marines sorted out whose flyer belonged to who, the entire force managed to get away. My techs are installing ID markers in all of your flyers as we speak. There will be no more confusion."

Kalen clenched his fist. "One of these days, I'm going to grab Jenna and nail her, hide still attached, to a wall and find out who she is, and why she's so bent on killing us. Quintin, I'm sorry about this. I should have realized when we interfered with Maria's plans again, she would retaliate. By now she knows she needs my father's computer and the key to access the data. She must believe they are hidden here. I should have known she'd come after them."

"Kalen, don't go blaming yourself," Quintin said. "If you and Mayla hadn't been together, we would all be dead. At least no one was killed."

"Catherine came close, too damn close." Kalen clenched his jaw as a wave of guilt swept over him. Looking to the house he said, "I want to help pay for the repairs."

"Kalen, I don't need your help. I–"

"I don't care if you need the help or not!" Kalen smacked his palms on the table. "I won't stand by while you suffer this kind of abuse and not help out. You're in this danger because you've accepted me into your family. So, am I family or not?"

"You are. You are also your father's son." Quintin managed to smile. "I'll accept your help. I can use it to hire more men."

"Thank you." Kalen settled back.

"I placed a call to Paddy," Cal said. "He's on his way down with twenty men and some additional equipment."

"Quintin, what do you plan to do?" said the commander, while fidgeting with his comm.

"I was going to make repairs." Quintin, glancing toward the estate, sighed and shook his head. "But the structure is too badly damaged. Between the explosives thrown at us and," he nodded toward Cal and Kalen, "you two blowing holes in the walls, we'll start over."

Cal and Kalen lowered their eyes and grinned at Quintin's mention of their use of the Lexicon's weapons.

"I have a few ideas that should make this a more secure compound and keep us a little safer. With the men you're supplying we should make short work of the reconstruction."

"Kalen, it looks as if you're going to help out in more ways than one," Cal said. "Quintin's going to put your skills to work."

"Fine by me."

"I'll need your mining skills too, Cal."

Surprise filled Cal's face. "What do you have in mind?"

"I haven't got it all worked out yet. The first order of business is to finish Kalen and Mayla's house. We'll need somewhere for the women and children to live while we rebuild the estate."

"That's still going to take a month or more."

"No, Kalen, all the materials to finish your home are ready. Albert completed them yesterday. He and the workmen are delivering them as we speak. I will put the crews to work around the clock and get the house completed in a few days. In the meantime, we'll go about recovering what we can from the rubble, then I can tear it down. While we're busy with the reconstruction, Liana and Lily are going to the capital to file a formal complaint with the Central Council. Liana will demand an official inquiry be started."

Neil leaned forward. "Do you think that is wise?"

"I do. We have some of the attackers' bodies, my injured grand-children, and the destruction of the house as proof something is going on. If we don't demand an investigation," Quintin slapped the table. "I'm willing to bet the Council members will find a way to put a spin on this and downplay the whole thing. They may even try to sweep this under the carpet like they've managed to do with the Crystal Lake conspiracy. Liana will present her formal request during the Council's monthly public broadcast. But even with public awareness, the Council may not listen, they seem to forget who they represent and who they work for!" Quintin paused. "Enough about the Central Council. Kalen, we will need a place to hold your wedding."

"With all that's happened, Mayla and I thought we'd put that off for a while."

"No, Kalen. We are not going to allow these terrorists to run our lives."

"Have you any idea where you will hold it?" Cal said.

"Liana has already thought of that."

Cal was about to ask where when a Marine came running from the staff housing.

He pointed at the citrus grove and said, "Commander, there's a flyer approaching."

The men scurried from their seats in time to see the Marines taking cover in the trees and behind rubble, their weapons pointed at the incoming flyer.

Santiago Estate
Post Attack

Chapter 44

A Fly in the Ointment

The black and green flyer hovered, south of the estate over the citrus grove. Sergeant Miller came to Neil's side, his weapon at the ready. "Commander, it looks to be one of the local Roving Patrol vehicles."

"It is," Neil said, without taking his eyes off the vehicle. "Sergeant, has the officer identified himself?"

Miller glanced to his left and called to his comm operator. "Corporal, have you made contact?"

"Yes, Sergeant! The pilot says his name is Lieutenant Castellano."

Quintin moved closer to his brother-in-law. "Neil, tell your men it's okay. I've met him during the Solana District Council meetings. He's a good officer."

Commander Elano nodded and said, "Sergeant, give the order."

"Stand down!" Sergeant Miller shouted.

The soldiers relaxed their stance, but didn't break cover. Kalen noticed the men's weapons remained at the ready, safeties off, including the Sergeant's.

Neil held up his arm and signaled to the RP officer.

The flyer moved closer, passed overhead, flew across the ruins, then turned and landed. The RP officer exited his vehicle, approached Quintin with his hand extended. "Good day, Mister Santiago."

Quintin stepped away from Neil and shook the officer's hand. "Not really, Lieutenant."

The officer pressed his lips together and nodded. "My staff just learned of the fires and the attack on your family. I came as soon as I was informed. Was anyone injured or killed?"

"The attack forced my daughter-in-law into labor." Quintin's eyes flashed with anger. He released Castellano's hand. "Our doctor was compelled to operate."

"She's all right, isn't she?" The officer's face showed genuine concern.

"Catherine is recovering." Quintin let out a frustrated sigh. "And we have two new additions to our family."

"What about the rest of your children and grandchildren?"

"Two of my grandchildren were seriously injured. The rest of them are bruised and frightened. There may be others. I don't have all the information from my doctor yet."

The police officer scanned Neil's troops. "Normally, Mister Santiago, I'm a curious man, but I'm not going to ask you what these troops are doing here." He turned and faced Neil. "Commander Elano, my condolences on the loss of your father. He was an excellent trial judge."

"Thank you, Lieutenant." Neil's eyes narrowed with curiosity. "How is it you recognize me?"

"Let's just say, I have my sources, Commander. The Central Council believes the warden at the prison's name is Daniels and his assignment is overseeing the facility. They haven't bothered to ask questions. As long as you're here on CCMF prison business I have no problem with your presence. You are here on prison business, Warden Daniels?"

"Of course, Lieutenant." Neil's face remained neutral. "I would have no other reason for being here."

Lieutenant Castellano turned to face Quintin again. "Could you tell if it was the same people from the assault on your granddaughter?"

A puzzled look crossed Quintin's face. "How did you find out about the attempt?"

"Your son, Jamie, told Officer Marcos, before your little group decided to start their own investigation into the women's disappearances."

"I'm afraid that was my doing, Lieutenant." Kalen rubbed the back of his neck and cringed. "Are the officers in trouble?"

"Yes, I'm aware of that fact, Mister MacKenna." A smile pulled at the corners of his mouth. "Officially, yes, but your little shindig made more progress in one day than the rest of my task-force did in a full Colonial Period." The Lieutenant sobered. "They've been suspended, and placed on paid leave for two cycles, as has Officer Nolan."

"A just punishment," Commander Elano kept his voice level, "for such flagrant disregard of protocol."

"Exactly." Lieutenant Castellano paused and searched the faces of the group, for what, Kalen couldn't tell. "Let's get back to my question. Was this attack carried out by the same people who assaulted your granddaughter?"

"We can't be sure it was the same people. The first attackers were all men. Last night, the entire force was female. Since they came looking for my granddaughter, I must assume it's the same group of people."

"Whoever did this is serious about taking your granddaughter."

Quintin, his voice flat, said, "Not serious enough, they failed."

"Mister Santiago, I have informed the Central Council of the attack. Councilwoman Acosta wishes me to investigate this incident and report back to her."

"Lieutenant!" Cal stepped closer to the officer. "Look around you! Does this look like a bloody incident? We were attacked by a force of fully armed women, bent, it would seem, on kidnapping Zavier's oldest daughter, and killing anyone in their way. We have half a dozen bodies to prove it. By the way, where were your men last night? You're the first Roving Patrol we've seen!"

"Cal, take it easy," Quintin said. "The Lieutenant has a job to do."

"I don't see anyone doing it! Otherwise, all the noise and fires should've attracted the attention of the Roving Patrol!"

"Ever since the CC assigned me to lead the task force, Acosta has kept me on a short leash." Lieutenant Castellano's expression darkened. "Yesterday, I was ordered into the Barrera Wilds on a rescue mission by Councilwoman Acosta. I see now the timing is suspicious."

"You think the assignment was a deliberate attempt to leave the area unguarded?"

"I believe now, it was." The officer looked at the faces surrounding him. "Because the Council did nothing after the last attack on your estate, I don't see any problem with you employing your own private security forces. I must, however, give the Central Council a report, so tell me what you can. I will fill in the kinds of details that tend to warm the cold corners of our politicians' hearts."

A smile pulled at the corners of Quintin's mouth. "Very well, Lieutenant." He turned and led the way to the table. Once seated he said, "First, Lieutenant Castellano, tell us about this sudden assignment."

The Lieutenant dropped into the offered chair. He removed his blue uniform cap and ran his fingers through his dark brown hair. "The assignment is of little importance. What is important is that Councilwoman Acosta made the request personally."

Cal leaned against the table. "For what purpose?"

The Lieutenant looked at him and asked, "And you are?"

"Forgive me, Lieutenant," Quintin said. "This is Cal Devers, Kalen's best friend. They are down here preparing for Kalen's wedding."

A look of recognition played across Castellano's face. The officer nodded in recognition. "Getting back to your question, that's what I have been asking myself. Now I find this estate attacked while we were pulled away from our assigned area."

"You can't believe the CC had a diversion staged?" Cal stood, and circled the table.

"Mister Devers, Councilwoman Acosta checks on every move I make. She gave me a detailed account, but what I found out there wasn't anything close to her description. Apparently, she knows more about the going-ons down here than she should."

"Then we have a spy watching our movements." Neil glanced at his brother-in-law. "Quintin, how well do you know the people on your staff?"

"Most of our people have been with us for at least ten years."

"We are still going to have to look into the backgrounds of anyone connected with you. The men you are bringing in to help rebuild the estate will also have to be vetted. Lieutenant, may I suggest that you start checking into your people?"

"I've already begun, Commander, as soon as I suspected the

assignment was a diversion."

Drumming his fingers on the table, Kalen said, "Lieutenant, may I ask you a question?"

"Go ahead, Mister MacKenna."

"Our little shindig, as you called it, only came about because your assistant told Officer Marcos you were too busy to question two viable suspects."

Lieutenant Castellano glanced at the men surrounding the table. Rubbing his chin, he said, "This must go no farther than this table, Commander."

"Understood, Lieutenant," Commander Elano said, answering for the group. He turned and glanced over his shoulder. "Sergeant, take your detail and assist Mrs. Santiago with the cleanup."

"Yes, sir." The sergeant gave the order and the men trotted off, disappearing through the ruined courtyard gate.

The lieutenant glanced around. "My so-called assistant never told me of the suspects."

"How did she explain herself?" Neil leaned forward.

"She didn't." Lieutenant Castellano clenched his hands into fists. "Shortly after Officer Marcos contacted her, she vanished."

Kalen started at the revelation. "What about Michael and Flin? Have you questioned them?"

The officer shook his head and grimaced.

"Why not, Lieutenant?" Kalen stared at the RP officer, his gut cramped. "They could supply you with some valuable answers."

"I had every intention of questioning those two buffoons when I returned from your little party. However, I was too late. I arrived at the barracks to find Michael and Flin dead in their cells."

"How?" Kalen said, jumping up from his seat. "How did anyone get to them?"

"While I was en route to Solana, their mid-meal was poisoned. I've questioned the staff, but since all meals are brought in, we've arrested the vendor."

Too stunned to speak, Kalen dropped into his chair. He found himself thinking of young Flin. *The lad deserved better.*

The discussions for the lieutenant's report and additional security continued for another half hour. When the meeting ended, the lieutenant stood. "Mister MacKenna, may I have a word with you?"

"Of course, Lieutenant." Kalen rose, a knot in his gut. He followed the officer until they reached his Roving Patrol flyer.

The lieutenant turned and faced Kalen. "I had to pry the information out of Officer Marcos. When I did, he admitted the momentum for the trip to Avila came from you. Why?"

Kalen leaned against Neil's black Corsair fighter, and rubbed the back of his neck. "After the attack on Zavier's daughter, I had a feeling we needed to follow up, since it didn't look like you were going to. I didn't know about your assistant, nor the two investigators you had out there."

"They were out there investigating for six cycles. You managed to open up that nest in just a few hours. I asked to speak with you because I wanted to warn you to watch your back."

"My back? Why?"

"Councilwoman Acosta may micro-manage my task force, but that has allowed me to keep track of her and the council. She is aware you're connected to both the Crystal Lake raid and rescuing the women in the Eastern Arm." Castellano balled his left hand into a fist. "Since it's obvious to anyone, but a fool, your involvement helped expose problems. The council can't move against you without raising more questions, but I get the feeling they're looking for a way."

"What would you suggest I do? I can't ignore what I see."

"I wouldn't want you to, but the next time you have a hunch, call me."

"Really, you'd listen to me?"

"I would and will."

"All right, Lieutenant. I can do that."

The lieutenant tossed his uniform cap into the flyer.

Kalen could see the officer had more on his mind. "What is it, Lieutenant?"

"I don't want you to take this the wrong way, Mister MacKenna, but I'm well aware of who you are."

"And you think I'm guilty?" Kalen steeled himself against the old familiar accusations.

"On the contrary. I was still in school when your trial took place. My grandfather, a detective with the Andalusian Roving Patrol at the time, followed your story. At first he couldn't believe you were arrested. He told our family the evidence against you was circumstantial at best."

"Not enough to prevent the prosecutor from moving ahead."

"No, and that surprised my grandfather. Your conviction was an even bigger shock. Do you have any idea what made Judge Elano sentence you as he did?"

Not sure how much to trust the lieutenant, Kalen decided on a simple explanation. "I have to believe my conviction didn't sit well with him."

"Well, I'm glad it didn't. Although, since your reanimation, there's been a lot of strange occurrences."

"Really. What have you noticed?"

"Mostly policies and laws the CC is ignoring, but never mind that. What I wanted to tell you is, I'll warn you if I learn the CC's preparing to move against you." He glanced at the estate. "Though I've done a poor job, so far. I would appreciate knowing of any other hunches you have or anything you learn in the future." He extended his hand.

"I'll do that." Kalen shook his hand. "Thank you, Lieutenant."

Late in the day, Kalen caught up with Mayla tending to the wounded in the field hospital Neil's men set up on the estate's north side. He walked through the tents and found the Marines had moved the children to an isolated section out of sight of the wounded soldiers. None of the children escaped injury. Mariah had a deep laceration on her left arm from flying glass. Caesar sat up in a bed playing with the insta-cast on his fractured leg. Laney lay next to him, her head on his uninjured leg.

"Hey, Caesar. How are you doing?"

"I got hurt," the boy said, pointing to the clear cast on his leg.

"I'm sorry that happened." Kalen reached down and patted Laney's head. "Don't worry, girl, he'll be good as new. Thanks for looking out for him."

The dog huffed in response.

"Aunt Mayla says I can't run around." Caesar frowned. "I have to stay in bed."

"And you're going to listen to her," Lily said, while tending to Lucas and Dulciana.

"Yes...Mother." He stuck his lower lip out and Kalen laughed.

Mayla finished examining Mariah when Kalen caught up with her. He took her arm and turned her so she faced him. "You look exhausted."

"I'm fine." Mayla snapped at him

"I don't think so, Luv. You look haggard."

"Thanks." Mayla clicked her tongue. "That makes me feel so much better."

"I'm sorry, but it's the truth. You've got dark circles under your eyes. When was the last time you ate anything or slept?"

"I'm all right." Mayla tried to pull away. "I'm not hungry." "Meaning no disrespect to you, Captain." Lieutenant Saint James came in from tending to the wounded soldiers. "Mister MacKenna, I would suggest you take her somewhere and make her lie down, before she falls down."

"Lieutenant, is it fair to say you can handle things here, for a while, without my fiancée?"

"Of course. I've managed to get several hours sleep and Captain Santiago has already seen everyone at least twice."

"Lieutenant." Kalen grinned and winked at Sandra. "Do you have a hypo handy? We might need to administer a sedative to the good Captain."

Mayla looked up and glared at Kalen.

"Hey, I'm only following my doctor's example." Then he echoed her words from a few weeks before back at her. "It may be the only way to slow you down long enough so you can rest."

Mayla's glare faded. "Touché. Sandra, wake me if anything happens?"

"Of course, Captain."

"Mariah, you lie still and I'll see you later."

"Yes, Aunt Mayla."

Kalen gave the child a warm smile, slipped his arm around Mayla's waist and drew her away.

"Would you have really have hypoed me?"

Kalen grinned, but didn't answer her.

"You would have!" She gave him a playful punch in the arm.

"Since you cooperated, I guess you'll never find out."

She hooked her arm in his and they walked toward the house.

Kalen repeated his conversation with Lieutenant Castellano. When he finished, Mayla stepped in front of him and stopped. "That's odd."

"Should we be worried?"

"Worry won't help, caution will. Make sure Uncle Neil's aware of the lieutenant's warning, he'll know what to do." Mayla turned her head, put her hand to her mouth and yawned. "Excuse me. What will help right now is sleep. Did you find someplace quiet for us?"

"Out on the western edge of the groves. I've set up two tents. It's not much, but the staff quarters are pretty noisy and crowded. At least, this way, you'll sleep without being interrupted."

Reaching the estate, they moved past the kitchen. Mayla glanced through the open doors and let out a heavy sigh. "This is going to kill Dani."

"I know, she really loves the place."

"She'd live here year-round if she had her way. Zavier told me she has no love for farming."

They moved away from the house. Reaching the western edge of the groves, Kalen stopped in front of the tents. "Like I said, it's not much."

Mayla made a grateful sigh. "Right now, this looks like heaven. Thanks for coming to get me." She turned and kissed him. "I'll be glad when we only need one tent, though."

"So will I. Are you sure you don't want to clean up first?"

"No, I am too tired." Mayla looked around, leaned closer and whispered, "Unless you've a waterfall in your pocket."

"Fresh out at the moment, Milady."

"What are you going to do while I'm sleeping?"

"Find the commander and tell him everything Lieutenant Castellano said. After that, your father will keep me busy."

"Better than lying around."

"Get some sleep. I'll come and get you for last meal." Kalen left, laughing to himself. *I'm not going to disturb you. You'll sleep straight through until morning.* He hurried through the grove and spotted the commander talking to Lieutenant Commander Cooper. By the time Kalen reached the commander's side, the two officers had finished speaking.

"Did you convince Mayla to take a break?" Neil said.

"Yeah. She's in the tent I set up." He repeated his conversation with Castellano.

"I will have to keep a closer eye on the Central Council." Neil scratched his cheek, "It is a good thing Dani wasn't here. You might not have been able to stop Jenna from taking her."

"They're spending so much time looking for her they're ignoring everyone else," said Kalen. "Seems her change in my itinerary was inspired. I wonder why she's so important to Maria?"

"I don't know, but It feels to me like she's a pawn in this game."

"You do realize, Commander, with the right moves, even a pawn can bring down a queen."

Commander Elano nodded. A quick smile pulled at the corners of his mouth."Let's hope it doesn't come to that. One thing is for sure, Maria's people have no idea where she is."

Kalen shifted his gaze westward. "Let's keep it that way."

The commander patted Kalen's back. "On a cheerier note, there is only a cycle until your wedding."

Kalen nodded. "That's thirty-two days too long for me. I should go and find Quintin. I'm getting married, and there's a lot of work to do before then."

Continued
In Book Four

Appendix

Kalen Russell MacKenna: Only child of Russell and Alannah MacKenna. Framed for the murders of his father and wife, he is sentenced to Cold-stasis as punishment instead of the death penalty. From the moment of his reanimation (Revival), his life is constantly sought. Prophetic title in the Crosskey Prophecy is 'Child of the Promise.'

Cal (Hobbs) Devers: Kalen's childhood friend. He is sought out by Mayla when Kalen disappears from the Crosskey Inn. Married to Shannan Kavanaugh-Devers. He discovers the Crosskey Prophecy spoken by his mother-in-law forty Colonial periods (years) ago to Alannah MacKenna.

Mayla Liana Santiago: Youngest child and only daughter of Quintin and Liana Santiago. She was raised on the Wyndimere Colony by her uncle, Commander Neil Elano. Holding the rank of captain in the CCMF, she is a doctor and surgeon. Her skills are tested at least three times throughout the saga. She is referred to in the Crosskey prophecy as 'The Hidden One.'

Quintin Santiago: Husband to Liana Elano-Santiago. Father to Zavier, Abel, Jamie, and Mayla. He is grandfather to Zavier's and Jamie's ten children. Quintin is a builder who constructs houses in what is called by Arrisian society the old style (Post and Beam). At the start of the saga he is about sixty periods (years) old. When he meets Kalen there is a family schism Kalen knows nothing about. Kalen's knowledge of his own family helps him to smooth things over, bringing peace to the Santiago family.

Richard R Draude

Liana Elano-Santiago: Daughter of Judge Arturo Elano, the man who preserved Kalen's life. Wife, mother and university professor, Liana is the heart and soul of the Santiago clan. She is loving and kind, but stern and unbending when it comes to certain traditions, the Arrisian wedding game being chief among them. She is especially close to Daniella (Dani) Santiago, her first grandchild. Her family turns to her for her wisdom and advice.

Zavier Quintin Santiago: First born child of Quintin and Liana, Zavier is a gentle giant, standing 203 centimeters (six foot eight inches), and weighing 132 kilos (290 pounds). He farms the family land holdings on Mesa Escarza. He is husband to Lilianna (Lily) Rancano-Santiago. Father to Daniella, Lucas and Dulciana (twins), Caesar and a future child. After settling the family schism, he becomes a fast and loyal friend to Kalen, defending him against any and all slander.

Abel Santos Santiago: Second son of Quintin and Liana, husband to Georgina, an outworlder from the Selwyn colony. No children. Not much else is known about him. After his attempt on Kalen's life, he separates himself from his family and turns his back on them.

James (Jamie) Arturo Santiago: Third and youngest son of Quintin and Liana. Husband to Catherine McMasters- Santiago. Father to five children: Mariah, Quintin (named after his grandfather), Kaitlan, Sonija, and twin boys, James and Arturo. The family practical joker, he is close to Kalen's actual age and they become great friends.

Lilianna (Lily) Rancano-Santiago: Wife to Zavier Santiago. Mother to Daniella, Lucas and Duiciana, Caesar and a child born in a later book. She has dark hair, blue eyes and stands 190 centimeters (six foot three inches) tall. She is close to Kalen and he turns to her at times for advice. She has degrees in botany and horticulture. Her experiments surround their Mesa Escarza home.

294

Catherine McMasters-Santiago: Wife to Jamie and mother of Mariah, Quintin, Kaitlan, Sonija, and twin boys born in this novel. Her family are landholders from the northern tip of Mesa Verde. She is a petite woman with pale, pale blue eyes (almost white) and light blonde hair. She holds a degree in mechanical engineering and robotics. She is a constant source of teasing for Kalen.

Daniella (Dani) Liana Santiago: Oldest child of Zavier and Lily Santiago. She is the first grandchild, headstrong and a bit spoiled. At first she resents Kalen's intrusion into the family's life, but later finds him a caring person. Her life changes when Kalen and Mayla disappear and Connor O'Dell appears at her grandparents' Lake Solana mansion.

Connor Shamus O'Dell: Son of Amin and Deirdre O'Dell, he is employed by Cal (Hobbs) Devers. He appears in the first novel *Dreams and Deceptions.* Upon spotting Dani eavesdropping on the adults, he is smitten with her and she with him. Connor proves himself to Zavier and Lily when he takes on a bully mocking the Santiagos and speaking ill of Dani.

Commander Neil Elano: Son of Judge Arturo Elano, brother of Liana Elano-Santiago. He is in charge of the stasis prison (under an assumed name, Warden Daniels) when Kalen is brought out of stasis. He keeps his true identity a secret while watching over Kalen. Later he saves Kalen's life during a mid-air battle and another time saves Kalen and Mayla in a similar situation.

Lieutenant Sandra St James: A rehab specialist, and a top fighter pilot, Sandra appears briefly in the first book as Kalen's Rehab Tech and caregiver during his reanimation. Standing 180 centimeters (five foot eleven inches), blonde, with brown eyes. She reappears in this novel after the mansion is attacked, assisting Mayla with Catherine's C-section and the other wounded. In love with Commander Neil Elano.

Richard R Draude

Lieutenant Commander Cooper: Sent by Commander Neil Elano to intervene in the attack on the Santiago estate. He will take over command of the prison later on.

Lieutenant Castellano: Roving Patrol officer in charge of uncovering the reason for the disappearances of Arrisian females. He grows suspicious of The CC and turns a blind eye to the sight of CCMF Marines at the Santiago Estate sfter the second attack.

Officer Eli Marcos: Roving Patrol officer and friend of Jamie Santiago. He is key in helping Kalen track down some of the missing women.

Officer Al Jennings: With Eli when he helps Jamie and Kalen interfere with the kidnapping of a woman. The two men fly cover for Kalen and Jamie when they attempt to uncover the identity of the person kidnapping and buying Arrisian women.

Officer Mandi Ryan: Officer Ryan is drawn into Kalen's plan to trace the missing women. Wounded during their battle and escape, Mayla takes her home to tend to her injuries. Still on suspension, she is at the mansion when Jenna attacks. She helps rescue Caesar and becomes an accepted member of the Santiago family.

Jenna: Tall, blonde, mysterious woman, chasing and trying to kill Kalen and Mayla. Up to this point the journals never mention her last name.

Maria Atwood: Daughter of prominent member of the Governing Quorum, Lionel Atwood. In disguise, she goes by the name Nara Killian, leader of the people trying to destroy Arrisian society.

Asilyn Ryan: Friend of Danielle (Dani) Santiago. Girlfriend of Jimmy O'Hanlin. A target of Maria Atwood's kidnapping plot, foiled when her friends see her fall and interfere in the criminal act.

Dela Ryan: Widowed mother of Asilyn. Seen once in the third book and mentioned several other times. She in favor of Jimmy as a son-in-law and wonders why he hasn't asked Asilyn to marry him. She is pleased when she sees him propose at the hospital.

Jimmy O'Hanlin: Asilyn Ryan's beau. Appears in the first chapter of book three and is only mentioned in later books.

Skylar Covenington: Maria Atwood's henchman in charge of collecting the woman she wants kidnapped. Kalen described him as a whip thin man with a nasal Salwynian accent. His attempt to kill Kalen, Mayla, Jamie, and Mandi fails. Jamie and Mandi in Kalen's Imperial Flyer kill him in an aerial battle. Protecting Kalen and Mayla.

Richard R Draude

PLACES

Crystal Lake: Located in the central Muro Verde Mountains, its name, chosen by Shawn MacKenna, was so named in honor of the great reservoir created by the Silvan people on their home world, Asperia.

City of Crosskey: One of the earliest settlements in the Muro Verde mountains. At their annual fair, Russell MacKenna and his wife, Alannah, happen across the tent of a pair of foretellers. Here, Alannah requests a future-teller for a reading, thinking it all in fun. In the young woman's tent the Crosskey Prophecy is given.

Armagh: City located in the western Muro Verde mountains, the home of Cal Devers. His wife is Shannan, and their daughter, Neela. Cal's mines are outside the town. Mayla first meets Cal and his men at an inn north of the town. Connor O'Dell lives south of the city, on his family's homestead.

Mesa Verde: The easternmost mesa on the central continent. It is also the name of the Arrisian capital city—home of the Arrisian Central Council.

Andalusia: Large fertile area of the Outlands. Also a city in the south central part of the Outlands where Quintin and Liana Santiago have a home.

Solana and Lake Solana: Town in the eastern portion of the Outlands. The town of Solana sits at the extreme southern tip of the freshwater lake. The Santiago estate, *Hurtos de Cielos* (Orchards of Heaven), lies on the western shore, ninety kilometers north of the city.

298

Avila: City-slum situated on the extreme south-eastern edge of the Outlands. Once a semi-prosperous town due to the populace being employed at nearby copper mine. The town went belly up what the CC refused to renew the mine owner's operating permits. Kalen, Mayla, Jamie, and Mandi, travel to this remote area in hopes of recovering the kidnapped woman.

The Crosskey Prophecy

Revealed to
Alannah MacKenna
by
Evalyn McMurry-Kavanaugh

Behold, the Child of the Promise. This day shall he be born.

He shall have two lives and death shall stalk both. He shall be nurtured by the love of goodly parents, but they shall be taken, and his first love torn from him.

In cold captivity shall he be saved.

When death's cold sleep releases him, again will his life be sought, but he shall escape alive.

From danger shall he flee, to rescue the Hidden One.

Grief shall haunt him, but he will triumph over it.

Death will stalk him, but shall not catch him unawares, for the

Hidden One's eyes and ears are ever alert.

After his heart is healed, he shall face suspicion and anger, but wisdom and understanding are already within him. Without foreknowledge of the grandsire's deeds, his words shall ring true and make whole again that bond which that elder one sundered.

The knowledge the child seeks is hidden among the artifacts.

As the child seeks to unlock the past, the Angry One shall overtake him. Filled with pride and hatred and believing the slander still, he shall steal the Child away, fill him with falsehoods,

then flee to seek his revenge in secret. He shall fail, and fall from on high, destroying his line from this world. Yet, amidst the carnage, the Child of the Promise shall live.

Freed, but filled with loathing and sorrow, the Child shall wander, alone and desolate. From danger shall he flee and in the swiftness of his flight he shall overtake those who enslave and shall uncover their secret designs.

Into jeopardy shall he fly, there to discover the Angry One's lies and be reunited with the Hidden One.

Into the barren wilderness shall the Child and the Hidden One be cast to die, but the Guardian is ever aware. He shall appear suddenly to guide the Faithful Ones, and they shall deliver the Child and the Hidden One from death's icy jaws.

The Child and the Hidden One shall come forth, bound in love.

They shall covenant together and with the rejoining of those two houses is the breach sealed and the foundations of the enslavers shaken.

Then is the Guardian revealed and with the Faithful Ones he shall hunt those who seek to prevent the continuation of life.

Peace for the Child shall be but for a moment, for evil shall rear its head another time. With unfamiliar faces shall they steal away the cherished treasures. Their lies shall corrupt many, but not all.

Beware, for even among the trusted, there is one set against the Child of the Promise He turns his vision inward, seeking only to satiate his own vain ambitions.

From the brink of death shall the Child of the Promise return to lead the hunt and stalk the betrayers of liberty and the wardens who fill their captives' hearts with lies.

After many attempts, shall a cherished one be taken into captivity, but her wardens shall not claim her. There is another whose love and determination stands as a bulwark between her and the enslavers.

The ensuing battle to free her and the other cherished treasures shall expose Avarice for his hatred and murders. By the hand of his own will he be destroyed, for that one is not guiltless, and the blood of many worlds stains his hands. When Avarice is no more, then shall the slander be revealed, *proving false the words condemning the Child.*

Beware of the one who hides behind two faces. She is as a grand tomb, beautiful to behold, but filled with corruption. Her true nature and hatred will be made manifest. Though she be revealed as the stealer of life, yet in evil, will her own support and embolden her.

And still, not all truth shall be known. Long have those who enslave, labored in shadows and in secret chambers. Their plans, alliances, and truest desires are yet veiled in darkness.

The Child shall have little time to rest, for freedom's battle is eternal. It will leave behind for a time the Hidden One. The Child, now freed of the lies and guided by the Guardian, will journey far with the Faithful Ones. Together they shall stalk the enslavers, discover the corrective and make the truth manifest in the place their forefathers struck freedom's blow first.

Beware!

Fortify the resolve of the Child of the Promise.

Guard well the life of the Hidden One.

For when all lies are ripped away and the final truth exposed, should the Hidden One be bereft of life, the will of the Child of the Promise shall fail. If this comes to pass, she who hides behind two faces will accomplish her designs and true freedom will be destroyed, sealing the doom of all mankind for ten thousand years.

Some minor changes to the Prophecy's wording were made due to further study of the journals, and clarification of the language.